The Garderobe of Death

ALSO BY HOWARD OF WARWICK

The Domesday Book (No, Not That One)

The Chronicles of Brother Hermitage:
The Heretics of De'Ath

The Chronicles of Brother Hermitage

The Garderobe of Death

Howard of Warwick

First published in 2014 by
The Funny Book Company
Dalton House
60 Windsor Ave
London SW19 2RR
United Kingdom
www.funnybookcompany.com

ISBN 978-0-9929393-1-1

Cover design by Double Dagger
Typeset by Lodestar Editorial
Printed in the UK by Albury Books

CONTENTS

Midnight: Death Takes Norman

HESE WERE VERY DARK AGES. Thus mused Henri de Turold as he stumbled through one of the very darkest bits and stubbed his toes on a beam of worm-ridden English oak. Cursing the ghastly country and its truly awful people to an eternity of pain, he hobbled on down the corridor.

'But we're emerging from the darkness, sire; these are modern times,' learned men gabbled on all the time. To Henri's way of thinking, emergence from the dark would be a lot quicker if he set fire to England and all the learned men in it.

It had to be said that Henri's way of thinking was slow and laborious at the best of times. If anyone wanted goose feathers putting on their arrows, they would turn to Henri de Turold. If they wanted a decent conversation, they'd turn to the goose.

Yet the Norman made up for this absence of brain with a huge portion of good looks. Towering five foot nine if he was an inch, he had a chest like a barrel – the inside of one – and a stomach that couldn't muster the strength to reach his belt, let along hang over it. When he stood up straight his knees were so far apart that he didn't so much mount a horse as overwhelm it.

His face was normally an example of Norman power and grandeur, having been hit very hard, many times, by horses' hoofs. This had re-arranged his features into that pattern most favoured by the ladies of the Norman court. At this particular moment, however, his visage was contorted into a grimace of disdain that made him look almost English.

This strange moment of the night saw him stumbling through the very strange castle of his fellow Norman, and intellectual equal, Lord Robert Grosmal. Henri appreciated that Grosmal deserved the estate as reward for slaughtering the women and children of Hastings, but why had he filled it with darkness? England's darkness might not be actually darker than anywhere else, but he always felt it was ignoring him at best, if not actively conspiring against him. Not like Norman darkness, which was friendly and welcoming, and allowed you to get up to all sorts of things without being spotted.

To rid himself of this cursed gloom, Henri held a candle in front of him – one that seemed in league with the murk and strangely reluctant to help. It was admittedly a long, fat thing with a flame on top, but those were all the candle-like qualities it was prepared to accommodate.

The candle maker of Robert Grosmal had a reputation, and it wasn't a good one. The thing guttered and spluttered and dropped about enough light to illuminate its own shaft, which, being made of something truly unspeakable, was best not illuminated at all. No one knew quite what it was the man did to a candle, but they all knew it was horrible. They were the only variety that could make a moth leave a room.

'What the hell am I doing here?' Henri mumbled for about the third time. Drips of almost sentient wax did their best to cling on to the life of the candle before dropping towards the floor, swerving strangely as they went and landing with a soft, hot splash on his naked toes.

Walking naked through the halls of this disgusting house in January was clearly mad – but so was walking anywhere naked in January. Normally de Turold took off no clothes at all between October and May, and even then was considered outlandishly hardy. His only splash of common sense was the floppy yellow cloth hat on his head. Perhaps this would postpone the moment he froze to death.

For earlier that evening his desires, long dormant or satisfied by killing things, had taken control of his body, and he was only obeying orders.

Over dinner the Lady Foella, a Saxon beauty of such distinction she almost looked French, had hinted that if he were to walk naked from his chamber to hers there might be a warm welcome for him...

Henri's reverie was broken and dragged to the present by an odour, slinking out of the opening to Robert's new fangled garderobe. The Norman paused for a moment to consider his bowels, or rather they grabbed his attention by rattling like six squirrels in a sack of walnuts. Mindful of all the trouble he had been having down there lately, he decided to visit the facilities before descending, literally he hoped, on Lady Foella.

A testing clench of his muscles released a scent that would have made a pig of little discernment vomit, never mind a lady of refinement. The odour of ordure did brief battle with the scents drifting from the garderobe, but soon gave up an unequal battle and retired from the field. If Henri had been visiting a serving girl she could have been told to clean up afterwards, but Foella had class.

Nipping quickly into the room, he followed one of the garderobe night lights as its disgusting smoke seeped into the air. There were two planted on the stone paving by sides of two holes, badly knocked into the chamber floor. He could have sworn his candle flickered at the others, probably just the wind.

Above the holes, propped off the ground by lumps of wood, were two slabs of stone with matching holes, optimistically described as seats by Lord Robert. The candles burned in the room as a courtesy to light the way for visitors, or at least to stop them doing it on the floor by mistake.

Setting himself down on the nearest ice-trimmed hole, he prepared to let drop. He didn't need to prepare long as his lower intestine wanted rid of its contents faster than Henri wanted to get at Lady Foella's.

Henri put his own candle at a safe distance. Then he bent to move the other so the fumes would find some direction of travel other than up his nose. This candle had got firmly stuck to the floor by its own excreted wax, and so he gave it a tug. He frowned for a moment as below the noise of his own evacuation he could have sworn he heard something. One second later he was dead.

Five-o-clock: Norman Noble

I T WAS TO BE A BRIGHT AND SPARKLING winter's morning, and the harmonious, pre-dawn swoop of owl song and delicate scent of pine drifting in from the all-encompassing forest had its usual effect on the Lord of the Manor. It imbued him with a sense of enormous contempt for the world and everything in it.

Still, this was the day King William would visit. Yes, it was only an overnight stay as his Majesty travelled north. Yes, he would arrive after dark and leave before dawn. Yes, he had sent word that he did not want to be bothered by anyone or anything. And yes, private word had been sent that Robert Grosmal may call himself Lord of the Manor, but he had better bloody well keep out of the King's way. But still. The King.

This put Robert in the mood for a good gloat over the conquered English, and so he set about a tour of his ever-expanding demesne.

He was young to have been gifted land, but he had two qualities William of Normandy valued on the battlefield. The first was the insane violence of the young who believe no harm can come to them, no matter what horrible things they do. The second was that no harm had come to him – pretty miraculous, really, as he had done some very horrible things.

Robert left his chamber, naturally the largest in the castle, and beckoned the two cleaners, who had been waiting outside his door all night, to begin their work. As the place was the largest in the castle it took longest to clean, particularly after Grosmal had spent a night in it. The cleaners exchanged looks of sympathy, took simultaneous deep breaths and dived in.

His lordship prowled his property. He growled at servants, snarled at guards and abused a couple of the permanent builders who had been expanding his castle from the moment that King William gave it to him. He wove his way through the growingly complex corridors and chambers, and by this journey discovered Henri de Turold.

He didn't do so immediately, of course. He went to the garderobe, stood next to Henri and did his business, left and went to the great hall to warm up. Then he asked where Henri was.

A servant was sent to look, and it was he who noticed Henri was dead, and had been for some time. This man was far too humble to deal directly with the master, so he got the major domo to come and look. He also valued his life too highly to be the bearer of tidings such as these.

The senior servant looked de Turold up and down with a frown on his brow, nicely balanced by a large grin. To the consternation of his companion he knelt behind the still seated Norman and peered up under the garderobe seat.

'Oh dear,' he said in sophisticated and insincere tones, 'our master is not going to like this.'

◆　◆　◆

In the great hall the senior retainer dragged words through his teeth as he approached the breakfast table. 'My lord?'

'What do you want?' The lord snapped, grinning at the humbled Aethelred, the previous owner of the castle, who had been reduced to a servant. At least Robert hadn't executed him. As he pointed out several times a day. He insisted on calling him Ethel, though.

'Henri de Turold is dead,' Ethel said with blank glee.

'So?' Grosmal took another bite of blood-red venison.

'He seems to have been killed.'

'Really?' Robert asked with the curiosity of an enthusiast. 'Who killed him?'

'I thought you had.'

'No,' said Robert, as if accused of spilling milk, 'at least I don't think so. Anyway, he was a complete arse, so good riddance. All that going on about him and William. The King and I did this, the King and I did that. Well, he won't be doing anything with the King now, will he? Ha ha.'

'Well, if you didn't do it I have absolutely no idea who did.'

Grosmal sighed impatiently. 'Just bury him then – we don't want the place stinking out.'

Aethelred didn't move.

'What's the problem, Ethel?' Robert now looked up from the table and gazed with so much contempt that the air between the two men scuttled quickly out of the way.

'Henri de Turold has been murdered in your castle.'

This bought no response.

'In your garderobe.'

'I presume there is a point to all your meanderings?' Robert asked, returning to his undercooked deer.

'The complete arse who kept going on about him and William? The King's personal Fletcher and favourite hunting companion? The same King who is due here at nightfall? He's the one who appears to have been murdered in your garderobe.' It was Ethel's turn to gloat.

'Oh, shit,' said Robert, finally grasping the gravity of the situation.

There were very few people Robert was afraid of – mainly because his mind didn't work properly. The King was number one. Grosmal was terrified of anyone who had more power than he did. King William could inflict that most hideous of punishments: taking away his castle.

◆　　◆　　◆

Ethel watched as thoughts struggled their way through the head of the Norman. They were not nice thoughts and it was not a nice head. Ethel was bright enough to realise this opinion was not founded on his blind hatred of all things Norman. Well, not totally founded there. Of course Grosmal had the stupid Norman haircut, but then they all did. The tops of their heads had plainly been replaced by something completely different. Something round and covered with a mat made of hair. Not human hair at that.

This particular Norman head was most disturbing because it looked as though someone had sharpened it. It was clear from his behaviour the man was stupid – everything he did and said confirmed it – but the cause was also clear. There wasn't enough room in his skull for a normal sized brain. His chin was as wide as a horse's arse, but everything narrowed after that. His mouth was a touch too small for the chin and the nose was too small for the mouth. The eyes were too close together for comfort. Then the head simply tapered off.

The rest of his body followed the lead and got wider as it went down. Narrow shoulders surmounted a widening chest. Stomach and hips spread further, and he even had fat feet.

While the shape of his head probably explained the absence of intelligent thought, living with his looks probably explained why Robert was an unbalanced, dangerous loon. His father probably rejected him, although his mother must have loved him. His birth would have been easy. Unless he had come out backwards, of course.

As Ethel gazed, he noticed the man had actually started to shake.

◆　　◆　　◆

Throwing a nearby table to one side for effect, Robert grabbed his retainer by the arm and made haste to the garderobe. After a couple of missed turnings, corrected by the simple expedient of following their noses, despite their noses' objections, the sight which greeted their arrival was bizarre.

The very first rays of the sun were creeping into the room, probably hoping to leave again almost immediately. They illuminated a scene best left in the dark.

'Good God, he's got no clothes on,' was Robert's first response to the naked Henri de Turold. The Norman sat as if still giving vent to his bowel problem, ready to get up at any minute. It was only time that made any impression on an observer. When the look of startled surprise on the ex-nobleman's face remained static, the onlooker started to have doubts. Soon after this the grey pallor, normally so greasy, also caught the eye, and the dryness of the skin made one wonder what was going on. After a few more moments of complete stillness on the part of the defecating de Turold, the facts of death became clear.

'He is dead, isn't he?' asked Robert.

'Let's ask him, shall we?' replied the irrepressible Ethel.

'But why's he got no clothes on?' This point was obviously disturbing the lord. 'I mean, for Christ's sake, who the hell would wander around with no clothes on in the middle of January? He wasn't some sort of pervert, was he?'

Ethel arched his eyebrows at this statement of the obvious.

Casting around the room Robert located the dislodging pike, kept close at hand for any motions that missed their target. Keeping its crusted point away from him, he gave his erstwhile guest a gentle prod on the shoulder. Henri gave what appeared to be a resigned shrug and gently toppled forwards on to the floor. This did not appear to bother him in the slightest.

As the body slumped, Robert saw his chances of avoiding a conversation with King William diminishing rapidly. There were no marks on the body, no sign of any sort of struggle, no hint that Henri had made a valiant but ultimately doomed attempt to fight off his attackers, no sign of any violence done to the body at all.

15

Apart from the arrow sticking out of his anus, of course.

'My God.' Robert stared. 'No wonder he's dead. How on earth did he eat a whole arrow?'

Ethel sighed expressively. 'I think we'll find the arrow is on its way *in*, not out.'

Robert frowned as he tried to take this in. 'Ow, what a way to go,' he said with true feeling.

'The point is that he has gone, and it is an issue we have to deal with,' said Ethel patiently, gazing down at the puzzled Norman.

Ethel was a tall man who carried a tall staff as his constant companion. In a dull light it could be hard to tell man from stick. He had the constant Saxon smell under his nose, which helped him to look down on everyone he came within sight of. If Ethel's family hadn't known your family, you were as the dust upon the ground. The fact that none of Ethel's family was in a condition to know anything at all any more didn't stop generations of inbred condescension finding a natural outlet.

'Well...' Robert paused as he thought. The process was clearly an effort. 'We could bury him and that would be that.'

'Until the next time the King wants to go hunting and calls at Henri's manor. "Is Henri in?" he'll ask. "Afraid not," replies the guard, "he got murdered at Robert Grosmal's place. Didn't anyone tell you? Oh, I say, how rude."'

'OK, we'll just tell the King he died.'

'Of?'

'Of course.'

'No, I mean what did he die of?' There was sincere concern in Ethel's voice. His lord might stand to lose his castle, but Ethel's fate would make Henri's death look like a mild rebuke.

'Old age? I mean, it's not as if there are any holes in him that weren't there before.' Robert was rather enjoying this.

'How old was he?' asked Ethel.

16

'Oh, positively ancient,' his master replied. 'Twenty-five, something like that.'

'Old, but hardly at the close of life, eh? The problem as I see it is this.'

Robert listened intently. It was a very disturbing sight, but Ethel had got used to it.

'We can't think of any natural causes that would account for Henri's death. He was a fit young man, wealthy and a favourite of the King. Such men usually live to at least forty. He might have caught a chill or ague of some sort, but I think when we pull that arrow out of him it's going to make rather a mess.'

'Couldn't we just push it in some more?'

'An excellent suggestion, sire, but if the rumours I hear are true the King may well want to examine the deceased's parts most closely.' Ethel left the suggestion hanging in the air.

Robert picked it up. 'Oh, they're true all right.'

'So we have to tell the King not only that Henri is dead, but that he was killed.'

'Well, you have to tell him actually,' said Grosmal, without a hint of worry.

'Indeed, my lord', Ethel simpered, 'it occurs to me that one option may be to present the King not only with Henri's body, but with his killer as well. That may redirect the King's rage away from me, I mean us.'

'Oh, excellent idea, Ethel. Who did it then?'

'That's just the point,' said Ethel, despairing irritation at Norman stupidity creeping in to his tone. 'We don't know.'

'Doesn't matter,' said Robert. 'We can just choose someone, kill them and give their bits to the King, well tortured. That ugly cousin of mine now, we could say he did it. I've never liked him.'

'A further problem occurs to me, my lord,' said Ethel, having just saved a young man's life.

'You are really boring today, Ethel,' said Robert, idly picking at his fingernails. He had clearly lost all track of the serious situation.

'If we present a dead body to the King, he will ask how do we know it's Henri's killer? Not just someone we decided to kill and say he was the murderer...'

'Yes, the King does know me rather well, doesn't he?' Robert gazed at the floor and drew circles in the dust with his boot. 'Remind me to punish the garderobe dusting hags,' he commented.

'It would be best,' said Ethel slowly, 'it would be best if we could find the real killer and offer him alive to the King to confess his guilt. By this means we might get away with a minor beating for poor security.'

'Great,' said Robert, as if it was all decided and he could get back to his meal. 'All we have to do is find someone who'll say they did it and dangle them in front of the King. Who shall we choose?'

'I don't think it will be that simple, sire,' said Ethel, talking to the most simple thing in the castle. 'It isn't the sort of role anyone is likely to volunteer for.'

'Oh, well, that's easily solved.'

'How?'

'Find out who really did it,' his lord and master commanded with disarming simplicity. 'By tonight.'

The Lord of the Manor strode from the stinking room. He did not see Ethel's knuckles whiten as the Saxon gripped his staff. Nor could he see inside Ethel's head, where thoughts were of dealing with the master by putting his staff where Henri kept his arrows.

There was one thought that was clear in Ethel's head. If this death had to be unravelled, there was a good chance the person doing the unravelling would end up in nearly as much trouble as the corpse. In situations like this there was only one solution. Get someone else to do it.

Hard on the heels of this consideration, an idea of where to get this someone else popped into his head. It was impudent, controversial and borderline insane, but it cracked the man's face into a malicious smile. Where better? he asked himself, while simultaneously thinking of a dozen places better. Grosmal wouldn't realise until it was too late.

He had some preparations to make though. He certainly wasn't going anywhere near that place on his own.

Caput III

Five-o-clock: Saxon Lady

LSEWHERE IN THE CASTLE of Lord Robert Grosmal the great beauty Lady Foella was being not very beautiful at all.

'Where's that stinking puss hole de Turold?' she screamed, her charmingly even face and wide brown eyes pinched into fury, drowning under waves of auburn hair.

Her maid, Eleanor, kept her distance. 'I don't know, my lady. I didn't see him last night,' she squeaked in her 'don't blame me' voice.

Eleanor had in fact lain awake in her straw most of the night, expecting the Norman to burst in at any moment, eager to fall upon her lady. While their chamber was ample, it wasn't as large as Grosmal's, and Eleanor's place at night was on the floor, close to her lady's bed. She had wanted to make sure she wasn't fallen on by mistake. Or as well. Only when the first, faint glow of approaching dawn crept into the room did she start to feel safe. That stopped with her mistress's first scream of the day.

'Well, why the hell not?' Foella demanded.

'I'm sure I don't know, my lady.'

Foella drew breath for another scream.

'But I'll find out,' Eleanor pre-empted, and scuttled from the room.

She closed the door gratefully on the familiar sound of things being thrown about. Many of them far heavier than a lady ought to be capable of throwing. At one point she was sure she heard the bed move, but surely that wasn't possible, not even for Foella at the height of her fury.

Muttering her usual litany of complaint about mistresses who were unfair, inconsiderate, harsh and plain loose in the head, Eleanor headed off in search of information. She hitched her thick skirt up a couple of inches to avoid all the varieties of muck on the floor and started looking for her favourite guard, William.

♦　　♦　　♦

William le Morton was happy with his lot as a very minor guard in the employ of Robert Grosmal. He led a pretty unremarkable life and had a fortunate name, as his mother had perfectly well realised. Before 1066 William le Morton had been called Erik Slaymonger; he had enjoyed a safe life as the supposed descendant of a horribly violent Viking who might just pop back at any moment. It was a pity that his family was blissfully unaware that he was, in fact, a direct male descendant of Julius Caesar. Once the Normans arrived Erik swiftly became William, making himself available for various guard duties as required.

He was also a handsome young man, just Eleanor's type. He was big and burly, but as soft as week-old milk. And as pliable. She was seventeen now, and with him already twenty-two she could have a good few years and then be a respectable widow.

William was just the man for this job. There was no way she was going to approach de Turold's personal household to find out what was going on. That consisted of one grizzled old Norman who spoke no English, but had hands which could reach places she didn't know she had.

As usual she found William carefully guarding the fire in the keep. He was even holding his palms towards it to prevent it leaping from the grate.

'What's going on?' Eleanor hissed as she sidled up, flicking her long blond hair expertly towards him.

'Oh, 'ello,' said William, shifting from the warmth of the fire towards the warmth of Eleanor.'Big trouble.'

21

'What?'

William looked around to check no one was listening to them. 'De Turold's dead. Murdered, they say.'

'Oh no.' Eleanor paled and slumped in shock.

'Oh, I'm sorry,' William said, obviously surprised at the reaction. 'Were you close?'

"No, of course not, but he was supposed to visit my mistress last night.'

'And did he?'

'I don't think so. I kept awake as long as I could and he didn't turn up. If he had done, I'm sure the noise would have woken me'

'Perhaps he arrived and they were quiet?'

'My mistress doesn't do quiet.'

'Perhaps he turned up and she killed him,' William joked.

Eleanor took the question seriously. 'She wouldn't. Not till after they were married, anyway.'

'Married?' It was William's turn to be knocked back.

'I know, horrible thought, but she's desperate. She'll lose her father's estate to King William if she can't find a husband on the winning side pretty soon.'

'Good looking woman, your mistress. Shouldn't have any trouble, I'd have thought.'

'Oh, sure, nice enough to look at, but you try talking to her…'

'Difficult?'

'Doesn't even begin to describe her outer ramparts. She can scare the skin off a weasel, that one.'

'But de Turold was willing.'

'Oh, he didn't know. She might have told him on the wedding day. And once she's made her mind up, that's that. No point in arguing that he never agreed to marry her or nothing. Mind you, if he turned her down she'd get pretty cross.'

'And she kills people when she gets cross, does she?' William exaggerated outrageously.

'Not usually.'

'Usually?' William choked.

'Well, there was this once with a young nobleman.'

'She really killed him?' William whispered and shouted at the same time.

'Nothing was ever proved, but they were both in company and were alive...'

'Yes?'

'And then they were alone together and he was dead.'

'Good grief.'

'She kills animals for no reason at all. She's probably like them creatures what kill their mates after they've done it.'

'Spaniards?'

'That's them.'

William frowned. None of this sounded good. 'So you'd better tell her he's been found, see what she says.'

'Not me.'

'Who then?'

Eleanor stroked William's arm. 'You're a big, strong chap.'

William looked shocked, but he didn't take his arm away. 'But she's your mistress.'

'Yes, but you've probably got armour and stuff. I bet you have. Chainmail and that. And a pointy helmet.' Eleanor sighed in happy reminiscence. 'I like a man in armour.'

'Armour? You must be joking. The likes of me don't get expensive kit like armour. Our head guard says the best way to avoid someone stabbing you is to stab them first.'

'Sounds fair enough,' said Eleanor. The topic of men in armour and stabbings gave her a lovely warm feeling inside.

'It would be if they give us any knives to stab with. All I get is me long stick.' William picked up a long wooden staff which would have been a pike staff if it had a pike on the end. It didn't. He held it out to Eleanor.

'Just the job for keeping my Lady Foella at a safe distance.' Eleanor stroked his staff thoughtfully.

William was thinking too. 'I'm sure she'll find out soon enough – it's all over the castle. Just keep your head down here long enough, then you can pop back once she's heard.'

Eleanor shook her head. 'No good, she doesn't do castle gossip.'

'Too high and mighty, eh?'

'Nah – just that no one'll talk to her.'

William folded his arms. 'You got a problem then.'

'You could escort me.' Eleanor batted more eyelids than she actually had.

'Eh?'

'Yeah. There's a dangerous killer on the loose and all helpless women are to be escorted by guards. She wouldn't kill me if you were there.'

William looked very doubtful.

'You wouldn't have to say anything, or do anything. Just stand behind me, looking guard-like. I'll tell her and then get out of the way.'

'You reckon?' His tone said no. William was not stupid. He was not going to do it.

◆　　◆　　◆

A few moments later they approached Lady Foella's door, having planned the approach.

They walked slowly, then in the last few steps rushed to the chamber, making as many loud and hurried footstep noises as they could. Eleanor knocked once and threw the door open.

'My lady, grave tidings,' she called out in a panic, looking around.

Foella was sitting by the window, looking out on to the courtyard below, her red winter gown spread around her just like a damsel in a tapestry. Not the rude sort of tapestry either. Her hair hung loose and her neck was at just the right angle to catch the beams of the rising sun. Her beauty was turned away from them, but it penetrated the room like an aura, slipping from her pose to impress all those who gazed upon her.

'What?' Lady Foella snapped, turning and pulling the final legs off the spider she'd been playing with.

'Henri de Turold is dead,' Eleanor announced, faking a slight swoon back into the protective aura of William, who had himself taken a step back.

At the news Foella's face became expressionless for a moment. It was just a pause on route to becoming a thing of horror. She didn't look as if she was just about to bite the head off a kitten; she looked as if she had just done so. Eleanor had seen that look before, on the face of a particularly stupid guard who had thought that kitten decapitation would impress her. It had, actually, but it made him taste funny when she kissed him.

'My lady,' said Eleanor with worry in her tone. 'What are you going to do?'

'Robert,' was all Foella would say, but she didn't say it in a very nice way. 'Where's Robert?'

'My lady, don't do anything rash. Lord Robert is very powerful.'

So was Foella. She stepped across the room very quickly indeed and picked Eleanor up by the scruff of her neck. Then she threw her into the straw on the floor and strode to the door.

Striding to the door involved brushing the large and heavy William aside with one arm, before sweeping out.

'Where's Grosmal?' The lady screamed as if the stones would answer. They didn't, but they rattled a bit.

Eleanor got up and joined William. They watched her disappear down the corridor.

'She's going the wrong way,' William said.

'Good job,' Eleanor responded. 'This is not going to end well.'

'I'll kill him,' wafted down the corridor from Foella's departing form.

'See what I mean?'

William did.

◆   ◆   ◆

The Lady Foella's journey through the Castle Grosmal was a testament to its design. It was long, repetitious and largely pointless. She had been given the full guided tour when she arrived, but had been so fundamentally bored by the whole thing she hadn't paid much attention. Now she cast about wildly, trying to find some recognisable landmark from which she could plan her search.

She clearly found each opening and passageway increasingly irritating as she mumbled and swore at them. Eventually settling on a direction for no particular reason, she pressed on.

The corridor Foella had chosen was narrow and curved slightly off into the distance so she could not see its far end. This had been shown to Foella as an example of the castle's most accurately built and plumb passage, but that memory had been despatched.

A guard, whose duty it was to make sure the riffraff did not trespass into the nicer bits of the castle, saw Foella's approach and prepared to avoid bumping into his lord's most welcome lady guest. His first ever lady guest, in fact. Well, the first who had stayed more than one night.

Foella saw the guard as well, but he had about as much impact on her senses as Eleanor's personal problems – such being the way of the noble class. It was pure, inbred, unconscious reaction which delivered the appropriate words for the encounter.

'Get out of my way,' she snapped, without realising that she'd said anything at all.

The man backed away frantically as Foella got nearer and he managed to corner himself against an old door. The only way he could think of to avoid contact was to open the door and slip through it. He knew Foella's reputation. If he impeded her in any way, obstructed her or, God forbid, bumped into her, she would be on to his lordship. The life of a newly created corpse did not appeal.

He didn't have a clue what was behind the door, though. If he interrupted Lord Robert himself his death would be a lot slower, a lot more painful and probably very rude.

He pushed hard at the door, threw it open and stepped quickly backwards through it. The Lady Foella swept past without a sideways glance. The guard made a very interesting discovery and took a downwards glance.

For some weeks Robert's resident builder had been trying to find the door he knew he had built, but just couldn't remember where. It was supposed to open on to a balcony above the main gate, which would give a commanding view of the countryside. He had never done a balcony before, and so his search had not been conscientious.

The thought of the great contribution he was making to the development of Castle Grosmal never even entered the guard's mind. Instead he plummeted all thirty of the feet to the stones below, where his mind mingled with the straw and manure.

Those living in the courtyard below, those passing through the courtyard below and those who were just having a quick look at the courtyard below took absolutely no notice of the event. This sort of thing was happening all the time.

◆　　◆　　◆

Lady Foella, quite oblivious of the life she had just despatched, carried on with her randomly brutal meanderings. She found herself eventually in the minstrels' gallery above the main hall, where she was lucky to find a piece of sound flooring to stand on. The first time some minstrels had been sent to the gallery the only entertainment they had been able to provide was falling in harmony.

Casting a glance around the room below that would have put the shivers up a wolf, she lighted on a figure sitting in a large chair in front of the roaring fire. Bobbing up and down like a woman of loose virtue in a hurry, she craned her neck to see who it was.

'Robert!' she bellowed in frustration.

The figure in the chair stirred and looked up. It was indeed the master of the house and he waved a friendly greeting to his guest before getting up and strolling over to stand underneath the gallery.

The massive fire, which occupied the space of a fair sized house, burned through trees at an alarming rate and had to be kept going, day and night, in case the master got a bit cold. No one else was allowed to warm themselves in front of it, of course, even if they were freezing to death.

The remains of Robert's breakfast lay scattered around the room, as if each bit had made a separate bid for escape. Venison bones, with enough meat left on them to feed a family, were laying under the table. Half a loaf of bread was dropped by the chair, and another substantial chunk had somehow found its way on to a rafter. This would provide a surprise meal for a family of mice, who never expected to find anything so wholesome quite so far from the ground.

Only the flagon of ale was as it should be, nurtured in the hands of Grosmal as he took regular swigs.

He sat in solitude, his mind wandering wherever it went in moments of relaxation. There was much speculation in the castle about where his mind went, and about where it deserved to go. None of the speculation was very pleasant, and it certainly wasn't shared.

Putting his thoughts aside, for which they were probably grateful, he stood underneath the gallery and gazed up at his guest.

'Ah, my lady,' he said in an ingratiating voice which still came across as menacing, 'you will have to remember how you got up there. Some of my idiot workmen claim to have lost the way to the gallery. But then, that's Saxons for you,' he said, forgetting that Lady Foella was Saxon, or not caring.

'Come closer, my lord,' said Foella in a voice that would have given a starving beggar indigestion. Robert duly approached, however, and stood under Lady Foella. The thud of the dagger descending at some speed from the gallery and embedding itself in the great table next to Robert seemed to cause him not a whit of bother.

'Bugger, missed,' said Lady Foella.

'My lady is in playful mood today,' opined Robert.

'I'll kill you,' screamed Foella.

'Why?' Grosmal asked, reasonably enough.

'De Turold is dead.'

Robert stared at her. 'How did you know?' he demanded in rising panic. 'It's supposed to be a secret. Did you do it?'

'My maid told me.'

'So she did it, eh? What's her name?'

'How should I know?' Foella snapped back, thinking that she did know the name of her maid, but couldn't immediately bring it to mind. 'You killed my husband.'

Grosmal frowned at this statement, which seemed to come out of nothing. 'Very likely,' he shrugged. 'He shouldn't have been at the battle in the first place.'

'What battle?'

'That big one, down south somewhere. A field with a hill in it.'

'What's that got to do with anything?'

'It's probably where he got killed.'

Foella shook her head to get the confusion out. Things were getting out of hand and this rambling Norman seemed to be completely mad. Why wouldn't he pay attention? Then why's he here?'

'Who?' Robert shook his head now. Nothing was making any sense to him – which was hardly his fault. These Saxons really were an odd bunch. He glanced around the floor, spotted a joint of half-eaten venison nearby, and stooped to pick it up. He gnawed absentmindedly.

He returned to the conversation between a mad woman and an idiot.

'De Turold, that's who,' Foella spat.

'De Turold is dead.'

'I know that.' Foella was losing what little control she had ever had of her brittle, insensitive and demanding nature. She was also starting to look more alarming than normal, which was not a pretty sight.

'As well as the man in the battle?' Grosmal puzzled easily.

'What man at the battle?'

'Your husband.'

'I've never been married.'

'But you said I killed your husband.'

'And you did.'

Grosmal gave this some profound thought. 'How? If you've never married.'

'None of your business.'

'My lady seems confused,' Grosmal patronised, safe below. Bored with his venison now, he threw it back where it had come from.

'Did you, or did you not, kill Henri de Turold?'

'Not that it's any of your business, but I did not.'

'Oh.' Foella was confused and disappointed by this reply.

'Did you kill him?' Grosmal asked. 'We're looking for who-ever did. If it was you, it would save a lot of time and effort.'

'No, I did not,' Foella screeched at such a pitch and intensity that the mice on the rafter ran for cover.

'Hum.' Grosmal wasn't convinced. 'We'll find out who did,' he said in a tone laced with meaning and threat. Then he returned to surer ground. 'And I might have killed your husband,' he offered.

'That's him.'

'Who?'

'De Turold.'

'Really? Your husband? He never mentioned it.'

'Well, he nearly was. He would have been if he wasn't dead.' Foella paused. 'Perhaps I'm his widow.'

Robert gave up. His head ached. So did his ears. This woman was so far out of her tree, the best woodsman wouldn't find her in a month. 'Well, in Normandy we tend not to marry people after they're dead,' he explained. 'God knows what you Saxons get up to. You all seem a bit weird to me.'

'We're weird?'

'And if you are his widow, perhaps you did kill him.'

'How dare you.' Foella's voice dropped in tone now. It took on a low grumble, which Eleanor would have recognised as the signal to get as far away as possible.

'Well, it wasn't me, and you're claiming to be his wife. That makes you the most likely. Typical Saxon – marry a fellow and then kill him.'

'I never got round to actually marrying him.'

'Probably killed him out of anger when he refused you then.' Robert was getting the measure of Foella. 'Now you come to mention it, I wondered what you were doing, following him round all the time. Probably just looking for your opportunity.'

Foella threw her hands up in frustration. She pointed at Grosmal. 'Stay there, I'm coming down.'

'Good luck,' Grosmal mumbled.

They turned their backs on one another.

'Bleeding idiot,' they both spat.

Foella left the balcony to begin the completely hopeless task of finding a way down to the hall. Once there, she would be able to do to Robert in person all the things she'd only been thinking about. And being Foella, she'd been thinking about a lot of things. If she considered for a moment she'd realise that every one of them would get her into an awful lot of trouble. Foella had never indulged in considering for a moment.

Caput IV

Seven-o-clock: Monk and Weaver

N THE NORTHERN PARTS OF LINCOLNSHIRE, immeasurable time and irresistible nature had combined to create a pocket of beauty in a harsh landscape. A gentle swelling of hills hid the place from the worst ravages of winter. Tall growths of trees dappled shade on to the ground in the summer, keeping the place cool and living with moisture. Delicate and colourful plants thrived, insects buzzed and the natural rhythms of life played out undisturbed.

The place had been known for generations, but never owned. The undulations of the ground made it too awkward to farm and, being scooped from the higher land on all sides, it had no strategic value.

It was also recognised as a place of charm – perhaps thought magical in older times. The landscape had a real presence, to be at least undisturbed, maybe even revered.

Even in these sleeping months of winter, this dingle remained poised and alert. Life could be felt building strength under the ground, ready to burst out upon the air once more.

The subtle power and majesty of the place had been recognised many years ago by one visitor – a Norman called William. But he had been a man of peace, a man of knowledge and purity of spirit. He was the first to take possession of the land – if such a fleeting presence as a human could be said to own somewhere like the dingle.

Upon his passing, unnoticed by a single tree over which he claimed dominion, William De'Ath left the wondrous place in bequest. He would have a religious community established here to acknowledge the debt mankind owed to God for such beauty.

That's where it all started to go wrong.

The resultant building, the monastery of De'Ath's Dingle, squatted on the site like a foetid toad. It eyed the perfection of nature spread out before it, just waiting for the perfect moment to jump forward and flatten the lot.

It had been put up by William De'Ath's son in accordance with his wishes. Also in accordance with the son's wishes to find some custom for a stone quarry, the only thing he'd been left.

As a result the monastery was a massive and disturbing presence. Not only because it was completely inappropriate for its surroundings, but also because it was simply massive. It was far too big to be of any real practical use. The population was not great in these parts, but the monastery of De'Ath's Dingle could have fitted them all in the meat store. No one had ever built a monastery of stone before. Now they knew why.

The religious community was also small. A monk could wander about the place all day, with the strong possibility of not meeting a single other Brother. Which was usually a good thing, as most of the Brothers of De'Ath's Dingle had reputations. Many of them were really not very nice. Refectory discussions, developing over the course of another coarse and disappointing meal, frequently broached the topic of putting the local population in the meat store and doing something comprehensively sinful with them.

There was no doubt this ghastly place was the work of man: that is to say it *had* been constructed on purpose, it just didn't look like it sometimes. It was only a few years since the work was completed, but already the monastery had somehow slumped. Its shoulders had sagged and it had started to let itself go. Bits fell off the higher walls quite regularly and unfortunate bulges were appearing, as if the belt holding in some monstrous stomach was beginning to fail.

It wouldn't be many more years before a casual passer-by might miss the place altogether, wondering instead who could have dumped an unhealthy-looking pile of old rocks in such a nice place.

Not that the monastery in De'Ath's Dingle had any to speak of. Casual passers-by, no. Determined avoiders moving quickly on, yes.

The whole ambience of the monastery sowed discord. There were contradictions between the building and the wonders of nature at which it glowered; between the intention of the bequest and the practices that went on inside; between the enduring order and pattern in the forces of nature and the visible decay in the works of man.

Inside the oppressive walls, in these first hours of light, a remarkable conversation was underway. It was between two relatively normal men, both appearing to be rational and intelligent. It was clearly between people who didn't belong there.

'But Mister Wat, you can't leave.' Brother Hermitage, the young and enthusiastic monk of the monastery, was not issuing an order. He was not politely asking a valued guest to stay longer. He was certainly not threatening a prisoner with prolonged incarceration. He was begging for his life.

This conversation had been repeated several times over the last few weeks, and Hermitage had so far prevailed on his friend to stay. He worried there was now more determination in the other man's voice.

This time they were even strolling towards the main gate. Wat had his pack across his shoulders, his walking boots on his feet, and it was the opening of the day, the perfect moment to start a journey. All of these facts combined to make Hermitage believe the weaver really meant to leave.

'You know what Abbot Athan will do to me if you go...'

Hermitage put on his best 'scared rabbit' face – the one he wore most of the time. His blue eyes widened and his clear, well ordered face would make a puppy with a spare tail look like a mongrel with fresh fleas.

Wat the Weaver ran a hand through his dark curly hair and rubbed his hand over a stubbly chin. Only a year or two older than Hermitage, he watched as helplessness poured from the monk and made a puddle at his feet. He shrugged his shoulders.

'I can take a guess,' he said. 'But Hermitage, I can't stay any longer. I've been here for months, it's costing me money. I've got commissions to complete, new tapestries to order from the workshop. I've said before, come with me.'

'I'm not allowed.'

'I know, not allowed by the man you think is going to kill you.'

'He will kill me.'

Hermitage still could not believe his misfortune. He had exposed a murder. A real live, or rather not so live, murder. In a monastery. He had even done so in front of King Harold, who was about to deal with the matter when he rushed off to the battle of Hastings. Rushing off to the battle of Hastings had become a euphemism for, well, dying horribly at a really inconvenient moment. Old Jack was mending his roof when he rushed off to the battle of Hastings. Young Alward, who'd ended up between the old bull and the cows, also got rushed off to the battle of Hastings. That sort of thing.

Brother Athan, who had only been prior then, had not taken the revelations around the murder well. He was a difficult man. Difficult in the way only an ugly man could be. A short ugly man of five foot three, whose first proposition in any discussion was to line his opponent up and hit him.

As soon as King Harold left, the original abbot of De'Ath's Dingle did likewise, in hot escape from a whole heap of trouble. He had turned out not to be who he said at all. Hermitage had really struggled to take in all of this deceit and wrong doing. These were churchmen, for goodness sake.

With King and abbot gone, Athan installed himself as community leader. He was waiting for the coast to clear before doing something 'really horrible' to Hermitage as punishment for bringing all this trouble on their heads. He'd even used those words. In a sermon. Apparently talking about God's retribution for sinners, but all the time staring at Hermitage and pointing at him, twice. The young monk knew it was only Wat's presence that held off the inevitable.

'But if he's going to kill you, you shouldn't stay. In fact as you know he's a sinner, I don't see why you have to obey him at all.'

'With the abbot vanished, Athan's in charge.'

'Monks.' Was all Wat said.

'Obedience,' Hermitage reluctantly admitted.

'If he told you to cut your own head off, would you?'

'I'd have to try.'

'God, you're an idiot.' This was the sort of thing Athan usually said, but at least Wat said it with good humour.

'Look,' Wat went on, as they drew closer to the gate and their pace slowed, 'the abbot vanished, so why shouldn't you?'

Hermitage was horrified. 'The abbot was our superior,' he said. Wasn't that enough?

'Your superior who was just as deceitful as the rest of you. As soon as the King turned up, the man scarpered. And you still have to obey these people?'

'Of course.' Hermitage often wondered where Wat got his strange ideas.

'So you won't leave?' Wat's question had the ring of finality in its tone.

'I can't.'

'Then I shall have to leave you and wish you good luck.'

All Hermitage could do was let out a slight whimper. The puppy had just lost both his spare tail and the original. He cast his head down and lifted his eyes to Wat.

The weaver shook his head in despair at the young monk's response. 'Don't give me the look,' he sighed. 'What if I speak to Athan before I go?'

'What good will that do?'

'I could tell him that I want you looked after, that I'll be coming back, and if any harm comes to you I'll hold him account-able.'

'That's what King Harold said before he left.'

'Yes, but I'm not going to a battle, am I?'

'Well, if you think it would help…' Hermitage was disconsolate.

'Oh for goodness sake, Hermitage pull yourself together. You've decided not to leave and this is the best I can offer. You want me to stay here forever?'

'That would be nice.'

'Excellent, no problem.'

Hermitage brightened enormously.

'You can pay me the penny a day then.'

'A penny a day?' Hermitage gasped at such wealth. 'Every day?'

'That's what I'm losing by being here.'

'Oh dear.' Hermitage's head fell.

'Come on, let's go and see Athan.'

◆　　◆　　◆

Wat led the way through the meandering stonework of De'Ath's Dingle towards the abbot's chamber. Hermitage followed, impressed that Wat had learned the ways of this rambling place in as little as five months. He even knew to avoid the passages where the stonework had recently collapsed under its own weight. Its weight plus the complete absence of planning, skill or mortar in its assembly.

As they went the weaver greeted a number of monks personally, even exchanging a few pleasantries. This was more than Hermitage had achieved in two years at De'Ath's Dingle. He was lucky if a week went by without some practical joke being played upon him.

There was even an exchange with Brother Stoop, who complimented Wat on the fine stitching of his jerkin. They stopped for a few minutes and discussed the finer points of cloth work, Stoop obviously having some experience of the trade.

Hermitage felt bitter that this was the same Stoop who regularly sat through the orders of the day poking Hermitage in the side with a specially sharpened stick. Keeping the young Brother's mind on the Lord, he called it. If that was the case, Hermitage felt, there was no need to cackle with every poke.

As they parted Stoop produced the stick from somewhere in his habit. He waved it at Hermitage with a grin.

◆　　◆　　◆

Drawing closer to the abbot's study, occupied by Athan within five minutes of the previous owner's departure, Hermitage started to feel more nervous than usual. For most people this level of terror would be debilitating, but it was pretty normal for him.

It had been bad enough visiting the study when the old abbot was there. But then that man was just plain insane, so there was no telling what he was going to do. Hermitage knew what Athan wanted to do. The man had even offered to learn to write just so he could give Hermitage a note about it.

'I'm not sure about this,' his voice quavered in Wat's ear.

'Don't worry.' The weaver clapped a bracing hand on Hermitage's shoulder.

'Oh, don't do that,' the monk cowered away.

Wat did the shake of head in despair which had become almost automatic. Hermitage, who had come to recognise the gesture over the months, tried to do as Wat instructed him.

Breathe deeply, close your eyes and let the fear flow out of your fingertips. The only trouble was whenever he closed his eyes someone did something to him. Or put his fingertips in something unpleasant.

He couldn't understand how Wat approached situations without an apparent care in the world. He answered people back, spoke when he wasn't spoken to and pointed his finger at people much bigger than him. Remarkable.

Wat demonstrated his style by knocking firmly on the study door, then pushing it open before he'd even been invited.

Hermitage drew in his breath, ready to hold it for as long as necessary. He entered the room and let it out straight away. He didn't recognise the place. It was clean and didn't smell of piss any more. The holes in the walls and ceiling had been patched, fresh straw was scattered on the floor and a fire even had the temerity to dance in the grate. Athan had gone soft.

Most alarming of all, there was a stranger in the room. There had never been strangers in the study. This put Hermitage completely off his stride. It knocked his attention off his immediate peril and kicked his brain into action.

The stranger was very well dressed and as thin as ink. He had been in conversation with Athan, but when Wat and Hermitage burst in he moved his head rather slowly round to face them.

'Ah, what luck,' said Athan. The friendly smile on his ugly face really put the wind up Hermitage. 'These are the two I was telling you about.'

'Good morning,' the stranger intoned in a very educated Saxon accent. 'You must be a monk,' he said to Hermitage.

'Er, yes.' Hermitage looked at his own habit and wondered why there was any question.

'And how long have you been a monk?' the stranger asked, making polite conversation.

'All my life,' Hermitage responded naturally.

'Really? I didn't know you could do that.'

'I had a previous life, but that is gone now.'

'Ah, I see, very commendable. And you, mister er...'

'Wat.'

'Indeed. And I see you are not a monk.'

Athan butted in. 'He says he's a weaver. Not that anyone's seen him do any weaving.'

'Wat the Weaver, eh?' The visitor recognised the name, and seemed rather disdainful of it. 'I think my brother commissioned, erm, a piece from you.'

'Really?'

'Yes. Aethelingus of Saxmundham?'

'Ah yes, I remember the work.' Wat spoke directly to the man. 'In all its detail.'

Hermitage was fascinated by the tone of this conversation. It seemed a good chance to try the new technique Wat had told him about. 'Paying attention', he called it. He said it might avoid Hermitage getting into difficulties quite so frequently with his fellow monks.

In this case he thought Athan's guest was insulting Wat somehow. He certainly didn't have a high opinion of the weaver's work. The word 'piece' had come out as if it was a piece of something really rather nasty.

Wat's response had also been very pointed – as if somehow blaming the stranger's brother for the work. It must be a fascinating tapestry. Hermitage would have to ask Wat about it later. The weaver was always reluctant to describe his work to the monk. Modesty, Hermitage supposed.

The stranger went on. 'I'm surprised to find such as you in a place such as this.' He nodded to indicate the monastic garb worn by Athan and Hermitage.

This really was fascinating. The stranger was suggesting that De'Ath's Dingle was too good for Wat. How bizarre. De'Ath's Dingle wasn't too good for anything Hermitage could conceive of.

'Ah well, strange chain of events really. And if you're Aethe-lingus's brother, and therefore a freeman, I'm surprised to find you here as well. Did you miss the King's call to Hastings?'

'I had other commitments.' The man dismissed Wat's insinu-ation with a wave.

'I never got to meet your brother in person; he had people to do most things for him. How is he?' Wat seemed keen to press the subject home.

'Dead.'

'Ah.'

'Like so many.'

'But not all.' Wat raised his eyebrows, apparently wondering why Aethelred wasn't dead as well.

'Shall we get on, or are we going to start reminiscing about the good old days of the Vikings?' Athan brought the conversa-tion back to the present with a thump.

'Absolutely,' the stranger nodded.

Athan waited.

The stranger smiled.

'Perhaps you could explain?' Athan said, glaring at the tall man in that way he had. The way that always made Hermitage take a step back.

'Ah yes, of course. Allow me to introduce myself. I am Ae-thelred of Baernodebi.' The man said this with an upward lift of his head, as if announcing his arrival at court.

The nearest village to the monastery would not have held any court. The place was not as grim as the monastery, but it was even more pointless. It only existed as a marker on the route from Lincoln to the Humber: a single small manor house, the Castle Grosmal and a collection of hovels. A small collection at that.

'Don't they call it Baernodebi le Wold now?' Hermitage asked innocently.

'Some do.' Aethelred let the words drip out.

'And what is that brings you to De'Ath's Dingle, Aethelred?' Wat asked.

'There has been an incident.'

'An incident?'

'Well, a bit of a death really.'

'A bit of a death?' Hermitage was puzzled. 'Don't they come in wholes?'

Wat and Athan exchanged the look of despair.

'It's a figure of speech, Hermitage,' Wat explained. 'But what can this have to do with us, or this monastery? We're not associated with the village.'

'Oh, absolutely. It's just that the Lord of the Manor where it took place wants matters resolved.'

'I'm sure the local priest could carry out a burial,' Hermitage offered.

'Resolved?' Wat said, emphasising the word. 'What do you mean, resolved? When you say a bit of a death, do you mean a bit of a suspicious one?'

'Ah, yes. Well, to the nub of it, eh?'

'Who's dead?' Wat was being quite blunt now.

'Chap called de Turold.'

'Never heard of him.'

'Well, I don't expect you move in King William's personal circle.'

'Oh dear.' Wat seemed to consider this to be very serious.

'Quite.'

'What?' asked Hermitage, for whom subtlety was a word beginning with 'S'.

'Hermitage,' Wat said, facing his friend, 'you have really got to start paying attention. I know this sort of thing is new to you, but try and learn something, particularly after the last occasion.' At this he cast a significant glance at Athan, who stared back, daring him to go too far.

Hermitage started to ponder. 'I shall think it through.'

'That's the spirit, and try not to think the best of everyone while you do it.'

'So we're faced with a death, which it appears is suspicious,' Hermitage began.

'Good.'

'And the victim, this de Turold chap, seems to be known to King William.'

'Therefore?'

'One of King William's circle has possibly been murdered, and the King probably doesn't know yet.'

'And when he finds out?'

Revelation dropped in on Hermitage. 'He won't be happy. And if the King isn't happy, he'll do something to someone. So we need to find out what did happen so that we can tell the King. Before he finds out.'

'Are you sure about this?' Aethelred frowned at Athan as Hermitage's reasoning gathered pace.

'Once he gets going it's quite impressive,' Wat said.

'Well, I hope he gets going a bit quicker than this. The King is due to arrive tonight.'

'Ah,' said Wat in a very knowing sort of way.

'Where was de Turold when he died?' Hermitage's tone was much more business-like now.

'What does that matter?' Aethelred snapped back.

'Ah, somewhere significant then? Was he at home, does he live in Baernodebi le – er, village?

'No, he was visiting.'

'Did many people know where he was?'

'A few, I suppose. I don't follow.'

'Well, if the murder, let's assume it was a murder,' Hermitage almost added 'just for fun' as he was enjoying this, 'if this murder took place when few people knew where de Turold was, it narrows the possible suspects. Unless it was an accident, of course?'

'No, no accident,' Aethelred replied, squirming slightly.

'I see.'

'Well, I won't detain you further,' Athan jumped in. 'You all clear off and deal with this little matter and, erm, let me know how it turns out. If you have to.'

'I can leave?' Hermitage's spirits leapt and he shot a pleadingly hopeful look at Wat.

'You can both leave,' Athan replied. 'I've recommended the pair of you for this, er, mission. Hermitage can sort it all out and mister Wat can make a tapestry out of it.'

'Why us?' Suspicion dripped from Wat's words.

'Aethelred here is looking for learned men to study the event and find out what happened. Naturally he came to a monastery.'

'This one?' Wat was aghast.

'Watch it,' Athan hissed. 'We were closest,' he explained. 'Naturally when I heard the tale I thought of Hermitage and his little weaving friend, and their remarkable powers of investy-whatnot.'

'Investigation,' Hermitage explained.

'Exactly. Who better to send?'

'Send where exactly?' Wat said slowly.

'The site of the death, of course,' Athan said with a very large grin.

'And that would be exactly?'

Aethelred replied, 'The home of my...' He paused and managed to drag the word out, 'master.'

'Please, someone, give me a name?' Wat looked to them both.

Simultaneously, one in happy tones and one very far from that, Athan and Aethelred replied, 'Lord Robert Grosmal.'

There was a silence which Hermitage broke with a sob. 'Jesus save us.'

Caput V

Half past Seven: Monk to Castle

ROTHER HERMITAGE DIDN'T REALLY KNOW what to do with himself. He was naturally delighted to be escaping the clutches of Athan. He knew what those clutches were like, and what damage they could do.

He was also delighted he would be spending more time with Wat. He recognised his reliance on the weaver for his supply of information on the norms of behaviour outside of the monastery. Or common sense, as Wat called it.

Wat himself had not seemed so keen on the passage of events. Obviously the poor man wanted to get back to his trade and this expedition would be a distraction. Hermitage had helpfully suggested that the new Norman nobility might like to commission works from Wat, and the weaver agreed this was a possible upside. If they liked what he did, and some of them were bound to, there would be a whole new market to cater for.

However, as Wat had then unhelpfully pointed out, the Normans had so far shown a pattern of seeing things they liked and simply taking them. Usually leaving the previous owner in a very poor condition.

All of Hermitage's positive thinking was being rudely brushed aside by the recognition that he had another journey in front him. Even though this would be a very short one, he did not like journeys. If they didn't start badly, they ended badly. Or they had bad bits in the middle. Sometimes all three. It was only Wat's intervention during his last excursion to Lincoln that had saved his life. At least he would have the man with him from the start this time.

There would also be Aethelred, of course. Not that he seemed fully engaged with anything. Hermitage knew he could be a bit distant at times, but Aethelred was positively vacant. He answered questions and engaged in conversation, but his mind always seemed elsewhere. The events around him were real enough, but he just wasn't interested in them.

'So,' Wat announced as he appeared at the opening to Hermitage's cell, 'ready?'

'Absolutely.' Hermitage picked up a small bundle from his cot. Or rather from the space his cot used to occupy until it disappeared one afternoon. It was only as he looked down at the vacant space that he remembered some of the firewood in Athan's study had looked very familiar.

'Let's go then.'

Hermitage could tell from Wat's tone of voice that he was not happy. This was one of the new skills he had picked up from the weaver.

As they left the cell and headed for the main gate Hermitage spoke up. 'You're not happy.'

'Well done, Hermitage. No, I'm not.'

'Why?'

'I should have left weeks ago when I first said so. Then I wouldn't have been here when the skinny Saxon turned up and I'd be back at my workshop now, making money.'

'And I'd probably be dead,' Hermitage added, 'crackling on Athan's fire to keep his feet warm.'

'There is that, I suppose,' said Wat. It didn't sound like he found the argument persuasive.

'I don't actually see why you have to go,' Hermitage said as he thought about their situation.

'Eh?'

'As far as I can see Aethelred came here to get a monk to look into this death. I'm sure Robert Grosmal,' at the name he crossed himself, 'isn't expecting a weaver as well. I could go on and you can go to your work.'

Wat frowned. 'A moment ago you were begging me to stay.'

'Ah yes, but that was because of Athan who wanted to kill me. Aethelred doesn't want to kill me and Robert Grosmal,' another cross, 'hasn't met me, so won't want to kill me for ages yet.'

'The murder's got to be solved though.'

'I can do that.'

'Really?' Wat didn't sound convinced.

'Probably.' Hermitage didn't sound convinced either. 'I could give it a go.'

'The place will be full of soldiers and Normans and ordinary people. The type who aren't open to a reasoned argument or a well turned debate. The type who stab first and ask questions later. If they bother to ask questions at all. I'd feel worse leaving you in a place like that than I would leaving you to Athan.'

'How far away is your workshop?'

'Derby.'

'Well, that's not too far. You could head off there while we go to Baernodebi and then catch up with us later.'

'Not too far? Derby? Have you any idea of geography?'

'Not really, no.'

By this time they had reached the main gate where the gatekeeper, Mad Thomas, hopped about shouting at the gate and the people gathered around it.

There were a lot of people gathered around it. Ordinary working people in ordinary working rags. Aethelred stood out like a stick in a field without any other sticks in it.

'What's going on?' Wat asked as they drew up to the man.

Aethelred gave them his usual disinterested look. 'We're leaving,' he said simply, 'aren't we?'

'What, all of us?' Wat gestured to the throng that was gathered.

'I wanted to travel light. Speed of the essence and all that.'

'Who are all these people?' Hermitage asked.

'Oh, just the usual,' Aethelred gestured vaguely, 'victuallers, camp managers, porters, cobblers, tailors.'

'Tailors? Baernodebi's only round the corner.' Wat found this incredible.

'One has to keep one's clothes in good order.'

'Oh, one does,' Wat agreed. 'And what about them?'

'Ah yes.' Aethelred acknowledged the presence of a good sized contingent of armed men. They were clearly Norman, they were well equipped and be-weaponed, and they looked ugly. Obviously they were all Norman ugly, but there was an underlying ugliness of spirit which rose like steam from a herd of sweating horses. Something in their movement said they were looking for something to be ugly to. Probably a Saxon something.

'I suppose they came along for the ride?' Wat asked.

'Lord Grosmal wanted to make sure the journey was completed safely.' Aethelred shrugged.

'I bet he did.'

'At least we'll make it,' Hermitage put in.

'I wouldn't bank on that,' Wat commented. 'I really don't think I can leave you with this lot, Hermitage.'

'Of course you can't leave,' Aethelred said, a hint of worry in his voice.

'And that would be why exactly?' Wat folded his arms and faced the thin man.

'This is Lord Grosmal's personal guard. Well, some of it anyway. They accompanied me here and their vassal was involved in my preliminary discussions with your abbot.'

'He's really only a prior,' Hermitage said in high dudgeon.

Aethelred waved the objection away. 'He knows I'm to return with Brother Hermitage and a chap called Wat.'

'And if you don't return with them?'

'Out of the question really. I think if any of us consider going anywhere other than Castle Grosmal we'll incur the vassal's displeasure.'

'And he's a decisive sort of chap, I imagine.' Wat glanced over at a very large Norman who was hitting some of the other Normans.

'Ghastly man,' Aethelred explained. 'In my day I wouldn't have trusted him with the blunt end of a horse.'

'Not your day any more, though.'

'No, indeed,' Aethelred sighed

'At least that solves my problem. I'm coming with you, Hermitage. Perhaps I could get your travelling cobbler to stitch my boots.'

Hermitage followed Wat and Aethelred out of the gate and into the train of people. They had sorted out bags, carts and horses and were now ready for the road. This was it. They were off. He turned to look back at the monastery.

'I shall miss the place,' he said.

'You are joking,' Wat responded.

'It's been my home for two years.'

'Yes, a horrible one as far as I can gather. You've been mistreated, attacked, had your property stolen and your superiors did their very best to execute you. I'd be happy to go if I were you.'

'Perhaps I'll come back one day.'

'Not if you've got any sense,' said Wat. Then he smacked himself on the forehead as if he'd said something ridiculous.

◆   ◆   ◆

The journey to Castle Grosmal began uneventfully and was very well ordered. The vassal and his band of decidedly un-merry men kept everything and everyone in order.

Wat found that Aethelred's caravan was very well provisioned and feasted rather well from the back of a cart, out of sight of the Saxon. Hermitage was horrified, but Wat reasoned, really rather well for a weaver, that they were performing a function for the castle and so were entitled to be fed.

Hermitage turned the argument over in his mind before reluctantly accepting a small piece of crust from one of Wat's loaves.

His stomach turned over a very few minutes later as it was full of chicken, cheese, mutton and a rather nice pickled swede.

His guilt nearly made him bring the lot up as they passed the outlying districts of the monastery, where one or two hardy idiots still waited for alms from the monks. The starving locals emerged at the sound of a passing caravan, doubtless hoping that some generous spirit would spare them a morsel or two, and so keep death from their doors for another day.

They needn't have worried. The caravan spared them not a second glance, but one of the carts did run over a dog, so they all ate that evening.

◆　　◆　　◆

It was only a matter of half an hour later, with the sun still struggling to top the lower trees, that the train approached the castle demesne. As the parade of Norman might and Saxon luxury which had cosseted their journey drew close to the edge of the woods, the lead Norman shied his horse to one side.

His fellows followed suit and there was much shouting and pointing in French. The shouting was in French, the pointing was universally understood.

'Oh, what is it now?' Aethelred huffed from the place on his carriage, from which he looked down at the walking Wat and Hermitage.

'There seems to be some disturbance,' Hermitage commented, craning his neck to try and see what was going on.

Aethelred climbed down and the three of them advanced,

Wat muttering bitterly at the damage the path was doing to his boots.

When they arrived at the sight of the trouble, the Normans were gathered in a huddle far away from one tree in particular. They seemed to be arguing with themselves over something.

Hermitage looked at them and then at the tree.

'Oh, it's the Green Man,' he said in a very relaxed and untroubled voice. He went over to the tree in question and indicated a large carving that had been made in the trunk. It was a man's face with a curly beard which went round and round until it came back on itself.

'Rather a good one,' Hermitage said as he traced the carving with his finger and admired the effort that must have gone into it.

As soon as he touched the thing, the Normans gasped as one.

'What's wrong with them?' Wat asked.

'They think it's an evil spirit,' Aethelred replied with some contempt, sniffing his nose at the panicking Normans. 'They reckon if you see the Green Man you'll die.'

'What nonsense,' Hermitage scoffed. 'They must have the Man in France, or something similar. It's a common image, very ancient. Obviously the underlying theology is fundamentally dangerous and evil and its protagonists will be punished by God, but some pagan concepts are understandable.'

'Really?' Wat was surprised. 'I thought men of the Church burnt pagans.'

'Some do.' It was Hermitage's turn to scoff. 'But they are as ignorant as the pagans themselves. There is much knowledge of nature and the like which we could usefully harness.'

'I think if a Churchman heard you saying that he'd burn you first.'

'Very likely,' Hermitage nodded. 'Obviously the Druids and the like have fallen from the path completely and will burn in the fires of hell for eternity,' he said equitably, 'but there are some groups who care for the country without all the heresy.'

'Really,' said Wat, with declining interest.

'Oh yes. In fact I made quite a study of the various groups at one time. An old abbot of mine said I could leave the monastery for many weeks to gather as much information as possible, so that appropriate prayers could be constructed to ensure their damnation.'

Wat just shook his head and granted himself a wry smile.

'There was The Ancient Gathering of Woodmen, The Circle of the Tree, The Green Man's Acolytes, The Brotherhood of the Sward, The...,'

'Yes, yes I'm sure,' Wat interrupted. 'Whatever they do, they're scaring the life out of the Normans.'

'Foolish fellows,' Hermitage concluded, 'be off with you.' He shooed them along the path.

The guards eventually gathered themselves together, taking not the blindest bit of notice of Hermitage and hurried on. They completely forgot their charges and were keen to get back to whatever it was guards got back to.

◆　　◆　　◆

As they emerged from the shadow of the woods Hermitage gazed in wonder at the building which leapt up before him. It was already abuzz with people coming and going, with guards guarding and with builders building. He thought he recognised a massive figure wandering among the tradespeople, holding his ruler up here and there to measure progress.

There were very few people in the world Hermitage found irritating, but Chirk the builder was one of them. The investigation into the death of Brother Ambrosius at De'Ath's Dingle required Hermitage to ask Chirk some questions. What appeared to be a simple task had driven him to real anger, as confusion, obfuscation and plain stupidity poured from Chirk like a leaky bucket. He hoped the builder wasn't involved in this death, but it was a bit of a coincidence.

Trying to ignore Chirk, Hermitage found the view of the castle a marvel. Stretching away on either side of their approach the main walls towered into the sky. They were still being extended, but they must have been at least six feet high. Directly in front of them, terminating the track they were on, was the drawbridge.

As far as Hermitage could recall, the usual Norman approach to building was to put up a pile of all the soil and rocks for miles around and stick a crude wooden fortification on top. There would be a moat of sorts around the pile and that was that. This construction was taking the whole concept into new realms.

At the bottom of this pile of soil and rocks there was a wall, going all the way round. Well, Hermitage was sure it would go all the way round when it was finished. In the middle of the wall was an arched gateway. A most unusual arch, being a half circle supported on two pillars built into the stonework. These Normans really were a peculiar people.

The main pile itself was simply huge. In years to come, people would probably mistake it for a hill. It must have taken the Normans months to build it – or rather it must have taken the Normans months to tell the Saxons to build it.

There was still a moat on the outside of the walls, a green and dank-looking moat, and it coagulated before the main entrance. The drawbridge was required to get across this filthy obstacle, but Hermitage couldn't actually see how it would draw. There were no ropes or chains attached, nor any holes in what must be the main gatehouse from which to pull it up. He put this down to his lack of knowledge.

Inside the arch of the gate, workmen were building what appeared to be a latticework of wood and iron. Hermitage had heard of these things, and was staggered to see such a sophisticated piece of equipment in real life. A portcullis. This would be a magnificent defensive mechanism. When it was finished. And installed. Hermitage could see the carpenter and the blacksmith directing the construction. Or at least he assumed they would be directing it once they stopped arguing.

He was slightly puzzled about how it was going to fit as it currently looked much too small for the gate. Probably they were still building it.

He also thought the moat might be less than effective as a group of children were playing in it, paddling up to their ankles.

Behind the walls, on top of the mound constructed for the purpose, the main tower of the castle emerged. Wooden scaffolding surrounded it and piles of stone lay around waiting to be hoisted into place.

To Hermitage's untrained eye, bits of this tower appeared to be slipping down the slope, as they created unsightly bulges and deformities in the main shape. In places it even looked as if the builders had given up on the main construction and started again, further down the hill. It was very hard to tell which was a deliberate building and which simply a store of stone. Again he put this down to his lack of knowledge of the art of the builder, but the place did remind him a bit of De'Ath's Dingle.

Wat came up beside him.

'What a dump,' the weaver commented.

'Really?' Hermitage asked.

'Saxon's revenge,' Wat whispered.

'Where?'

'Here.' Wat gestured at the castle.' I mean, look at it. One puff of wind and the whole place will come down. The drawbridge won't work, the towers are wrong and that portcullis isn't going to fit.'

'I thought it looked a bit odd. But why?'

'I'm sure Chirk and his friends are taking their cut. Do a shoddy job the first time round and then get paid to do it again.

Better still, get a contract to keep coming back and fixing things for years.'

'That's dishonest.' Hermitage was horrified.

'Certainly is. Better still if you can do it to the invaders. They might have taken your land, but you still can make them pay.'

'A bit risky, I'd have thought.' Hermitage nodded towards the last of the guards as they entered the castle.

'It is a bit. Good chance the lord will spot what you're up to and have your head. For the place to be in this much of a mess, they must have sized up Lord Robert as a complete pointy arse.'

Wat had a further thought. 'In which case the place might be good for business after all.' He rubbed his hands.

'But Grosmal's reputation is horrible.'

'It might be on a battlefield. Dealing with hardened soldiers and the thick of war is one thing. Getting a bunch of builders to do what they're told calls for much sterner stuff.'

They looked around for Aethelred to see what they should do next. He was nowhere in sight. The porters and victuallers were unloading the carts they'd only loaded up an hour earlier, while the cobblers and tailors went off muttering to themselves. As they passed Wat and Hermitage they raised eyebrows into foreheads in the universal gesture of those who are dealing with fools.

More scanning the site eventually located Aethelred coming out from behind a pile of masonry, obviously stacked and waiting to be put to use in the walls. Or waiting to be made into something that looked a bit more like masonry and a bit less like a pile of rock. The man was in earnest conversation with another. The second man wore a close-fitting cloth hat almost over his eyes. He was still a thin fellow, but when he stood next to Aethelred he looked positively porcine.

The two were in deep conversation, heads close and voices low. When the discussion finished the second man looked all around him. Then he slipped away from the site and off into the woods.

'Now what do you suppose that was all about?' Hermitage asked.

Wat put his hands on his hips and gazed at Hermitage without speaking.

'What?' Hermitage was bewildered.

'Hermitage, I'm proud of you.' Wat patted Hermitage on his shoulder. The young monk stood up straighter and glowed.

'Really?'

'You're becoming suspicious. Well done.'

'Oh.' Hermitage's shoulders fell slightly. 'That doesn't sound like a very good thing to be.'

'Depends on the circumstances. You don't want to do it all the time, but it can save your life. Work on it. What are you suspicious of?'

Hermitage knew that Wat meant well, but this felt like a very backwards step somehow. Wouldn't it be better if he just stuck to people who didn't do suspicious things?

'A secret,' he said reluctantly. 'Aethelred's behaviour tells me he has a secret. He didn't want to be seen or heard talking to that fellow. The fellow didn't really want to be seen or heard at all, and is plainly not part of the castle household. None of which would be of the remotest interest if there hadn't just been a murder. And if Aethelred was not obviously a well-bred Saxon in a castle full of Normans.'

Wat gave a very respectful and polite round of applause.

'Marvellous,' he said

'Awful,' said Hermitage. 'Imagine thinking such things of people.'

'I'm afraid the number of people to be treated with suspicion outnumber the rest of the population,' Wat shrugged.

'Truly awful.'

'Question is, what do we do about it?' Wat prompted.

'Gosh, er, keep an eye on Aethelred?'

'Go on.'

'We don't know what they were talking about or who the fellow was. It could be entirely innocent. Aethelred might have been ordering new hose and doesn't like to discuss that sort of thing in public. If we notice him behaving strangely, then perhaps we, erm, follow him?'

'Good.'

'Or listen in on his conversations?'

'Excellent.'

'It's all rather rude, isn't it?'

'More rude than killing people?' Wat asked.

'I suppose not,' Hermitage admitted. 'I don't see Aethelred as a killer though.'

Wat nodded. 'Interesting. Why not?'

'Well, he's a noble.' Hermitage thought this bit of reasoning would be obvious to a sheep.

'Was a noble,' Wat corrected.

'Oh yes. Still, I imagine he's not capable of doing anything himself. He might order someone else to do it, but does that count?'

'I think if you're a noble, even an ex noble, you can decide what counts.'

Hermitage nodded acceptance of this fundamental truth.

Aethelred was approaching now.

'Here's another option,' Wat whispered to Hermitage as the Saxon joined them.

'Who was that then?' Wat asked brightly.

Hermitage gaped at his insolence.

'I beg your pardon?' Aethelred responded.

Hermitage's new-found observational skills could tell that Aethelred was completely thrown by the question. He was probably thrown by someone questioning him at all.

'That chap you were talking to. Well, whispering to. The one who snuck off into the woods after checking no one had seen him. The one you were hiding behind the masonry talking to.

58

That one. Who was he?'

Aethelred now took all of the questions in and drew his bony shoulders back. From his great height he looked down at Wat and gave his answer. 'None of your business,' he said and strode off into the castle, beckoning them to follow in his wake.

Wat grinned at Hermitage and Hermitage found himself grinning back. Then he felt ashamed again and stopped grinning.

What if Aethelred had something to do with the murder of the Norman? The Saxon would certainly have, what was the word he was looking for? Motive. That was it. Aethelred would have a motive to kill a Norman. Probably any Norman, given his fall from power, but particularly a Norman who was building a castle all over what was probably his old home. It might be too dangerous to kill Lord Robert himself, but finishing off a visitor might be just the thing.

Caput VI

Half past Seven: Lady to Castle

ADY FOELLA'S PERAMBULATIONS of Castle Grosmal were inconclusive. Leaving the minstrels' gallery, she followed her own idea of the route down to the main hall. She even took a couple of flights of steps downwards before ending up back in the gallery. She peered down to the hall once more, but Robert had gone. The place was deserted.

Growling her frustration she set off again, this time turning right at every opportunity.

Gallery again.

Next time it was left.

Gallery.

The apparent impossibility of her journey did nothing to assuage Foella's violent temper. She seriously considered jumping over the parapet, but the drop to the hall floor was just a touch too far. She screamed a few times for Eleanor. If she could only get the stupid girl into the hall, she could jump on to a servant for a nice soft landing.

No response. She set off once more, determined to escape this maze if she had to batter the walls down with her bare hands.

Following exactly the same route as before, she found herself in a different corridor. She stopped and glared at it, daring it to be there.

The impudent passage defied her, even presenting a door she hadn't seen before. Knowing that this would be the exit she marched towards it, grabbed the iron ring handle and threw the thing open, ready to berate whoever was on the other side.

It took her a few moments to realise that the floor she stepped on to sloped. It sloped viciously downwards, and it took her feet from under her. Sliding down a polished shoot on her aristocratic backside, Foella screamed.

She screamed in surprise and in shock and, of course, in anger. How dare this castle treat her in this manner? How dare there be a slope behind a door? How dare the slope make her fall – didn't it know who she was? How dare the world be created like this? If she'd met God at that moment, she'd have wrung his neck.

◆   ◆   ◆

Her slippery slope came to an abrupt end, depositing her on a large log. What the hell was a log doing in her way? She would have it burned later.

She was sitting astride the log in a most undignified manner. Good job she wasn't in company. Foella looked for something else to put her feet on and saw another log. She widened her gaze and saw more logs on the floor of this place. In fact, all she could see was logs. This unexpected sight calmed her slightly and she looked around.

She had fallen into an inner courtyard of some sort. It was a square about fifty feet across, open to the sky and entirely floored with logs. Not carefully laid and jointed logs to create an interesting feature. These logs had been simply thrown into this space and left where they landed. If this was the log store for the castle, it was as poorly designed and managed as the rest of the place.

Choosing a log to the side, Foella clambered off her mount and pushed her skirts back down over her legs. She could have sworn she heard a brief moan of disappointment from behind a particularly large pile of logs which occupied the centre of the space.

Not wanting to investigate further, her ladyship staggered to her feet, balanced on the large timber. She looked out into the dull winter light of the log yard and tried to see how the hell she got back inside.

All around her were the steeply rising walls of the castle which kept this place in permanent shadow. They were dotted with the irregular arrow slits and just plain gaps that set Castle Grosmal apart from anything she'd experienced before. As far as she could see, there was no way out. The ramp she'd slid down was as smooth as ice and far too steep to be climbed. The gaps in the walls were too high to be reached and the walls were all encompassing.

Events had gone badly. They were still going in that direction and looked likely to carry on.

Foella scanned the site for any sign of another entrance or exit. Her attention was drawn to the large pile of logs in the middle of the space. Peering at it more closely, she wondered if it was actually some sort of building. It resembled a simple collection of old logs that had been left rotting for so long they had taken root and happened to have grown into the shape of shed.

Then again, perhaps it had been built as a shed and was reverting to logs.

Not wanting to think about it too much, Foella realised the place was starting to give her the creeping shivers. Picking her way gently over discarded lumps of rotten and rotting logs and vegetation, she made towards the nearest outcrop of stone walling, some ten feet to the left.

The floor of this yard was becoming a small wood in its own right. Mounds of sawdust, bits of unwanted wood, chippings and seeds were starting to create a little world. It wasn't a pleasant world, shaded from the strictures of the weather and the goodness of the sunshine. Things were growing which didn't look like they ought to be alive.

She tripped and stumbled, and once trod on something that seemed to move of its own accord. Eventually she grasped the solid stonework of the castle, some of which naturally crumbled away in her hands. Seeing that one direction was no better than any other, she started to shuffle along to her right.

'I wouldn't go that way if I were you, my lady,' said a very civilised voice which none the less made Foella nearly jump back out of her skirt.

She spun round as best she could spin on the wobbly ground, and saw a man standing by the shed.

'What?' was all she could think of.

'I said I wouldn't go that way if I were you, my lady,' the voice repeated. Foella relaxed a little as she recognised the gentle and rounded tones of a well-spoken but rather dim-sounding Saxon. 'The floor does get rather treacherous in that direction. And there's a bit of a bog in the corner.'

This was the sort of voice Foella had associated with in the days before the Normans. It was the voice of the rich Saxon idiots that her father had tried to marry her off to. At least the invasion got her out of marrying that moron Douglas – very good blood, but as poor as some poor people she'd nearly seen once. From a distance. Apparently his name meant 'dweller by the dark stream', and if Foella had her way she'd have drowned him in it. Not suitable material at all.

She found herself feeling nostalgic for the gentle touch of a Saxon noble, or at least for the way they always asked first. Still, business was business. Now she needed a Norman.

Anyway, this fellow didn't look like a rich Saxon. He looked more like one of the logs, dressed in brown from head to foot with moss growing here and there. She couldn't tell his age, but he wasn't far off her own twenty.

Then she remembered the disarray of her dress when she appeared on the log shed floor.

'How long have you been here?' she demanded.

'Oh, months, I think. One loses track really.'

This was not the answer Foella had been expecting.

'Months?'

'Probably. What's the date today?'

'Erm.' Foella had never been very good with numbers. 'January, I think.'

'Missed Christmas again, then,' said the man.

Foella now gingerly made her way back towards the log shed. At least this strange person should know the way out.

Noticing the direction she was taking, the man spoke again. 'And I wouldn't come this way either if I were you, my lady.'

Foella's natural reaction to instructions came to the fore. 'Just who the hell do you think are you, what are you doing here and why can't I walk where I please?'

'Who am I?' said the man as if the question had never occurred to him before. 'They call me Logs, but I don't think that's my name.' He paused for a moment, thinking hard. 'I live here.' Another pause. 'And if you walk straight towards me you will almost certainly step on my dead crows.'

'Mad as a Norman,' Foella mumbled as she ignored his directions. Like so many others, this soul had obviously been humiliated by the invaders and left to rot. In his case, literally.

Stepping reasonably carefully through the rough ground of the courtyard Foella made her way towards the rotting Saxon in the middle of his rotting little kingdom. She was brought up short by a pile of dead crows.

'Ahhyeuch,' said Foella as the smell inveigled its way into her nostrils. She skipped quickly around them and up to the man. She did think for a moment of asking why he had a pile of dead crows, but quickly decided it would cause more trouble than it was worth. She probably didn't want to know anyway.

'How,' she panted, 'do I get out of here?'

'Why would you want to do that?' said the man in obvious puzzlement.

'Well,' said Foella using her talk-to-an-idiot voice, 'it is cold, damp, smelly and dirty. There is no food, no clothing, no fire and no servant. And I think you may be mad.'

'Ah,' said the man, accepting this completely.

'So?'

'So what?'

'Tell me how I get out of here before I scream for a guard or hit you with something myself.'

The man seemed to pause for several moments, carefully considering this plethora of offers. He weighed up, in what was left of his mind, which would be for the best.

'Would you really do that?' he asked, checking the situation.

'Yes,' said Foella in a very convincing voice.

'Oh well,' his mind made up, 'the guards come every now and again and throw their trees out of that hole.' The man gestured to a door some fifteen feet above the ground, below which was a patch of bare and clear earth. Around its opening the remnants of branches could still be seen, as if it was a messy eater.

'What about the door I fell through?' Foella pointed at her arrival gate.

'Yes, they used to use that, but then some builders built something on the other side and they stopped. Anyway, I then chop the trees up into logs and push them down that hole.' He pointed again towards a hole much nearer to them and a lot closer to the ground.

'And that's the way out, is it?' Foella asked.

'Don't know,' said the man, 'but it's the hole that eats my logs.'

Despite herself Foella was curious. She had to know some more about this man.

'Have you always been a logsman?' she said.

This obviously caused some trouble in the Saxon mind. The answer took a while to arrive.

'Ah no, actually I don't think so. I used to live in there,' he gestured to the walls, 'but it all looks different now.'

'You mean you used to live in the castle?' This all made some sense.

'Only it wasn't really a castle then, I think.' Logs seemed perfectly at ease relating his past as if it was all a new revelation to him. 'More a sort of house thing.'

'Before the Normans came, then,' said Foella in what she thought was an encouraging voice, 'this was your house. Probably quite a big house.'

'Yes, I think that's about right. And then the French types came along, knocked down the house and gave me the job of logman here.' Logs sounded as if these events had been a marvellous career development handed to him on a plate by those nice Normans.

'That's about all there is to tell, eh, Logs?' said another voice. Foella was getting a bit fed up with jumping all the time.

The new voice belonged to a tall figure who emerged from the log shed and who Foella felt strangely sure had witnessed her fall and done nothing about it. It was equally Saxon and sophisticated, but a lot more educated. And devious.

'Allow me to escort you from this horrid place, my lady.' The tall man took two steps forward, grasped Foella's arm quite firmly and almost carried her over to the log hole. The grip on her arm was strong and the man was well built. He was dressed far better than Logs, and his face was a lot less vacant. He looked like a man who was used to being in control. He was older and more grizzled, as if he had been through a lot just to get here. Foella considered getting here was pretty much a failure, so no wonder the man looked grizzled.

'Just a minute,' Foella began, thinking that for a log dump this courtyard was strangely crowded. Before she got any further with her enquiries she found herself at the lip of the dark hole which wormed its way into the rotten body of the Castle Grosmal. Her balance deserted her, and only the strong grip of the tall stranger prevented her from falling.

'Logs is quite happy doing his logging, my lady. We look after him and there is no need for you to be concerned about his wellbeing.'

'We?' Foella thought about saying that she was not in the least bit concerned about his wellbeing, but decided that there probably wasn't time.

The man ignored her question.'At the bottom of the hole you will see a door to your right. If you go through that and then take three turns to the right, you will emerge on the outer wall by the gatehouse. And my lady?'

'Yes?' Foella felt somehow completely helpless in this man's grasp, and then realised she was.

'I wouldn't stay in the castle if I were you. I'd go home now.'

'I'm sure you would,' Foella found her tongue, 'but I shall do as I please. Let me go.'

'Please take my advice seriously. You are one of us.'

'I most certainly am not,' Foella snapped back, with a frosty glare around the log store.

'I mean a Saxon.'

'Oh, yes, I suppose so.'

'And it doesn't do to mix with these invaders. They are doing great damage to our country and their time will come.'

'What do you mean?'

'I cannot give you details. That would be to risk discovery.'

'Discovery?' Foella sounded surprised. 'You're in the castle log store, you're bound to be discovered,' she pointed out.

'Not that sort of discovery.' The man was losing patience. 'The discovery of what is happening.'

'Why, what is happening?'

He squinted mysteriously.'That I cannot tell you.'

'I think you've been in the log store too long.' Foella cast a suspicious glance at him.

'Just because the Normans have invaded doesn't mean the matter is closed,' the man explained.

'Too right it doesn't.'

'And there are those of us who are prepared to take action.'

'I was taking action until the idiot got killed.'

'Henri de Turold?' The man asked.

'How did you know?'

'Many things come to the log store.'

Foella looked about.

'Oh, for goodness sake,' the man said, 'not literally.'

'Well, what then?'

'Information.'

'Well, if you get any information about other Norman nobles of marriageable age, let me know.'

'You're planning to marry one of them?' The man was disgusted.

'Not for long,' Foella defended herself.

'Ah, I see,' the man returned to his mysterious tone, 'a devious plan and one demanding great personal sacrifice on your part.'

'I hope not,' Foella was pretty clear on that. 'You're being very mysterious,' she complained.

'I'm trying to be mysterious. Things are mysterious. And if you don't take care, some of the mystery might rub off on you,' he nodded very significantly.

Foella started nodding too, in sympathy. 'I see, well, really must be going.'

'Don't forget, my lady.'

'How could I?'

'Beware the Normans. We'll watch out for you now we know your plan, but you watch out for us.'

'Oh I will, don't worry about that. Now if you would kindly let me go?'

The man kindly let her go.

◆   ◆   ◆

She fell straight into the hole and landed with a bump at the bottom, fortunately into a large heap of discarded leaves and bark.

She looked back up the way she had come and saw the last of a covering of some sort being put in place over the hole.

'Wait a minute, do you know who killed de Turold?' She got no answer.

Foella waited for a few moments to let her eyes get used to the gloom. What had he said? Door to the right and then three to the right, or on the right or something? Or three doors to the right?

There was a faint scrabbling in the dark and leaves were pushed aside by a creature of some bulk. Foella was in the dark. She couldn't see where she was going. Her main target was dead and she couldn't identify any other opportunities at the moment. The whole visit had been awful and this morning had taken it not just downhill, but to the very the bottom. Into a bog. A bog of floating logs.

There were few times in her life when she craved comfort and companionship, but this was turning into one of them. All she wanted to do, right at this moment, was go home. She knew, of course, that her home no longer existed. That all of those who might have offered her comfort and companionship were dead. That there was no longer any home for a Saxon to go to.

Such thoughts and cogitations might give birth to a justifiable sob, if not a few moments of understandable tearfulness and self-pity.

They just made Foella really, really angry.

Caput VII
Eight-o-clock: Castle Grosmal

THE SAYING 'DON'T JUDGE A PRIVY BY ITS HOLE' did not apply to Castle Grosmal. The outside was a shoddy shambles, and any hope that this hid an interior of efficiency and quality was quickly dispelled. If the exterior was an example of the unqualified using the unsuitable to construct the unstable, the theme carried through the gates, where it met a philosophy of 'it'll do'.

If great buildings were going to travel down the centuries, and Hermitage thought the new Cathedral in Lincoln was a fine example, they would be leaving Castle Grosmal well behind. It would be lucky to make it to next Michaelmas.

The pointlessness of most of human activity struck Hermitage forcibly as he gazed about. His thoughts leaped forward, and he imagined that in a thousand years people would look on his time as he looked on the Romans. And they would marvel. They would think great craftsmen had worked tirelessly to create the masterpieces which still stood. They'd have no idea about piles of rubbish like Castle Grosmal and useless builders like Chirk. They'd be lost to history. Good job too.

The courtyard was confused. It was more than that. Perhaps it was the very Platonic form of confusion, the essence from which all confusion in the world emanated. People were walking hither and thither in seemingly pointless but frenetic activity. The hubbub of conversations and orders being barked was a mess, while the buildings themselves were completely at odds and out of sorts.

They seemed to have been caught in the middle of a game of

statues. Most had been trying to get into the right place when the music stopped, but hardly any had made it home.

Even the disorder lacked consistency. The styles of the buildings, if such a word could be applied to this mess, was as random as the layout.

The stable block merged perfectly with the side wall of the main gatehouse – except it wasn't joined to the side wall of the main gatehouse. Next to the keep was what looked remarkably like another keep, only smaller. It was another keep, only smaller. Its builder, having got the hang of one, thought it was easier to just carry on. His financial skills were similarly refined, and he later attended a routine creditors meeting where he was routinely stabbed to death. The maintenance died with him.

As the three men entered the place and Aethelred was noticed, caps were doffed and curtsies curtsied.

'Almost like you run the place,' Wat commented – rather cruelly, Hermitage thought.

Aethelred made no response.

'Morning, master Ethel,' a large Norman guard called. Probably the head guard, judging from the cleanliness of his accoutrements.

'Ethel?' Wat enquired.

'Master Grosmal's choice. I think he has trouble getting his head round Saxon names. Or any word with more than two syllables, come to that.'

Wat sniggered slightly.

'Don't,' said Ethel, with the first sign of a real person lurking under his frigid exterior, 'don't even start.'

He led them up the hill, through a door of sorts and into the ante chamber of the main hall.

'Wait here while I find the lord.'

'Hermitage,' Wat said, when Ethel had gone.

'What?'

'Let me do the talking. Please.'

'What talking?'

'The talking to Grosmal. When he asks us anything, you let me reply.'

'What if it's a question on the interpretation of scripture?' Hermitage asked brightly.

Wat sighed. 'If he asks a direct question on the interpretation of scripture, you can answer,' he promised.

'Thank you.'

'I'll also bite my own ear off,' Wat grinned, then gestured Hermitage to silence.

'You may enter.' Ethel reappeared through a half-open door. 'But don't touch the door,' he said, indicating that it might fall off its hinges at any moment.

They squeezed through the space and stood in the farthest corner of the great chamber of the castle of Robert Grosmal, awaiting their interview.

Ethel strode to the other side of the room and talked quietly to his master. He suddenly gestured vigorously for Wat and Hermitage to join him. They scuttled over as quickly as they could and stood, just catching the end of Robert's softly spoken sentence.

'...find the individual, is that clear?'

Ethel indicated most persuasively that they should just say yes.

'Yes,' they both said together.

'Good,' said Robert and he rose from his chair to face them.

'Because for all I know, it could have been you two.' Hermitage assumed that this was supposed to make some sort of sense.

'And if you muck up, it probably will be.' Lord Robert stared into their faces. Hermitage leant backwards. Wat held his ground.

'So,' Lord Robert began, 'why are you still here?'

Ethel quickly grabbed one handful of habit and another of fine cloak and dragged the two away.

✦   ✦   ✦

Once out of the room the retainer beckoned they should follow him. He led the way through twisting corridors, which weren't supposed to twist, past small openings in the walls, which weren't supposed to open, and eventually up a winding flight of uneven steps to a small turret room.

This was clearly Ethel's chamber. It contained a cot with straw mattress, a log for a chair and another larger one which seemed to be playing the part of a desk. It had a quill on it, but no parchment. Or ink.

'Sit down,' said Ethel as he sat on the log. Hermitage went to sit on the desk, but the look on Ethel's face made him change his mind. He joined Wat on the cot.

'Let me tell you what has happened.' And Ethel related the sad end of Henri de Turold in all its revolting detail. At one point he produced the arrow, recently removed from the Norman's nether regions. Both he and Wat had a jolly good laugh at that.

'And we're supposed to figure out who killed him?' said Wat. 'Who fired an arrow? Not easy.'

'There are a number of interesting facts which might help our considerations,' said Hermitage as he sat on the cot with a very puzzled look on his face.

Ethel and Wat looked to one another, and then to the monk.

'Such as?' said Ethel. He absentmindedly took up the arrow from Henri's darkest hole before he remembered what it was. He put it down quickly.

'Well, the arrow itself to begin with. May I?' Hermitage held his hand out for the murder weapon.

Ethel picked it up gingerly and held it towards the monk.

Hermitage grabbed it and happily examined it closely. Ethel turned his nose up. Even Wat looked askance.

'This tells us a lot.'

'I can still smell some of it,' Ethel put in.

'I mean, look at it. It's not from a Saxon longbow. It's too short.'

'You're right.' Ethel now looked at it more closely. 'Well, well, I wouldn't have thought of that.' The Saxon raised his eyebrows.

Wat seemed about to say something, but thought better of it.

Hermitage beamed with pride. 'Are you sure it's complete?' he asked.

The eyebrows came down again. 'I wasn't about to go digging for any more of it. It's got a point on one end and some feathers on the other. I believe that constitutes an arrow.'

'In which case, why is it so short? I can't imagine any bow small enough to fire this.'

'A child?' Ethel suggested.

'Could be, but I can't imagine a child able to deliver enough force to finish someone off in so, erm, so personal a manner.'

They sat in silence for a few moments until Wat spoke.

'You are joking?' he asked.

'You have something to add, Mister Weaver?' Ethel dribbled his disdain.

'The arrow,' Wat pointed at it, 'is not an arrow.'

Ethel guffawed. 'Mister Wat, I may not be familiar with all the contrivances of manual labour, but I think I recognise an arrow when I see one.'

Hermitage was enthralled. He held the thing at a distance and looked at it in wonder. 'What is it then?'

'It's a crossbow bolt,' said Wat, in the tone of one stating the mindblowingly obvious. 'Perhaps some of Ethel's men had some. When they were his men, of course. In any case he's probably paid for quite a lot,' he added through his guffaws.

'There's no need to be rude,' Ethel snapped.

'Of course, a crossbow,' said Hermitage, trying to mediate. 'Why didn't I think of that?

'Because you've got good reason not to know a crossbow from a crooked mile. You're a monk.'

'Ah yes,' said Hermitage, as if he needed reminding. 'Anyway, I'm sure we'll find out more as we investigate.'

There was a further pause as Wat grinned and Ethel grimaced.

Hermitage broke the awkward silence. 'So we now have a crossbow as the murder weapon. Easier for a child to fire, I suppose. The next question, of course, is what was Henri doing naked in January?'

'Pervert.' Wat again stated the obvious.

'Possibly,' said Hermitage. 'And the honoured noble was still sitting on the privy?' This was to Ethel.

'Honoured noble?' Ethel questioned. 'Oh, Henri? Yes. I don't think I'm going to forget that sight.'

'So,' said Hermitage, 'someone must have been below the garderobe, lying in wait for their victim.'

'I don't think they'd have lain,' said Ethel with disdain.

'All right, stood in wait for Henri. Then they shot him in the, er, er, garderobe, and ran off.'

Hermitage gazed out of an arrow slit in thought. Or rather gazed out of the hole in the wall which he assumed was meant to be an arrow slit. 'The question is, why? Did Henri have any enemies?'

'Do Normans burn down the woods?' said Ethel, indicating the stupidity of the question.

'Then we are really no further forward. It could have been anyone,' Wat said

'Well,' said Ethel, rising, 'this has been really useful. If you'd like to go away and find the killer now, I have work to do.'

'What if we can't find out who did it?' asked Hermitage, thinking that they might expect a bit more support than that.

'I'd be happy to notify your next of kin,' said Ethel.

There was an uncomfortable pause.

'I think that we should look at the garderobe,' Hermitage said eventually.

'Why?' said Ethel.

'Because that is where the murder took place, there might be evidence.'

'Heavy what?'

'Evidence. Something that might tell us who did it.'

'What, like a note or something?'

'Well, a note would be good, but not likely, I think.'

'Whatever you like, just do it quickly. The King will arrive tonight and we'll need to know by then.'

'Tonight!' Hermitage was appalled.

'Well, of course. How long did you want?' Ethel was puzzled. 'And didn't you hear Grosmal say?'

'I couldn't catch what he was saying, to be honest.' Hermitage had caught Wat's shrug.

'Well, he said tonight.'

'Resolving the death of Brother Ambrosius took the best part of a week.'

'A week?' It was Ethel's turn to be shocked. 'I suppose you can have a week if you want.'

'Thank you.'

'But you'll be dead for the last six days of it.' He ushered them out of the chamber. 'I suggest you get a move on.'

◆　　◆　　◆

'I suppose running away is out of the question,' said Hermitage once they were out of earshot, strolling carefully along the top of one of the castle walls, looking for the way down.

'I think so,' said Wat. 'If it was just Ethel I'd say yes, but that Grosmal has the look in his eyes.'

'The look?'

'You know – the look the mad people have when you can tell they're capable of doing something horrible for no apparent reason and with no warning.'

'Ah yes,' Hermitage nodded. He knew the look well. He was disappointed to hear that it belonged to mad people. Most of his Brother monks had it at one time or another.

'And Grosmal is a noble. He's got soldiers and weapons and authority. People like that who also have the look are best dealt with carefully. If you can't avoid them all together.'

'I am sorry I got you into this,' Hermitage said with sincerity.

'Not your fault. Teach me to hang around too long.' Wat peered over the edge of the castle wall with great care.

'But you only hung around because of me.'

'And as it turns out that could be a good thing.'

'How?'

'I don't want to be rude, Hermitage, but I think if you were trying to sort this lot out on your own, you'd probably be dead by tonight.'

'You're probably right,' Hermitage nodded.

'So we have to solve the crime. Again.'

'So it seems.'

'We'll be getting a reputation if we're not careful.' Wat gave a grim smile.

'People from all over the land could be seeking us out to re-solve their mysteries. Murders, thefts and the like.' Hermitage sounded a bit dubious.

'So,' said Wat, reaching some sort of inner conclusion, 'if we do get out this one alive...'

'Yes?'

'If we do sort out who killed de Turold and escape in one piece?'

'Yes?'

'We split up, go into hiding and never mention it to anyone.'

'Suits me.' Hermitage nodded wholehearted agreement.

'To the garderobe then,' said Wat. He spied a castle guard.

The guard was walking very tentatively along the parapet,

prodding the floor in front of him at regular intervals with a long pole. Hermitage approached.

'Excuse me,' he said politely. The guard nearly jumped out of his boots and off the edge of the unprotected wall.

'Oh God, don't do that,' said William le Morton, 'you nearly had me off.'

'Aren't you supposed to ask us who we are and what we're doing here?' said Wat.

'You're the two who've come to investigate the murder of Henri de Turold,' said William simply. 'You have to keep ahead of the news in this place, otherwise it comes up behind you.'

'Er, yes,' said Hermitage. He saw William's point. 'Can you tell us where the garderobe is?'

'Well, I can,' said William, 'but why don't you use the straw like normal people? The garderobe's only for Lord Grosmal's personal guests.'

'We are his personal guests,' said Wat, which brought a look of huge respect and fear to William's face. 'We don't want to use it, anyway – we just want to look at it. Apparently.'

'Oh, right,' said William, 'please yourself.' He took a cautious half-step away from the pair. 'Second tower on your left, up two flights, second opening on the right.'

'Thank you,' said Hermitage.

'Down the long corridor, past the tapestry, don't touch it whatever you do, down two steps and then up one, first left and it's on your right.'

'I think we'll find it,' said Wat, pulling Hermitage away.

'Just follow your nose if you get lost,' said William, genuinely trying to be helpful.

◆　　◆　　◆

They didn't really need to follow their noses as, from the moment they stepped across the threshold into the second tower on the left, the smell assailed them. It then assaulted them, abused them and told them that it knew where they lived and never forgot a face.

It had grown up until it wasn't really a smell at all any more. Now it was a sort of tangible, palpable thing with a mind of its own and a lot of very strange ideas.

A fresh breeze bearing the tangy bite of pine cones had wafted across the grassy sward, bringing with it the scent of the dew, and had started to freshen its way into the tower. It was told in no uncertain terms that it was not welcome.

Hermitage and Wat moved carefully over the rough stonework, following the direction their noses told them the thickening atmosphere came from. Their minds and bodies told them to get the hell out.

Eventually they came to the threshold of the stinking chamber and entered.

A single candle burned in the gloom, but the gloom was winning. Arrow slits in the wall let a little light in, but it stopped before it got too close to anything unpleasant.

'So this is Lord Robert's garderobe. God's holy trousers, what a stink,' Wat exclaimed. He pulled a piece of scented cloth from his sleeve and slapped it firmly across his nose.

'It is pungent, isn't it?' Even Hermitage, who was used to the pretty horrible smells of De'Ath's Dingle, had a pronounced wrinkle on his nose.

'This is worse than doing it in the corner of the room,' Wat mumbled through his cloth. 'Tell me again what the advantage is supposed to be?'

'It's all wrong,' said Hermitage, looking around as if he was checking the spelling in a scriptorium.

'Are you on to something already?' Wat asked.

'No. This garderobe, it's all wrong.'

'It certainly smells it,' said Wat with feeling. He moved over towards an arrow slit in the wall, noticing as he did so that it looked too small for an arrow to pass through. 'Mind you, I've never really been one for new-fangled inventions.'

Hermitage was being quite revolting. He strode about the room, examining it closely. He even went over to the seats and peered into the holes. Wat gagged slightly at the prospect.

'I read about these things in a book on architecture the old Bishop of Lincoln had,' Hermitage said, all enthusiasm, gazing in wonder at the construction around him.

'Good God, what are the ropes for?' Wat spluttered from behind his mask.

Two fairly sturdy ropes were tied to the upper stones of the seats. Their ends dangled into one of the holes.

'Straining ropes, I imagine.' Hermitage tested the strength of one of them. 'When your need is urgent, but things are not, erm, progressing well, you hang on to the ropes for extra purchase.'

Wat coughed deeply into his mask.

'I'm sure it's wrong, though. The seats are supposed to be in the wall, allowing the, erm, material to fall to the ground outside the castle, from where it's taken away. You're not supposed to keep it. Especially not indoors.'

'When you look at the state of this place, do you think the builders would get anything as sophisticated and complicated as this right?' Wat was edging back towards the entrance.

'I suppose not. But you'd think someone would spot it wasn't working properly.'

'I suspect Robert's list of talents doesn't include thinking.'

'Hum.'

Wat was now back at the entrance and anxious to move away into the fresh air. Hermitage had not moved at all. He was still looking around the place.

As he looked at the holes, and weighed up the overall construction of the facility, the monk started to picture the chain of events. He stood open mouthed in wonder as his mind reconstructed an unfamiliar landscape. Real, practical things done by real practical people.

Just as he could untangle an argument, given the appropriate universal truths, it only now occurred to him to do the same with actions. If someone walked into a room, they had to walk out again. Or not, in the case of de Turold. What a marvellous revelation. He wanted to try it out straightaway.

'What are you doing?'

Hermitage realised that Wat was talking.

'Like we did with the death of Brother Ambrosius, I'm re-creating.'

'Ambrosius was in a nice clean refectory.'

'In De'Ath's Dingle?'

'A relatively clean refectory. Relative to this place anyway.'

'But this is where de Turold died.'

Hermitage came over to the door, turned his back on it and walked into the room. He bypassed the candle and sat on the nearest seat.

'Interesting,' he said.

'Really?' Wat was not convinced.

'Oh yes. De Turold would have sat here.'

'Why?' asked Wat.

'Nearest to the door and closest to the candle. Who'd want to go on the next seat, further into the dark?'

'Not me.'

Hermitage looked about and hummed, pretending that he was using the facility. He moved about a bit to get comfortable. He then started to get up, feigned a look of intense pain and shock and collapsed back on to the seat, head drooping.

'So I was right,' he said, 'the arrow did come from down there.'

Hermitage parted his knees and pointed downwards into the hole.

Wat really did gag this time.

'And given that there is a chamber below, rather than the outside air, whoever shot at Henri may have left some trace. Footprints perhaps.'

Wat gave up all pretence and hurried to the spare hole. He hung his head over it and threw up.

'I bet no one ever thought of using them for that,' said Hermitage, fascinated.

'Can we leave please?' Wat said as he righted himself.

'Of course,' said Hermitage. 'You never had this trouble when we were examining the corpse of Brother Ambrosius.' He looked at his companion with a mix of curiosity and sympathy. 'That'd been decaying for days.'

'I can do death, rotting vegetables, silage, gangrene and putrid pheasant. I cannot do poo.'

'Oh dear,' said Hermitage with some weight to his words.

'What do you mean?' Wat asked with suspicion.

'Well, we need to continue the investigation.'

'Yes?'

'Move to the source of the instrument of death,' Hermitage gestured to the holes. 'Down there,' he said, with some glee.

Wat returned to deposit the rest of his stomach contents.

Caput VIII

Nine-o-clock: Lady to Guard (small)

ADY FOELLA HAD CALMED DOWN somewhat. She followed the directions, after a fashion, and emerged into the populated parts of the castle.

She picked on the first person she saw, a small, humble-looking man, and demanded to be taken to her chamber.

The small, humble man didn't speak a word of English, but recognised the threatening nobility when he met them. He trotted along random corridors, hoping he was meeting this alarming woman's requirements in one way or another.

'Stop,' Foella eventually shouted.

He understood this.

'Do you have the faintest idea where we are?' she yelled.

'Je ne comprends pas,' he shrugged.

'Oh, bloody marvellous.' Foella waved her arms about in frustration, clipping the man on the side of the head in the process.

'Bloody well find me someone who speaks English,' she shouted even louder.

He shrugged again, but she pushed him away down a passage. 'Go on.'

The humble man still didn't have a clue what she wanted, but being pushed away was always a good thing. So he went. As fast as possible.

'I speak English, my lady.' A voice came round the corner of the corridor. It was an odd combination: someone was trying to sound powerful and gruff, but didn't have the lungs for it. It sounded more like a boastful crow than anything. It was definitely Saxon though.

Foella peered, and the voice was soon followed by a guard. A much smaller one than was normal.

'At your command, my lady.' The small guard was laying it on thick. 'We need to stick together.' He bowed low, at the same time tapping his nose.

'What is it with this place and Saxons crawling out of the woodwork?'

'Have you met others?' the guard asked, quickly.

'I've only just got away from a couple of them in the log store.'

'Really?'

'Yes,' Foella said clearly, 'a stupid one and a devious one. Which sort are you?'

'Straightforward, my lady.' The guard sounded offended and stood up as straight as he could. As this meant his head came to somewhere around Foella's chest, it wasn't much of a statement.

'Well look, straightforward Saxon, I am not in a good mood. I have been looking for the idiot Grosmal, but have got lost and ended up in a woodshed. Now I'm accosted by a miniature guard. When I'm not in a good mood, bad things tend to happen to those around me. I now want to get back to the main part of this God-awful so-called castle, and you are going to show me. Are we clear?' The retelling of her short adventure was kindling to the fire. Foella's temper started to bubble once more.

'As water that's not been pissed in, my lady.'

'Good.'

The guard leant forward and checked the corridor for listeners. 'But I am not a guard.'

Foella relaxed. 'Well, I'm not surprised really. I didn't like to say anything, but I shouldn't think even Grosmal is stupid enough to employ guards who can't see over the battlements.'

The small not-a-guard was clearly annoyed at this. 'I mean, I am in disguise. I am not in Grosmal's employ at all.'

'Does he know?'

84

'No, of course he doesn't know.' Not-a-guard was getting huffy. 'What would be the point of that?'

'Don't you get clever with me.'

'Sorry, my lady,' the guardish one controlled himself. 'I trust you won't tell him?'

'Certainly not. I have as little to do with jumped-up peasants like him as possible.'

'But you're his honoured guest.'

'It's not much of an honour, believe me. And we don't have much choice about things any more, do we?'

'No, indeed, my lady.' The guardly one seemed happy with this. 'The fact is, I have infiltrated the castle.'

'Well, that's not exactly hard. The gate doesn't work and anyone can wander in as far as I can tell.'

'Be that as it may, my presence in the castle is of significance.' He narrowed his eyes and nodded gently.

Foella looked the man up and down, which didn't take long. 'No, it isn't,' she said, explaining the situation to him with as much sympathy as she could muster. Which was none at all.

'You don't seem to be grasping the situation. Can you be trusted, my lady?' He leant forward and whispered as conspiratorially as possible.

'How dare you?'

'Of course, of course.' He scanned the corridor yet again. 'I am in fact Lord Grosmal's enemy.'

'Also not hard. I think most of the county's included in that band.'

The guard nodded knowingly, but paused for breath as he was clearly intending to say something significant. 'I am of the Brotherhood of the Sword.'

'The what?' Foella missed the significance.

'The Brotherhood of the Sword,' the man hissed.

'Never heard of them.'

'We are a secret society.'

'You certainly are.'

'Dedicated to the overthrow of the Norman invader.'

'Really? Which one?'

'All of them.'

'Fat chance,' Lady Foella snorted. 'There's hundreds of them. Are those log store men Brothers of the Sword then?'

'Log store men? Of course not. Whoever they are. We are men of action – we don't skulk around in log stores.'

'You're skulking in a corridor.'

'That's different. If they were Brothers of the Sword I'd know.'

'How? If they're secret?'

The man had clearly not expected this sort of conversation and he shook his head to make it stop. 'They are not the point. I shall deal with them later. I am in Grosmal's castle on a mission.'

'What, to convert him?'

'Not that sort of mission.' The small non-guard was showing signs of frustration and a temper of his own.

'What sort, then?'

'I can't tell you.'

'Not you too. I think those log men are your Brothers, you just don't know.'

'Why?'

'Because they think they're up to something and they can't tell anyone either. It's no good having a plan if you don't know what it is – you won't be able to complete it.'

'I know what it is, for goodness sake. I just can't tell you.'

'Why? Is it in French?'

'Oh, heavens. Look, I am a Saxon on a secret mission against Grosmal. I'll show you where you want to go and then get back to business. I had thought, as you're Saxon, you might be interested and want to help. I can see that's probably not a good idea. What were the men in the log store up to?'

'Haven't I just told you they wouldn't say? Why don't you have some sort of meeting? You can all work out what the hell it is you're supposed to be doing and get on with it.'

'I might just do that.'

'Are you going to kill him?' Foella asked seriously.

'Who?'

'Grosmal, who do you think?'

'I can't say.'

'Not again.'

'Sorry.'

'Only if you were going to kill him, I would like to help.'

'Why? You're living the good life with him.'

'Hardly. Here out of necessity and the necessity's just been done to death.'

'My lady?'

'Henri de Turold.'

'Oh yes,' the small man nodded and smiled. 'Nasty.'

'I was here to wed him.'

'Also nasty.'

'Just to save my family estates,' Foella justified herself. 'Now he's dead and I'm sure Grosmal had something to do with it.'

'Why?'

'Because he has something to do with most deaths around here.'

'True.' The man nodded and there was a moment's silent contemplation of the deaths that the Norman plague had brought to the country.

'He probably had an argument with Grosmal over something,' Foella speculated. 'Which one had the bigger sword, that sort of thing. Grosmal got offended and killed his mate. Happens all the time.'

'But killing Grosmal will leave you even worse off.'

'I'll feel a lot better, though. And if you killed him I wouldn't get the blame.'

'Thanks very much.'

'I've got to give him some sort of horrible fate for putting me to all this trouble.'

'Why don't you marry him then?' The Brother of the Sword couldn't stop himself.

'Who?' asked Foella, missing the barb of the comment completely.

The man stumbled on. 'Grosmal? He's got a castle, well sort of. He seems well thought of by the king.'

'But he's not noble, is he?'

'He could be soon. William's taking titles off everyone at the moment and dishing them out to his friends. Grosmal's already got estates in France, I hear. He could be in line for something.'

Foella was all ears now. 'Do you think so?'

'Very likely.'

'But what if he's married already?'

'Him?' The guard was aghast.

'Could have some ghastly French mare somewhere.'

'No, I've heard the servants talking. Apparently he was married once, but the Pope annulled it.'

'Really? Why?'

'Turns out the bride was his sister.'

'Gosh, and he never knew?'

'Oh, yes, he knew.'

'Why did he marry her then?'

'Fancied her apparently.'

Foella shivered and pulled a face which expressed her heartfelt loathing of Normans, of Grosmal and everyone to do with him and of everyone else as well. The look stayed on her face as she contemplated the things this despicable Norman was capable of, and how loathsome they all were. The foul-minded, stinking, deceitful, murdering dung heap drew upon wells of hatred in Foella which were seldom plumbed. Just to picture the appalling man's face was enough to inspire waves of nausea.

'So he's not spoken for then,' she said brightly.

'Marry 'em while they're still alive.' The man tapped his nose again.

Another figure appeared down the corridor, a full-size guard this time. Foella and the small no-guard began a gentle amble along, talking about the weather.

'Here we are, my lady,' the small man said, gesturing that she was back in the main upper hall of the castle. Her chamber was along here somewhere.

'Yes,' said Foella; her upbringing rendered her incapable of saying thank you. She checked the corridor now. 'And don't kill 'em until they've been married, see?' she hissed.

'I'll see what I can do, my lady.' The small man tapped the side of his nose in an overly familiar manner and pattered away down the corridor.

Foella pondered as she made her way back to her chamber. Wasn't it amazing how a day could start with a dead husband and have a new one installed before breakfast? Yes, Grosmal was truly revolting in so very many ways, but if he was revolting, married to her and dead, that would be fine.

She would just have to make sure that the small guard did his part of the job before the horrible thought of consummating the marriage got anywhere near Grosmal's pointy head.

Ten-o-clock: Monk to Garderobe

ILLIAM LE MORTON HAD BACKED OFF as far as he could, but the crumbling stone was stopping him going any further. 'You want to do what?' His eyes were wide and his voice was squeaking.

'It's a simple request.' Hermitage wasn't going to repeat himself a third time.

'You want to go into the garderobe? The bottom bit?'

'Exactly.' Hermitage folded his arms and waited for his wishes to be met.

'Why in God's name would you want to do that?'

'None of your business,' Wat stepped in. 'What is your business is making it happen. Either that or we go and ask Lord Robert to find a more cooperative guard.'

'All right, all right.' William gave in. 'I'm as cooperative as the next man, but there are limits,' he mumbled.

'You want to go down through the hole? Like a turd?'

'Preferably not.' Hermitage thought the fellow was being unnecessarily crude. 'I imagine there is another way in, as the space below used to be a chamber?'

'Oh yes,' William nodded knowingly. 'It was the priest's room in the old house. Grosmal just built on top of it.'

'Just like a Norman to kick a priest out of his own chamber,' Wat snorted.

William snorted louder. 'More like a Norman not to tell the priest what was happening until he realised it wasn't blessings raining down on him.'

'Oh, my goodness.' Hermitage felt his horror at what men

were capable of was fully justified.

'Anyway,' William went on, 'the old entrance is outside the castle, on to the field.'

'Not very defensive,' Wat observed.

'Tell me about it. Why Robert is turning this place into a castle is beyond me. It's useless.' William shrugged and led them away.

He took them by a circuitous but probably direct route round the outside of the tower to a small wooden gate in the castle's outer defences. The 'outer defences' were in fact two small wooden fences which could be easily climbed over, making the gate largely superfluous. However, Robert's outer defences had to have a gate, and so they got one.

'You two,' William beckoned to two more dozing guards who should have been marching briskly along the defences. 'Lord Robert's personal guests have a task for us.' The sentence contained all the words necessary to generate the proper level of engagement.

'I think we'll need torches,' Hermitage said. 'It's going to be pretty dark in there.'

'What's going to be pretty dark in where?' one of the guards asked.

'You don't want to know,' William replied.

One of the men ran off to get the torches while William led the way round the field. He brought them to the door which opened into what had been the priest's parlour, and which was now the access to the garderobe depository.

◆   ◆   ◆

It was a normal door. Vertical planking braced by cross pieces and a large round iron ring for a handle. It was patterned and worn with age and weather, and in fact looked rather dignified. A perfect counterbalance to what lay inside.

It was as difficult to open as the sort of door that keeps

91

secrets should be. The second guard returned with the torches which he stuck into the ground.

William stood back and took some pleasure in directing the work of the others. The two burly guards, who had been hired for their burl not their brains, pulled on the old door handle for a few moments. Eventually they sorted themselves out and synchronised their efforts.

After a few hefty tugs the door began to move. Once there was a small gap, the garderobe smell – appalling at high level, but positively sentient in the depths – made for the outside world. Burly Guard number one was breathing out at the time, but his colleague was breathing in.

'Get him out of the way,' said Wat. He watched with some surprise as one of the burliest people he had ever seen slid unconscious to the floor.

'Perhaps you'd better step back a bit, mister Wat,' said Hermitage, realising what was about to emerge from the chamber.

Wat did so. He turned on his heels and ran a good forty yards away.

William now joined the remaining guard to give one last tug. Neither the door nor its crude hinges had been built to withstand this sort of treatment. It gave up the ghost and came off completely in the hands of the surprised men.

Wood in hand, they staggered several steps backwards, straight into Hermitage who had been standing behind them. Burly guard number one, William, investigative monk and large door slid backwards on the wet grass for a few feet. Then all of them, except the door, looked back towards their feet to see what effect they had had on the tower.

The sight that met their eyes stayed with them for several years after the event. The stuff piled up behind the door stayed exactly where it was; it even had a perfect impression of the inside of the door embossed upon it. It took the eyes a moment to register the fact that the original door had in fact gone, and had not simply changed colour.

After several tense moments the contents of the room started to move. They did so slowly and cautiously, but with inexorable intent. As if testing the way, as if doubting that the route was safe or that its new-found freedom was real, the stuff shifted forward an inch or two.

With a noise that could only be described by those who were there at the time, and only then after many strong drinks, the contents of the garderobe made a comprehensive, if incomprehensible, deposit on the field. The territory was never to be reclaimed.

Hermitage ran over to join Wat who was again covering his face with his scented cloth. It was more scent than cloth at the moment.

A number of other guards from the castle appeared to see what all the fuss was about. They saw one colleague lying prone by the tower and two others backing away slowly with eyes wide, as if the ground were about to leap up and chase them. The two guests of Robert were looking on.

The captain of the watch brushed through the ranks of his men, furious at having been woken so early.

'What the hell is going on out here?' he yelled as only he could yell. He spotted Wat and Hermitage and changed his tone. 'Any trouble, sir?' he asked.

'We need some new men for the torches,' said Hermitage, putting the events of the last two minutes behind him with remarkable ease. He beckoned towards the stumps of two torches which were burning merrily close to the door.

'Eeuuucchhh,' said the captain as he took a gentle sniff of the air.

'Is that –?'

'Yes, it is,' said Wat. 'Just get the torches.'

Gagging into his hand, the captain staggered away and selected two of the men he disliked most.

'This is not good,' Hermitage said to Wat.

'My friend, you are a master of understatement,' Wat mumbled through his cloth.

'The evidence will have been disturbed. I should have thought of this. Hermitage, you idiot.'

'Eh?'

'If there was any footprint, or trace of the killer, it will have washed out of the door with all the rest of the, erm, material. We should have gone down through the hole like William said.'

'I don't think we'd have fitted, Hermitage,' said Wat with commendable restraint. 'The holes weren't meant to let whole people pass through.'

'Perhaps not. Anyway, we can still examine what remains, to see if there is anything of interest.'

'*You* can still examine what remains,' Wat corrected him.

'Ah yes.'

◆   ◆   ◆

Word spread quickly about what had happened and some of the night guards came to join their colleagues at the foot of the tower. Two reluctant souls appeared with hastily-made cloth masks covering their noses and mouths. Hermitage waved them towards the tower door.

Ethel appeared at Wat's side. 'What is going on?' he asked, frowning at the mess that had been made of the field.

'We're getting into the bottom of the garderobe,' Hermitage explained.

'I hope you're going to put it all back.' The Saxon sniffed uneasily.

Looking helplessly towards their captain for respite that they knew would not come, the two guards gingerly approached the tower, trying hard to tread in as little of the stuff as they could manage.

They reached the torches without event, plucked them from the ground and held them in front of their faces, as if the flames would frighten the smell away. With more caution than they had ever used before, they approached the door in the castle wall.

The rudiments of chemistry had long since been forgotten in eleventh-century England. This was a shame. If a Saracen had been to hand he could have warned them about the effects of thrusting a lighted torch into a confined chamber full of extremely combustible gases. As it was, the resulting explosion took the now large gathering by the biggest surprise of most of their lives. It was certainly the messiest.

Not even soldiers had invented a word to describe the event.

'Well that's that, then,' Hermitage snapped in disgust, as the contents of the garderobe launched themselves into the sky before raining down again, very unlike rain. 'We'll never find anything now.' He turned to Wat, only to spot him running away again, this time back to the castle.

As he looked further he noticed that everyone was running back into the castle, guards, captain, William, the lot.

'"As people being ashamed steal away when they flee in battle,"' he quoted resentfully. 'Two Samuel, book nine chapter three,' he added. 'Useless bunch of....'

He grumbled as he stepped towards the tower to see if anything of value remained.

Picking his way as carefully as he could, he lifted a smouldering torch which lay nearby and coaxed it into a gentle life. He reached the opening of the tower. The old wooden door was nowhere to be seen, having been comprehensively buried.

'How fascinating,' Hermitage said, examining the wreckage. Several parts of the stonework had been destroyed and there were large burn marks all around doorway. He rubbed these with his finger tips and smelled the result of an intense fire.

'There must have been some violent humour inside the room

which reacted with anger to the light of the torches. This warrants further investigation.'

With extreme caution, even for Hermitage, he held his low burning torch at arms' length. Slowly he moved it into the room, hiding as best he could behind the stonework. It didn't occur to him for a moment that he was being extremely brave. Nor that he was being incredible stupid. The torch leapt into life, but there was no further eruption.

He poked his head into the chamber and noticed that the worst of the smell had gone. 'So the smell and the humour are one and the same thing. I wonder if there could be some practical use for this process?' He pondered some more. 'If a whole series of mobile garderobes were built, they could be moved to a forest, for example. Then, when the trees need felling, we simply throw in some torches and let the humours do the rest. It would save days of chopping.'

'Unless, of course, the humours set fire to the forest,' he reasoned with some disappointment.

Then, casting his mind to the Normans, he wondered if there might be some use for this effect as a weapon of war. Intriguing, but not something for a monk to pursue. And he couldn't see Wat coping with the finer details. Oh well.

'Back to the matter in hand.' He now climbed into the room, made largely vacant thanks to the violent humours. Still taking care where to put his feet, and not a little nervous of the torch, he looked around.

Nothing. Hermitage's shoulders sagged.

The room was by no manner of description clean, but there was very little left of what used to occupy the space.

He held the torch up and peered towards the holes in the ceiling. He moved under the one which had supported de Turold's last moments and looked closely around. Nothing on the floor or walls gave any indication of presence. There was certainly no child's bow or crossbow lying about.

He was about to give up when the light of the torch cast a strange, thin shadow on the wall. As Hermitage moved, the shadow wavered. He moved the torch around until he located the source. Some thin filament was dangling from the hole above, perhaps a remnant of Henri's gizzards.

He had just taken hold of it when his arms were grabbed by strong hands.

'Right,' said a gruff and ignorant voice, the sort of voice that was usually attached to strong hands, 'you're coming with us.'

Hermitage dropped the torch in shock. He was unceremoniously dragged backwards, the heels of his sandals most effectively scooping up the floor of the chamber and thoroughly coating his feet.

Caput X

Ten-o-clock: Weaver and Saxon

AWN'S CHAOS HAD DESCENDED into the mere mess of a morning at the Castle Grosmal. After breakfast – a much later and lighter meal than normal for anyone who had witnessed the destruction of the garderobe – Ethel sent for Wat and Hermitage.

The weaver arrived in the retainer's tower looking pale and bilious.

'Where's the monk?' Ethel asked with the usual disdain in his voice.

'Brother Hermitage,' Wat replied, emphasising the fact that his companion had a name, 'is investigating the garderobe.'

'Well, let's hope he investigates a little less vigorously this time. We won't have much of the castle left. What happened?'

'No idea. I'll have to wait for Hermitage to come back. He was going to examine the chamber below to see if there was any indication of who committed the crime.'

'If killing Normans is a crime,' Ethel said with considerable sincerity.

Wat frowned at him. The man was obviously a snooty, arrogant, self-important dung bucket, but he had been taken down several notches by the invaders. There was no one like a snooty, arrogant, self-important dung bucket for bearing a grudge. And nothing like a noble for taking a grudge to extremes. Especially an ex-noble with little hope. Wat had better discuss this with Hermitage.

'And what are you supposed to be doing?' Ethel asked.

'Well, I would be investigating as well if I hadn't been summoned here.' Wat folded his arms. He might have taken this condescension from Aethelred Saxon noble, but Ethel the servant could stick it.

'Well, get on with it then. And find your monk before he does any more damage. If he's looking in the lower chamber, you'd better check the upper one. You can see if there's been any damage there. And if there has I can arrange for you to tell Grosmal.'

'"Grosmal" eh?' Wat observed sardonically. 'Yes, I will go and have a look. Then maybe we can both go and see your lord and master. I imagine you're responsible for the fabric of the building.'

Wat turned and strode from room without looking back and certainly without bowing.

'Dung bucket,' he muttered as he left the tower.

◆　　◆　　◆

On reflection, he reluctantly admitted that looking in the garderobe again was probably a good idea. The big fire that had blown out the lower chamber might have done some damage, but it might also have revealed something of interest. Wat didn't have a clue what something of interest in a garderobe would look like, but it wouldn't do any harm to check. Apart from having to put up with the smell, of course.

Making his way back to the garderobe he passed William again, quietly walking up and down the battlements.

'Ah,' Wat began.

'Oh no,' William got in quickly, 'not again. I can't do anything for you, I'm busy,' and he scurried off.

'Don't blame you, mate,' Wat muttered. He followed his previous path until he came to the chamber.

He was very pleased to note that the worst of the smell had gone. The odour of the place was now no worse than the average dwelling.

This gave him the courage to enter the room and look around. The place looked pretty much as it had before. The seats were still there, in their proper place, the walls were as intact as he imagined they were supposed to be and the floor of the place was as grubby as it had been.

He went over to the nearest hole and peered in. Daylight was streaming in through the missing door below and he could see the floor of the lower chamber.

'Hermitage,' he called, 'are you there?'

There was no reply which puzzled him. It was unlike the young monk to leave a scene of interest until he was physically dragged away from it. Perhaps he had found something and was at that moment looking for Wat.

The weaver leant over a bit further and tried to see the whole of the lower room.

He was nearly knocked down the hole when a large object fell from the sky and crashed across his shoulders.

'Ow, bloody hell!' He leapt back and looked up. A large portion of the lower garderobe's contents had clearly been blown up through the seats when the torches went bang. It had liberally coated the ceiling and Wat's first thought was that he hoped no one had been sitting here at the time. His second was that a large portion of something had just fallen on his clothes.

He hopped about, brushing his shoulders with his hands. Then he realised what he might be brushing.

He looked round on the floor to see what had fallen. One rather heavy, entirely man-made object had clearly come up through the hole with the filth. It had been stuck to the ceiling and had chosen this moment to fall down. Wat didn't like to pick it up. Or touch it. Or go anywhere near it. But he knew it was of vital importance.

Sighing loudly, he wrapped his hand in his piece of scented cloth, picked the object up and went to find Ethel.

◆   ◆   ◆

The retainer himself had been summoned and was dragging himself across the great hall.

'What's going on?' the lord of the castle demanded. 'Noises, smells, people running about shouting – bloody mayhem in here.'

'It's the garderobe,' Ethel said, without batting an eyelid.

'Who is doing what in my garderobe? I'll have their heads.'

'The monk and the other one are trying to determine how de Turold was killed. They were examining the lower chamber of the garderobe when there was some sort of fire.'

'A fire?' Grosmal panicked for a moment. 'In my castle?' A worse thought occurred. 'In my garderobe?'

'It went out again straight away, but it left a bit of a mess.'

'Looking into the garderobe?' As usual, Grosmal was a few steps behind. 'It's not for looking into, you know, it's for putting stuff in.'

Ethel laughed lightly at his master's terminal idiocy and explained.

'They have been trying to find out who killed de Turold, as you ordered.'

'Oh, excellent. Who was it then?'

This rocked Ethel a bit. 'I don't know yet, they haven't found out.'

'Well, that's not very good, is it? I asked you to do that hours ago.'

'They've got to find some evidence.' Grosmal looked blank. 'Clues,' Ethel explained. 'Something that might tell us who the killer was.'

'What, like his name on a piece of parchment or something?'

Ethel laughed contemptuously, neatly side-stepping the fact he had thought the same thing himself a little while earlier. 'Well, that would be ideal, obviously. A little bit of paper saying I did it, signed William, that would be really handy.' Ethel's tone was so laced with sarcasm that it could barely walk. However, it could have jumped up and down on the spot singing that popular number 'Let's Kill the Normans and Cook Their Heads in a Pot' and Robert Grosmal would have missed it.

'Oh, it was William was it?' He paused. 'William who?'

'No, it was not William. I was just giving you an example. I was trying to indicate that a piece of parchment was an extremely unlikely thing to find. I was trying... oh, I give up. I think they were going to look for something like a footprint, or a piece of clothing that came off, maybe a spare arrow, or the bow left behind, anything at all really.'

'And what did they find?'

'Nothing.'

'Nothing? In the garderobe? That's not possible. I've been going in there for months, there must have been something.' Robert sounded as if he was about to abandon the hunt for the murderer and re-direct his efforts towards finding the contents of his garderobe, which had obviously been stolen.

'Clearly there was something, there was a huge amount of something. The trouble was that it all fell out of the door when they opened it, and then when they tried to look inside it all went bang.'

'Bang?'

'Well, more a sort of Whhoooommfff really. But the end result was that the contents of the garderobe were scattered all over the field and any clues there might have been were lost with it.'

'So who's cleaning up the field?' asked Robert, with disarming simplicity.

'Well, er.' Such deft logic was not what Ethel had been expecting. 'No one really.'

'Can't do that,' said Robert as if it was perfectly obvious. 'Can't have smelly stuff all over my field, makes it look untidy.

Have someone clean it up. And tell those monks to bring me the killer.'

Ethel was dumbfounded. He felt it really wasn't worth the effort of explaining to Grosmal that the one not dressed as a monk was not, in fact, a monk.

The moment was disrupted by a clattering noise outside the chamber door.

'I shall press them for a resolution.'

'Yes, you do that, or I shall press you. Very hard and with something very heavy.'

'Yes my lord,' Ethel grimaced.

Wat appeared at the chamber entrance, holding his new-found object at arms' length.

'Who's that?' Grosmal demanded.

'That's the one who isn't a monk,' Ethel explained. He beckoned Wat to join them.

As he came closer Grosmal recognised what Wat had in his hand.

'Where did you get that?' he demanded viciously.

'I found it,' Wat replied.

'Found it? Found it?' Grosmal seemed very disturbed by this.

Ethel stood back, observing but out of the firing line.

'Where did you find it?' Grosmal snapped.

'In the garderobe.'

'Impossible. You're a liar. Ethel, hang this man.'

Ethel took a step forward with a slight smile.

'I found it in the upper chamber of the garderobe, but it started in the lower one.'

'And it jumped up all on its own, I suppose?' Grosmal was clearly angry.

'No, was thrown up when the torches made the big fire. I think this is what killed Henri de Turold.'

That made Grosmal stop in mid-flight. 'What?'

'Well, it's clearly a crossbow.'

'No, it isn't.'

Wat was too stunned at this to respond immediately. He looked at the object again. 'Yes, it is,' he said, as it was blindingly obviously a crossbow. 'I don't know whether you've ever seen one before, but this is just what they look like. The arrow sits in here,' he gestured to a slot down the top of the body of the thing, 'and the string went across here. It's broken now.'

'Just a toy,' Grosmal said dismissively. And unconvincingly.

'No, it isn't. It's a real crossbow. What is the problem with it being a crossbow?'

'It's a secret,' Grosmal said.

'Secret?' Wat felt like he had walked into entirely the wrong conversation. 'What's a secret? That this is a crossbow? I can see it's a crossbow. A man dies on the garderobe with a crossbow bolt up his arse. In the chamber below there's a crossbow. Not much of a secret to that.'

'There is, if I say so,' Grosmal said. Points danced on each of his words.

'The arrow that killed him must have come from the pit underneath, and this was in the pit underneath. It also means someone was in there to fire it.'

'Nobody should have one of those.' Grosmal gestured to the dirty bow.

Revelation dawned on Wat. 'I get it,' he said, 'you think cross-bows are a secret. You think the Saxons don't have them.'

'Of course they don't. King William assured us that the Saxons had no weapons at all to speak of. And certainly nothing like the magnificent Norman crossbow.'

'We've had them for years,' Wat delivered the plain truth.

'No, you haven't,' Grosmal responded with his plain truth.

Wat shrugged. The man was in charge – let him have whatever truth he wanted.

'So no one could have shot de Turold from below, with this

weapon.' Wat feigned deep thought. 'Oh, except a Norman, of course.'

Ethel took a step back.

'What are you suggesting?' the lord of the manor asked. His tone indicated that Wat had better not be suggesting anything at all.

'Just that someone had this weapon in the garderobe and shot Henri with it. If no one is supposed to have one except a Norman, then it must have been a Norman.'

'What sort of thinking is that?'

'It's called intelligence,' Wat explained. 'It's all the rage. Hermitage uses it all the time.'

'Who's Hermitage?'

'The monk,' Wat prompted.

'Oh yes, where is he?'

'He was examining the lower chamber of the garderobe.'

'Disgusting.'

'And I think if the thing hadn't gone bang he'd have found this down there.' Wat waved the bow.

'So he was down there. Perhaps he did it,' Grosmal suggested.

'Not again,' Wat groaned before he could stop himself.

'What do you mean, again?' Ethel jumped in now.

'Hermitage is a monk. A real, believing, honest and innocent monk. Hard to believe there is such a thing, I know, but there you are. He was accused of something before and he didn't do that either.'

'So he has a reputation?'

'Yes – for not killing people.'

'But he was down in the garderobe looking for his bow.' Grosmal was in accusatory mode.

'Today he was looking for a bow. He doesn't possess one of his own, and even if he did he wouldn't know how to use it. Especially not something like this. Anyway that was just now. De Turold was killed last night when Hermitage was with me in the monastery. So he couldn't have done anything.'

'And that's more of your intelligence, is it?' The Norman was contemptuous.

'No, that's called common sense,' Wat replied.

'Perhaps you're in it together?'

'You sent Ethel to get us!' Wat's patience was wearing thin. 'And that was when de Turold was already dead.'

'So you say.'

'No, so *you* say.'

'You could have been in the garderobe already, waiting for your moment. You kill de Turold, run back to your monastery and wait to be summoned.'

'No,' Wat said simply. He looked at Ethel. 'When your servant arrived we knew nothing of the death.'

Ethel had found something fascinating on the ceiling to look at.

'Perhaps Ethel was in the garderobe, killed Henri and then came to get us.'

That got Ethel's attention all right.

'Ethel?' Grosmal burst out laughing. 'Don't be ridiculous. Ethel was a weak-willed, ineffective girl's bonnet when we arrived. He didn't even have the gumption to defend his own house. He certainly couldn't sneak up on a Norman and kill him. I doubt he even knows which end of an arrow points forwards.' The laughter went on for some time.

Wat regarded Ethel with eyebrows raised. The servant stood in silence, but his lips were tight enough to strangle a horse.

Grosmal eventually calmed down. 'Well, this is all going terribly well.'

'Is it?' Wat asked.

'Of course. I've got you and the monk. If no one else turns up I'll tell the king you did it and we can all get back to normal. You are Saxons, after all, it was most likely one of you. It's been ages since I executed a monk.'

106

'And where did we get this thing?' Wat dropped the bow on to the floor.

'Clearly stole it from somewhere.

'But if we find who really did it?'

'You can if you like. If no one's come up by tonight, then that's that.' Grosmal dismissed them with a wave.

'I think we need to talk,' Wat hissed to Ethel as they left the chamber.

Caput XI

Half past Ten: In My Lady's Chamber

LEANOR!' THE LADY FOELLA slammed the door to her chamber and her dulcet screams ran from the room to circulate the castle, kicking the stonework and abusing the ears.

'My lady,' Eleanor replied, emerging from the small dressing area which was part of the room.

'I've been calling you for hours.'

'Really, my lady? I've been here.'

'And I've been stuck somewhere in this ghastly castle. Wandering around lost, calling for my maid who was nowhere to be found.'

'Sorry, my lady.'

'In the breeches of some guard or other, I shouldn't wonder.'

'My lady! Did you find Lord Robert?' Eleanor seemed keen to change the subject.

'Yes, I did. He claims not to have killed de Turold, but I don't believe him for a moment.'

'Why not, my lady?'

'He's a liar.'

'Ah yes. But you didn't, erm, do him any harm?'

'Not yet. He even had the temerity to accuse me of murdering the man.'

'Ah,' Eleanor paused for a moment. 'And did you?'

'No, I did not.' Foella stared at her impudent maid.

'Well, there was that business with the son of Urik of York.'

'That was an accident, as everyone agreed.'

'Eventually.'

'What are you suggesting?' Foella demanded.

Eleanor sighed. These conversations were always difficult. Sometimes her mistress could be a howling demon to whom saying good morning was a risk to life and limb. At other times, and this seemed to be one of them, she could be reasonable and engaging and would talk to Eleanor as a friend and confidante. Well, perhaps just a confidante. The problem was she would leap from one state to the other without any indication of what was coming.

'Just that it was suggested the son of Urik turned down your, erm, advances before he had his accident.'

'So?'

'And your temper may have got the better of you.'

'I have got a temper, haven't I?' Foella almost giggled.

Eleanor took a breath and a step away. Giggles were never a good sign.

'You have, my lady,' she agreed, 'but no one believed a woman could do what Urik's son had done to him. If Henri de Turold turned you down as well, you may have got...' Eleanor searched for the right phrase, 'carried away?'

'Stop saying people turn me down,' Foella snapped, almost back to normal now.

'Yes, my lady.'

'Anyway de Turold did not turn me down. He didn't even turn up. You know that.'

'I was asleep some of the time, my lady.'

'Well, he didn't.'

'That's what I'll say if anyone asks.'

'Who the devil is going to ask?'

'Oh, there's some people arrived who are trying to find out who killed him.'

'Why?'

'We're not supposed to kill Normans any more.'

'Oh yes. Well if they do ask, you make sure that's what you

do tell them.' Foella fixed her maid with a steely glare.

'Yes, my lady.'

'Or I'll make sure you have trouble talking at all any more.'

'Yes, my lady.'

'And now,' Foella brightened straightaway, as if the previous conversation had never taken place, 'get my gentlemen's gown out.'

Eleanor looked surprised. 'The gentlemen's gown? The one with not much top and the unfortunate tear down below?'

'The fortunate tear down below. That's the one.'

'I've only just put it away from the last outing.'

'It worked on de Turold – let's see if it'll work on Robert.'

'Grosmal?' There was real horror in Eleanor's voice.

'Going to be a noble, I hear,' Foella explained.

'My lady, he's awful. He's ugly, he smells, he does horrible things to people and even worse ones to women. I've heard of all the servants Robert Grosmal has ever had, the dead outnumber the living.'

'Going to be a noble,' Foella repeated.

'But, my lady, surely he's married.'

Foella beamed with the good news. 'Only to his sister. That doesn't count.'

Eleanor didn't bother trying to untangle that one. 'Will he take kindly to a bride who's just tried to kill him?'

'Who cares? Just get the gown.'

'Yes, my lady.' Eleanor went to retrieve the gown, notorious for revealing far more of Foella than was necessary.

'Shame it doesn't reveal the inside of your head,' she muttered as she opened the rough wardrobe where her mistress's gowns hung.

Her own scream rent the air as she leapt back from the door, tripping over her own heels and falling on to her back.

Lady Foella, hearing her maid's agonised cry, did absolutely nothing. A man stepped from the wardrobe and leant forward to help Eleanor up.

'You get away from me,' Eleanor squealed, scrabbling backwards across the stone floor.

'Come, my dear,' the man said, 'let me help you.'

His voice was warm and authoritative. He was reasonably well dressed in a thick jerkin and matching trousers. He had rough leather shoes with no holes and he was tall and big and strong. So far, so good. Eleanor let herself be helped. She was helped so much that once she was on her feet she fell into his arms.

'Eleanor, put him down,' Foella instructed. 'What are you doing here?' she asked, recognising the man from the log store who was now standing in her chamber.

Eleanor stepped back from the comforting strength and looked at her mistress.

Foella was standing, hands on hips, in her insistent stance. Most of her stances were insistent, but this one was for people who weren't going to be allowed to leave until they explained themselves. And maybe not then.

'I have come to warn you, my lady,' the man said.

'You do a lot of warning me. Why don't you stay and play with your logs? How did you get in here anyway?' Irritated, Foella looked around. 'Were you in my wardrobe?' she demanded, as if the man had been caught fumbling in her underskirts.

'There are many secret paths in the castle. Some known to many, some known to a few.' The man from the log store was still mysterious.

'And what's the one to my wardrobe? I do hope there hasn't been a troop passing through.' Foella clearly intended to get the names of the troop so they could be eliminated.

'Known only to me, my lady, and I have not used it until today.'

'Hum.' Foella didn't sound convinced. 'What do you want?'

'Don't marry Robert Grosmal,' the man said simply.

111

'Yes, thank you very much. Good morning.' Foella gestured that he could return to the wardrobe.

'It will do you no good, my lady.'

'I think that's for me to decide.'

The man walked over to a window rudely knocked in the castle wall and gazed out of it. Mysteriously.

'I appreciate your plan for the Norman, my lady, and of course I approve.'

'I don't recall asking for your approval, or needing it.'

'Indeed, but the case of Grosmal is unique. I must give you more information that I would normally release. I realise that I should have told you more at our first meeting, and so I am here.'

'Well, you can shut up now and bugger off,' the Lady Foella suggested.

'You think that marrying Grosmal will protect your estates and give you a title. A title to be enjoyed in your widowhood, which we all hope would be speedy.'

'So far, so obvious.'

'I have to tell you that we have plans for Grosmal.'

'What, you and the man who's turning into a log? I think I'll take my chances with Grosmal.'

'There are more of us.'

'In the log store?'

'No, not in the log store.' The man came away from the window, a touch of exasperation getting the better of his mystery. 'All over the land.'

'The Brotherhood of the Sword?'

The man stepped back and looked at Foella in real shock. 'How do you know? Not that it's pronounced quite that way.'

'Never mind how it's pronounced. I've already met one of your number. Well, probably half of one, come to think of it.'

'Where?'

'Oh, I don't think I can tell you that. It's a secret after all.' Foella was enjoying herself.

The man did his best to recover his composure. 'Well, that's good, you know that we are real and that we are active.'

'Not that I can get anyone to tell me exactly what any of you have done or are going to do. You just go round telling everyone you're a secret. So secret you don't even know one another.'

'It's vital for our safety.'

'Even if you're in the same castle.' Foella adopted her famous 'folded arms in contempt' pose.

'Obviously. The point is that Robert Grosmal is not going to be a noble.'

'From what I hear of your aims I can't imagine you have much influence over King William.'

The man spat on the floor at the name.

'I hope you're going to clean that up,' Foella snapped at him.

The man ignored her. 'Our plans for Robert Grosmal mean that William the Bastard will never ennoble him.'

Eleanor had been standing looking backwards and forwards between Foella and the man, not having a clue what was going on. She coughed to let them know she was still there. She didn't want to hear any more of this. Plans and nobles and secrets always led to sorry ends. And when the nobles came to a sorry end, they usually took their servants with them. That's if they didn't actually send them on ahead.

'Get out,' Foella helpfully proposed.

Eleanor scurried out of sight. But not out of earshot. It was best not to be involved in any plans, but knowing about them could be a life saver.

'You can do what you like to Grosmal after he's ennobled and I'm his ennobled wife,' Foella said quite distinctly.

'That is not our plan.'

'Make it your plan.'

'We must make an example of Grosmal so that his kind will see the error of their ways. They are destroying our country. He will die in ignominy at the hands of his own people.'

'And how are you going to make that happen?'

'The death of de Turold,' the man began, and then stopped himself.

'What about it?'

'I have said too much.'

'Well, say some more. What about de Turold? Did you kill him?'

'Suffice to say the death of de Turold will be the lever which tips Grosmal to his doom.'

'Very devious, I'm sure.'

'It is. Death is too good for Robert Grosmal.' The man said this in a very dramatic voice and took a slow step back towards the wardrobe. He felt for and opened the door and put his left foot inside. As he stepped back into the cupboard, he let his words ring out. 'For his crimes he will be utterly destroyed. He will be shamed and disgraced and we will have our victory.'

He started to close the door behind him, but Foella stepped forward and gave it a good kick.

'Ow,' the man screamed as his fingers were smacked by the heavy oak door.

'Just stay out of my wardrobe,' Foella shouted at the furniture.

As if frightened into following Foella's screamed instruction, the wardrobe threw its handle on the floor.

Caput XII

Eleven-o-clock: Monk to Woods

ROTHER HERMITAGE FELT HIS HEAD had been slammed in a door. Being dragged backwards from the garderobe was not comfortable, and he had tried to struggle to his feet.

'If you don't stop struggling, I'll club you,' the rough voice had said.

Hermitage stopped struggling, but the rough voice had clubbed him anyway.

◆   ◆   ◆

Now he was waking up and his head pounded with the blow. He found he was propped against a tree. A painful opening of his eyes revealed the edge of a large clearing, in what appeared to be a substantial forest. The clearing was only some hundred feet square and contained a few tents of various designs and condition. The condition was consistently poor.

One of the tents occupied the centre of the space and caught Hermitage's attention. It must have been rather grand in its day – probably during the reign of King Alfred.

It was tall and had an opening high enough to let a man walk in without bending. At its crown was a carved wooden boss. From the front, two poles held a canopy over the doorway. The thing wouldn't have looked out of place at a king's joust, if its colour hadn't faded to match the mud in which it stood. The ragged tears in the side would be unacceptable to any self-respecting king, though, while the few remaining tassels, dangling from the edges of the roof like bodies from a gallows, had been growing their own moss for some considerable time.

Hermitage looked up and gauged that it was still only morning. He had not travelled far. A small fire was burning away the last of the night's chill and a couple of men were lounging by it. Another was just bringing some wood in from the forest.

Hermitage assumed the rest of the camp must be either still asleep or off on some errand or other. He didn't like to think what sort of errands the people who lived here might get up to.

He raised his arms and gently touched the back of his head. The contact made him wince and he brought his hands to his face, expecting to see blood. There was none, but his fingers told him a lump the size of a second head had sprouted where he had been hit.

'Aha, with us again then, monk? You have a monstrously thin skull for a thinking man.'

This was the rough voice again, although it was a lot less rough now. It was clearly Saxon and belonged to a man who was striding across the clearing from the tents.

Hermitage appraised him quickly, anxious that a matching blow might be about to land on the front of his head. The man was clearly ready for a fight. He was very stocky and of average height, wearing an extremely thick jerkin which looked like it could turn an arrow in flight. The way his arms could not rest at the side of his body but stuck out slightly, as if he was about to wrestle a boar, told Hermitage that most of the stock was muscle.

The legs were like pillars and the whole image was topped off by a completely shaven head. Where the hair had been removed, a nasty, aggressive-looking tattoo had been made which showed a snarling boar. Probably one the man had wrestled.

The tattoo was showing signs of age, and the man was not young any more. He was still more than a match for Hermitage – but then who wasn't? The lines on his face may have said the very best of his fighting days were behind him. But the fighting days still in front were enough for Hermitage. He recognised the type and cowered as best he could.

'And you're thin as a boar's nipple, no weight to you at all.'

The man now arrived at Hermitage's resting place and held out his hand to pull the monk up. Hermitage took it and was yanked upright with such strength and speed that the inside of his head stayed where it was. He swooned slightly.

'For goodness sake, monk,' the man was not impressed. 'No guts inside you either, I'll warrant.'

The man stood back for a moment while Hermitage got his senses back and was able to look the fellow in the eye.

'Sigurd son of Sigurd, Brotherhood of the Sword.' The man introduced himself with a thump to his chest.

Hermitage's mind leapt to wakefulness. 'Brotherhood of the Sward? How fascinating. I've made quite a study of your…'

'What?' Sigurd stopped him.

'I said, I've made quite a study of…'

'No, no. Brotherhood of the what?'

'Oh.' Hermitage paused for a moment. He knew fighting men didn't require great knowledge, but he thought remembering your own Brotherhood for five minutes was a reasonable demand. 'The sward, Brotherhood of the Sward.'

'What do you say it like that for?'

'Because that's how it's pronounced: s-w-a-r-d.'

Sigurd looked puzzled now. 'No, it isn't. I mean I know monks are learned and all that, but really. A sword is a sword, not a s-w-a-r-d.' To emphasis the point he patted the sword hanging at his side.

'Oh you mean sword?' Hermitage realised his mistake.

'What else would I mean? What's a sward?'

A simple 'sorry, my mistake' would have sufficed at this point. But if there was a complex option available, Hermitage would choose it every time. 'It's the life all around us, the fields, the pas-

117

ture, the trees,' he explained.

Now Sigurd really was lost. 'And have they a Brotherhood then?' The concept was beyond him.

'Oh yes.' Once more Hermitage prepared to deliver a detailed report on his studies. 'Many of the Brotherhood's fundamental tenets revolve around the need for people to live and work as part of their surroundings. They see the role of man as subservient to the spirits of nature. All of man's activities, his constructions, his behaviours, even his thoughts must be natural.'

'Erm.' Sigurd looked like he wanted to stop Hermitage, but didn't know how. Many would have sympathised with him. Wat, for a start.

'The clear flaws in their system of belief stem from a number of Druidic interpretations…'

'Ha.' Sigurd saw his moment. 'Druids.' He beat his chest.

'Oh, they aren't actually Druids, but…'

'Druids,' Sigurd repeated, more loudly. He felt on sure ground now.

Hermitage wasn't sure whether 'Druids' was a good thing or not. But it seemed to mean quite a lot to Sigurd – who was, after all, the big man in front of him with a sword. He finally realised that this was the moment to stop talking.

'Druids.' Sigurd leaned forward and said the word with significance.

Hermitage didn't have a clue what the significance was, so he just nodded. 'Indeed,' he said, not knowing what he was agreeing with.

'Do you have a name, monk?'

'Er, Hermitage,' Hermitage replied, with a modest bow of the head.

'Odd name for a monk.'

'I suppose it is,' Hermitage replied, not really wanting to engage in any more conversation with this fighting machine. 'Brotherhood of the Sword, you say?' He thought moving the conversation on to Sigurd's ground might help.

'Aye, fighting off the Norman invader.'

'But I thought they had invaded. And conquered.' Hermitage reasoned.

'No need to stop fighting,' Sigurd replied with enthusiasm.

Hermitage thought it was a very good reason to stop fighting, but also thought it best not to say so.

'Why have you brought me here?' he asked instead. 'You obviously don't want to kill me or you'd have done it by now.'

'Kill you? Good Gods above, we don't want to kill you. Quite the opposite.'

Hermitage was about to point out that 'quite the opposite' of killing someone was bringing them back to life, but this fellow had already demonstrated a lack of interest in intellectual matters.

'Good,' he said instead.

'You're a hostage of the Brotherhood of the Sword.'

'A hostage!' Hermitage's voice squeaked with surprise and alarm. 'Good heavens, who's likely to ransom me?'

'That boil on the pox-ridden arse of his race, Robert Grosmal.'

'Oh, I don't think so,' Hermitage said brightly, although he immediately thought he probably shouldn't have. He imagined people who were held for ransom, who turned out to be the wrong people, didn't get held for long. And they probably didn't get released either. He gulped. 'Presumably you think Grosmal would pay reparations for the recovery of someone he valued.'

'Absolutely, it's a grand plan.'

Hermitage tried not to say anything, but his deep frown gave him away.

'You think not?' Sigurd asked, in quite a reasonable tone.

'I think your plan falls on two main pillars.' Hermitage couldn't stop his tone of instruction sneaking out.

'Really?' Sigurd looked a bit puzzled now and Hermitage reasoned that erudite debate had probably not played much of a part in his upbringing.

'Yes,' said Hermitage. He knew he would have to choose his next words carefully. He also knew that choosing words carefully hadn't been part of his upbringing. 'You see, Robert Grosmal is not the sort of person who would pay reparations for anyone he valued. This is primarily because he doesn't seem to value anyone. I have met him and he strikes me as the type who would sell his own children.'

Sigurd didn't seem worried about this. 'Ah well, who hasn't sold children at some time or another,' he chuckled. 'But seriously now, we've heard all the Normans are making sure they don't go to hell for invading God's own place on earth.'

'Jerusalem?' Hermitage was puzzled.

'England.' Sigurd spoke as if this was obvious.

'Ah.'

'Aye, and they're keeping priests to pray for them night and day.'

'Not in Grosmal's case.'

'Bastard.'

'Indeed. And even if he was, and even if I was praying for him, he wouldn't pay anything for me. We've only met the once, and if I don't do what he wants he's going to kill me himself.'

Sigurd looked puzzled. 'But you're his priest.'

Hermitage knew his next comment was not going to help the situation. He knew quite clearly that he should be saying yes, he was Grosmal's priest. Yes, he would be sorely missed by the Norman and yes, he would doubtless pay a vast sum of money to get his priest back. This lie would be perfectly justified as it would keep Hermitage alive.

'No, I'm afraid I'm not,' he said instead, which was the truth. Which must be always a much better thing to say.

'You were coming out of his priest's chamber.' Sigurd seemed offended that Hermitage was contradicting him.

'That's true, but it hasn't been his priest's chamber for some time. It's his garderobe now.'

'His what?'

'Garderobe. It's a sort of privy that you have inside a castle.'

'Ye gods.' Sigurd was clearly horrified at the very idea.

'And this garderobe wasn't even built properly. All the muck fell into what used to be the priest's chamber and it was still there.'

Sigurd contemplated this for a moment. 'I thought the place was a bit of a mess, but then who knows what filthy habits Normans have got? What the hell were you doing in it then?'

'That's complicated.'

Sigurd looked at Hermitage with a mixture of suspicion and disgust. He then threw his muscular arms as high as they could go and walked in a small circle away from Hermitage and then back again.

'I told Scarlan this was a stupid plan. We should have just attacked.'

'Grosmal does have lots of guards,' Hermitage informed his captor.

'That's what Scarlan said. Coward.'

Sigurd stared hard at Hermitage as if some revelation would spring from the monk.

'So Grosmal won't pay for you?'

'No.'

'Or give us weapons and victuals?'

'Definitely not.'

'Or surrender the castle and leave this land taking the Norman horde with him?'

'That one's a bit optimistic, isn't it?'

'That's...'

'What you told Scarlan,' Hermitage finished off. 'No, I'm afraid not.'

'Bugger.' All the enthusiasm and energy had fallen from Sigurd. He looked at Hermitage with his massive shoulders sagging.

Hermitage didn't like to ask the next question, but as usual he couldn't keep his questions to himself. 'Erm, what are you going to do with me then?'

Sigurd gave him the look people give lame donkeys. He shrugged. 'Kill you, I suppose.'

The bottom fell from Hermitage's bottom. 'Oh, er, do you have to?' he squeaked.

'I suppose we do. You know too much.'

'Not really.' Hermitage's reasoning had a pleading tone. 'I've no idea where we are as you hit me on the head. I've only seen you and have no knowledge of your plans. Anyway, I may not be a priest, but I am a monk, and you're really not supposed to kill monks.'

'Hum.' At least Hermitage detected a hint of doubt in his captor's mind.

'And there's nothing to gain from killing me now.' Hermitage had put himself in the position of a kidnapper. He was rather proud of managing this. 'If I was a hostage and had been paid for, you'd have given me back to Grosmal alive.'

Sigurd frowned in deep concentration. 'I don't think that was Scarlan's plan,' he said with another shrug.

'That's very deceitful,' Hermitage said in a disappointed tone, realising that he'd missed a whole plank of a kidnapper's personality.

Sigurd hung his head slightly. 'Well, what do you suggest?'

'You could just let me go.'

'Then you'd find out where we are and tell Grosmal.'

'Oh, I wouldn't do that, I assure you. As I said, he's no friend of mine.'

'Yes,' Sigurd said slowly, thinking slowly as well, 'you said he was going to kill you if you didn't do something. What's that all about?'

'I'm investigating a death.'

'Yeuch,' Sigurd spat, 'first a room full of poo and now fiddling with dead bodies.'

'No, not the body, the death. I'm investigating the death.' Hermitage could tell that the word meant nothing to Sigurd. 'I'm trying to find out who killed someone else.'

'Ah, a trial.' Sigurd brightened as understanding arrived.

'Sort of.'

'By combat.' Sigurd smacked his own chest again.

'No, there's no combat involved.'

'Oh.' Sigurd was clearly disappointed. 'Who's dead then?'

'Henri de Turold.'

'Never heard of him.'

'He's a Norman.'

'Excellent, a dead Norman. I like them.' Sigurd's thought processes went on a bit. 'Why do you care who killed him?'

'I don't care. Robert Grosmal cares.'

'I thought you said he didn't value anyone.'

'That's very good reasoning.' Hermitage was impressed – at least the man was taking something in. Sigurd's chest swelled a bit.

'The problem is Grosmal values himself. It turns out this de Turold was a friend of King William. If the King finds out that de Turold is dead and it was partly Grosmal's fault, he's likely to take it out on Grosmal.'

'Get one thing straight, monk.' Sigurd was all seriousness now and had hold of the scruff of Hermitage's habit. 'William is not the King.'

'Ah no,' Hermitage gurgled, 'of course not.'

Sigurd put him down again and was calm once more. 'Anyway, if William the Bastard does Grosmal in, so much the better. Two dead Normans is an even better outcome.'

'Not for me. If I don't find out who did it, he'll do something horrible to me.'

'Hm.' Sigurd stroked his stubbled chin in thought. 'How was the Norman killed?'

'He was, erm, shot. Arrow.' Hermitage didn't like to go into the personal details.

'Ah well, probably us then.'

'You?'

'Yeah, Brotherhood of the Sword. We're always killing Normans, we are. It's what we do.'

'I see.' While Hermitage thought it couldn't be this straightforward to find out who the killer was, his heart rose for a moment. It fell again when he remembered where he was and that he wasn't in a position to do anything about it. If the killer came forward and presented his dirty shoes, Hermitage could hardly take him to Grosmal. He imagined the rest of the Brotherhood would be rather cross if he tried something like that. They would probably do something to him which involved swords.

'We'll ask Scarlan. He knows who kills most of the Normans round here.'

'Ah, marvellous,' said Hermitage, although he felt the opportunity to meet such a man was not very marvellous at all.

Sigurd scanned the clearing until he saw the man he wanted. 'Scarlan,' he yelled, and beckoned a figure to join him.

Hermitage followed the gesture and saw what appeared to be a large weasel on two legs standing by the main tent.

The man, for it plainly was a man, being too big for a real weasel, raised his arm in acknowledgement. Hermitage watched him approach and took an intellectual interest in the man's extraordinarily short legs, paddling back and forth under a body that must have been stretched on a rack. The arms were shorter than normal as well, but the man's head did him the worst favour. Rather pointy with a long nose and small eyes, it was also questing forwards all the time, as if smelling the air.

As Hermitage watched, he concluded that someone should tell Scarlan not to wear a light brown coat which didn't close at the front. This revealed his pale cream jerkin, very effectively completing the weasel ensemble.

A thought entered Hermitage's head that this man should be followed by a skipping band of real weasels, dancing in the wake of this giant of their race as he led them to weasel paradise.

He shook his head to get this bizarre thought out. Perhaps the blow on the head was still having some effect.

'I see our captive is roused?' The giant weasel whined in the sort of voice that should come out of a giant weasel.

'Aye,' said Sigurd, 'but not good news. He says he's of no value to Grosmal.'

'Well, he would say that, wouldn't he?'

'I suppose so, but he says he's doing something with a dead Norman.'

'Investigating,' Hermitage explained.

'Investigating eh?' Scarlan pointed his beady eyes at Hermitage. 'Interesting word. From the Latin *vestigare*, to track? Why are you tracking a dead body? I shouldn't think it's going anywhere.'

Hermitage was impressed. He castigated himself for making a judgment about this fellow based solely on his appearance.

'I am tracking the cause of his death so that the person responsible can be brought to justice.'

'Oh, we don't want that,' said Scarlan. 'We don't want people who kill Normans brought to justice. Want them rewarded.'

'Er, yes, absolutely.' Hermitage nodded his best enthusiastic agreement. 'It's just that Grosmal said I should find the killer or I'll be the next body.'

'Typical Norman reasoning,' Scarlan spat on the ground. 'If you're the suitable person to investigate, how can you do it when you're dead?'

'Exactly,' said Hermitage. He was warming to Scarlan.

'Still, you're out of it now. Let him look for the killer himself. Not that he'd be capable, of course.'

'Ah.' Hermitage saw where this reasoning was going.

'You can stay with us. We need a priest.'

'There is a problem,' Hermitage reluctantly put in.

'Explain,' Scarlan instructed. He didn't know how much Hermitage loved explaining. Wat could have warned him.

'I have a companion who is still at the castle. He and I were staying at De'Ath's Dingle.'

'Gods above,' Scarlan interrupted, crossing himself. Even Sigurd looked a little shocked.

'It's not that bad really.' Hermitage felt obliged to defend the place. 'Anyway, we'd dealt with the death of Brother Ambrosius, so when Mister Aethelred...'

'Traitor,' spat Scarlan and Sigurd in unison.

Hermitage looked at them in disappointment. 'When mister Aethelred came calling, we were sent to Grosmal. You got me out, but Wat's still there.'

'Casualty of war,' Scarlan concluded.

'I can't leave him. He'd would be lost without me.' Hermitage felt a little guilty at this untruth, but it served a greater good.

'And what does this Wat do? He's your servant?

'No, he's a weaver.'

'A weaver?' Scarlan seemed very surprised. 'A weaver called Wat? Wat the Weaver? *The* Wat the Weaver?'

'Well, I only know one weaver and he happens to be called Wat.'

'Bloody strange, Wat the Weaver hanging out with a monk,' Sigurd seemed to think the pairing was absurd. 'If it is *the* Wat the Weaver.'

'He saved my life from brigands one day. We met again in Lincoln and sort of worked together ever since.'

'Have you seen any of his tapestries?' Scarlan asked, very pointedly.

'Well, no, not actually. Although they seem to be very popular. Everywhere we go people have heard of Wat. Even mister

Aethelred had heard of him.'

'I bet he had,' Sigurd said in a very crude tone, and winked at Scarlan.

'My abbot once had a tapestry that was rather shocking,' Hermitage put in, feeling that he was being left out of something.

'If you've still got your eyes in your head, it probably wasn't one of Wat's.'

Sigurd was getting bored. 'What do we do then?' he asked Scarlan.

The weaselly man thought for a moment, but it was only a short one.

'We can't leave Wat the Weaver to the Normans.' He held his hand to his heart and spoke in the direction of the trees. 'They may take our land, they may take our people for slaves, they may leave our worth in the ruts of their carts, but they will never, never take our spirit. Wat the Weaver embodies that spirit, the spirit to express ourselves as Englishmen, to flick our fingers in the face of authority and to plough our own furrow. To weave tapestries of whatever we damn well like.'

'Yargh,' Sigurd yelled, beating his chest.

Scarlan looked back from the trees to two men who were looking at him from the fireside. 'Gather the men, Sigurd. We're going on a rescue.'

Sigurd immediately strode off the camp shouting 'to arms,' or something very similar. Hermitage looked at the encampment and waited for the rest of Scarlan's men to burst from the tents at the call. All that happened was that the two men by the fire picked up swords.

'Is that it?' Hermitage asked, not really intending to speak out loud.

'Quality men,' Scarlan responded, although he didn't sound too sure.

'Two?' Hermitage's disbelief at the paucity of the band was

clear. He quickly appraised the men by the fire. One was large, but looked awkward and he was not holding his sword quite properly. The other looked like he was trying not to hold his sword at all. As far as he could see, Sigurd was the only fighter among them.

'A rescue mission,' roared Sigurd from the middle of the camp.

'Oh dear,' mumbled Hermitage, but he smiled at Scarlan.

From his brief experience he knew that the Castle Grosmal was a disorganised shambles of a place. He suspected that a half-decent, well planned and executed mission might well extricate Wat from Lord Robert's clutches.

However, there were two problems. First, getting away from the Norman probably wouldn't do much good as he would only come after them – or send some people with swords. Second, from his extremely brief experience of Scarlan's band, he suspected they couldn't organise the rescue of a maiden from the middle of an empty field – a field owned by the maiden who had planned the whole thing herself.

Half past Eleven: Weaver to Saxon

 HOPE YOU'LL FORGIVE ME if I speak plainly,' Wat said as he and Ethel walked back towards the retainer's chamber.

'What am I saying? I don't give a donkey's fart whether you forgive me or not. I don't know what you're up to, Aethelred, and I don't think I care. I don't know if you really have given up completely and are happy to be this Norman no-brains' lackey, or if you have some secret scheme going on. You could be poisoning his water for all I care. In fact if you are, I'll carry the jug. What I am not going to do is get either Hermitage or I dragged into this murder.

'We're here to try and find out who did it. If I detect even the slightest hint that we are being sold out I will make sure the Norman believes you killed de Turold, interfered with his mother and pissed in his milk. And he seems stupid enough to believe anything.

'For all I know you did kill de Turold. Perhaps it's part of the secret scheme. I wouldn't blame you for exacting revenge, but if you did do it we need to know. Perhaps we can work something out.'

Wat looked to the thin Saxon for some response. There was none.

'Or we will find out who did it by this evening, tell Grosmal and leave you to your fate.'

Wat stopped and folded his arms, staring hard at Ethel.

The Saxon stopped as well and looked at Wat. 'I'm sorry, did you say something?'

Wat contained the urge to slap the man in the face. Or pull a knife and stab him in the head. Both were tempting. 'You know bloody well I did. I know your sort, Ethel,' Wat emphasised the Norman's derogatory name for his servant, 'but you're in no position to walk all over everyone around you any more. King Harold may have let you do what you want, but he's not King any more. As far as your wellbeing is concerned, I'm the King. Think on that.'

Ethel looked at Wat without an expression on his face. For a moment Wat thought he was going to walk away. Instead the Saxon gave the shrug of a man who is already dead. 'What do you suggest?' he asked.

'That's better,' Wat grinned. 'Come on, man, we can run rings round this Norman idiot.' He clapped Ethel hard on the shoulder.

The Saxon retainer looked at Wat as only a noble who has never been touched without invitation could look.

'Back to the garderobe,' said Wat.

'Do we have to?' said Ethel as if he'd been asked to go into a room that smelled of poo. 'You've already examined it at close range. From both ends.'

'That was before the Normans' crossbow turned up. We need to find Hermitage anyway – he's probably still examining the chamber.'

If Ethel could have turned his nose up any further he'd have smelt his own neck. 'Oh, very well,' he said, 'this way.' He walked off.

'I thought it was this way?' Wat beckoned to the tower.

'Not if you want to go directly,' Ethel replied in a tone that spoke highly of Wat's idiocy.

The weaver shrugged and followed Ethel. They went along a path, through a hole in a wall, down a short tunnel, out a hole in another wall and up a short flight of steps which looked more like mistakes in the stacking of the masonry. This led to another series of holes in walls, the last one of which opened outside the garderobe entrance.

Wat turned and gazed at the way they had come.

'The whole place is riddled with mistakes,' Ethel explained, 'apart from the ones living in it, of course.'

'What is your game, Aethelred?' Wat asked before they entered the garderobe. 'What are you up to?'

'Mister Wat.'

'Yes.'

'You say you know my type?'

'That's right.'

'The old order. The way things were?'

'Yes.'

'So there's absolutely no possibility of me revealing any personal details to a tradesman, is there?'

Wat couldn't stop himself grinning widely. 'I suppose not.'

'Let's just get on with whatever it is we're getting on with then, shall we?'

✦ ✦ ✦

The room was occupied.

'Oh, I beg your pardon,' Wat started, before realising the occupants were just two old hags trying to scrub the place clean.

The ghastly apparitions, wearing rags which put the function of the room to shame, had got some sort of ladder, or rather a pile of planks loosely bound together with twine. They were using this, and some sticks with even more hideous rags tied to the ends, to try and relieve the ceiling of its bowel problem.

As the explosion had forced a goodly quantity of the garderobe contents up through the seats, so the hags had to get it back down again. Not an easy task.

As the larger lumps of material fell from the roof the hags had started with shovels, which were still propped by the entrance. Now they had moved on to leather cloths, dipped every now and then into a bucket containing a liquid only slightly less revolting than the muck they were trying to clean away.

'What are you doing?' Wat asked

'We're hollowing out this huge turd to make into a house,' one of the hags responded, with creditable sarcasm.

Ethel stepped neatly forward and banged his knuckles on the back of the hag's head until she lay down.

'Now,' he said to the remaining hag.

'Cleaning the place up, sir,' said the second hag, recognising authority when she saw it hitting someone. 'Lord Grosmal likes the place neat.'

Wat walked gingerly across the still stained floor toward the two privy seats, above the slightly larger holes in the chamber floor.

'I was right.'

'Delighted to hear it,' Ethel responded, without interest.

'Hermitage was feeling bad that he'd set light to all the evidence, but I said these holes weren't big enough for anyone to get through and I was right.'

'I'm sure you're very happy.'

'Which means,' said Wat, trying to get the message across to Ethel that this was important, 'that no one went down there to shoot de Turold.'

'Ah,' said Ethel, actually showing signs of interest. Very dim signs, but signs none the less.

'And no one went in through the bottom door. That hadn't been opened for years.'

'Very wise.'

'So how was de Turold shot?'

Ethel shrugged his shrug of resignation.

'Unless he was shot first and then put in the garderobe?' Wat asked the very direct question of Ethel.

'In the arse? A remarkable shot.'

'Well, what do you suggest?'

'Perhaps it was a child?'

'A child?' Wat was horrified at the suggestion. 'Someone sent a child down a garderobe with a sophisticated weapon to shoot a Norman up the back passage?'

'Sounds like a plan to me.' Ethel seemed to think it was rather a clever one as well.

'Ridiculous.'

'Or a very thin person?' Ethel offered.

'Like you,' Wat observed.

'I think not,' Ethel replied.

Wat accepted immediately that Ethel wouldn't have even contemplated going down the hole. No matter how much he hated the Normans.

'Hermitage said de Turold was sitting on this particular hole when he was shot,' said Wat, closely examining the one closest to the door.

'He was,' Ethel confirmed, 'but what does that matter?'

'Don't know, but it might be important.'

'It was definitely that one, sir,' said the conscious hag, fawning shamelessly. But then she was mopping up a garderobe, so shame probably didn't trouble her much.

Peering into the hole, Wat could see into the chamber below again. The door below had still not been put back, partly to air out the smell and partly because no one in the castle could be persuaded to take on the job.

'Where is Hermitage?' Wat asked as he peered all around below.

'Perhaps he's on his way up?'

'That's what I thought last time I was here, but there's still no sign of him. He wouldn't go wandering off on his own.'

Ethel sauntered over to the hole. 'I can see that it would have been easy to shoot him. All the killer would have to do would be to stand down there, wait for Henri to sit and then fire.'

'The child?' Wat said, 'who would have to be lowered down

through the hole and then wait?' He tutted. 'I may know little about investigating and clues and evidence and such, but I do have a clue about shooting people. When was the Norman shot?' he asked Ethel.

'We found him in the morning. Presumably it was some time during the night.'

Wat frowned in thought. 'Presumably the hags work all night?'

'Of course they do.'

'Eeeek,' the hag squeaked, as hags do when grabbed. Wat reluctantly held on to the filthy rags and shook her a few times to make some words fall out.

'When did Henri de Turold get shot? Was it light or dark?'

'Dark,' screeched the hag. She followed the screech with a flutter of her eyelids at Wat. 'I was on the night clean and saw him wandering about.' She giggled unpleasantly.

'What do you mean, "wandering about"?'

'Well he was walking to the garderobe, but his clothing was … unusual.'

'We know.'

'He didn't have any at all,' the hag cackled. 'So I sent for Mabel here,' she gestured at the still unconscious hag, 'and we both had a good look.'

'So – in the dark,' said Wat, dropping the hag in her bucket of swill. 'How did they shoot him?'

'With the bow,' said Ethel. He was losing interest again.

'If he was here at night, when it was dark, how did anyone down there see that there was anyone up here, let alone shoot him? Or do we have a child-archer-bat who can see in the dark and hit a target smaller than a dingleberry?'

'There's the night candle which always burns here.' The hag gestured towards the stub of stuff that lay on its side by the privy seat. 'Henri had a candle as well.' She cut herself off quickly and instantly returning to her wiping. Then she stopped wiping as

Wat had helped her to her feet by pulling her hair.

'How do you know?' he enquired.

'We saw him carrying it,' said the hag, 'and when we was bought in to clear up, we found it in the muck and stuff.'

'Where is it?' said Ethel, in the tone of those who know wrongdoing when they hear it.

Delving into clothing which even the most parasitic, starving flea would avoid for fear of infection, the hag lifted her skirts, deliberately giving Wat a flash of her shapely legs. They were certainly shapely – just not leg-shaped. She retrieved the remains of the candle and presented it to Wat.

'Don't break it,' she said. 'We was going to give it back.'

Wat just frowned and held the candle in his hand. 'This thing weighs a ton,' he commented. 'What's it made of?'

'Oh, I don't think you want to know that,' Ethel said with distaste.

Wat examined it. He could find nothing of worth in its appearance. The texture seemed a bit odd. It reminded him of something, but he felt that he didn't want to remember quite what. It seemed to have been cleaned of the poo in which it must have landed. Reluctantly, he put it to his nose.

It is said that one can never smell in a dream, but this was an age of serious smells. If you had smelt De'Ath's Dingle once, that cloying, persistent, evil and somehow impertinent odour stayed with you forever. It would follow you around everywhere, even into your sleeping hours.

The smell of the garderobe of the castle of Robert Grosmal, as has been indicated, was of a comparable presence, albeit of a somehow more natural origin. But the smell of a candle of the castle of Robert Grosmal could blunt arrows. Wat's head swam and he staggered back, dropping the candle into the outstretched hand of the hag.

'Good gods above,' he said, shaking his head to try and make the memory go away. It only responded to this taunting by settling in more deeply. He took a couple of deep breaths which he immediately regretted.

'Right,' he panted, valiantly trying to get the world back in the right order. 'We know that Henri had a candle with him. If someone was in the garderobe, they would have been able to see the light of the night candle coming down through the privy seat, and when Henri arrived as well.'

'And perhaps,' said Ethel, following the line of reasoning, as if the practice was new to him, 'as soon as Henri sat himself down the light would have gone out. Then they'd have known to shoot.'

Wat considered. He acted out standing in the garderobe with a bow pointing upwards. 'We still need a child to do the job, but I can't see how else it was done. In any case it would have been difficult to see what you were aiming at.'

Wat turned to the hag. 'How big was Henri de Turold's backside?'

'Ohh sir,' said the hag. She assumed a greasy mock shyness.

'Was he a big fat Norman or a skinny weasel Norman?' Wat asked, accurately describing the two most common types.

'Very slim was Lord Henri. Very nice cheeks...' The hag's mind had wandered off into its own perversions.

'I think we need to try something out,' said Wat. 'We need to go down there again.' He gestured through the privy seats.

Wat was still rather pale from the bouquet of Robert's candle and felt positively bilious at this prospect. He was about to follow up with a very reasonable explanation for why his own suggestion should be ignored. Then Ethel intervened.

'Yes,' he agreed, with an unlikely enthusiasm. 'If we can show that no one could have shot de Turold from below, it means he was killed first and then put there.'

'Which doesn't make finding the killer any easier,' Wat observed.

'But it would mean we need to trace his earlier steps. Maybe we could find out that it was another Norman.' Ethel seemed positively excited by this idea.

'That would be a good thing?'

'Of course – there have been enough Saxon deaths already.'

'But if it was a Saxon?'

'As you say, Master Wat, perhaps we can come to an arrange-
ment.'

Wat frowned at the man. Ethel seemed to have woken up
somehow. Was the reality of the situation finally dawning on
him? Was he really interested in finding out who did it and pla-
cating Grosmal? Or was he worried that if the truth came out it
might not do him any favours? Nothing in the insouciant arro-
gance of the man was giving anything away.

'I'll go below and you wait here,' said Ethel.

At least that was a relief. Wat knew the smell up here wasn't
too bad now, but he suspected the room below would go straight
to his guts and invite them out to play.

The hag wandered over to the privy hole and stared down to
see Ethel appear. She looked at Wat as if this was some sort of
perverted parlour game.

'You can get on with your duties or I can throw you down the
hole,' Wat observed.

'I wouldn't fit, you said so.' The hag was an impudent one.

'I could jump up and down on you a few times,' Wat suggested.

The hag returned to her duties.

After a few minutes Wat heard noises below and peered into
the privy. He could see Ethel at the door at the base of the tower
looking up.

'Right, I'm here,' he said.

'I can see that. Which makes me wonder again where Hermitage has got to. Now, can you get in the tower and stand under the privy seat?'

Ethel didn't move.

'Is there a problem?'

'It's not actually very nice down here. There's rather a lot of, erm, dirt on the floor.'

'I should expect so,' Wat grinned to himself. This was clearly beyond anything the Saxon ex-noble had experienced before. 'You don't have people to do everything for you any more. You'll have to, erm, muck in.' Wat couldn't restrain a laugh. At least it was a cheap one.

'Very amusing, I'm sure.'

Slowly and reluctantly Ethel put a tentative foot into the chamber. He sighed in relief when it did not sink into something truly revolting, and gingerly advanced into the room. The old priest's desk was still half-submerged in the corner, rather like the tower of a church emerging from the waters of some demonic flood.

'Can you pull the door across behind you?' Wat asked

'Good idea,' Ethel responded without enthusiasm. He tugged at the battered wooden door, which had been propped back near its home, until he was alone with his thoughts in a dark chamber full of poo, looking up through a privy seat.

'I can see through both holes into the chamber,' Ethel said with some disappointment. 'So if someone was down here they'd have been able to spot de Turold.'

'Not necessarily,' said Wat. 'I'll sit down and you tell me if you can see my arse.' He wasn't sure he wanted to put his nice clean leggings on the sort of garderobe seat arrows came through, but these were unusual circumstances.

'Right.' Ethel's voice became muffled as Wat's body blocked the hole.

'Well?'

'Yes, I can see you.'

'Ah, but it was dark wasn't it? Just the light of the candle which was by my side.' Wat reached forward and grabbed the hag, who was busy scrubbing nearby. He lifted her from the floor with one arm and planted her on the second privy seat beside him.

'Oh?' she said. 'One of them, eh?' and she started to lift her skirts. Wat cuffed her lightly on the side of the head and called to Ethel.

'Can you still see me?'

'No, can't see a thing,' came the muffled but rather triumphant reply – followed by a plaintive, 'I think I'll leave now.'

A very short space of time later a very grateful Ethel was back in the company of Wat.

'So,' Wat said, thinking very hard indeed, 'if it was dark, which we know it was, and the killer couldn't see Henri's backside, which we know he couldn't, how did he manage to hit him?'

'Could he have taken aim when the candle light was visible – and then just fired when it got dark?'

'It's possible,' said Wat, 'but he'd have to be a damn fine bowman.' Wat searched his memory for instances of people being shot in the dark. There were a few, but they were mostly mistakes. In fact it was pretty hard to shoot someone even in broad daylight. In the hands of most people the modern bow was hopeless. Killing someone on purpose was like trying to hit the moon with a sheep.

He could never understand poaching: the only real way of killing a deer was to creep up on it with a rock. Anyone who could finish one off with an arrow deserved a prize. He found it hard to believe the crossbow was any better.

Killing someone with one shot was unheard-of. Apart from Harold and Hastings, of course – but then that was most likely an accident.

That gave Wat pause for thought. The thought hurried off pretty quickly as he realised that shooting someone in the backside while they were sitting on the privy was highly unlikely to be an accident. No one would be cleaning their bow in the garderobe chamber when it accidentally went off.

And that brought him back to the size of the killer.

'This is just too odd,' he said.

139

Before Ethel could respond, the first hag, counting them in the order of being hit, began to stir.

'Where's my candle?' were the first words she uttered on rejoining the world.

'Don't panic, you evil, thieving wretch, it's here,' said Ethel. He picked up the distasteful object from the side of the privy and waved it in the air.

The first hag put her hands in her clothing, delved about for a bit and came out with a few more flea bites and another candle. 'Ah, here it is,' she said, as if she had just found her baby alive and well after a horrific carting accident.

'It's a third candle,' said Ethel, as if he was taking stock of the things.

'So?' Wat thought that the fewer of these things there were the better.

'Why is there another candle? Why would Henri have had two candles?'

'Maybe this is the killer's candle,' said Wat. 'If he was in the garderobe with his own candle, he would have been able to see Henri. He then fired, climbed out through the hole and brought the candle with him.' He paused for a moment. 'This child is getting cleverer and cleverer.'

'But surely,' Ethel questioned, 'if he lit a candle down there the whole place would have gone bang, like it did this morning?'

'Good point. And it still doesn't get over the problem of this child climbing into a garderobe, operating a crossbow in the dark and killing a Norman with one shot. Which he must have done – not much chance of climbing up to finish the victim off before the alarm was raised.' Wat paused again for another thought. 'Mind you, if de Turold had finished his business and then saw a child climbing out the privy hole, the shock might have killed him…'

'This is getting ridiculous,' Wat huffed, unable to see how all the strange facts could fit together. Maybe Hermitage would get it.

Ethel was carrying on regardless. 'If it was the killer's candle, why would he leave it here? It would have been pitch dark. How would he have got out of the room and escaped through the darkened castle without a candle?'

'I think we've got to back to the beginning.' Wat shook his head. 'There are too many confusions in this.'

'And you do this sort of thing regularly, do you?' Ethel sounded contemptuous of Wat's skills.

'Only the once,' Wat replied sharply, 'and then we found it was the man in authority who did it.'

'Really.' Ethel didn't seem concerned.

'The only thing we know is that de Turold is dead,' said Wat.

Ethel didn't reply.

'We do know that, do we?'

'Well, he wasn't breathing, his heart wasn't beating, he was cold and pale and didn't flinch when he smashed his head on the floor.'

'Good.'

'I thought so, yes.'

'I don't think there's any more to be done here,' Wat said. 'I need to sit down and think this through. I need to talk to Hermitage as well. Can you send some men to find him?'

'I suppose so, although I don't know what a monk can add to this.'

'He's very good with facts and reasons. He puts them together in odd ways. If we give him this lot he'll have an answer in no time.'

'I do hope so, because by this evening no time is exactly what we'll have.' Ethel looked at Wat and raised his eyebrows. It seemed the Saxon wasn't really bothered about being killed by Grosmal, but he assumed Wat would have some objections. He was right.

They left the garderobe and were immediately assailed by a furore from below. There was a commotion in the courtyard of

141

the castle and the noise drifted up to their walkway. Wat stepped very cautiously towards the edge of the pavement to see what was happening below.

Ethel stayed back, very unwilling to follow.

A group of guards had gathered in the middle of the courtyard and were raising their voices at a figure who was in their midst somewhere.

'I demand entrance to this castle,' the voice of the figure whined its way into the air.

'I recognise that voice,' Wat said in puzzlement. He couldn't quite place it, but he knew it had been recently, and he knew the recollection was not welcome.

'But you are in the castle,' the most senior guard was insisting. 'You don't need to demand anything. And you don't need to push my guards around.'

'They are clearly incompetent and have no idea who they are dealing with.'

'I really do recognise that voice,' said Wat. His stomach was sinking, but the memory would not come. Perhaps it didn't want to.

'Look,' the castle guard was saying, 'the door is wide open, anyone can just walk in. You're welcome. If you stand outside shouting at the walls we're bound to think you're some kind of loon and send the guards.'

'Your master shall hear of this.'

'Of course he will – he probably has already, you're very loud. If I was you I wouldn't seek him out, but that's up to you. If you insist on getting him, it'll be on your own head.'

A hand appeared from the small throng and waved everyone away. A monk was revealed and Wat's heart sank at the cut of the habit. The cowl was thrown back and a face pointed its way into the daylight.

In a fine counterpoint to Lord Grosmal's head which pointed upwards, this one went forwards. And it didn't point to the air in an interested or intelligent way. A thin skull, sallow cheeks and narrow, contemptuous eyes lent their support to a monumental nose which pointed at the world in front of it as a noble points at a leper. It pointed out the world's failings and inadequacies, and then it sneered at them.

'Bring your master to me,' the pointy head demanded. 'I am Brother Simon, the King's Investigator,' it announced. 'I have heard of a murder and I am here to dispense justice.'

'Oh bloody hell,' Wat said slowly and with deep feeling.

'Who's he?' Ethel asked.

'We have to get to Grosmal before he does.'

'Really?'

'Oh yes. If he gets your master's ear we'll be dead by midday, never mind sunset.'

The morning was well into its prime and Wat had thought he was making some progress. A simple chat with Hermitage and a discussion of the facts could well see the whole business dealt with before nightfall.

And now this. If there was one individual guaranteed to take your progress and wreck it completely, he had just walked into the castle.

It was just what the murder of Henri de Turold in the Castle Grosmal needed – another idiot.

Midday: Lady to Norman Noble

ERE'S THE GOWN, NOW PUT IT ON.' Foella emerged from the dressing room with the gentlemen's gown draped over her arm. She clearly had not a clue what to do with it.

Eleanor took the gown and, interpreting the instruction correctly, laid it out on the bed. She was ready to get her mistress into it – or at least as much of her mistress as could be squeezed into its confining spaces.

'What are you going to do, my lady?' Eleanor asked, having heard all the details of the discussion with the mysterious man from the wardrobe.

'About what?' Foella asked, lightly, as if she'd just been asked whether she wanted boar or swan for dinner.

'About the man from the wardrobe,' Eleanor heard her exasperation squeak into her voice, 'telling you not to marry Lord Grosmal?'

'Have you been listening to my conversations?'

'I was standing right there, my lady.'

'You still shouldn't listen.'

'No, my lady.'

'I shall ignore him as I ignore all men who hide in my wardrobe.' A frown crossed Foella's face. 'Make sure he's not still there.'

Eleanor returned to the wardrobe and opened it. There was no one inside, but she now saw there was a rather large hole in the back which led off into the stonework. She was surprised that she had noticed it when they arrived. Not quite the sort of thing you expect in a wardrobe.

'No, he's gone, my lady.'

'Good job too – who knows how long people have been traipsing in and out of my furniture? And God knows what they've been getting up to in there.'

'Yes, my lady,' said Eleanor, frustrated that the conversation was drifting away from the subject. 'Lord Grosmal, my lady?'

'What, is he in there as well?'

'No, my lady. I meant what are you going to do about Lord Grosmal?'

'Not that it's any of your business, but I shall not be taking any advice from my closet.'

'But if they do have some devious plan for Lord Robert?'

'Devious? You do know the man from the wardrobe lives in the log store.'

'Maybe he's fond of wood?'

'And he lives there with some Saxon imbecile who is turning into a tree.'

'Ah.'

'They call themselves the Brotherhood of the Sword or something, and there's another one of them running around the castle. He has to run because his legs are so short. If he swung his sword he might take your knees out, but that would be about it. These are not people who have ideas in their heads, let alone devious plans.'

'But…'

Foella had had enough. 'Get this gown on me and I shall go to see Grosmal and see what he's got to offer.'

'At least in this gown he'll be able to see what you've got to offer.'

'That is the general idea.' Foella held her arms out, waiting for Eleanor to do as she was told.

Eleanor's shoulders sagged. The matter seemed lost. Not that the marriage to Grosmal was in the bag. A million and one things could go wrong between here and the altar. All she had to do was think of one or two of them.

She helped her mistress out of her day gown, reorganised the undergarments so that they didn't obscure the view and then put the new gown over the top.

Several bits of her mistress tried to escape their new constrictions. With an ease borne of practice, Eleanor pushed them back into their proper places and stood back to look at the results. She stepped forward to adjust a hem here and fluff up a sleeve there before finally admiring her work.

'Disgusting,' she said politely as she appraised the fleshy bits of her mistress, most of which were on the outside of the dress.

'Lord Robert's the disgusting one,' Foella retorted as she flounced from the room. 'Men are all just disgusting,' she muttered as an afterthought, twitching her gown and preparing to enter the fray.

◆   ◆   ◆

There were many ways in which a man could be disgusting, and Lord Robert Grosmal had mastered most of them.

His personal habits, hygiene, food and the like were enough to ensure that personal servants never stayed very long. They normally left to take up more wholesome careers as slaughtermen or turd harvesters.

Robert's personal retainer Brolard, the ancient and grizzled Norman whose wandering hands had alarmed Eleanor, was so absent in the head that he forgot who Robert was the moment his master left the room. Only this complete lack of memory enabled him to welcome Robert back into his presence.

Grosmal's powers of thought were so limited that he was incapable of silent contemplation. If he had an idea, he said it out loud. Thus everyone knew his ideas were disgusting. Whether they revolved around punishments for poaching, what diseases to give political opponents or possible uses for dead peasants, they were all horrible.

With everything he did, everything he said and everything he thought being disgusting, it was a surprise to find that sex was missing. It was as if nature, realising what it had done in bringing the triangular babe into the world, had tried to make amends by removing any desire for reproduction.

This didn't stop the noble doing disgusting things in this area of life, but it was usually just to see what all the fuss was about. He heard tales from battle and its aftermath and tried his best to fit in with his comrades, many of whom were comprehensively more disgusting in this area than others.

Robert was completely at ease with these 'I wonder what would happen if' adventures, as he called them. He wondered what would happen if he did x, or if someone else did y, or if four people got together and did z while hanging from a tree.

He did some of these things to women, or even with them if they were paid enough, but he appeared to draw no particular distinction between the sexes. Or the species, come to that. As long as it moved. On a couple of occasions even that line had been crossed.

But despite all of these activities, he never really saw the point. He would come away from another excursion in which a variety of people had been roundly humiliated, vaguely wondering what it had all been about. The only person he would tell any of this to was Brolard, on whose discretion he could always rely.

Brolard was always horrified at what he heard, but then he simply forgot it.

◆　　◆　　◆

At this moment Grosmal was in the main hall of his castle, sitting on a long bench pulled up to the great fire. He wasn't in his usual comfortable chair because he needed to get at his feet to pick his toenails. Even when he had nothing to do, Robert was disgusting.

When Lady Foella entered the main hall, all of her assets on display, Lord Robert barely looked up from the piece of hard skin which was his current focus of attention.

'My lord,' said Foella, in her best come-hither voice.

Robert stayed thither, unmoved.

'Yes?' he said, eventually checking the alluring figure of Foella up and down.

She wiggled slightly.

'No knife now, then?' Robert observed, going back to his toe-nail.

'Er, no.' Foella was clearly disappointed at the reaction. She stepped closer and sat next to Grosmal on the bench.

'How goes it, my lord?'

'What?'

'How goes it?'

'Yes. How goes what?'

'Oh, you know.'

'No?'

'Well, erm, the, erm…' Foella floundered around for a topic of conversation. Murder seemed the best option. 'De Turold?'

'Still dead.' Robert left his toe at this. He looked Foella straight in the eye, which wasn't where he was supposed to be looking at all. 'You said I'd killed him.'

'Ah, well. We all make mistakes.'

'And that he was your husband.'

'Husband to be.' Foella fluttered her eyelashes.

Grosmal looked at her with a slight frown, as if she had something in her eye.

'But when one door closes…' she suggested.

'What?'

'When one door closes.'

'Which door?'

'It's an expression. When one door closes, another one opens.'

'Are they connected somehow?'

'It means when one opportunity has gone, another one presents itself.' Patience was not Foella's strong suit, but this was a special occasion.

'Does it?'

'Oh, yes,' said Foella, in a sultry tone of voice intended for another time and place all together.

Grosmal at last noticed her gown. 'What's happened to your dress? If one of my staff has damaged it, I can have them punished.'

'It's supposed to be like this,' she said, showing him particularly which bits were supposed to be like what.

'Aren't you cold?'

'My lord,' said Foella in a very business-like way, putting her hand on his knee.

◆　　◆　　◆

'My lord,' Ethel called as he and Wat scurried into the room through the kitchen door to the hall.

'What do you want?' Foella shrieked. 'Get out.'

'But my lord,' Ethel pleaded to his master.

'Out.' Foella's shriek, which couldn't have got any higher, got higher.

Grosmal shrugged, indicating Ethel had better do as the lady wanted.

The retainer took Wat by the arm and led him back out of the room, the weaver whispering fiercely in his ear.

'Where were we?' Foella asked Grosmal, who was the last one to know.

'My lord,' a whining, simpering voice slid across the floor from the main door and disturbed Foella again.

'O-u-u-t-t-t!' she yelled and stamped her foot for emphasis.

The voice took no notice at all.

'I am the King's Investigator, Brother Simon,' the voice intoned.

Foella was about to scream again when the word 'King' penetrated Grosmal's head. He brushed away Foella's hand, which had made quite a significant ascent from the level of the knee, and stood up.

'King's what?' He asked.

'Investigator.' Brother Simon imbued each syllable with its own pomposity.

'What's an investigator?'

Brother Simon seemed a bit puzzled by the question. 'I am commissioned by the King to look into things.'

'What sort of things? Boxes and the like?'

'No, no. Matters.'

'Matters?'

'Matters.'

'People who make mats?'

Something akin to a giggle emerged from the doorway through which Wat and Ethel had recently passed.

'No, no my lord. Matters. Matters of import, matters of mystery, matters of question. Those sort of matters.'

'And the King wants these things looked into, does he?'

'Oh, yes, my lord.'

'Well I don't think I've got any matters here, so I'll bid you good day. My regards to the King.'

'But my lord, I have heard of a death in this place.'

'So? People are always dying, all over the place. I don't think that counts as a matter.'

'An unusual death, my lord. Possibly a murder.' Brother Simon gave this word all the significance he could.

Grosmal paled considerably. 'Did the King send you to look into it?' he gulped.

'Not directly, my lord. Fortunately I was in the district, giving instruction to the monks of De'Ath's Dingle. Brother Athan, who seems to have installed himself as abbot – with little authority that I can detect – reported the event to me and suggested I should hurry to assist.'

'Ha!' burst from Wat, before he could stop it.

'And why are you a monk? In fact, why are you all monks?'

Simon looked around, apparently puzzled that there weren't any other monks in the room.

'It is my calling, my lord, but there's only me.'

'What about the other one?'

'Other one?'

'Yes. Ethel got me another monk to look into matters. I don't think I need two. Surely the first one can tell you what happened and then you tell the King?'

Simon frowned heavily. 'What is the name of this other monk, my lord?'

'How the hell should I know? I don't keep a book of monk's names.'

'This is very suspicious. Did this other monk have anyone with him?'

'Yes, there were two of them, but the other one wasn't a monk.'

'The monk was a rather young and stupid fellow?' Simon asked. 'And was the one with him well dressed and impudent?'

'That's them.'

'Oh, my lord, I fear we have a serious problem. But we may have the answer to the murder.'

There was a clatter behind Simon which made him turn. The sight of Wat the Weaver with a most unfriendly look on his face made the King's Investigator step back towards the safety of Grosmal.

'King's Investigator, eh, Brother Simon?' Wat asked as he advanced menacingly on the monk, ignoring Grosmal, Foella and Ethel.

'Indeed, you know this to be the case, Mister Weaver,' Brother Simon sneered.

Grosmal stepped between them and beckoned Ethel. 'If you

have business with the King's Investigator, you shall answer to me,' he glared at Wat. His glare was always most effective, being that of a madman.

'Which King?' Wat asked mildly.

'Eh?' Grosmal didn't understand the question. 'King William, of course.'

'I think not,' Wat responded. 'Why don't you explain, Brother Simon?'

'There's nothing to explain. I am the King's Investigator.'

'The King who doesn't know you're here and doesn't even know he has an Investigator?'

'You said...' Grosmal started, turning to Brother Simon.

Wat interrupted. 'And I recall you being replaced by the King. Because you were useless. Remember that?'

'Nonsense.'

'Who was King when he was appointed?' Ethel asked Wat in all innocence, seemingly as a matter of polite conversation.

'Oh, erm, let me think. I know. It was, erm, oh, what was his name? Began with an H. Harold. That's it, Harold,' Wat responded.

At the sound of the name Grosmal changed. The lurking beast that floated like scum on the pools of his vacant eyes woke and took control.

Ethel gently tugged Wat backwards out of the way as Robert Grosmal launched himself at Brother Simon.

'Eek,' the King's Investigator said. He neatly side-stepped as the Norman hurtled by.

Grosmal turned back towards his prey, crouching slightly with arms outstretched as if to prevent Simon escaping. He was breathing heavily and had turned a strange shade of crimson.

'There is no King Harold,' he snarled.

'No, no, of course not,' Brother Simon whined as he swayed about, trying not to be wherever the next attack was going to land.

'The King of this God-forsaken, frozen, piss-puddle of a country is William.'

'Yes, yes, King William. God bless him,' Simon said very hurriedly.

'So you claim to be King William's Investigator?' There was a slight undertone of sanity in the Frenchman's voice now.

'Of course, of course.' Simon nodded with enthusiasm.

'He says not.' Grosmal pointed at Wat, keeping his eyes all the time on Simon.

'I er, I became his Investigator as soon as our gracious Lord William became King.'

'Eh?'

'I sort of go with the job. I was King's Investigator under King, er, the previous incumbent, and so I get passed on to noble, valiant, all-conquering King William.' Simon seemed quite pleased with this reasoning.

'That doesn't follow,' Grosmal growled.

'Oh?' A squeak came from Brother Simon.

'A lot of people who were something under the usurper are nothing now. Isn't that so, Ethel?'

Ethel simply stood, expressionless.

'In fact,' Grosmal went on, relatively calm now, 'a lot of people who were something under the usurper aren't even people any more. Well, not living ones. Why should you be different?'

Simon looked around the room for help. It certainly wasn't coming from Wat or Ethel, and Foella was looking on as a completely disinterested observer. So disinterested that she had started fiddling with her gown to see if she could show off any more of herself.

'Well, I, er, wasn't appointed directly by the usurper, of course, it was purely an administrative post. My appointee was the Bishop.'

'Which one?' Grosmal asked, his voice heavy with suspicion.

'The Bishop of Lincoln, Odo.'

'Also not what he used to be.'

'Really?' Simon's voice was getting higher and higher.

'Not a Bishop any more. Still living, I think, but not very well.'

'Oh, ah, well, if, erm, circumstances have changed then naturally I am at my lord's disposal.' Simon's thinking found some solid ground and he planted his feet on it. 'In fact, I am only too glad to wait noble King William's pleasure to confirm my position.'

'Really?' Grosmal insanity was being reigned in.

'Oh yes. And if in the meantime I am able to offer my humble service to your lordship in this matter it would be most gratifying.'

'Oh, knock it off, Simon.' Wat was contemptuous.

'What services?' Grosmal asked.

'My investigation skill.'

'Hermitage says it's investigative,' Wat interrupted with a snort.

'And what good would that be exactly?' Grosmal's eyes narrowed.

'I could investigate this murder for you, my lord.'

'I've already got someone doing that.'

'Ah, but not someone with my experience. Surely you don't have someone who really was appointed by the usurper?' He threw this question sideways to Wat, who kept his peace. It was clearly a struggle for him, but he kept it.

'And anyway,' Simon went on, 'I already know who committed the crime.'

'You do?' Grosmal was impressed now, 'this is more like it.' He glared at Ethel. 'Who was it, then?'

Simon drew his spindly shoulders back and thrust forward his spindly nose. 'He did.' He pointed at Wat.

'You idiot,' Wat retorted in despair at Simon's stupidity.

'Him and the other monk.'

Wat put his hand on his hips. 'Simon, you've only just walked in the place. You don't know who's dead, how he died or where anyone was at the time. Who knew him, who hated him or who benefits from his death? You know nothing. But then that's pretty normal, isn't it?

Simon ignored him. 'They are a notorious pair, my lord. Had you but been involved with the matter I have resolved at the monastery in De'Ath's Dingle…'

'Ha!' burst from Wat again. He felt he had several more to come.

'If you had just resolved the most heinous crime perpetrated by this man and his supposed companion, you would have no doubt.'

There was a silence in the room. Wat was shaking his head in disbelief, stunned by the barefaced dishonesty. 'You had nothing to do with it and you know that for a fact. I'm afraid, my Lord Grosmal, that you have before you a monk who lies.'

Simon was standing with a smug look settled comfortably on his face. Ethel was as neutral and disinterested as usual. Foella had finished undoing her dress and was smiling at Grosmal. The lord of the manor was thinking.

It was clearly a complex task and was taking up most of his capacity. There wasn't enough power in his head to do thinking and keep an expression on his face, so his features had dropped and his mouth hung open. As the thought processes wound their way to completion, his head moved. Slowly his features rolled themselves up again. He looked from Wat to Simon and back again.

He drew breath. 'I knew it,' he said, staring hard at Wat. 'Guard, take this murderer away.'

Caput XV
Midday: Wood to Castle

BROTHER HERMITAGE WAS DISAPPOINTED with the rescue party. He would have been disappointed had the gathering been a party in the scriptorium to celebrate his old mentor Brother Timothy's completion of page four of the Book of Genesis. And Brother Timothy was a notorious recluse who had taken a vow of silence.

That it even constituted a party at all was a matter of debate. There were six of them eventually, including Hermitage.

Only six was a worry, and Hermitage thought there ought to be a minimum requirement for this sort of activity. The best first principle he had to go on was that two was company and three was a crowd. On this basis Wat was going to be rescued from a heavily defended Norman castle by two crowds. One of these contained Hermitage himself, and he had to admit castle-storming and rescuing were not skills he could call upon.

He had read about them, of course, but in recent times he'd discovered that reading about things was insufficient preparation for when the things themselves turned up. Things in real life were very complicated and had never read the same books.

He was sure castle-storming should have more people. He tried to consider what the collective noun for a crowd would be, and was quite pleased with his reasoning until he came up with a crowd of crowds. And even that was only nine people.

On several occasions Hermitage had tried to point out that Wat wasn't in fact a prisoner, that he was just at the castle to investigate the death of de Turold and so didn't really need rescuing at all. Strangely this seemed not to matter to Scarlan.

He had suggested they just go up to the gate and ask to speak to Wat. Someone would probably go and get him. Again, this was not good enough for Scarlan. He said that Wat was a symbol and this was the time for action.

His little band of men were roused by this, and Hermitage rather suspected that was the point. They had all looked a bit lacklustre and frankly bored when Hermitage had first seen them. They clearly needed a purpose in life, and Wat was providing one.

Hermitage's concern was that while the cause may be glorious and just, as Scarlan insisted, their lives would be pointless and short if they tried to extract someone from a fully armed fortress. Someone who didn't need extracting in the first place.

Sigurd was in the vanguard, of course, and he matched the requirements of the role perfectly. Hermitage imagined he could climb ladders, leap across gaps, hit people, everything the modern castle-stormer required.

Scarlan drew up the rear and Hermitage did not find this surprising. The man was clearly intelligent and would be directing activities from a place of safety. All well and good, but with Scarlan and Hermitage out of the mêlée that left Sigurd plus three.

The three did not bolster Hermitage's confidence that their assault on the castle would do anything to the Normans other than entertain them.

The two he had seen by the fire were Durniss and Cotard. Durniss looked like a man of the fields – strong as an ox, and with about the same level of tactical skill and mental prowess. Hermitage was sure he could despatch a few guards, or knock down a door or two, but once he was through the door he would likely have to wait for someone to point him in the right direction. He seemed to need reasonably clear instruction on how to put one foot in front of the other.

Cotard had begun the campaign by offering to stay behind and look after the tents. Almost every step of the way he raised the topic of another essential task at the camp which he had really better go back and complete. He had gone into the bushes to relieve himself at one point, only for Sigurd to have to go after him when he was spotted a quarter of a mile away heading in the other direction. Hermitage suspected he was not fully committed to the rescue.

It was the last of their number who nailed the lid on the coffin of Hermitage's hopes. This was another Sigurd, son of the larger Sigurd, who was clearly being raised in his father's image. He would be a great warrior and would vanquish all who stood before him. He would be just the sort to storm a castle and rescue a prisoner, leaving a trail of destruction in his wake. That time was for the future. The present worried Hermitage, as the new Sigurd son of Sigurd was only four.

Sigurd, father of Sigurd son of Sigurd, would hear nothing of Hermitage's objections to taking a small child on the mission. He pointed out that he had stormed his first castle when he was six, although Hermitage's brief interrogation revealed that had been in a company of six hundred. Young Sigurd had been escorted into the castle and been allowed to kill a guard of sorts. This appeared to be a guard dog which was already wounded and was held down by three large women.

Scarlan seemed confident their mission would be a success despite these shortcomings. Eventually he told Hermitage to shut up whining and concentrate on their magnificent journey.

Their magnificent journey, the great trek that would take them across hostile territory, under the eyes of the enemy and the constant threat of death, was completed after half an hour's stroll through a rather nice wood.

Hermitage's forebodings came to full and vibrant life as the band peered out of the woodland at the questionable sight of Castle Grosmal.

Cotard's oft-stated concerns at the perilous nature of the journey were transformed to a frosty silence by the vision of the enemy stronghold. A frosty silence warmed by his regular breaking of wind.

Durniss thought nothing of the place and had to be told to stop walking when he got to the tree line. 'Castle,' he accurately observed.

Sigurd gave a low snarl as his foe was presented to him.

Scarlan looked across the open space between woodland and castle and stroked his chin.

Sigurd son of Sigurd threw twigs at some rabbits.

'There's a lot of them, eh?' Hermitage commented, pointing out the Normans who patrolled the castle. There must have been a dozen in sight at this moment, all in uniform, armoured heads shining in the weak winter sun. Several had swords at their waists and others carried large pikes. Real pikes with spikes on top.

'Where's Wat likely to be?' Scarlan asked Hermitage, squatting down at the edge of the wood and throwing some grass in the air – as if knowing which way the wind was blowing would help defeat a lot of men in armour with pikes.

'No idea. We were looking all over the castle. The garderobe, Ethel's chamber, the great hall.'

'He'll be in the dungeon,' Sigurd explained, with confidence in his knowledge of situations like this.

'Why?' Hermitage asked. 'He hasn't done anything. He's helping Robert Grosmal. Why would the lord put someone he needs in the dungeon?'

'Norman,' Sigurd explained simply.

'We need to know before we attack.' Scarlan was clear.

'Attack?' Hermitage was horrified. 'Us? Attack them?' He gestured first at their own band, using his arms to very effectively illustrate the paucity of their military resources, and then at the Normans, demonstrating that theirs were much bigger.

Much, much bigger.

'He's right,' Cotard said, clearly prepared to leave immediately.

'Not head on,' Scarlan explained, 'not man to man combat.'

'Ah,' said Cotard with some relief.

'Oh,' said Sigurd with disappointment.

'We have a man,' Scarlan nodded his head, indicating it had a secret inside it.

'Just the one?' Hermitage asked.

'On the inside. We have a man on the inside.'

'Inside what?' Durniss asked, looking round at the trees and eventually at his own large frame.

'Inside the castle. A spy.' Scarlan whispered the last word as if the wind would carry it to the wrong ears.

'But we're here and he's there,' Hermitage pointed out, emphasising the large space between Scarlan and his spy. A space currently full of Normans.

'We can signal to one another. There's a routine established. We'll get a message to our man. He'll find out where Wat is, then we can sneak in and get him out.'

'Sneak?' Sigurd was appalled at the word.

'Why don't I just walk up to the gate and ask for him?' Hermitage proposed.

'Pah.' Sigurd was dismissive.

'They know me, they're probably expecting me. I can just ask where Wat is and we can pop out.'

Sigurd seemed to have run out of contemptuous terms and just shook his head in sorrow at 'pop out'.

'And as I tried to explain,' Hermitage went on, 'even if we do get Wat out, what do we do then? We can't just leave. Grosmal wants us to sort out the death. He's not likely to just say goodbye. He'll send men to bring us back. Lots of men. With weapons.'

'We leave him to rot. Hide in the woods and let him sort out the death himself.'

'I don't think mister Wat will want to hide in woods. He has a business to run. He got very bored in De'Ath's Dingle, and there was plenty to do there.'

'This is war.' Scarlan was losing some patience. 'We don't get what we want in war.'

He seemed very sincere in this and Sigurd hefted his sword, so Hermitage thought better of pointing out that the war had already been lost.

'There's the signal,' Scarlan called.

Hermitage looked to the castle, but couldn't see anything.

'Our man is on the battlements. He goes there every hour. I'll use our secret sign language to tell him what to do.'

◆　　◆　　◆

Scarlan stood up on the very edge of the wood and raised his right arm. 'Good, he's seen us.'

Hermitage peered hard at the battlements and couldn't see anyone. There was a Norman guard strolling along, not looking in their direction. Certainly no sign of a spy exchanging signals.

Scarlan was waving his arms and moving his body in a way that was anything but secret. Anyone looking in his direction would assume some loon was pretending to be a tree in a high wind. Maybe that was the secret, Hermitage thought. Very clever. No one would expect this bizarre show to be an exchange of information.

Mind you, if the spy in the castle was behaving in the same manner, he wouldn't be a secret very long.

Scarlan settled down from his extravagant gyrations and leant forward to read the reply.

'He already knows of Wat, and of you, it seems,' Scarlan announced.

Hermitage really did look very hard at the battlements and couldn't see a thing. He looked askance at Scarlan, wondering now if the man really was a loon and this was all in his head.

After a few more moments watching, Scarlan turned to Hermitage with his hands on his hips. 'Well,' he said in a very told-you-so tone.

'What?' Hermitage was all innocence.

'We know where mister Wat is. The dungeon.'

'Ha!' Sigurd was triumphant.

'The dungeon? Who put him in the dungeon?'

'I think the lord of the manor usually does things like that,' Scarlan pointed out.

'Yes, but why?' Hermitage really hated it when new facts turned up without invitation.

Scarlan turned back to the battlements. 'It's just coming through,' he said, squinting.

They waited a moment or two.

'Murder, apparently,' Scarlan shrugged, 'of de Turold.'

'That's impossible.' Hermitage dismissed the message as an error. 'Wat was with me at De'Ath's Dingle when de Turold was killed. We didn't even know he existed until Ethel came and told us he didn't exist any more.'

'That's Normans for you,' Sigurd explained.

'I don't understand,' Hermitage shook his head. Why did events have to make themselves happen all the time?

'I'll see if I can get any more information.' Scarlan turned to the battlements and his waving dance.

'Ah,' he said, 'yes. I see. Oh, really? Well, well.'

'What?' Hermitage demanded when the exchange had finished.

'Turns out some other monk has turned up.'

'Other monk?' Hermitage couldn't imagine which of his Brothers would voluntarily visit Robert Grosmal.

'Yes. I couldn't quite make out the title. King's Master Baker or something.'

'Master Baker?' Hermitage found people who gabbled nonsense at him difficult to cope with. If they didn't have a full and comprehensively referenced source for what they were going to say, why didn't they keep quiet?

'Why would a baker turn up? And why would a baker be a monk? He ran the syllables through his head until the bottom dropped out of his stomach.

He turned to Scarlan and his voice shook. 'Did he say "King's Investigator"?'

'Ah yes, could be.'

Hermitage looked at the castle and then back at the sorry band. There were four now as Cotard was nowhere to be seen and Sigurd son of Sigurd had climbed a tree to do a wee.

Hermitage took hold of Scarlan by the scruff of the neck and looked deep into his eyes. 'We have got to save Wat.'

One-o-clock: Noble Takes Weaver

VEN AS HE WAS CARTED AWAY to the dungeon, Wat could not really believe what was happening. He explained again, in very simple terms, that he could not have killed de Turold. He explained it to Grosmal and to Ethel. He even explained it to Foella when she happened to glance in his direction.

He explained it loudly to the two guards who lifted him by his arms and carried him from the room. He even explained it in his poor French. He explained it to the gaoler who scratched an 'x' on the wall to remind him to feed the prisoner in number two – in a couple of days.

His most pointed and sincere explanation was for the defective idiot whose job it was to lock the doors of the cells. It was pretty clear this boy either didn't speak English or French, was deaf, was pointedly ignoring him or was so stupid he couldn't understand the noises that came out of people's mouths. The outcome was the same. Wat was thrown in the dank and dark cell and the door was locked.

'This is ridiculous,' he explained to the darkness.

◆　　◆　　◆

Up in the main hall Brother Simon was giving his own explanation to a rapt audience. Well, Robert Grosmal was rapt. Foella was just loitering as near to the lord as she could get and Ethel was being Ethel – as inscrutable and invisible as he could get.

'And so my reasoning is sound.' Simon was rambling away.

'Your what?' Grosmal asked.

'My reasoning, sire. The chain of thinking which moves from one event to another.'

'Fascinating.'

'You see Wat and Hermitage were closely involved in the death of poor Brother Ambrosius at De'Ath's Dingle, and I always had my suspicions. I managed to get Brother Hermitage locked up, but then the abbot of that place, who was an insane fellow, insisted he be released. Well, no sooner could you say jack to a rabbit than there was another death.'

'No!' Grosmal's raptness was undiminished.

'Indeed. The connection seemed obvious, but others were not capable of following my thinking. Eventually the King, erm, usurper turned up and Hermitage was able to worm his way out of the accusations.'

'Disgraceful.'

'So it is matter of no little thought at all to see the connection to events here.'

'Is it?'

'Of course. There was a murder in De'Ath's Dingle: Hermitage and Wat were there. There was a murder here: Hermitage and Wat are here. Therefore they did both murders. You see?'

'Marvellous.' Grosmal actually clapped his hands like a child. 'So this is reasoning, is it?'

'It is, sire,' Simon bowed low, 'a wonderful new weapon in the armoury of the intellectual. This particular instance is called a principle. Where one thing happens and another one is always there, we can conclude that God has connected the one to the other. Of course, we all know every event in the world happens at God's will.'

Ethel coughed.

'What?' Grosmal snapped at him. 'You don't cough unless you've got some interrupting to do.'

Ethel bowed his patronising bow and tried to sound humble.

'I was as impressed as any by Brother Simon's erudition.'

Brother Simon accepted the compliment.

'And, of course, following his example, it seems that he was at both deaths as well?'

'So?' Grosmal didn't get it.

'It would appear by this Brother's reasoning that anyone who was at both sites must have been the killer?'

'Not at all.' Brother Simon snorted with contempt. 'You clearly are not capable of following my intellect either. I think you should stick to your domestic duties, my man.'

'Surely God has connected you to the deaths as surely as mister Wat?' Ethel politely pointed out.

Thought was struggling across Grosmal's face again. 'But,' he said and paused while another concept crawled slowly through his mind, 'you did say that this Wat and Hermitage were at both places and so they had done it.'

'I did.' Brother Simon obviously didn't get it either.

'But, as Ethel says, you were at both places as well.'

'Sire,' Simon nodded his head.

'So you did it too.'

Simon stopped for a moment and let the proposal pass through his mind. His brow furrowed and look of worry appeared for a moment. It was soon dispatched.

'Ah, I see where you've gone wrong, my man,' he said to Ethel. 'I am, er, was the King's Investigator. I was there in an official capacity, not a personal one.'

'Does that matter?' Ethel queried.

'Does it matter?' Simon was shocked. 'Does it matter? Of course it matters, my foolish fellow. Instead of interfering with the work of your betters, why don't you go and clean something or other?' He turned to Grosmal.

The lord's face had cleared. 'Of course,' he said, 'I see.'

'In any event,' Simon went on as if he had just thought of another excuse, 'I didn't arrive at De'Ath's Dingle until some considerable time after the death of Ambrosius. In fact I was only sent there by the bishop's office after the event.'

'Just like mister Wat being summoned here after de Turold was already dead?' Ethel proposed.

Simon and Grosmal got thoughtful again.

Eventually the lord's face cleared. 'I know how to solve all this,' he said brightly.

'Really?' Ethel asked, a lot less brightly.

'Of course, we'll go and interrogate the prisoner. They always tell you what you want – in the end.'

'If they make it to the end,' Ethel observed.

Grosmal ignored him. 'Besides, it's such fun.'

He left the room, followed closely by Simon. Foella hurried after them and Ethel tried to catch her eye to see if she was going to be any help. She saw his look, stopped and slapped his face for his impudence.

Ethel stood alone in the empty chamber. His head sagged and he buried his eyes in his palm. He ran his hand down his face, sighed loudly and stood straight. He took his dagger from his belt, looked it up and down and tested the point with his finger. He looked from the dagger to the door through which the interrogation party had left. He considered the dagger again before sighing once more and putting it back in his belt. Then he headed for the dungeon.

◆　　◆　　◆

The gaoler was just starting his afternoon nap, having had a busy time with his lunchtime doze and his morning sleep, when his lord arrived. He leapt to action and summoned the boy to open number two.

Wat was pacing up and down the chamber. One pace took him up it and the other pace took him back down again. Pacing sideways was out of the question as he could touch both walls by sticking his elbows out.

Grosmal entered the room, followed immediately by a bustling Simon. He pressed himself in after the lord, who in turn pushed Wat against the back wall. After that it was full and the occupants were in uncomfortable proximity.

Wat tried to back away from Grosmal, but there was no back left to move into. Grosmal tried to step away, but only found Simon's feet. Simon obviously wondered why they'd stopped and so pushed some more.

'Go back,' Wat called over Grosmal's disgusting head.

Simon now saw there was no room and attempted a retreat. This manoeuvre proved that Grosmal was standing on the hem of his habit. He tugged backwards without success.

'This is no good,' said Grosmal. He turned, releasing Simon's habit just as the monk tugged.

The Investigator staggered back out of the door into the approaching Foella.

She screamed at having a spindly, ugly monk thrust at her out of the darkness. She pushed him back, but her cry had already brought the gaoler at a run.

Simon, forced back into the cell, grabbed at Grosmal who was now coming in the other direction. They both came out of the cell, found Foella's feet in their way and fell to the floor. The advancing gaoler didn't see Ethel in the corridor, but his pace was enough to take them both into Foella. These three made a separate heap.

Wat stepped out of his cell and looked down at the wreckage. 'Shall I wait?' he asked.

'Take him to the interrogation chamber,' Grosmal ordered his gaoler from somewhere in the muddle of bodies.

'The what?' The gaoler asked from the other pile.

'Number four,' Grosmal barked as they all got themselves back to their feet.

'Number four?' The gaoler caught his breath before starting to roll up his sleeves. It was going to be a long session then.

◆   ◆   ◆

Number four was much more spacious, so they could all spread out a bit. There was a rude table in the middle of the room and even ruder iron implements lying scattered around.

'You will tell us the truth,' Grosmal growled at Wat, firmly held in the gaoler's grip.

'Of course I will,' Wat replied. 'In fact I already have.'

There was a pause while Grosmal looked at Simon. Eventually it sank in that the monk was supposed to take over.

'Master Wat,' Simon intoned.

'So far, so good. Well done,' Wat replied with an ironic grin.

'Do you deny that you were at De'Ath's Dingle when Brother Ambrosius died?'

'Yes.'

'What?'

'Yes, of course I deny it. I wasn't there. I only went to De'Ath's Dingle with you. Remember?' He asked this as he would an old crone who had forgotten where she put her cat.

'But now you are here, and there is another death.'

'No, there was another death and then I came here. Or perhaps I can kill people from miles away. People I don't even know.'

'Devilry, hah!' Simon crowed.

'Oh, don't be ridiculous. Look. De Turold died sometime last night, yes?'

Simon looked to Grosmal for confirmation. The Norman nodded.

'When I was at De'Ath's Dingle.'

'So you say.'

'Where were you, then?' Wat interrogated the interrogator.

'I was at De'Ath's Dingle as well, and I didn't see you.'

'Well, I was at De'Ath's Dingle and I didn't see you, so we've only got your word that you were there at all.' Wat folded his arms and stared accusingly at Simon.

The Investigator was clearly getting lost.

'In fact I wouldn't be at all surprised if you'd concocted this whole thing to make sure you stayed King's Investigator under William. Get a nice murder under your belt. Pretend to solve it. Job done.'

Lord Grosmal was looking backwards and forwards as if the two men were throwing a ball to one another.

'We're not talking about me,' Simon blustered.

'Perhaps we should be,' Wat retorted.

'How did you kill him?' Simon snapped.

'You tell me. You're the Investigator.'

'Shall we make him confess?' Grosmal asked with some enthusiasm.

'Wait a minute,' Wat held his hands out in an attempt to calm things down. 'How did anyone kill de Turold?'

'They shot him,' Grosmal snorted and grinned, 'in the arse.'

'Quite right, sire,' Wat congratulated the Norman, 'but how did they shoot him?'

'With a bow.' Grosmal nodded to the others in the room to confirm his quick wit.

'Right again, sire, but how? He was killed from below, but the killer didn't get out through the garderobe door because that had been shut for years. It was a struggle to get it open.'

'He must have come out through the privy seat then.' Wat carried on a two-sided conversation as it was clear no one in the room was going to follow this unaided.

'But the hole in the privy seat is too small for anyone to climb through. And if someone did manage that, how did they see in the dark to shoot?'

'They had a candle,' he chastised himself.

'Ah, but if they had a candle why did they leave it behind in the middle of the night?'

'Hum,' Wat considered his own reasoning. 'The candle doesn't make any sense anyway.'

'What have candles to do with anything, you fool?' Simon interjected. 'The killer may have had a box full.'

'But when a lighted torch was put in the chamber the whole place went bang. It would have gone bang with a candle. So the candle can't have been down there. Why take a candle to a murder and then not use it?'

'You tell me. Killer,' Simon snarled.

Wat ignored him. 'The mystery of the candle is bad enough, but I believe the privy hole is key.'

'Do you mind?' Foella put in, having sneaked up close to Grosmal once more.

'It's too small.'

Foella looked away.

'No one could have got down there. Not even Ethel and he's as thin as a – well, you know.'

Ethel bowed slightly to acknowledge the nicety.

'De Turold was shot from below, with a bow, which no one could have taken down there.'

There was silence in Number four.

◆ ◆ ◆

Foella was getting bored. The day wasn't going any better and the gentlemen's gown was proving a bit chilly for dungeonwear. Only half listening, she idly regarded the bits of ironmongery around the walls. Then, 'I know someone in the castle who's very small,' she said, as if she just wanted to be part of the conversation.

They all turned as one to face her.

'What?' she said, looking at the crowd, now looking intently at her.

'Who is very small in the castle?' Wat asked very carefully, as if he was sneaking up on a duck.

'The, erm, little guard, of course,' Foella rather hurriedly stated the obvious. They all looked blank.

'The little guard,' she repeated, 'you must have seen him. He's a guard. Except he's little.'

"I don't have any little guards,' Grosmal sneered at the thought.

'You do,' Foella contradicted playfully, as if Grosmal was hiding her Christmas present. 'A little fellow. He's a guard.'

'I can assure you, my lady, that I do not have any little guards. What would be the point?'

'Well, that's what I thought, but I didn't like to say anything. One doesn't like to be rude.' Foella smiled as one who very much liked to be rude.

'Where did you see this little guard, my lady?' Wat asked.

'In the corridors, guarding. Where do you normally see guards?'

'Did he say who he was?' Ethel asked.

Simon's head was going backwards and forwards now as he tried to follow the conversation.

'No, he did not say who he was. I don't invite conversation from the staff and I certainly don't talk to guards,' Foella said, looking down her high and mighty nose. 'Anyway, why would he say anything? I walk round the castle all day. I don't expect the guards to introduce themselves.'

'Then how do you know he was a guard?' Simon interjected, smiling at everyone and nodding acknowledgement that he had the situation under control.

'How do I know any of them are guards?' Foella snapped back. 'They dress like guards. They behave like guards. They're guards. I don't expect to interrogate the staff to make sure they are who they appear to be. I'm a lady, not a bloody peasant.'

'This is very significant,' Wat said. 'It seems we have someone who could have carried out the murder. My lady,' he turned to Foella, 'do you think the fellow was small enough to get through the privy hole?'

'What is this?' Foella glared at them all. 'First I'm supposed to get the names and addresses of the servants, now I have to know the dimensions of the plumbing?'

'Sorry, my lady,' Wat bowed.

'So I should bloody well think. Honestly!'

Wat addressed the others. 'We have a suspect,' he declared. 'All we have to do is find him.'

'Send out the guard to find a guard?' Ethel smirked.

'If he is an impostor, he won't hang around,' Wat made a move to the door. 'We'd better start looking.'

At a nod from Grosmal the gaoler put an arm out at around throat height and knocked Wat firmly to the floor.

'Oof,' said Wat, rubbing his throat and gasping his breath. 'What was that for?'

'Trying to escape, of course,' said Grosmal.

'But we have a good idea who the killer is, we should find him,' Wat protested.

'We have one possible killer,' Grosmal explained, 'who is not imprisoned in my cells. We have another possible killer who is imprisoned in my cells. I'm not likely to let the second one go, am I? In case we don't find the first one.'

'But...'

'When all this gets explained to William,' Grosmal began, then shook his head at the prospect. The explanation obviously wasn't clear to him, so how would he get on with the King? 'Point is, I've got to have someone to hang. I think I'll keep you for the time being.'

'Very wise, sire,' Simon said condescending from no very great height. 'After all, they could still be in league. The weaver and the little guard.'

'A plot?' Grosmal asked.

'Indeed, sire.'

'There we are then. You stay here – we'll go and look for the little guard. If he exists,' he said triumphantly.

'Are you calling me a liar?' Foella glowered.

'No, no, my lady,' Grosmal rapidly back tracked. 'I mean if he hasn't already made good his escape.'

The party left the cell with Foella mumbling obscenities at Grosmal's back.

The gaoler grinned at Wat and pulled the door closed behind him, sliding the massive bolt across as he did so.

Wat got to his feet and looked around. At least this place was larger than his last cell. And it had an ample supply of tools lying about. At a quick glance he saw several he could use to simply take the door completely to pieces.

For reasons that he failed to comprehend, many of Wat's very particular clients wanted tapestries set in dungeons like this. With implements like these. In active use. He'd done so many of them he felt like quite an authority on the places.

Caput XVII

One-o-clock: Wood to Castle II

HE RESCUE PARTY WAS READY.

There had been much debate about the benefits of sneaking. A lot of it revolved around pride and standards and the things a real man did, rather than effectiveness. The combined forces of the sneaking camp (Hermitage, Scarlan and the now re-captured Cotard) eventually won the day.

It wouldn't be the underhand sneaking of a thief in the night. Durniss's bulk made it unlikely he could sneak anywhere, while six people approaching the castle would not go unnoticed anyway.

When Hermitage said the sneaking in mind was more like deceit, even Sigurd the Elder came round.

Sigurd son of Sigurd said he could do a really good sneak and demonstrated by lying down and crawling through the grass making hissing noises. At the end of his sneak he jumped up and held his arms out. Prompted by Sigurd the Father, everyone applauded politely, whereupon Sigurd son of Sigurd ran round and round in circles for a bit.

With a plan that was more Hermitage's walk-up-to-the-gate-and-ask than anything, the troop left the safety of the wood and headed across open ground to the castle. They had agreed their story and who would do the talking.

Before they reached the ramparts they were approached by a couple of guards, patrolling the outer reaches.

The party held its collective breath as it prepared for the most daring part of the plan. They would have to be convincing or all would be lost. One word out of place, one wrong gesture or suspicious behaviour of any sort could see them condemned along with Wat. Even Sigurd son of Sigurd had been made to swear an awful swear that he would keep quiet.

The guards drew closer. They looked the group up and down. They appraised them and their eyes narrowed. They hefted their weapons.

As they drew level one of the guards suddenly threw back the visor of his helmet and spoke.

'Afternoon,' he said, glancing at the sun and seeing that was as near to midday as anyone would know.

'Oh, er, afternoon,' the rescue party mumbled.

'Nice day,' said the second guard. 'At least the rain's kept off.'

'Hello,' shouted Sigurd son of Sigurd, getting bored. 'I'm a rescuer,' and he jumped around to demonstrate.

The guards laughed and wandered on.

'Ha, ha,' Sigurd the elder roared under his breath, 'idiots.'

'I told you it wouldn't be a problem,' Hermitage explained. 'They're not expecting an attack or any sort of action at all. The Normans have settled in and it's life as normal. This is a working castle,' he waved his arm towards the gaping gate of Castle Grosmal, 'not the site of a siege.'

'Gone soft,' Sigurd mumbled again.

Cotard was quite cheerful and didn't hide his face in his hood any more.

'They want people to come in,' Hermitage went on. 'They want to get back to the country being as normal as possible, except with them in charge.'

'It'll never happen,' Scarlan sneered.

'I think it already has, to a large extent.' Hermitage smiled weakly, hoping this comment wouldn't lead to a physical reprimand from Sigurd. All remained peaceful so he went on as they walked.

'The Normans will want their taxes and tithes and the like, of course. But they won't get anything if the farmers can't farm and the traders can't trade, so they have to leave them alone. They're far more likely to murder a rival noble than they are the man who cleans out the gargoyles.'

'Our Saxon nobles.' Scarlan expressed his disgust at the notion.

'Were they good nobles?' Hermitage asked, trying to sound as innocent as possible.

'Bastards,' Cotard put in.

'You watch your mouth,' Sigurd pointed a finger.

'Well, they were,' Cotard responded, obviously confident that Sigurd wouldn't attack him in front of a castle full of Normans in the middle of a sneaky rescue.

'Yer,' Durniss added, nodding his great head.

'Mine took all the doors off my hovel, just 'cos he needed a new one for his cupboard,' Cotard whined.

'What?' Hermitage found this hard to believe.

'He did,' Cotard declared the truth of his statement. 'He'd had the carpenter build him a great closet for all his magnificent robes and the like. Bloody thing was bigger than most hovels. And of course he never paid the carpenter. Said it was his dues. Then when they come to the doors they need another one in a hurry.'

'Another one? How many doors does a cupboard need?' Hermitage asked.

'Well, I don't know. I've never had one, have I? All I know is they needed another door and so the Lord sent out for all the doors in the hovels.'

'And you didn't get them back if they didn't fit?'

'Course not. They used what they wanted and the rest was firewood.'

'Awful.' Hermitage shook his head at the greed of mankind and its ignorance of the needs of others.

'Only right and fair,' Sigurd said. 'Got to have nobles. Once you got nobles they can do what they like. Not for us to question.'

'Oh, I think…' Hermitage began.

'Not for us to question,' Sigurd said very slowly and deliberately.

Hermitage changed tack. 'For me there'll be very little change. Monastic life will carry on exactly as it always has. The Normans worship God the same as everyone. We'd never have a King who did anything to change belief or the status of the monastery.'

The party nodded acceptance of this eternal truth.

'And if I'd stayed in De'Ath's Dingle I probably wouldn't have noticed the change from Saxon to Norman until someone came and told me.'

'Yeah,' said Scarlan, 'but who'd want to stay in De'Ath's Dingle?'

The party snorted its agreement.

♦   ♦   ♦

By this time they had reached the main castle gate. Trying to look as nonchalant as possible they strolled across the drawbridge, nodding 'good afternoon' to the occasional guard.

'Now what?' Scarlan hissed as they stood in the courtyard. And they did stick out rather as they clearly had nothing to do. Everyone else in the place was either doing something or was rushing somewhere else. Here a man was adjusting a horse's bridle; there two more were carrying saddles away for storage. Still more were shovelling horse dung into a cart. And another group was unloading a freshly butchered horse for the kitchen.

'I'd heard it, but I never believed it,' Durniss rumbled to himself.

'What?' Cotard asked him.

'They really do eat horses.'

'Delicious,' Sigurd put in. 'Come on, monk, what do we do now?'

'Now we, erm.' Hermitage looked around for a suitable guard. 'Ah, just the fellow.' He led the group across to where Wil-

liam le Morton was guarding the castle walls – by holding them
up with his shoulder.

'Guard,' Hermitage called.

William looked up. 'There you are.'

Hermitage looked around to see who else had joined them.

'We've been looking for you. Where you been?'

'Looking for me?'

'Yes. Instructions from Ethel to find you. Him and that other
one of you. The one in proper clothes.'

'Wat.'

'The one in proper clothes.' William spoke more loudly.

'No, his name is Wat.'

'Why?'

'No, Wat.'

'No, why is his name Wat?'

'Why not? What's wrong with Wat?' Hermitage decided to
move on. 'I've been on an errand,' he explained, 'and I've come to
find Wat. So can you tell me where he is?'

William looked around cautiously. 'In the dungeon, I hear.'

'The dungeon?' Hermitage feigned shocked surprise.
'What's he doing there? Investigating some new aspect of the
murder?'

'What the what?' said William, thoroughly confused.

'What is Wat doing in the dungeon?'

'Not much, I should think.'

'Why is Wat in the dungeon then?'

'They don't tell me nothing. I just heard from my mate on
chamber duty that he got to cart this bloke off to the dungeon.
Lucky bastard.'

'Lucky?'

'Yeah, I never got to cart no one off.' William looked sullenly
at the floor.

'So,' Hermitage went on, 'erm, which dungeon did they put
him in? Er, cart him off to.'

'I'd heard it was number two.' William nodded at this significant point.

Scarlan poked Hermitage in the back. 'Get a move on,' he hissed, 'we're starting to attract attention.'

Hermitage looked around the courtyard. There did seem to be a lot more activity now. More guards were coming out of the buildings.

'Uh, oh.' William stood up straight. 'Here comes the head guard. I'd better see what he wants.'

Before Hermitage could ask any more, William ran off in a very military manner towards a well uniformed guard with a badge at his shoulder.

'Norman,' Sigurd spat.

The group tried to blend into the stonework of the castle. Hermitage and Scarlan turned their heads as if in deep conversation. Durniss stood and stared at the horses.

Cotard and Sigurd pretended they were bargaining over some intricate matter of trade.

Sigurd son of Sigurd poked some ants with straw.

'So,' Scarlan whispered, 'where's dungeon number two then?'

'No idea,' Hermitage shrugged.

'What?'

'We never got as far as the dungeons.'

'What good is that?' Scarlan demanded.

'I imagine they're downstairs somewhere. We'll just have to find a way in and look.'

'What, with the place crawling with guards? For a learned man you are particularly thick.'

'Well, pardon me,' Hermitage said, some shameful irritation creeping into his words.

Their worry was disturbed by the return of William.

'Now we've got to look for some small guard,' he said, shaking his head at the random stupidity of orders.

'A small guard? Why?' Hermitage asked.

'No idea. Don't think for a moment that we're ever told why we have to do anything,' William grumbled. 'The orders are to find a small guard, so a small guard we'll have to find.'

'How small?'

'Small enough to fit down a privy, apparently,' William shrugged.

'Filthy bastards,' Sigurd spat.

'Oh, I see,' said Hermitage, in the relieved tone he used when things became clear. Or slightly less totally obscure, at any rate. 'And is there such a small guard? Have you ever seen him?'

'Nah. Don't know that there is one. Could just be one of the Lord's whims. You know like, fetch me a peasant with one leg. Find a pregnant deer. All the weird stuff he gets up to. He probably just fancies a small guard. Rather the small guard than me.'

'Well, we'd better not detain you then. Could you just point us towards dungeon number two?'

'I'll come with you.'

'Really?' Hermitage tried to sound grateful, even as the rest of his party sighed at his ineptitude in inviting the enemy on the rescue.

'Yeah. I can say I'm searching the dungeons for the small guard. Otherwise they'll send me somewhere horrible to look.'

'Aren't the dungeons horrible?'

'This is Castle Grosmal. There are a lot more horrible things than dungeons here.'

William led the way. Sigurd followed with Sigurd son of Sigurd in tow. Durniss was pulled away from trying to count the horses by Cotard, while Hermitage and Scarlan brought up the rear.

Scarlan tugged Hermitage's habit. The monk leant over.

'This is a disaster,' said a very serious Scarlan.

'Oh, I don't know,' Hermitage replied brightly, 'we're on our way to find Wat. This guard's not a bad fellow. He's obviously

Saxon. I don't think he has any great loyalty to the Normans. He might even help.'

'No, not him, the small guard.'

'Oh well, as this fellow says, there probably isn't one.'

'There is,' Scarlan said pointedly.

'Really?' Hermitage was fascinated. He leaned in closer to Scarlan. 'Have you seen him?' he whispered, hoping that no Normans would overhear.

'He's our man,' Scarlan nodded significantly at the word 'man'.

Remarkably, Hermitage got it straight away. 'Oh lord. The one on the inside, signalling?'

'Yes. And we are now part of a Norman search party looking to expose our own spy.'

'Yes, I can see that's a bit awkward.'

'Awkward?' Scarlan tried to do extreme outrage while keeping his voice down.

As they followed the lead of William, the sights and smells of the Castle Grosmal introduced themselves. Hermitage had got used to them, but Scarlan's face twisted and grimaced as if it wanted to get away. He regarded a filth-man, carrying a bucket out of the castle with disdain – then caught a glimpse of what was in the bucket, and almost cried out.

A builder came their way, carrying a large piece of stone in his arms. It looked like the keystone of an arch, destined to play a vital role in the structure of the place. The man had his eyes firmly focused on its destination and nearly dropped his load when he bumped into Hermitage.

Swearing an oath never intended for a monk, the builder had to look sharp to save his own toes. Danger averted, he glanced up again to re-establish where he was headed. He frowned as he scanned the stonework, clearly trying to figure out where it was he had been going. He swore again as he turned and went back the way he had come, grumbling about having to start all over again.

Avoiding several piles of various substances which lay in their path, some natural and recognisable and others not, Hermitage and Scarlan caught quickly up to William.

'They clearly think your man's the killer,' Hermitage explained helpfully.

'What?'

'Oh yes. Why else would they be looking for someone small enough to fit down a privy?'

Scarlan's mouth opened, but he clearly didn't have any words lined up.

'But if that's the case,' Hermitage pondered, 'why are they still holding mister Wat?'

'Oh, this is great.' Scarlan was not impressed. 'Perfect plan, master monk. Now we've got both to rescue Wat and get our man out.'

Hermitage frowned. 'Do you think your man is the killer?'

Scarlan winked. 'Could be,' he admitted, with some enthusiasm.

Caput XVIII
Two-o-clock: Noble Takes Lady

 EANWHILE, LORD ROBERT GROSMAL was pacing up and down in the great hall. He had issued orders to his men and watched them rush off in search of the small guard.

As soon as he had issued the orders his questionable mind started toying with them – in the way a child who is going to grow up to be profoundly horrible toys with a beetle.

First he thought that he couldn't possibly have a small guard: why would he have appointed one? Then he started think what sorts of thing he could get a small guard to do. And what sort of places he could send him. Small ones, mainly.

He then wondered how entertaining a fight between a small guard and large one would be. This was followed by a fight between a child and a small guard, then a dog and small guard, then the dog and the child.

One of his most disturbing smiles played briefly across his lips, like the child who has found mice are more fun than beetles.

Foella, who was still standing close enough to be at hand, thought this was an indication that the Norman was at last paying her some attention.

'So, my lord,' she half-breathed towards his ear.

Lord Robert turned to her, and looked her and the gown up and down.

She smiled encouragingly.

'Are you still here?' Grosmal asked absently as he wandered back to the fire.

✦   ✦   ✦

Unfortunately Lord Grosmal's orders consisted of a lot of screams in colloquial Norman French. His own men had leapt into action straightaway, but there had to be a lot of to-ing and fro-ing among people with varying language skills before the message got across to the local recruits.

From Norman slang to court French, court French to Latin, Latin to English and English into the mumbling grumble that passed for speech in these parts.

William le Morton had got it pretty quickly, but some of the local boys, the ones who were farm hands a few months ago, still didn't have a clue what they were doing. They did know the loony Grosmal wanted them to run around looking for some-thing, however, so that's exactly what they did.

One of them even found something – but apparently it wasn't what they were looking for.

✦   ✦   ✦

'Even if we find the small guard,' Simon lectured his audience some time later as he stood with his back to the fire, 'I maintain it does not confirm this Wat fellow's innocence.'

'Eh?' said Grosmal, stopping mid-pace. 'You mean there were two of them down there?'

'Ah no, sire.' The condescension in Simon's voice almost pat-ted Grosmal on the head. 'The Wat fellow may be in league with the small guard. It may be that the weaver issued the orders. He could be the master of misdeed.'

'So we hang them both,' said Grosmal, cheering up enor-mously at the prospect.

'We shall have to see what the small guard has to say,' Ethel interrupted, from his usual place by the door. 'That's if we find him.'

'I told you I saw him.' Foella looked up from the table to snap

185

the retainer's head off.

Discussion during the wait for the result of the search had been ripe with the suggestion that Foella's mind was such that small guards might appear anywhere. Along with goblins, fairies and magic beans. She got quite annoyed at this, and was frustrated that there was no one to take it out on.

'Of course you did, my lady,' said Grosmal, but he still had a snigger in his voice.

'I saw him and spoke to him.' Foella stamped her foot.

She paused for a moment, clearly weighing up whether she should reveal more. It would be a ghastly breach of confidence if the little man really was part of an organised resistance against the Normans. On the other hand, people were laughing at her.

'He said he was part of the Brotherhood of the Sword,' she announced.

'The what?' Grosmal had resumed pacing, but turned to look at the lady.

'The Brotherhood of the Sword. Apparently it's some sort of club.'

'Never heard of it.' Grosmal resumed pacing.

Brother Simon raised his eyes to the ceiling in thought, taking in this new information and nodding as he accommodated it into his analysis. Had she said sword or sort? And if it was sort, what sort? Brotherhood of the sort of what? Or perhaps a sort of Brotherhood? He frowned as confusion got the better of him.

The look on Ethel's face was probably the one Death used just before he took a sinner's soul. It was directed at Foella and did not miss its mark.

It was a combination of shock, outrage and anger. Absolute, flaming anger. It was so effective that even Foella squirmed a bit, but eventually she found her old self and glared back.

Ethel's look did not soften, and if there had not been others in the room, one of whom was a mad Norman with a knife, something physical would have been done.

Ethel's look bade Foella to silence in much the same way as cutting the throat of a sheep is an invitation to stop bleating.

Her natural defiance at being told what to do by anyone would not stand for this onslaught.

'Yes,' she went on, 'that's what he said. Brotherhood of the Sword.'

'Some blacksmith's association, perhaps, my lord,' Ethel suggested.

'He was too small to be a blacksmith,' Foella countered.

'Well, what does my lady suggest?' Ethel attacked with all the innocence of a weasel babysitting rabbits.

'I don't know,' she parried. 'I don't concern myself with the pastimes of the staff.'

'Of course not, my lady.' Ethel bowed his head just the right amount to replace respect with impudence. 'But, as we have heard, Lord Grosmal does not have any small guards on his staff.'

'That's right,' Grosmal confirmed, 'and even if I did they certainly wouldn't be allowed to join a club. Not even a small one.'

'I didn't say there was a club, I just said it might be like one. They were a Brotherhood and they're up to something.'

Ethel stepped forward and approached Foella. He did so at a gentle pace and with natural grace, but he looked unstoppable.

'These have been tiring events. Perhaps my lady would care to retire to her chamber?' He made the invitation obligatory.

'No.' She tried to dismiss him with a wave of her hand.

'All this talk of swords and murders and,' he pointed the last word straight at her, 'death. It's perhaps not suitable for so delicate a constitution?'

'Delicate?' She laughed lightly, 'Oh mister, er, what was your name? I can deal with death at any time of day or night.' She glared her own glare.

'If this fellow is in a Brotherhood of some sort,' Simon cogitated, 'there may be others.'

'Other short guards?' Grosmal found this hard to believe. 'I can imagine not noticing one of them being short, but don't tell me there's a bunch of them wandering about the place.'

'They need not all be short, my lord.'

'I don't think you can have a small guard who isn't short. I thought you monks were knowledgeable types.'

'I mean that it may be a Brotherhood of different types. Not necessarily a Brotherhood of small guards. What did you say the name was again?' he asked Foella.

'Sword. Brotherhood of the Sword.'

'There we are, sire. It's a Brotherhood of People who have Swords.'

'Pretty big Brotherhood.'

'Or maybe they like swords, or collect them, or polish them or something?' said Simon, who clearly had very little experience of swords.

Grosmal stopped his pacing and looked at Simon with a blank stare. He passed the glance to Foella and Ethel. 'And this is getting us where exactly? He's small, he has some friends. Unlikely, I know, but it happens. I'm not interested in his Brothers. I want him.'

'Perhaps the Lady Foella knows his Brothers as well,' Ethel suggested lightly.

He got one of Foella's hardest looks. The sort that normally sent Eleanor running for cover.

She didn't grace the comment with a reply.

'My lady?' Grosmal asked.

'What?'

'Do you know this small man's Brothers?'

'No, of course I don't. It's ridiculous to suggest that I know the first one. I met him, that's all. For goodness sake, I wish I hadn't mentioned it now.'

'Too late,' Ethel said, with feeling. 'I believe you told us earlier that you didn't speak to him. Yet now you inform us he told you all about his Brothers.' He gave Simon a prompting look.

The King's Investigator watched it go by.

Ethel waited until the monk's gaze wandered aimlessly in his direction and grabbed it with a look of intent. Brother Simon's eyes resumed their pointless meanderings before a spark drew them back to Ethel.

'My thoughts exactly,' he said profoundly.

Ethel used his gaze to drag Simon's eyes over to Foella. He nodded an explicit 'go on then'.

Simon looked backwards and forwards a couple of times before Ethel's thought occupied the vacant space where his own ideas ought to be.

'It seems to be the case that one person here has both seen this small guard and spoken to him,' he said.

Foella gave him a warning look, but like all hints, suggestions and not-so-subtle indications, it passed through Simon as if he wasn't there.

'And it has been shown,' he went on in declamatory mode, 'that where knowledge of one part of a thing rests, there rests knowledge of the whole.'

'What?' This was beyond Grosmal.

'There is a great deal of learning that shows that if a person knows a twig he knows the trees.'

'Are you feeling all right?'

'I think the Brother is suggesting that our Lady Foella,' Ethel bowed with some sincerity towards the seated Saxon, 'knows more than she is telling.'

'How dare you?' Foella was on her feet now, her temper getting the better of her.

'And did not you mention, my lord, that the lady threw a knife at you earlier?' Ethel asked innocently.

'She did,' said Grosmal with some enthusiasm. 'She accused me of killing her husband or something. Or was it de Turold? I forget. Anyway, she definitely threw a knife. Threw it quite well actually, for a girl.' Grosmal nodded in satisfaction at the memory.

This latest round of accusation got the legs moving under Foella. Her arms stretched out nicely and the fingernails extended.

She went for Ethel.

To get him, however, she had to pass Grosmal, and he simply thumped her on the back of the head as she went by.

Lady Foella went down.

◆　　◆　　◆

'Guards,' Grosmal called, sounding rather resigned that he had to keep calling them to take people away.

It was a moment before two of the nearest guards, those who had engaged in the hunt for the small man with very little enthusiasm, appeared at the door.

Grosmal beckoned they should restrain the Lady Foella, who was now recovering her senses.

'You hit me,' she said in still-stunned outrage.

'Of course,' Grosmal shrugged. 'Can't have you damaging my property.'

Ethel was back to his calm self.

'Anyway, why would you attack him?' the Norman went on. 'Perhaps you are involved in this somehow.'

'My thoughts exactly,' Simon piped in. He liked this phrase – it had seemed to work last time.

'Involved in what?' Foella snarled as she returned to the bench, rubbing the back of her head. The guard stood close, preventing any further outbursts.

'You can explain, Brother,' said Grosmal, waving a hand towards Simon.

'Ah, erm, yes. Of course. Indeed, my lord.'

Ethel folded his arms and watched with some interest.

Grosmal made himself comfortable. The guards looked to

the monk for some sort of explanation for what on earth was going on. Foella did some more glaring.

'Well,' Brother Simon paced off around the room, 'what we have here is a most interesting situation.' He stopped and looked at each of the faces in the room. They looked back. He paced again.

'The small guard.' Brother Simon nodded with significance.

'What about him?' said Grosmal.

'Him being the possible killer,' Ethel helped along.

'Precisely.'

'And if the lady has knowledge of the small guard...' Ethel tried to lead the King's Investigator by the brain. It was a struggle.

'Yes?'

'She knows his friends.'

'She knows his friends,' Simon declared with a flourish.

'And if she knows his friends...' Ethel went on.

Simon hadn't expected more.

'Yes, yes,' he said, 'exactly. If she knows his friends...'

'She would know what's going on.' Ethel's control was tested to the limits.

'Absolutely.'

'The murder.'

'Aha, yes, the murder.'

'This is beyond me.' Grosmal looked from monk to retainer and back again. His thoughts were wandering back to the various bouts of combat he might arrange. All this thinking and talking was getting tedious – never mind being unintelligible.

'It's quite simple, sire,' said Simon with a sigh.

Ethel coughed.

'Lady Foella here is the only one who has seen the small guard. It can therefore be concluded that she's involved in the murder.'

'What!' Foella leapt to her feet, only to be pressed down again by the guards.

'Bloody Saxons,' Grosmal spat. 'Take her away.' He flapped a hand to indicate the guards should remove her.

The Lady Foella said a number of very unladylike things in a very loud and shrieking voice. She promised damage to Simon, Grosmal and, very explicitly, to Ethel. Even the guards winced when they heard some of her suggestions.

Foella kicked and spat and struggled, but it was no use. These guards were not small. They were large, and they lifted the lady between them, her feet swinging above the floor.

The noise slowly faded as the lady was taken below.

'Well, I never,' said Ethel, shaking his head in sorrow.

'It's all quite clear.' Simon nodded his head.

'I thought she was a bit mad, but really…' The lord of the manor sat down and stared into the flames of the fire. 'We still have one problem.'

'What's that, sire?' Ethel asked.

'It's what you said.'

'I?'

'Yes. I mean we've got two Saxons in the cells now, which is obviously good. But will this get us out of trouble with the King tonight? There's only one way I know to make sure they'll confess to William before we execute them.' Lord Grosmal rubbed his hands in a most alarming manner. His unhealthy grin and disturbing eyes were already selecting the right tool from number four to make his guests spill not just their beans.

Caput XIX

Two-o-clock: Wood to Dungeon

OWN IN THE CELLS the Wat rescue party had reverted to sneaking again. This time Sigurd son of Sigurd really was best. He was so light on his feet that he made not a sound. The problem was he would sneak in the wrong direction, or tiptoe in the most extravagant manner out into the middle of the corridor.

Eventually Sigurd picked his son up and clamped a hand over his mouth to stop the consequent squeals.

Scarlan peered around one corner and saw the gaoler sitting at his table, dozing. He gestured to Durniss.

The big man came up and looked. He looked back at Scarlan.

Scarlan nodded his head towards the gaoler. Durniss nodded back.

'Go on,' Scarlan hissed.

Durniss looked blank. Scarlan mimed creeping up behind the gaoler and thumping him on the head.

Durniss smiled and nodded. He crept up behind the gaoler and thumped him on the head with one of his barrel-sized fists.

The table on which the gaoler dozed collapsed under the impact, leaving the unconscious gaoler slumped in the wreckage.

Durniss looked on in horror at what he had done. He knelt and gently picked up pieces of the table and tried to put them back together.

Scarlan slapped his hands away and the rest of the party approached.

At this moment the lock-up boy appeared around a corner. He looked at the five people who had brought a small child to the dungeon. He looked up at the size of Durniss. Then he looked down at the body of his master in the wreckage of the table.

He assessed the situation and weighed up his options. He lay down on the floor, curled up, closed his eyes and started making loud snoring noises.

No one moved. The lock-up boy opened one eye, raised an arm and beckoned them to carry on with whatever they wanted while he went back to snoring.

Sigurd put Sigurd son of Sigurd down again. The little boy went straight to the sleeping form of the boy and smacked him on the head with a tiny fist. He turned and raised his arms in triumph. They all applauded politely, but very quietly.

"Where is Wat?' Hermitage asked Scarlan.

'I don't know. The man just said he was in dungeon number two. Place doesn't look very big, so he shouldn't be hard to find.'

The dungeon was indeed not very big. There were two doors opposite the collapsed gaoler and a short corridor to his left, in the middle of which the lock-up boy snored.

The party advanced and found the corridor revealed a dead end with two more doors in the wall.

Hermitage approached the door nearest to them, assuming that even Normans would put their numbers in the right order.

'Master Wat?' he whispered as loudly as he dare. There was no reply. Perhaps Normans had a different system of numbering. Perhaps in Norman two came before one? What a fascinating concept. What if every country used numbers in different ways, like they spoke different languages?

'Ow,' he hissed as Scarlan clipped him on the back of the head to get him out of his reverie.

He rubbed his head and made a note to think about numbers when all this was over. If he still had the capacity to think at all by then.

He moved on to the next door and repeated the process with

the same outcome. He completed the set and turned back to Scarlan. 'He's not here.' Hermitage looked worried.

Scarlan was standing with hands on hips. 'He's hardly likely to hear you through a cell door. Why don't you just open them?'

'There might be all sorts of people inside,' Hermitage fretted.

'Prisoners of the Norman invader, you mean,' said Scarlan with points.

'Ah yes, of course. Let's open the doors then.' Hermitage gestured that Scarlan could go first. Who knew what was inside these doors – there could be mad men and all sorts. Hermitage couldn't deal with either mad men or all sorts. Hopefully Scarlan could.

Scarlan drew the bolt of the first door and swung it open. The room inside was not much bigger than the door itself, but it was empty.

The second door was very stiff and Durniss had to help. The poor man seemed very nervous about damaging more furniture.

He pulled at the handle of the door without success. He then adjusted his stance, prepared his shoulders and heaved at the handle. He staggered backwards as the thing came off in his hand. He looked at the hardware in horror.

'Shoddy Norman workmanship.' Sigurd spat.

Durniss held the detached handle out for Scarlan. The leader knocked the thing to the floor. 'For goodness sake try and stop caring about horses and equipment. Care about your country and your downtrodden fellows.'

Durniss looked rather hurt.

'How will we open the door now?' Hermitage asked. 'Wat could be trapped in there for ever.'

They all gathered around the dysfunctional door and looked for some other way of opening it. Sigurd suggested setting fire to it. Cotard suggested that he should go back to the camp for a lever of some sort, and Sigurd son of Sigurd attacked it with hands and feet shouting 'ha' and 'yargh' and the like.

'We must do something,' Hermitage said anxiously, expecting guards to appear at any moment.

They all stood back and stared at the door.

◆　　◆　　◆

'Are you looking for me?' Wat's voice came from behind and made them all jump. Cotard stayed trembling for some time, while Sigurd son of Sigurd burst out laughing.

'How did you get out?' Hermitage asked, just resisting the urge to leap forward and throw his arms around the weaver.

Wat stood and held up the hammer and iron he had used to remove the hinges from his cell door.

'Decent of them to provide these,' he said, dropping them to the floor. 'Where have you been anyway?' he asked Hermitage.

'Master Wat the Weaver,' Scarlan cried, stepping forward, shaking Wat's hand vigorously. 'Great admirer of your work. Great admirer.'

'Ah,' said Wat in some embarrassment, glancing at Hermitage.

'The Coventry triptych.' Scarlan shook his head in awe.

'Ah, yes.'

'A masterpiece.'

'Thank you.'

'So many images in the one space. So much going on.'

'Is that the one of Saint Paul?' Hermitage asked. 'I thought that was a painting.'

'That one is,' Scarlan explained. 'I'm talking about master Wat's tapestry triptych. Full of detail and every square inch of it absolutely…'

'Yes, it did take a while,' Wat interrupted. 'What are you all doing here anyway?'

'We've come to rescue you,' Scarlan announced proudly.

'Rescue, rescue, rescue,' said Sigurd son of Sigurd, jumping up and down to give each word emphasis.

'Well, that's very kind,' said Wat, frowning at the presence of the small boy. 'I think I would have been all right though. They're all out looking for some small guard who could have done it.'

'I've heard about him,' Hermitage replied. 'Apparently he's one of Scarlan's men.' The monk nodded his head to indicate Wat's fan was Scarlan. 'He's obviously suspect.'

'Yes,' said Wat, 'but…'

'I rather think we should be leaving now?' Scarlan interrupted this time. 'Perhaps we could have this conversation somewhere other than the dungeon of a Norman castle?'

'Ah yes, said Hermitage, 'probably wise.'

'We camp in the woods,' Sigurd son of Sigurd explained with some enthusiasm.

'Do you?' Wat bowed to speak to the child.

'And we sneak and rescue and everything.'

'Very good.'

'And we'd better get back there about now,' Scarlan said, leading the way out of the dungeon past the still sleeping gaoler.

'I'm not sure just leaving is going to help much,' said Wat as he followed.

'Well, it's better than staying here,' said Cotard, with considerable enthusiasm.

'Grosmal will only send men after us. Well, after me specifically.'

'But he can't think you're still involved, not after he heard about the small guard?'

'There's a new factor you're not aware of,' Wat said seriously.

'What?' Hermitage asked, a trace of worry appearing as he saw the weight in Wat's face.

'Not a what, a who. Brother Simon.'

'I know.' Hermitage sounded worried. 'We found out from the small guard, er, spy, um, man. That's what prompted us to come. Heaven knows what will happen with Simon's, erm, how can I put it?'

'Idiocy?' Wat suggested.

'Perhaps,' Hermitage granted. He paused in contemplation for a moment. 'Brother Simon,' he sighed, 'dear God.'

'And he has the ear of Grosmal.'

'Who's Simon?' Scarlan asked.

'We must leave,' Hermitage responded immediately.

They had arrived back in the courtyard now. A few guards still wandered about, rather aimlessly looking for the small guard, but no one took any notice of the rescue party. Sigurd son of Sigurd was picked up and held quiet again. Scarlan pointed Durniss away from the horses and Cotard headed straight for the gate.

'Brother Simon presents himself as the King's Investigator,' Wat explained in a harsh whisper.

'But he's not.' Hermitage was clear.

'We know he's not, but Grosmal isn't sure,' Wat explained. 'The simple word "King" seems to have put the fear of God up him.'

'Investigator?' Sigurd asked. 'Scarlan said it was something to do with tracking?'

'I didn't know what it was until recently,' Wat responded. 'It's someone who looks into things. Murders and the like. Figures out who did what to whom. Follows their tracks, if you like.'

'Very clever. Then he kills them.'

'No, he hands them over for justice.'

'Ah, justice,' said Sigurd with enthusiasm, patting the pommel of his sword. Pretty much the same thing.

'And the King has his own, does he?' Scarlan asked, snarling out the word 'King'. It was clear that anyone who did anything for King William was as bad as the man himself and deserved the same fate. Which was something worse than death.

'Not this King.' Wat dropped his voice as a couple of guards ambled by, looking up as if small guards fell from the sky.

'It's a very messy picture,' the weaver went on as they walked out of the castle as nonchalantly as they could. 'There was a murder at De'Ath's Dingle. The bishop's office was involved and they told Simon he was the King's Investigator. Then, when it all got sorted out, the King himself turned up.'

'Harold,' Scarlan said in awe. 'You saw him?' His eyes were wide and watering slightly.

'Oh, I've met him before,' Wat dropped in.

Scarlan was speechless.

'Anyway, when the King turned up, the murder was solved by Hermitage.'

'Well, sort of,' Hermitage responded modestly.

'And King Harold sacked Simon, who he never knew about in the first place,' Wat went on, 'and appointed his own Investigator.'

'Not Simon?'

'Definitely not Simon. Brother Simon, as I say, is an idiot. An arrogant, overbearing, self-important dolt who wouldn't recognise a murder if it was his own. He just jumped at the title, not realising that people with more brains were simply using him. He hadn't got a clue what was going on. Just wandered about accusing everyone he saw. Now he's doing the same again.'

'So who did King Harold appoint?' Scarlan asked as they walked through the castle gate.

'Hermitage here,' Wat nodded to the monk.

Brother Hermitage smiled a weak smile and shrugged.

Scarlan stopped walking. He looked at Hermitage in awe and knelt, bowing his head. 'I never knew, sire, I never knew. We'd never have kidnapped you if we'd known.'

Sigurd stood by holding son of Sigurd, trying not to be noticed.

'Kidnapped?' Wat asked.

'Oh, my dear fellow, get up, get up.' Hermitage pulled Scarlan up by the shoulders. This was embarrassing as well as dangerous. Hermitage looked around, hoping none of the Normans had noticed.

'I'm not a sire, I'm not an anything. Just a monk who was able to help out.'

◆   ◆   ◆

They walked on, Scarlan now at Hermitage's side, gazing at him as if the sun was hidden in his habit.

'But the King's Investigatrum…' Scarlan breathed.

'Investigator,' Hermitage corrected, 'and it hasn't been much of a job. King Harold appointed me and then set off for Hastings. We all know how that turned out. It's just bad luck that this de Turold chap got killed right next door to De'Ath's Dingle. Lord Grosmal doesn't know I had anything to do with King Harold. I don't think he'd be very happy if he found out.'

'He shall not hear it from me, sire.' Scarlan bowed again.

'I told you, I'm not a sire. And if you keep bowing someone will spot us.'

'My lord?' Scarlan asked.

'Certainly not.'

'I can't just call you monk; it wouldn't be respectful.'

'My name is Hermitage.'

'Odd name for a monk.'

'Yes, a lot of people say that.'

'The Honourable Sir Hermitage?'

'Just Hermitage.'

'Well, I'll give it a go.'

'What's this about a kidnap?' Wat asked as they got so close to the woods that they could run if anyone came out of the castle after them.

'Ah yes,' Scarlan averted his eyes. 'Complete misunderstanding. We thought my lor–, erm, Brother Hermitage here was

Grosmal's priest, and that if we held him we could get a ransom.'

'Not from what I've seen of Grosmal.' Wat laughed a bitter sort of laugh.

'So we gather. Anyway, that's all forgotten now. We've got you out of Grosmal's grasp. We're free men again and never need to see the Norman pig again.'

'So what is the plan now?' Wat asked warily.

'The life of the honest outlaw,' Scarlan breathed out as they entered the shelter of the woods again. 'We take up life in the woods and forests and attack the Norman invader at every opportunity. We are the Brotherhood of the Sword, after all.'

'Excellent,' said Wat, stopping before they moved much further into the cover of the trees. 'Well, good luck with that. I think we'd better be off. Lots of business to see to. Just have to hope Robert Grosmal doesn't get out much. We shall have to avoid this part of the country, but it's the towns that provide the profit anyway.'

'You can't go,' Scarlan said, stopping as well and turning back to look at Wat and Hermitage with a broad smile, cheer in his voice. 'You'll become part of the band. You can make tapestries of our deeds which will live down the centuries. And Brother Hermitage, King Harold's Investigator, will be our priest.'

'No, no, really. It's very kind and I'm most grateful, but the weaving business won't run itself, and Hermitage really ought to get back to being a monk.'

Hermitage wasn't at all sure getting back to being a monk was a good idea. Particularly if it meant De'Ath's Dingle. He thought Wat seemed as anxious to get away from Scarlan as he was to return to his daily toil.

'I'm sure I can get a work depicting your band produced at some point though.' Wat gave a cheery smile.

'You can't leave.' All the cheer had gone from Scarlan's voice now, and Sigurd's hand was on the pommel of his sword as he stepped round behind Wat. 'Brother Hermitage will be our priest and you will make the record of our fight to the death.'

Hermitage let a small whimper escape. 'To the death?'

'Of course.'

'But Brother Hermitage is the King's Investigator. King Harold's own appointed man.'

'And an excellent martyr he will make. He'll probably get sainted.'

'But…' Hermitage felt the too familiar cold of fear shudder through his frame.

Scarlan was cheerful again. 'You said yourself Grosmal would do something horrible by this evening if you hadn't performed your duties. Look on the bright side: stay with us and you could live for days. Maybe even weeks.'

Hermitage noticed that Wat had become very serious in his appraisal of Scarlan. He turned once to look at Sigurd. The weaver's eyes narrowed and he was clearly weighing up action.

Hermitage took half a step away from Wat to give him room for whatever he was planning. 'If we were to return to Grosmal,' he said, dragging Scarlan's attention in his direction, 'might we not still act as spies?'

'And find out who killed de Turold? Scarlan asked.

'Well, yes,' Hermitage thought this would be a good thing.

'That would be a very bad thing.' Scarlan was sneering slightly.

'Really?' Hermitage wasn't sure why finding a murderer could ever be a bad thing.

'Of course,' Scarlan said.

Wat chose this moment to move. He took one step forward and pushed Scarlan back, while at the same time slipping his left ankle behind the Saxon's right. Scarlan went down, but Wat kept moving forward. After two more steps he turned and as expected faced Sigurd who had moved, albeit rather slowly.

Wat dropped backwards, reaching up to grab Sigurd by the waistcoat as he did so. He pulled the large man over as well, sliding neatly to one side at the last moment to avoid being crushed.

Sigurd son of Sigurd joined the fray, but Wat picked him up by the scruff of his neck and deposited him on top of his father – thus preventing Sigurd senior from getting up.

Wat grabbed Hermitage and they took three steps back towards the castle before they stopped.

From behind a tree a small man with a bright and pointing sword emerged. He held it at the height of Wat's stomach.

'Like I said,' Scarlan was in full sneer now as he got up, 'I insist you stay with us. We most certainly do not want you telling Grosmal who killed de Turold.'

'Why not?' Hermitage insisted.

The small man with the sword spoke as he waved his weapon in a flourish around his head. 'Because I did it.'

Caput XX

Half past Two: Lady to Dungeon

HE LADY FOELLA DID NOT GO QUIETLY all the way to the dungeon. Eleanor could have predicted that.

'Put me down,' she ordered.

'When we get to the dungeon we'll put you down. Then we'll throw you in a cell and lock the door. Then perhaps you'll shut up,' one of the guards said wistfully, in a lilting Norman French accent.

'I will not shut up.' Foella was outraged.

'Well, at least we won't be able to hear you, which is just as good.'

'I'll see you punished for this. I know who you are,' Foella growled through clenched teeth.

'No, you don't,' the guard said simply, 'your sort never do.'

They were at the steps down to the cells now, but the guard had more to say. 'It was me who brought all those wretched trunks up to your room when you arrived. Two days of solid work coming and going while you sat in the window seat shouting at your maid. And you still don't recognise me.'

'Well…' Foella began.

'Still, when Lord Grosmal wants your head chopped off and I volunteer to be axe man, you might bring me to mind, eh?'

For once Lady Foella was speechless.

◆　　◆　　◆

The guards were rather taken aback as well when they came across the wreckage in the dungeon, including the unconscious gaoler and the moaning lock-up boy.

'What happened here?' the guard demanded.

The lock-up boy moaned some more and held his head, and then his leg. 'There was an army of them. They attacked out of nowhere, we never stood a chance.'

'When Lord Grosmal finds out you won't have much of a chance either,' the guard observed. 'We'd better lock this harridan away and go and tell his lordship.'

'You can tell him,' the other guard responded. 'He likes you.'

'I told you,' his companion snapped back, 'that was only the once.'

'Look,' Foella piped up, 'I can see you've got a lot on your hands so I'll just wait here if you like.' She tried to smile, but it didn't come out right.

'The guard simply laughed. 'Number three for you, I think.'

'Oh, you bastard,' the other guard said with some feeling.

'What?' Foella cried out as she was bundled through a solid cell door and into the room. 'What about number three? What's special about number three?'

She continued to cry out as the door was slammed and locked and the guards went to find Lord Robert.

'Tell me,' she squealed, 'tell me what's special about number three?'

When there was no response her voice broke into a sort of whimper. 'Please tell me.'

The lock-up boy jumped to his feet and gathered his meagre possessions ready to leave and start a new life. Or at least keep the old one out of the hands of Lord Grosmal. He then paused, thought and helped himself to the less meagre possessions of his still prone master before scuttling up the steps.

Just as he left the dungeon itself he heard a high pitched scream from Lady Foella.

'Found out about number three, then,' he sniggered as he whistled his way out of the castle.

◆　　◆　　◆

Despite the news coming from a supposed friend, Lord Grosmal did not take it well. In fact he took it so badly the second guard had to take the rest of the day off to get his wounds seen to.

He hurriedly dragged Ethel, Simon and the undamaged guard back to the dungeon.

When they arrived, the gaoler was just coming round.

'So, my man,' Grosmal said, crouching down beside the clearly befuddled gaoler, 'where is my prisoner?'

It was asked very nicely, but it pressed a look of terror on to the gaoler's face.

'My lord,' the man mumbled, 'I was struck from behind by a massive blow. Look, it destroyed the table.' He gestured to the wreckage around him.

'And it looks like it took my prisoner away.' Grosmal gestured to the cell door which was propped up against a wall instead of stopping the people in the cell getting out.

'Ah.' The gaoler looked.

'Guard,' Grosmal called and the remaining guard stepped up. 'My lord.'

'Take this man outside and give him a massive blow on the back of the head. This time make sure he never wakes up.'

'My lord.'

The guard dragged the gaoler to his feet and took the protesting figure away.

A gentle and plaintive plea whispered into the silent chamber.

'Please let me out.'

'Ah,' said Grosmal, 'number three. Good choice.'

With no staff in support, Grosmal stepped up himself and pulled back the bolts of the cell door.

The Lady Foella tumbled out straight into his arms and looked nervously back at the cell.

'There there, my lady.' Grosmal was all comfort and solicitation, which was very disturbing. 'Let's have a nice chat and you won't have to go back in the nasty cell.'

'Nasty,' she shivered.

'Come, Master Investigator,' Grosmal summoned Simon, who had been hanging back by the steps. 'Let's go into number four and you can do your thing.'

'My, er, thing?'

'Yes, finding out about matters. I'm sure the lady has a lot of matters she wants to discuss now.'

'Ah, yes, of course.' Simon didn't sound very sure.

'All of which will lead to the inevitable conclusion that she knows about de Turold's death and will confess all before King William.'

'Will she?' Simon asked.

'She will.' Grosmal was quite emphatic.

The lord of the castle took the still trembling Foella by the arm and led her past the absent door of the interrogation room.

Simon followed, but he had to be ushered in by Ethel.

'So,' Grosmal said cheerfully, spreading his arms to encompass the impressive array of equipment in the room. 'Where would you like to start?'

'Oh.' Simon was looking around the room as well. Apparently for another exit. 'Erm, perhaps with some questions?'

'Well, obviously, but which tool do you want to ask the questions?'

'Tool?'

'Yes. Good God man, anyone would think you'd never asked any questions before.'

'Ha ha,' Simon laughed lightly and without authenticity.

'What's it to be then eh? The Dancer's Hearthstone?' He gestured to a large collection of metal shapes held together by chains. 'Sir Bringly's Brightener?' He pointed to a single spike with a winding handle on the end. 'Perhaps even the Iron Encumbrance?' This was a man-shaped piece of metal with holes in it at strategic points. Strategic and intimate.

'Oh, er.' Simon was paralysed with indecision.

'I have it.' Grosmal picked up a strangely shaped object which looked like nothing so much as the leavings from a blacksmith's apprentice on his first morning. 'My Lady's Grimace. Perfect and so appropriate. I've always liked this one.'

He handed the contraption to Simon, who cut his finger on it.

'I think we can achieve our ends without mechanical assistance.' He sounded sure, but didn't look it.

'Really?' Grosmal looked at Lady Foella, and then at his interrogation equipment. His face was that of a youth told to leave the hall before the roistering began.

'Oh yes, sire,' Simon had found his condescension again. 'Modern methods simply require the application of intellect. A few piercing questions will get to the truth.'

'Without any actual piercing?' Grosmal was not convinced.

'Absolutely.'

'Well, I must say this is extremely disappointing and I have to say suspicious. I've never heard of anyone asking any questions or getting any information out of anyone without equipment. Are you sure you're qualified for this job?'

'Of course I am, sire,' Simon huffed, 'was I not appointed by the King? Did I not solve the mystery at De'Ath's Dingle?'

'So you say. And you never used anything? Not even a tickling spike?'

'Absolutely not.'

Grosmal shook his head. 'Saxons are very odd. Have it your own way, but I expect results.'

'Of course, sire. Now if you could leave me with the lady?'

'Leave you?' Now Grosmal really was lost.

'Oh yes, sire, absolutely essential. The, erm, victim must not be distracted by others. I myself require the deepest levels of concentration and these are highly confidential methods.' Simon nodded significantly.

'Can't I even watch?'

'I'm afraid not, sire.'

'What do you make of this, Ethel?' Grosmal turned to his retainer.

'Highly unorthodox, sire.' The retainer spoke to Grosmal, but looked at Simon.

'No use of the questioning engines and now no one else in the room?' Grosmal thought and then a sly grin appeared on his face. 'What are you going to do to her then?' he asked Simon.

'I am going to put her to a severe test of reasoning. One which she will not be able to resist. The truth will out.'

Grosmal frowned in thought some more. It was not a pleasant sight. 'All right. I'll give you ten minutes.'

'It will take longer than that, sire.' Simon dismissed this ridiculous timescale.

'We'll come back after ten minutes, and if there's no progress we use something metal.'

With a wave of the arm Grosmal ended the conversation. The same arm gestured Ethel to leave the room and the door was propped back in place behind them.

The afternoon sun dappled through the shoddy brickwork of the cell. It danced on bits of equipment that had never been anywhere near a dance, and illuminated the place quite unnecessarily.

In the distance a bird tweeted its incongruous joy at the day, while a sheep coughed its throat clear of half-digested grass in a much more appropriate manner.

Motes of dust floated in the air, their lazy progress making it clear they had not the faintest idea what went on here.

All in all the processes of nature trod their path; slow, relentless and consistent. Probably just what Grosmal expected of the King's Investigator.

◆　　◆　　◆

Simon turned to Foella. She was standing rather still, but kept wringing her hands as her eyes darted about the room.

'Now, my lady,' Simon said as he approached her.

Her eyes found him. 'What?' She snapped her snap, but it was a nervous one with a quiver in it.

'I am going to ask you a series of questions. Answer each one honestly and openly and this will lead to the revelation of the truth of events.'

'What?' she snapped, and quivered again.

Simon sighed as talked down to Foella. 'I will ask you some questions,' he said very slowly. 'They may not seem connected to events, but will lead us on a trail of inexorable thinking. We will start with simple things, questions from the outlying reaches of your time here. Subtle questions which will slowly build up a picture of you, of the people here and how the time has passed. Questions, seemingly innocuous, which will create a picture. A picture of great detail, but a picture of the whole. When we have all the minute, inconsequential details we will stand back and look at what we have created. In that creation the circumstances of the death will be revealed. It will be clear and it will be unavoidable.'

Foella seemed to be emerging from her nervous state as Simon rambled on.

'Questions?' she said.

'Indeed.'

'Go on then,' she challenged him.

'Right, my lady.' Simon was not fazed. He looked Foella in the eye. 'Are you ready for the first question on our tortuous path to truth?'

'Yes.'

Simon drew his breath. 'Did you kill de Turold?'

'No, I bloody well didn't, you idiot.' Foella was now completely out of her nervous state and resumed her normal approach to life – attack.

'Oh.' Simon seemed lost now.

'That wasn't very subtle, was it? Where's the chain of inconsequential questions? The building of a picture?' She put her hand on her hips.

'That was a ruse,' Simon flustered.

'A ruse?' Foella's voice rose to a shriek.

There was a giggle from outside the cell door at the sound of the shriek. A giggle with a Norman accent.

'Yes, I was lulling you into a relaxed state before snapping out the key question. It's a common technique.'

'Relaxed? I'm in a bloody Norman torture chamber, you imbecile. How relaxed do you think I can get? I've just been released from a cell with, with things in it and threatened by a man with his own collection of pain makers. Is this really the best you can do?'

Simon looked nervously from Foella to the door and back. He then stole a glance at My Lady's Grimace.

'Don't even think about it,' Foella instructed. 'You even look at any of those things and I'll use them on you.'

'My lady,' Simon dropped his voice, 'Lord Grosmal is going to return at any moment and if there is nothing to tell him he most certainly will use these things.'

'So what do you suggest?' The contempt in Foella's voice was strong and direct – it headed straight for Simon.

The King's Investigator narrowed his eyes as if reducing the amount of light entering his head would make his thoughts work harder.

'You knew de Turold?'

'Of course.'

'Very well?'

'There was only Grosmal, me and de Turold here,' Foella answered, ignoring the hundred odd other people who were there as well. But then they were peasants, servants and guards, so didn't really count.

'He had a cousin knocking about somewhere, but they didn't get on so he kept out of the way.'

'So you knew de Turold? You had meals with him and conversations.' Simon nodded in a very knowing manner.

'Well done.' Foella was not complimentary.

'And we heard that de Turold was shot in the privy.'

'In the arse in the privy,' Foella corrected.

'Indeed, and did you know this place?'

'The arse or the privy?'

'The privy, my lady, the privy. I think you had better take this matter seriously.'

'Oh, I am taking the matter seriously. It's you I think are a joke.'

'Did you know the privy?' Simon asked. He ignored the comment, but hardened his gaze at Foella.

'Of course I did. You can't miss the place, it stinks.'

'And we also heard that you threw a knife at Lord Grosmal and accused him of killing de Turold, your husband.' Simon stopped talking as if amazed at his own powers of deduction.

'That wasn't it at all.' Foella tried to dismiss the suggestion, but the dismissive tone towards Simon had gone. 'It was merely that I liked de Turold. When I heard that he'd been killed, I was naturally upset. I thought Grosmal must have had something to do with it.' She shrugged.

'Your husband?'

'No, no,' Foella laughed a tinkling laugh. The sound was more like a horse's corpse being thrown through a window made of cheap glass than a tinkle. 'I got confused in the horror of the murder.'

'You got confused about who your husband was?'

'I don't have a husband,' Foella glared.

'Then there hardly seems room for any confusion whatsoever. I can understand a woman who sees two men in a darkened chamber being confused. If the men are of about the same size and shape and their faces are covered. And they don't say anything or move about. Then I can understand a woman being confused over which is her husband.'

'Yes, all right,' Foella capitulated.

Simon was on a roll. 'But if a woman entered such a chamber and did not in fact have a husband at all, she would not mistake either of them for her man.'

'Yes, yes.'

'Because, not having a husband at all, she would realise that neither of the men presented to her could be that man, because he didn't exist.'

'All right…'

'Perhaps if she entered an empty chamber she might confuse the emptiness for her absence of a husband.'

'Shut up.'

Simon shut up because he had driven himself down a rational dead end.

'So you thought you did have a husband?' Simon struggled to get back on track again.

'No.'

'Then what, my lady?' Simon demanded. 'You need to explain.'

'I need to do no such thing.'

'Then Lord Grosmal will return and use some of his own personal methods.'

Foella looked to Simon and to the stack of personal methods lying in wait. She sighed.

'I had thought that de Turold might be a suitable match.'

'A dead man?'

'Before he was dead. I think that weaver is right, you are useless.'

'That will do, my lady.' Simon bit the words.

'Naturally when I found that de Turold was dead my plans fell apart and I was, erm, disappointed.'

'So disappointed that you threw a knife at Lord Grosmal.'

'Just so,' said Foella looking Simon straight in the eye. 'I do that sort of thing when I get disappointed.'

'You attack people when they disappoint you? Interesting. Did de Turold know of your intentions?'

'He and I had a discussion of sorts over dinner the night he died.'

'And was he amenable to the proposal?'

'It wasn't a proposal, but yes, he was amenable. Well, amenable to taking the first steps.'

'What were those?' Simon was positively lively. This line of questioning actually seemed to be getting somewhere.

'He, erm.' Foella hesitated as she thought carefully about her next sentence.

'Yes, my lady? It is important that you tell everything. If you had nothing to do with the death then all the details you can give will ensure no action is taken against you.' Simon nodded encouragement for her to go on.

'He was going to come to my chamber that night.'

'Really?'

Foella actually blushed. Just for a moment before she forced it away.

'Yes, but he never arrived.'

'He was killed on the way?'

'He must have been.'

'I see.' Simon stroked his chin in thought. He even turned away from Foella and paced a little way up and down the chamber with his hands behind his back. He stopped pacing when he stubbed his toe on a set of Disturbing Irons.

'If he had come to your chamber you would have discussed arrangements for the marriage?'

'Yes, erm, something like that, I'm sure. Eventually.'

'This is very significant.'

The door was dragged back from its resting place and Grosmal walked back in. Ethel was at his heel as usual.

'So,' the lord rubbed his hands together, 'all sorted?'

'Oh, yes,' Foella and Simon said together.

'Remarkable,' the Norman commented. 'I only heard one shriek.'

'And that wasn't what you're thinking,' Foella snarled in disgust.

'Well, Master Investigator, what's to do?'

Foella folded her arms in smug satisfaction that she would soon be released.

Simon adopted a declamatory pose.

'She did it,' Simon's pose declared as he held out an arm and pointed at Foella.

'What?' Foella shrieked again.

Simon ignored her and spoke to Grosmal. 'By her own confession she made an assignation with de Turold to discuss marriage. I suspect he turned her down and so she killed him and left him in the garderobe. We've already heard the privy hole was too small for anyone to get through, so he can't have been killed there.'

Foella was beside herself. 'I have just explained, you cow brain, I couldn't have done it. De Turold never arrived in my chamber. Anyway, the privy hole is big enough for the small guard.'

'My lady, you have told us that de Turold did not arrive. You have told us there is a small guard in the castle. As King's Investigator I have an option in situations like this.' Brother Simon was all confidence with extra smug.

'Which is?' Foella's voice had got some of the tremor back.

'I don't believe you.'

Three-o-clock: Guard to Maid

HE GUARD WHO WAS SUMMONED to lock the Lady Foella back in the cell had a much easier time of it. She seemed shocked and her only request was not to go in number three.

Closing and barring the door of number two, the guard nodded to Grosmal, Ethel and Simon. As they left, the lord and the investigator were discussing whether they should have a gallows ready for when King William was told, or whether that might be presumptuous.

Once they were out of sight across the courtyard, the guard's demeanour changed. 'Eleanor,' William le Morton called out loud, as if the maid could hear him from the dungeon. With a look of worry on his face, he scurried away. 'They've locked up your mistress.'

Running and sliding around the corridors, William eventually arrived at Foella's chamber. He threw the door open to find Eleanor having a lovely time.

She generally had a lovely time when her ladyship wasn't there. Granted, Foella provided her with employment, food, shelter, protection and clothing. Without Foella, poor Eleanor would be just that – poor. Well, she was still poor technically, as she had no possessions of her own, but with Foella looking after her she didn't really need any.

Although she relied on Foella for absolutely everything in her life, Eleanor's constant wish was that the woman would simply go away. She had long tried to think of an expression which summed up her employer, although the relationship was more like owner than employer.

Eleanor was not an intellectual, but she wasn't stupid either. She used her spare time, and the moments when Foella was driving her to utter distraction to try to create a picture of her mistress, using the most apposite words in the English language. A picture she would be able to use to distract her when things got really bad.

Eventually she had it. It was simple and obvious, and she had clearly been over thinking things. She'd almost ended up with essays in her head describing all the details of the Lady Foella's appallingness. All she needed was one word. Useless.

The lady Foella was useless. She was a useless human being, a useless woman and a useless noble. She was no imaginable use to anyone or anything in any circumstances. If she vanished from the face of the earth, the whole of creation would breathe a sigh of relief.

An apple was useless for lighting a fire, but at least it was good for eating.

Foella wasn't good for anything.

Or if she was good for something Eleanor hadn't spotted what it was, despite years of watching.

She couldn't talk to people or engage with them in any way that didn't drive them mad. She complained about everything. She'd spent all this time trying to get a man, and couldn't understand why those she approached ran a mile. Eleanor half suspected de Turold had found out about her intentions, gone to the garderobe and shot himself in the arse just to avoid her.

She couldn't manage an estate or be a lady of the court. She'd been to court once, but King Harold had thrown her out after an hour.

She couldn't dress herself or prepare her own food. She didn't know where clothes came from or how to tidy a room. She couldn't sew or paint or play music, write poetry, do tapestry. She couldn't even just waft quietly about, looking beautiful.

Useless. Lady Foella was utterly, utterly useless.

But. She did have one overriding function which negated the rest of her pointless life. She kept Eleanor out of the cold.

Yes, she was useless and nasty and thoughtless and selfish, but she was Eleanor's lady. And there were times when she wasn't about, and they were good times. A lot better times than if there had been no Lady Foella to come back and ruin things again.

This was one of those good times. It was good for William, too, as Eleanor was in the middle of working her way through Foella's wardrobe, trying on everything that would fit.

'That's pretty,' said William, drawn up short by Foella's most expensive dress. The one that had taken a week just for the embroidery on the hem. The one that had finally cost the elderly seamstress her sight as it had to be completed for Christmas. The one Foella hated because it was too fiddly.

'Oh.' Eleanor jumped. She had her excuses ready. She had noticed a slight tear on the dress last time Foella had worn it, but had been unable to find it again. She had to try it on to see if she could locate the hole from the inside.

She saw it was William and relaxed.

'You nearly frightened my head off,' she accused him with a laugh.

'Nearly made you jump out of your dress, eh?' William winked.

'In your dreams.' She swished up to him and let the skirts fly out, just as they had been made to do. The way that made Foella complain they flew out too much.

William took her by the waist and swung her round.

'Maybe we can make it just fly off all on its own.'

Eleanor beat him on the shoulders with absolutely no effect whatsoever. Just as intended.

He brought her to a halt and their faces were inches apart. He looked down at the slim and weightless treasure in his arms.

He held her as if his strength could make her part of him.

She looked up at the shape that lifted her feet from the ground. She melted into his grip, becoming as soft and pliable as the dress itself.

They kissed.

Their eyes closed and the soft touch of lips was soon reinforced by the weight and presence of their bodies. Hands moved and limbs pressed. The kiss spread through them and prepared to move on.

'Oh, take me to your prison, you naughty guard,' Eleanor growled. William's hands explored the fine cloth of Foella's dress.

'Oh, bloody hell.' William withdrew, but didn't let go.

'What?' Eleanor had offence in her voice.

'I knew there was something.'

'There is, let's find it.'

'Your mistress,' William insisted.

'Where?' Now Eleanor withdrew as well and turned to look out of the window.

'No, no. That was why I come up here. They've locked up your mistress.'

'Who has?' Eleanor was slightly distracted.

'Grosmal and Ethel and that monk fellow.'

'Why?'

William paused for effect. 'They reckon she killed de Turold.'

'Oh, right.' Eleanor didn't seem shocked by this.

'She didn't, did she?' William was surprised by the reaction.

'Don't think so.'

'*Think* so!'

'Well, like I said, she could if she wanted. She's capable, believe me, but I don't think de Turold came to the chamber that night. Probably because he was already dead.'

'Perhaps because she'd already killed him?'

'She didn't sneak out while I was awake.'

'What are we going to do?'

'I've got a few ideas.' Eleanor swung the dress forward again.

William stepped back. 'They've locked your lady in the dungeon.'

'At least we know she won't interrupt us.' Eleanor tried to look seductive, and succeeded.

'But…' William said, before his mouth was covered by Eleanor's.

'But what?' Eleanor asked. She lowered her head, looked up at him and fluttered her eyelashes.

'Oh, nothing, I suppose,' William mumbled as he licked his lips. 'We'll have even more time after they've executed her.' He stepped forwards to take Eleanor in his arms again.

She had gone.

'They what?' she demanded, all affectionate intentions despatched.

'Execute her, of course.' William was getting confused by what seemed important and what didn't. 'If she killed de Turold and they've locked her in the dungeon, what do you think they're going to do? A night in the cells isn't enough for killing Normans any more.'

'We've got to get her out.' Eleanor had started pacing the room and wringing her hands.

'Don't be daft.'

'Yes, yes. You can let her out. You'll have the keys.'

'There aren't any keys, just a bolt,' said William, and wished he hadn't.

'Easy – you can just unbolt the bolt and let her out.'

'And then? What? She turns up again? Don't you think even Grosmal might notice? "Oh, there's Lady Foella, funny, I thought I'd locked her in the dungeons"?'

'Well, I don't know.' Eleanor was flustered and getting annoyed with William. 'We'll get her out and then think what do to.'

'We could get her out and then *you* could think what to do.'

Eleanor looked at William with disappointed eyes. 'I see. All right while I'm swishing round in my dress, but first sign of trouble and you're off.'

'It's not that at all.' William held out his hands in supplication. 'Of course I'd want to help. Be a bit difficult for me though 'cos I'll be dead for having released a prisoner.'

'Typical,' she huffed, 'one excuse after another.'

Eleanor thought some more. 'What if we get her out and run away?'

'We could, although I'd give Grosmal's personal guard about a day to find us and then we'll all be dead.'

'Oh, this is impossible.'

'I think that's the general idea when you lock someone in a cell.'

'We either leave her there to die. We get her out and you die, or we all run off and we all die.'

'That's about it. Personally I'd be in favour of the first option.'

'You would. Bloody men.' Eleanor despatched the sex.

'I thought you hated her?'

'Of course I do. She's…' Eleanor paused to give the favoured word the right emphasis, 'useless. But she keeps me in frocks. She won't be able to do that if she's dead, will she? She ain't going to leave me anything in her will. More likely leave me to someone.'

'Women.' William dismissed them all. 'Well, what do you suggest?'

'We've got save her.'

'We've been through that.'

'No, I mean save her. Get her out and stop her being executed.'

'Yeah,' said William with a hollow laugh, 'that would about do it, I reckon. So? How?'

'By showing that she didn't do it,' Eleanor said simply.

'But you said she could have.'

'Hum.' Eleanor saw her own problem. She walked to the window and back, kicking out in irritation at her skirts as they flew out in all directions.

'Then if she did do it, we convince people she didn't.'

'Lord Grosmal, Ethel and this monk chap?'

Eleanor just glared at him. She continued her perambulations of the room before coming to a dead end at the wardrobe. She kicked it too. The door swung slowly open.

Eleanor looked at it and put her hand to her mouth.

'William,' she called.

William came over and stood beside her in front of the wardrobe. Eleanor was pointing at the inside. He peered in.

'Very nice,' he said, 'but it's hardly the time to be playing with clothes.'

'No,' she was irritated at his lack of insight, 'the wardrobe,' she explained.

'Yes, love, it's a wardrobe.'

'The man in the wardrobe.' Eleanor was insistent.

William looked at her from the corner of his eyes and shied his head away slightly. 'That's right, there's a man in the wardrobe. Come and have a nice sit down and I'll get you a drink.'

Eleanor batted him away. 'Not now. There was a man in the wardrobe.'

'What your lady gets up to in her own time is up to her. Weird lot, nobles.' William had always thought so.

'There's a secret passage. A door in the back of the wardrobe. The man came through that and warned Foella not to marry Grosmal.'

'Blind me, she don't hang about, do she? I don't think she's got much chance there though.' William snorted.

'It'd be Grosmal who didn't have much chance if she'd made her mind up.'

'I think my Norman nutcase would beat your Saxon schemer.'

'Whatever. The point is the man who came out of the wardrobe claimed to be from the Brotherhood of the Sword or something like that. He should be able to help.'

'Uh, huh.' William was clearly not convinced. 'So what do we do? Recite a spell or something? I'm not taking my clothes off.'

'No, you dungstink. We walk through the door.' She gestured him to go first.

Humouring her, he put his head into the wardrobe. 'Bloody hell, there's a big hole in here.'

'Yeah, let's see if the one in your head will fit through it.' Eleanor pushed William forward and followed, closing the wardrobe door behind her.

As if to show its objection to all this non-wardrobe activity, the piece of furniture dropped its other handle on the floor.

Caput XXII
Half past Three: Dungeon to Wood

ON'T DESPAIR,' WAT SAID WITH SINCERITY as he and Hermitage sat with their backs against a tree, looking out at the shambolic camp of Scarlan.

'But I do despair.' Hermitage was very specific.

They had been left on the outskirts of the camp while Scarlan and his men discussed their next steps. Insult was added by the guard allocated to watch them.

Sigurd son of Sigurd marched up and down, a wooden sword over his shoulder. He told them he was a centurion, and if they tried to escape he would throw them to the lions.

Wat had moved once, thinking he could simply pick the child up and deposit him in a tree. They would then make their escape.

Sigurd son of Sigurd had screamed the place down. Sigurd the father appeared very quickly and informed Wat in some detail that even though his son's sword was made of wood, it would still smart a bit if it was inserted into the weaver. Which event would happen if he so much as breathed.

The captives sat quietly.

'I despair about everything,' Hermitage went on in a low moan. 'First they kidnap me, then let me go, then rescue you, then imprison us again. I mean, it's so inconsistent. Obviously this situation is not a good one. That causes me to despair about our countrymen and the paucity of consideration they give to their fellow man.'

Wat nodded.

'But then I despair more generally.'

Wat hummed vaguely and nodded.

224

'My despair goes all the way back to the business with Am-brosius at De'Ath's Dingle. Those in authority turned out to be corrupt. Virtually everyone was telling lies of one sort or anoth-er, and then the only man to cut through it all, the King, went off to Hastings and got, well, you know.'

Wat hummed vaguely again.

'And then we come here and there's more despair. Someone has most definitely killed another human being. The Norman seems to be so touched by evil he's invited it to move in. That Ethel fellow is probably hiding something, and no one seems to care a twig about the poor man who's actually dead.'

Wat was silent.

'In fact the small fellow is positively boastful that he commit-ted murder. I think I have every right to despair.'

Wat let out a gentle snore.

'Oh really!' Hermitage huffed. Even his despair put people to sleep.

'Oy,' yelled Sigurd son of Sigurd in a high-pitched squeal. 'No sleeping,' and he whacked Wat over the head with his sword.

Wat was awake in an instant. He grabbed the sword and yanked it from the child's hand. This brought the small shape into grabbing range and Wat wrapped one arm around young Sigurd and clapped his spare hand over the mouth.

Muffled mumbles and wriggles were easily contained by the weaver who stood up and beckoned Hermitage to follow.

'Ah,' Hermitage hissed with some relief, 'you weren't asleep at all. It was a ruse.'

Wat grunted.

'It doesn't help my despair, though, mishandling a child. It shouldn't be necessary.'

'A child who wanted to throw us to lions,' Wat replied in a harsh whisper. 'A child who has a massive father.'

Hermitage shrugged and followed Wat in a crouching run towards the trees.

225

They had nearly made it to the edge of the woods when a shout went up from the camp and there was bustling among the tents.

Hermitage dared a look back to see Scarlan, Sigurd and the small man emerge from a tent. The small man was carrying something.

'Stop,' Scarlan called.

'Why did he say that?' Hermitage asked as he continued to run. 'Does he think we're likely to bring an escape to a halt simply because he calls out from a hundred feet away?'

'Hermitage,' Wat panted, 'try running now, reasoning later.'

Hermitage did running.

'What are we going to do with the child?'

'We'll get a good distance and then let him go. It'll slow them down when they have to stop for him.'

'Awful,' Hermitage shook his head. The despair was still with him.

Just before they entered the wood, Hermitage noticed that the small man had raised the thing he was carrying.

'He's got a bow,' Hermitage called out a warning to Wat.

The pair of them ducked lower as there was a loud click from some way behind them and a swish through the air.

The shot went wide and a crossbow bolt thunked into a tree off to their left.

'Interesting,' Hermitage commented in his tone of fascination.

'Very,' said Wat. 'Running some more would be good now.'

They ran some more. When they were well into the woods Wat selected a suitable a tree and deposited young Sigurd on a high limb. It was too high for the child to jump down and Wat beckoned Hermitage that they must leave. Quickly.

They put more distance between them and the shouting horde of followers who had now entered the woods. The high pitched wail of Sigurd in his tree marked their way.

Hermitage was panting and out of breath. 'The child saw which way we went and will simply tell his father,' he called to Wat.

'Of course he will,' Wat replied, not very out of breath at all. 'That's why we'll carry on this way until we're out of sight and then head back to the castle.'

'Oh,' Hermitage was somewhat put out by the plan. 'Do we really want to go back there?'

'Just to put Scarlan and his bunch of the mad and useless off the scent. Once we're in sight of the castle they'll leave us alone. Then we stroll off.'

'I'm sure they'll still track us. They're probably used to this sort of thing.'

'Hermitage, I know you're in the middle of a nice despair, but try and be positive.'

Hermitage looked at the weaver ahead of him as they crouched and stumbled through the wood, pushing through undergrowth, which snagged and tugged at his habit. Wat was right. He really must try to be more optimistic. He often thought things were so bad the only option was to sit down and let them do their worst.

'But won't the people at the castle stop us and drag us back in?' He couldn't help himself.

'Not unless Grosmal himself is out patrolling, and I don't think that's likely. The rest of them will think it's part of the investigation.'

They stumbled some more until they came to an ancient ditch in the wood. It dipped sharply into a high-sided trench and ran off to their left and right.

'This'll do,' said Wat as he led the way down until they were out of sight of any pursuit.

Hermitage followed and tramped along in a thick carpet of leaves. Each year's fallings had simply piled one on top of the other, so the floor was at least a foot deep.

'Won't Lord Grosmal send his men after us?' Hermitage worried that there were too many connected and unconnected events going on at the same time. He could manage events in a nice, neat row, but all at once really was too much.

'Probably,' Wat spoke back over his shoulder, 'but with enough time he'll give up.'

'And what do we do in the meantime? And then when the meantime is over and we end up back this way?'

Wat waved his hand to indicate Hermitage should stop moving. The weaver listened carefully for any sound of Scarlan and his men, and child. Seemingly satisfied, he led Hermitage on more slowly and carefully than before.

'Hermitage,' he said, 'in my experience people never remember the things you think they're going to remember. There may be some horrible slight you think you've done them. You worry and fret over it for years, and then when you meet them again it's been completely forgotten.'

'Really?' Hermitage was amazed. He'd never had the opportunity to meet the same people after many years. He tended to meet people once, and then never again. Even those he positively remembered meeting claimed never to have heard of him. Perhaps Wat was right.

'Yes,' the weaver nodded ruefully, 'it's the things you've completely forgotten they want to kill you for.'

'Ah.'

'So there's no point in fretting over anything really. Just take each new event as yet another nasty surprise.'

'It seems a very cheerful, if rather fatalistic philosophy,' Hermitage mused.

'Sometimes the surprises are nice ones.'

'Oh good.'

'Just not often.'

'Ah.'

They had come to the end of the ditch now and the high

walls faded into the floor of the wood. This too was strewn with hundreds of years of leaves, which at least killed off all the undergrowth so the place was easy to walk in.

It was also easy to see through. Wat crouched behind a tree and looked out across the woods, back towards Scarlan's camp.

'Bugger,' he hissed.

'A nasty surprise?' Hermitage asked.

'That's the spirit,' Wat clapped the monk lightly on the shoulder. 'Scarlan's ignored the ditch and come straight through. Looks like he's split his men up, though. There's just him and Durniss. Sigurd and Cotard must have gone to the other end.'

'If Cotard hasn't gone back to camp for something,' Hermitage commented.

'Really?'

'Yes. He's, what can we say, reluctant to engage the enemy...'

'Right,' Wat nodded, 'that could be useful.'

Wat peered round the tree again. 'They don't seem to really know where we are. They're casting about all over the place. And they're still some way off.'

'But if we run they'll see us.'

'They will indeed.'

'Which will be a bad thing?'

'Normally, yes,' said Wat, thinking deeply.

'And what about the small man with the bow? Can you see him?' Hermitage asked.

'Good point. No, I can't. Don't want him sneaking up behind us with that thing. Not after the damage he did to Henri de Turold.'

'Yes, now about that.' Hermitage wanted to explore a new theory with Wat.

There was a rustle in the leaves behind them.

'Found you, found you.' Sigurd son of Sigurd kicked up a great flurry of leaves.

'Oh, bloody hell,' Wat swore, and started to move back to the small figure.

A second small figure appeared behind the boy. This one had a crossbow in his hand.

'Go.' Wat spat out the word, and he and Hermitage jumped from their hiding place and sprinted out into the wood.

They were immediately spotted by Scarlan, who gave a cry and set off after them.

Hermitage dared a look back and saw the small man drop to one knee and take careful sight along his weapon. Hermitage ran, ducked and grimaced at the same time as he wondered what being hit by a crossbow bolt would feel like. Very painful, he imagined. He just hoped the small man's target was not the same as in de Turold's demise.

The click came again, this time louder and closer. The sound of the bolt tearing through the close air of the forest was palpable. This time it ended in a flurry of leaves as the projectile fell to the ground off to Hermitage's left.

They had made good distance from child and man, and were keeping the space from Scarlan.

Hermitage looked over his shoulder again. He saw the small man heaving the loading pulley on to the crossbow, his foot in the cocking stirrup at the head of the weapon. He clearly didn't quite have the strength for a quick reload, and Hermitage's confidence grew.

'This way.' Wat swerved to his right slightly and led the way through trees and shrubs. 'Not far to the edge now, we'll make it.'

'Are you sure?' Hermitage gasped with the effort of the run.

'Yeah.' Wat was sure. 'Scarlan's no runner. Planner and orderer-about of other people. Doesn't do the dirty work himself. Durniss's built like a barn and probably runs like one as well. The child and the little man have short legs and won't catch up. Just got to hope Sigurd's too far away from the rest of the band. He's the only one I'm worried about.'

Sigurd was too far away from the rest of the band.

The problem was he was too far away right in front of Hermitage and Wat.

'Cheating so and so. He's run on ahead.' Wat frowned as they saw the bulky figure of Sigurd senior several hundred yards ahead. The man was on one knee, examining the floor of the forest for tracks. They slowed their pace, having left the rest of the pursuit behind.

'Yargh,' Sigurd called across the forest as he looked up at just the right moment. He stood and hefted his battle axe above his head. He started lumbering towards them.

Shouts from behind became clearer. It would not be long before they were surrounded.

Wat started walking straight towards Sigurd with Hermitage at heel.

'Er?' Hermitage knew that Wat must have a plan. He always did. He knew about situations like this and how to get out of them. He was sure Wat would tell him what the plan was. Any minute now.

Wat leaned over to talk quietly to Hermitage.

'When we get within about a hundred feet I'll give you a nudge.'

'A hundred feet?' Hermitage thought that was a bit close. 'Isn't that a bit close?' he asked.

Wat ignored him. 'When I give you the nudge, you go left. As fast as you can round the side of Sigurd. Keep a hundred feet away and then start to run round behind him.'

'What are you going to do?' Hermitage could not let his friend sacrifice himself like this.

'I'm going to run right. We'll see which one of us he really wants. At least he hasn't got that other fellow with him.'

'Cotard? No, I thought he wouldn't.' Another thought occurred to Hermitage which he knew wasn't appropriate for the situation, but he always had to let his thoughts out. They muddled up his head if he kept them in.

'Why a hundred feet?'

'I reckon that's about as far as Sigurd could throw his axe. He looks a bit worn out from the run and he is getting on a bit. Even then it won't be very accurate.'

'Very accurate. But perhaps a bit accurate.'

'Perhaps. But I suspect he won't be able to make his mind up which of us to go for. By the time he's decided it'll be too late.'

'Oh, good. And if he makes his mind up sooner, it might be too late as well.'

'True,' Wat shrugged, 'but what would you rather do? Go up to him and let that axe get really close?'

Hermitage contemplated. He was just coming to the conclusion that an axe a hundred feet away was probably better than one close up when Wat nudged him.

It was a bit much for a nudge and Hermitage stumbled slightly as Wat sprinted off away from him.

'Oy,' Sigurd yelled as Wat and Hermitage parted rapidly. The big man looked left and right at the departing figures, but only for a moment. He lifted his axe and hurled it as hard and as fast as he could. Having had lots of practice over the years, this was pretty hard and pretty fast. The deadly lump of iron sliced through the cool forest air as it made its way straight for Wat's head. It even made its way straight for where Wat's head was going to be when the axe arrived.

Sigurd had done this before. As soon as the axe left his hand he was off after Hermitage.

Fortunately it seemed as though Wat had done something like this before as well. Hermitage looked back in horror as the weapon set off on its inevitable journey. He then drew breath as Wat stopped for half a step before starting off again. The hesitation was enough for the axe to fly by, right in front of the weaver.

Wat stopped for another half step as he picked the axe from the undergrowth, where he found it had killed a squirrel.

Hermitage thought his running was going pretty well until he saw Sigurd had done running before too.

Rather than run straight after the monk, the man had set off on an intercept course, anticipating that Hermitage would try to get behind him.

Sigurd was closing even though Hermitage was young and fairly fit. His usual running away from people was restricted to the confines of a monastery, where wide open spaces were few and far between. Now there were acres to cross. Hermitage's short bursts of speed were being eaten up by Sigurd's inexorable energy.

Hermitage thought it rather unfair that when he had to stop to recover his breath, the wretched Sigurd kept coming.

He set off for about the third time when he heard a definite sword being drawn. It wasn't a sound he was familiar with, but it was unmistakeable. As the metal shivered from its sheath, Hermitage's back joined in.

The sound of steps in the underbrush was behind him now and he had really forgotten which way he was supposed to be running. All he knew was the sounds of Sigurd should be behind him. The awful man could be chasing him back into the arms of Scarlan for all he knew.

Now he could even hear the breath of the attacker. He knew some swords could be quite long, and so it wouldn't be a moment before he felt the cut of metal in his back.

He took one last desperate lunge and got behind a tree. He turned to look and saw the mighty figure of Sigurd with an even mightier sword raised for the blow.

The mighty sword fell. It made a mighty clang as it crashed into an axe thrown into the tree trunk above Hermitage's head.

'Now, now,' said Wat as he drew up to Hermitage and Sigurd, 'mustn't kill monks. Very bad form.'

Sigurd put his hands to his waist and bent double. He was panting hard and couldn't get his words out.

Wat considered him more closely. Sigurd was not young and it was his reactions which had pushed his body to a level of activity which was unwise, to say the least. The man was red in the face and looked in great pain. His gasps were snatched and uneven and had a horribly terminal ring to them.

Wat put a hand on each of Sigurd's shoulders and pushed the man over backwards.

Sigurd put up no defence and lay panting on the floor.

'Oh God, oh God,' he eventually got out, making no attempt to get to his feet.

'I think we've done for him,' Wat observed.

The observation was confirmed when Sigurd rolled over and was sick on the floor.

'He is getting a bit old for this sort of stuff. And he will insist on wearing all this heavy gear.' Wat himself was panting a bit, but nothing like the edge of death noises coming from Sigurd.

'You want to watch it, mate,' Wat said to the prone figure. 'Any more of this and Sigurd son of Sigurd will be just Sigurd.'

Wat took a deep breath and waved to Hermitage.

'Come on. Let's get back to the Normans where it's safe.'

Hermitage took one last look at sword and axe, crossed himself and followed Wat out of the woods.

Caput XXIII

Four-o-clock: The Guard, the Wench and the Wardrobe

LEANOR WAS MOST ASSUREDLY in charge of the adventure into the wardrobe. She was pushing William in front of her and slapping his back whenever he stopped. To William the slaps seemed to be getting increasingly impatient, frustrated and frankly rude.

He only stopped because it was pitch dark and he couldn't see where he was going.

Once through the back of the wardrobe itself they were in a rough tunnel. They had to bend to get into it and then couldn't stand up straight. They soon discovered bumping a head on the ceiling not only hurt, but brought lumps of the roof down on top of them.

The sides of the space were rough and crumbling. The floor was uneven and strewn with bits which should have been holding the rest of the place up.

Their passage damaged the passage further as they had to feel their way. The tunnel wound left and right, with obstructions in the floor and large bits sticking out of the walls. In places it was so narrow they had to squeeze, and in others it seemed to stretch into the distance away from them.

It was clearly a tunnel of mistake – simply a gap between other bits of the castle, rather than a deliberate construction.

They had only been going a few minutes, and hadn't got far as every step had to be explored, when William realised that he no longer had any idea where they were. Neither did he have any idea where they had come from, or where they were going. All sense of direction had fled in the twisting darkness, and the slippery fear that they might die in here and never be found began to prey on him.

'We should have gone back for a torch,' he hissed at Eleanor.

'And half a dozen other guards. Ones who aren't afraid of the dark,' she snapped

'I'm not afraid of the dark,' he bit back. 'The main problem is I can't see through it. My fault, I know, not being a cat and all, but perhaps you should have asked for a guard who could see in the dark?'

'Never mind the dark. When we find whoever's at the end of this tunnel, you can moan them to death.'

'At least if I'm between you and them they won't get nagged into their graves.'

Eleanor hit him again.

'And will you stop doing that?' William snapped, turning to her in the dark. 'It's not helping.'

'There's a light,' he said, as he turned back to face the way they were going, 'through a crack in the wall.'

He pointed ahead until he realised he couldn't see the end of his finger.

There was a very faint shimmer down low to their right. It damaged the darkness just enough to indicate that it wasn't absolute any more.

William got down on to his hands and knees, and crawled slowly forward.

'Where have you gone?' Eleanor hissed, unable to find her man.

'I'm down here,' William whispered back, afraid that the crack in the wall might be able to hear him.

'This is not the time,' Eleanor hissed.

'Oh, for goodness sake keep your mind on the job,' William said, as the thought did cross his mind to crawl back and locate Eleanor's skirts. 'I'm trying to see where this light is coming from.'

He crawled further and found that the light was coming from really very low on the floor. The masonry of the tunnel they were in was fundamentally poor, but just here there was sufficient shoddiness to allow the light from the neighbouring chamber to seep through.

William got his head low and pressed one eye against the hole.

'Oh dear,' he said as he drew his eye back. Quickly.

'What is it?' came Eleanor's voice.

'You don't want to know.' His voice had a shiver in it.

'Of course I do now you've said that.'

The skirts bustled forwards until Eleanor kicked William.

'Oy.'

'Get out of the way. I want to see.'

She lay down on the ground, pushing William to one side.

'You really don't,' William insisted, but he let her go ahead.

She pressed her eye against the hole.

'Oh,' she said in a serious tone. A tone devoid of all life and joy and hope. A tone which said it had been inside Eleanor's head and had left, taking the happy part of her with it.

'Is that…?' she asked, the tinkle of her voice tolling like a knell.

'Yes,' William replied. The darkness deepened further as he spoke.

'I never knew the Normans did that sort of, you know,' Eleanor's voice broke slightly.

'Don't think about it,' he said, finding her arm and squeezing it. She lay her hand on his in gratitude.

They sighed together and moved on as one.

After several more minutes of stumbling, turning and bumping into things, one of which moved out of their way and generated a shriek from Eleanor, they noticed a pronounced reduction in the darkness.

The next corner was visible, and from it came a vague recollection of daylight. A poor memory of the sun.

They edged around it and saw a door. It was a wooden door full of holes, and its construction matched the deplorable standard of the rest of the castle. It hung on one hinge, the other being completely missing, but there was definite light behind it.

It didn't look like welcoming and warm daylight. It wasn't even fresh as it had a dim and shadowed quality about it. But it was a darn sight better than staying in the eye-watering darkness of the tunnel. Perhaps it might wash the image of that other chamber from their heads.

William grabbed the door, gave it a light tug and stood holding it as the whole thing came off in his hand. They both stepped forward, still crouching slightly under the roof of the tunnel, and noticed that the floor on the other side of the door seemed to be missing.

They found some bits of wall which didn't fall apart under the lightest grip, and leant through the door to look down on to a large open space. They were some ten feet up the side of a wall and the door opened out on to an enclosed courtyard.

The floor was covered in logs.

One of the logs looked up and moved. 'Master, we are discovered again,' it called out, skipping away towards a giant log in the middle of the place, into which it disappeared.

William and Eleanor exchanged very puzzled looks.

'Ah.' A well-rounded and educated voice called up in recognition.

They looked down and saw that a more normal figure had appeared on the floor below.

As normal as any figure could be in a courtyard full of logs, that is.

'This is just Eleanor,' the new figure called comfort to his companion, 'the lady Foella's maid. And William the guard.' The voice was cordial and welcoming. The log man peeped out.

'You,' Eleanor called.

238

'Do you know him?' William asked. 'And how does he know me?' he added.

'Of course I know him. This is the one that came creeping out of my lady's wardrobe in the first place. So this is where the tunnel leads.' She looked the space over. 'What a dump.'

'The tunnel leads to many places, sweet Eleanor,' the man called up in good cheer.

'Oy,' said William, 'less of the sweet. And how do you know who I am?'

'I meant nothing by it, sir – William. And I know you as I know all in the castle. William le Morton now, but only recently, eh?

Eleanor was puzzled. 'What does he mean?' she demanded of William.

'Nothing, nothing,' he rushed out. 'What do you know of Lady Foella's imprisonment?'

The man shrugged. 'Only that it has happened.'

'Hum.' Eleanor was not convinced.

'And where she is held, how to get there and how to release her, of course,' the man added with a further shrug.

'What? Well, get her out then,' demanded Eleanor, who was not Foella's maid for nothing. She tried to wave a hand to illustrate the point, but nearly fell. 'Look, this is ridiculous. Can you come up? It's very off-putting, shouting from up here.'

'Logs, fetch the ladder,' the man instructed.

They all watched while Logs went behind the little house of logs and emerged with a construction made of logs. He put this on the floor of logs and propped it against the wall.

It was a ladder in as much as it had two sides with some rungs between them. But the whole thing looked like it had been grown especially, rather than manufactured.

'Come down,' the man called.

'I'm not getting on that thing,' Eleanor squeaked.

'It's perfectly safe, I assure you. Safer than being in the tunnel. It's always a bit prone to collapse around the edges.'

William clearly agreed as he took hold of the contraption and got one foot on to it. 'I'll go first,' he said, holding out a hand to help Eleanor.

William climbed and Eleanor grumbled down the ladder until they reached what passed for the floor.

'Right.' Eleanor had hands on hips and was in combative mood once more. 'Just who the hell are you and how quickly are you going to get my mistress out?'

'My name is not important and I can't get your mistress out,' he shrugged his shrug.

'If you shrug once more I'll kick you so hard in such a place that your shoulders will never come down again.'

'What would be served by getting your mistress out?' The man seemed to take the threat to heart.

'She would be got out, you idiot. A bit less prone to execution?'

'And then Grosmal will execute someone else. If not a lot of people.'

'A lot of people are not my problem. My mistress is my problem. And right now I am your problem.'

'Very clearly argued, I'm sure, but not persuasive.'

'My lady did not kill Henri de Turold,' Eleanor said with some emotion.

'We don't know that,' said the man among the logs. He almost succumbed to a shrug, but resisted.

Eleanor narrowed her eyes. 'I bet you do.' The narrow eyes were trying hard to pierce the man, like the arrow that had done for de Turold.

'Not at all,' the man dismissed the accusation.

'You kept going on about how much you knew, and how mysterious you were. If you don't know who killed de Turold I would be very surprised.'

The man said nothing.

'In fact I'd be very disappointed. Not much of a mysterious creeper-about if you don't know about a murder. The only murder to have happened in recent days.'

'We have other interests.' The man nodded his head towards Logs, who grinned at everyone.

'And what might they be?' Eleanor's determination was bristling.

The man drew his shoulders back. 'We are the Brotherhood of the Sward,' he announced.

'Sword,' Eleanor corrected.

'No, sward.' The man corrected the correction.

'Very nice, I'm sure. Meaning?'

'We are a Brotherhood.'

'With you so far.'

'And we protect the Sward.'

'What Sward?'

'The Sward.'

'What? Like the Greensward?' William spoke up with a healthy load of disbelief.

'Exactly.'

'All of it?' William was incredulous now, as well as disbelieving.

'As much as we can protect.'

'Protect it from what?' It was Eleanor's turn to address the man as if his brains had been trampled into some sward.

'Normans, just at the moment.'

Eleanor shook her head to get rid of some patently daft ideas. A couple of twigs and a bit of the tunnel dropped from her hair. 'You are protecting the fields from the Normans?'

'Not just the fields. The forests, the animals, the whole of everything.'

'And the Normans are doing what exactly? Walking on it heavily?'

'They are despoiling it with their foreign ways. If we don't take action it will be gone.'

'The whole of everything will be gone?' Eleanor checked the man's reasoning.

'Precisely.'

'Mad. You are precisely mad. This thing here,' she gestured to Logs, who grinned, 'we can see he's mad. He looks it. He talks like it. He behaves like it. Full deck. You, on the other hand – you look normal, but then you go and open your mouth.'

'Say what you will, Eleanor. In the days of the Saxon we had respect for the land. We nurtured it and worked with it. It supported us.'

Eleanor's look was suddenly full of understanding. 'Druids,' she laughed, 'you're a bunch of bloody Druids. Why don't you go and live in a tree with one of your spirits instead of bothering the normal people?'

'As it happens I am not a Druid, but I have a lot of sympathy for their ways.' The man had got very defensive.

'I bet you do. Danced naked round any mulberry bushes recently?'

William sniggered.

Logs looked offended.

'That is a myth. Honestly, there are so many rumours around Druidic ways. Usually made up by people who should know better.'

'So the Normans are chopping down the wrong trees, killing the wrong animals. There's a lot of them out there and when you chop one down a new one grows.'

'And there are many Normans. All of them busy despoiling. If we don't act, who will?'

'No one. I think that's the point. Anyway, what's all this got to do with my mistress and de Turold?'

'We are all chaff in the wind.'

'Speak English.'

'The needs of individuals are nothing compared to the needs

of the Sward.'

'Excellent. In that case you as an individual can go and tell Grosmal you killed his mate. You're so weird he's bound to believe you. My mistress will get off and you can become a bit of the chaff.'

'My duties to the Sward prevent that.'

'I don't think the Sward will miss you. You'd make a bit of extra soil after a few years in the ground.'

'It cannot be.' The man folded his arms with some finality.

'So what is it you actually do?' William asked patiently.

'I'm sorry?'

'This protecting of the Sward? What does it involve?'

'We protect.' The man sounded grand.

'Yes, but how?' William persisted. 'I mean, what is it you do when you get up in the morning to protect things? Where do you go? What do you...', he hesitated as he couldn't think of a better word, 'do?'

'We confuse the Normans.'

'You confuse me,' Eleanor put in.

'I mean we confuse their schemes. Where they go hunting, we scare away the animals. Where they plan to fell the forests, we invoke the spirits.'

'That mulberry bush again.' Eleanor was contemptuous.

'No,' the man insisted, 'we put up symbols and images to enhance the spiritual strength and frighten the Normans away. We carve the face of the Green Man. The Foliate Head is powerful.'

'It is if you're eating the right mushrooms,' Eleanor mumbled.

'You'd be surprised how easily we can worry the average Norman with a few well-placed dolls and masks.'

'So why are you in here?' William asked, 'I mean I'd have thought you'd be out there in the Sward. Looking after it and all. Being in a Norman castle's a bit, well, off, isn't it?'

'We have our missions here as well. This place was not always Norman. It retains a good spirit for the time being. Their developments must be halted though.'

'So set fire to the logs,' Eleanor suggested.

Logs gasped.

'Or at least get my mistress out. That would confuse them and damage their plans.'

'Hardly.'

'She's a Saxon lady. She's part of the spirit, isn't she? If the Normans kill her that'll be more damage to the precious Sward.' Eleanor was getting exasperated.

'It's not the same thing at all.'

The man's mind seemed made up. If Eleanor could pace up and down she would. Unfortunately the ground was made up of uneven logs and any pacing would likely lead to a broken ankle. A thought did occur to her though.

'She wants to marry Grosmal.'

'I have already advised her against that path,' the man nodded sagely, 'and she'll make a rather poor bride if the groom executes her before the ceremony.'

'Not if you let her go and square it with Grosmal. Look,' Eleanor was contemptuous, 'I work for Lady Foella. I'm with her every day. I am the closest thing she has to a confidant, friend and advisor. When times are difficult she discusses issues with me. I give what help I can from my meagre experience and my lowly position. She listens to me.' Eleanor paused for the finale. 'Then she takes absolutely no notice whatsoever and does exactly what she wanted in the first place. Believe me, she's not going to do anything Grosmal says. In fact she's more likely to do the opposite. If she got out and did marry him, that would aid your plans.'

'How?'

'You'd have a Saxon in charge again. She'd exert her influence over Grosmal the way Vikings influence unarmed villagers. 'Course you wouldn't be able to tell her what to do exactly.'

'Why not?'

'No one can. But you could drop hints in her ear, suggest that Grosmal wanted some trees chopped down, for instance. First thing she'd do was say the trees were hers and if he touched them she'd do something horrible to him. She's good at that. Doing horrible things to people.'

The man frowned. To Eleanor it was a good frown. It meant he had something to think about.

'Grosmal is a Norman. He wouldn't change anything,' he argued.

'Pah,' Eleanor dismissed the objection. 'He'd be married to Foella. Have you any idea what that would be like?'

Logs and the man exchanged glances. There was quite a bit of apprehension in them.

The man waved the plan away with a hand. 'We have our own designs for Lord Grosmal.'

'Yes, blame him for de Turold's death somehow.'

The man's eyebrows shot up. 'How do you know that?'

'You told me. In Foella's chamber, remember? You've spent too long with the trees.'

'Ah, yes,' the man relaxed slightly. 'We will arrange it that Grosmal is blamed for de Turold's death and his reputation will be destroyed.'

'Problems,' Eleanor said as if she had a list.

The man sighed with reluctant resignation. William shifted his feet and spotted a log which looked safe enough to sit on. He sat.

'One. I don't think you're capable of influencing one of your logs to lay still. How you think you're going to persuade any of the Normans, let alone King William, that Grosmal is a bad lot is beyond me. He's probably exactly how the King likes him.

Two. If Grosmal is shamed by some massive stroke of luck, who are you going to get in his place? Pardon me, but I don't think King William will say "Gosh, that Grosmal chap was a bit rough, wasn't he? I know, I'll put the Saxons in charge again. Better still, let's give the estate to the Druids. They'll look after it nicely".'

'Three.' Eleanor paused. 'Three is one plus two, there you are.' She folded her arms.

'Very entertaining, young lady. There is still no reason to release Foella. At this point in our plan Grosmal will simply capture her and put her back. Or he'll pick someone else. Once he is shamed, your lady will be released.'

'If she isn't dead by then,' Eleanor snapped. 'Gods of the bushes, I hope you get shot up the arse like de Turold.' She plonked herself down on the log with William and buried her face in her hand.

There was a silence in the log store.

Eleanor was disturbed by muttering. When she looked up Logs and the man were engaged in a heated but whispered conversation.

They noticed Eleanor was watching and the man turned back to face her.

He tried to do nonchalant, but it had a distinctly worried flavour. 'Er, shot up the arse like de Turold?' he asked, as if making conversation in a chapel.

'Yes,' Eleanor said, 'didn't you know?' Her tone climbed a notch to superior. 'Mister clever, mysterious, "I know all that's going on, we have plans". Did you not know how de Turold was killed?'

'The details are not a concern. The fact is sufficient. As long as he's dead the outcome will be the same for Grosmal. Who cares how it happened?'

'Well, you do by the look of it. Yes, de Turold was shot up the arse.'

'By a crossbow,' William added.

This caused more whispered and insistent conversation.

'And, erm, just out of interest, where exactly did it happen?

I mean we know, of course, but I just need to check that you do and are telling the truth.'

'Yeah, right,' said Eleanor with a cartfull of contempt.

'He was killed in the garderobe,' William explained. 'Horrible, it were. I weren't there meself, but I heard from the staff that Lord Grosmal himself found the body. Still sitting on the bog. Stark naked, with an arrow up 'is whatnot.'

This set the man and Logs to a flurry of shouting at one another in heavily controlled whispers.

'Well, thank you for your time,' the man said quickly. 'Logs will show you out. We have some, er, business to discuss.'

'Oh no. We're not going anywhere. There's more to this. What do you know about de Turold and the garderobe?'

Eleanor never got an answer. She hadn't noticed Logs disappear from his place behind the man. He had walked silently round behind them, as if he were part of the floor himself. Then he hit them on the head with some logs.

Caput XXIV
Four-o-clock: Wood II to Castle II

ERMITAGE AND WAT'S discreet emergence from the woods surrounding Castle Grosmal lasted about five seconds. Then all plans of a quiet 'wander off' were slaughtered...

'There they are,' a shout went up from a patrolling guard.

Within moments a large contingent was heading their way.

'Not likely to notice us unless Grosmal himself is patrolling, eh?' Hermitage asked as he prepared to surrender.

Wat was frowning. 'Very odd. I wonder what's happened that they want us this badly?'

'May I speculate that it isn't good?' Hermitage asked.

'Please do,' said Wat as the leading guard came up. He was very big, very ugly and very Norman.

'We've been looking for you everywhere,' the man said. 'Where've you been?'

'Oh, here and there,' Wat said casually, 'you know, out and about.'

'Yeah, well, time to come in now,' the guard said as he drew his sword, not very casually.

'We've been investigating,' Hermitage explained as they walked back across the grass to the castle.

'Dirty buggers,' the guard spat.

'It involves thinking,' Hermitage retorted, rather amazed at the words and tone coming out in his own voice, 'not a requirement for guards, I would surmise.'

Wat nudged Hermitage and gave him a supportive wink. It didn't drive the shame from the young monk.

248

'Disgusting,' the guard muttered.

'So,' Wat said brightly, 'what's going on that you're looking for us?'

'That Ethel bloke said we was to look for the monk. He'd gone missing, apparently,' the guard responded. 'Now we know why, don't we?' he sneered.

'Looking for Hermitage?' Wat was surprised. 'But that was hours ago. I've been imprisoned, rescued, imprisoned again and escaped in the time you've been looking for Hermitage.'

The guard stopped and faced his captors. 'Well, obviously it took us this long to find him as we've only just found him.'

'That's very reasonable,' Hermitage put in, trying to get some charitable thoughts back in his head.

'And it turns out he's been investigating in the woods with some other bloke,' the guard looked Wat in the eye, 'which, as I say, is disgusting. If I wanted to do investigating with another man I'd hide in the woods as well. Now come on.'

Wat gave Hermitage a resigned look and they followed the man back to the castle.

Once inside the gates the guard made them stand against a wall. He instructed one of his men to go and find Ethel and the rest of them to stay and guard the captives.

'And no investigating one another,' he instructed.

'My good man...' Hermitage was ready to embark on a comprehensive explanation of investigation covering etymology, grammar, declension of the original Latin verb and a number of observations of his own on custom and practice, drawn from his recent experience.

The guard walked off.

'Well, really,' Hermitage commented.

'It's all right,' said Wat. 'It was me who asked Ethel to find you in the first place – when you went missing from the garderobe.'

'Ah, I see. Yes, Scarlan and his band captured me and wanted to ransom me to Lord Grosmal.'

'Yes about that,' Wat insisted. 'I thought you'd joined their band.'

'Oh, good heavens, no. A rough lot. It was only when I explained that Grosmal would probably pay for the entertainment of watching my execution and that I knew you they changed their mind.'

'Hermitage,' Wat whispered fiercely, 'it would have been helpful to know all this.'

'Really?' Hermitage ran this over his head. Making connections between events as they happened had always been tricky. Getting them written down and having a few weeks to consider the documentation was much more straightforward.

'Yes, really. If I'd known you were under duress we could have got rid of them before they carted us off into the woods for some light tying up.'

'Ah,' Hermitage nodded with new understanding. 'Yes, I can see how that would have been useful.'

'Oh good.' Wat drilled the lesson into Hermitage with a harsh glare.

Hermitage filed this new concept away with the others he had accumulated since meeting Wat on the Lincoln road all those months ago. It was turning into quite a collection. He pondered for a moment and concluded that the weaver was probably getting less out of these experiences than he was. There was so much Hermitage could tell him, but the man never seemed interested in the latest theological thinking. Or even developments in domestic monastic rule.

Still, give it time and a few more lengthy conversations. Something must give.

Hermitage's musings were brought to a halt by the arrival of Ethel.

'What the devil are you doing here?' the retainer demanded. For once driven by a bit of tangible passion.

'Oh, you know,' said Wat, 'just passing by. Trying to help here and there. Thrown in a dungeon on the say so of an idiot in a habit.'

'I say,' Hermitage objected.

'Not you, Simon.'

'Oh. Right.'

'I've been abducted by mad woodsmen and tied to a tree. Escaped at peril of our lives, captured by a fresh bunch of guards, marched here against our will,' he stopped and gave Ethel one of his hardest glares, 'the usual.'

The manner, tone and content of the little speech did not go unnoticed. 'We had you in the dungeon,' Ethel hissed back, 'you escaped – what the hell would you come back here for?'

Hermitage thought he detected a hint of jealousy in the retainer's tone. As if he wished he'd escaped. And if he had, he wouldn't have come back.

'Believe it or not, the bunch who got me out of the dungeon are just as deranged as the people on the inside. The problem was they were closer. And please believe me when I say that this is the last place I want to be.'

'Me too,' Hermitage put in, feeling that he ought to say something, and it ought to be supportive of Wat.

'After all,' the weaver went on, 'going back into the dungeon and facing execution for a murder I didn't commit wasn't on my list of things to do today.' He folded his arms and waited for the response.

'Oh, that's all sorted,' Ethel said, relaxing and turning his stare away from Wat. 'Mind you, in Lord Grosmal's eyes breaking out of the dungeon will be pretty serious. Damaging the door is probably worse.'

'What do you mean, sorted?' Hermitage asked.

'We know you didn't do it.'

'Well, thank you.' Wat was put off his offensive stride.

'Oh yes,' Ethel went on, 'Grosmal's got Foella in the cells now. She's been found out.'

'Really?' Hermitage was surprised at this. Even Wat looked put out.

'Apparently.' Ethel sounded surprised as well.

'And what is Lord Grosmal going to do?' Hermitage was worried. The sanction for killing de Turold seemed to be pretty consistent, no matter who was accused at any particular moment.

'What do you think? You're the investigator,' Ethel sneered.

'Oh dear, oh dear,' Hermitage fretted, 'I hate to say this, but I think we need to see Lord Grosmal. I have some more news about his murder, er, the murder,' he corrected himself.

'Voluntarily?' Ethel asked.

Hermitage shrugged and Wat sighed.

✦   ✦   ✦

Ethel led the way once more into Grosmal's presence. He was a little less cautious this time; the noble was in a better mood now there was someone in his dungeon again.

'My lord,' Ethel announced as he entered the room with Hermitage and Wat failing to hide behind his inadequate figure.

'Ah, Ethel,' Grosmal turned from the fire.

His face had reddened as he warmed himself and Hermitage couldn't keep the thought out of his head that the man looked like nothing less than a swede. Perhaps a turnip, but certainly a round root vegetable. One that was cooking nicely.

The image took away some of the fear of meeting this man again. Only some of it.

'What are they doing here?' Grosmal demanded.

'We found them, sire.'

'I can see that. The one who escaped from my dungeon, and broke my door? He should be dead. The monk? God knows what you do with monks.'

'They have news about the murder,' Ethel announced calmly.

Grosmal sighed. 'I've had all the news about the murder I

want. Every time I talk to someone I get more news about the murder. The next person who opens his mouth about the murder will probably tell me it was someone else, and frankly I'm getting bored of the whole business. I've got the woman in the dungeon. Let's say that's that.'

'But she didn't do it, sire,' Hermitage spoke up, despite his trembling.

'The King's Investigator said she did,' Grosmal declared.

'No, I didn't,' Hermitage responded automatically. He glanced sideways and saw that Wat had his head in his hands.

'What?' Grosmal said slowly and with intent. And not the good kind of intent.

'Oh, you mean Brother Simon,' Hermitage made great play of this revelation, 'of course. The King's Investigator. I understand now.'

'Well, I don't,' Grosmal growled. 'Are you saying he isn't the King's Investigator and you are?'

Hermitage's mouth hung open while he waited for some words to fill it up. 'Erm' wasn't a very good word, but it was all that came.

'Ethel,' Grosmal barked, even though the retainer was standing right next to him.

'Yes, sire,' Ethel responded calmly.

'Get the other monk.'

Ethel bowed his non-bow and left.

'Are you the King's Investigator?' Grosmal asked again. 'It's quite a simple question. Yes or no will do the trick.'

'It's not quite that simple, sire,' Hermitage began.

'It was a long time ago,' Wat stepped in to explain, 'at the monastery of De'Ath's Dingle...'

Grosmal held up his hand. 'Are you the King's anything?'

'Well no, not really, although I did do some work for...'

'Then shut up. You've already broken my cell.'

'I can fix that,' Wat offered.

'Me too,' Grosmal said with a more permanent solution in mind. 'Now. Monk. Are you the King's Investigator?'

'No,' Hermitage said with confidence, having had the chance to think it through a bit.

'Then why did you say you were?'

'Because I was. Briefly.'

Grosmal stepped closer to Hermitage. 'Let me tell you, monk, I have a large collection of tools in my dungeon which I use for asking people questions. They always answer. I haven't had a chance to use my tools for a long while. Shall we go and see if my Tongue Waggler still works, or are you going to explain now?'

Hermitage gulped. 'I'll explain now please.'

'Oh dear. Well, give it your best shot and we'll see.' Grosmal sat back on his bench by the fire and folded his arms.

'I *was* King's Investigator,' Hermitage said, 'but the King is William now and he didn't appoint me, so I can't be.'

'Nice answer,' Grosmal nodded.

'But I was appointed by King, er, by the previous occupant of the, er, job?'

'And the other monk?'

'Well, he was appointed too.'

'So you're both King's Investigators. Ex-King, that is?'

Hermitage knew that a simple 'yes' would suffice here. It would bring things to a speedy halt and stop any potential unpleasantness. He also knew that his answer wasn't quite the whole truth. That didn't so much rankle with him as render him totally incapable of keeping his mouth shut. If he had a truth inside him, he had to let it out. Wat had criticised him many times for this fundamental failing, but he couldn't help himself.

'Well, yes, and no,' Hermitage had to say.

Wat, who had been smiling, stopped smiling.

'You see, Brother Simon...'

'Who?'

'The other monk.'

'Oh, him. Yes?'

'He was appointed by the Bishop of Lincoln.'

'Ex bishop.'

'Ex bishop, yes. In fact, he wasn't even appointed by the bishop. He was appointed by the bishop's man Nicodemus. There is some question about the authority to make such an appointment, but I haven't had the chance to carry out the necessary researches to determine the truth of the situation. I'd need to get to the archives in Lincoln and consider various volumes of...'

'Yes, yes.' Grosmal shut Hermitage up.

Hermitage looked at Wat, who was nodding encouragement. Wat never encouraged him to talk about such matters.

'And then King, er, the ex, previous King appointed me directly. But, as I say, he's gone now. Perhaps King William has his own Investigator?' Hermitage finished.

'I doubt it,' Grosmal sighed. 'In fact, I hope not if they're anything like the two I've met so far.'

Hermitage shrugged apology for his own nature.

'Back to the question in hand,' Grosmal said, having clearly lost all motivation to ask Hermitage any questions using his tools. Or even having any more discussion with him at all.

'You say the lady in the dungeon didn't do it?' Grosmal asked the question, but it was clear from his tone he didn't really want an answer.

'That's right, sire.'

'And how do you know this?'

Hermitage was about to answer immediately when he realised he would be betraying a fellow countryman to the Norman. Could he really do that? Granted it would save a lady from a horrible fate. And a Saxon lady at that, so the betrayal would really be an even outcome. As far as Saxons being executed was concerned.

But if the lady thought she was doomed anyway, was it fair

to doom someone who thought they were safe in order to un-doom someone who already thought they were doomed?

It was a fascinating question.

'Well?' Lord Grosmal was bored with Hermitage's fascination.

New thoughts came to Hermitage. He would be betraying the person who had shot at him. Twice. He would be telling Lord Grosmal that a man killed de Turold when that man was boasting about it to everyone. Surely it was only a matter of time before word got to Grosmal anyway? Hermitage would only be shortening that time.

These justifications gave his some comfort. A more shameful comfort came from the thought he'd be sending a man to his doom who jolly well deserved it. He drew breath.

'Because the person who did it confessed to me,' he announced.

'Are you supposed to tell what people confess to you?' Grosmal looked rather worried.

'Oh, not that sort of confession,' Hermitage explained, wondering briefly what sorts of things Grosmal had confessed to priests that he wouldn't want repeated. He wondered as briefly as he could as he was sure they would all be pretty horrible.

'So?' Grosmal demanded.

'I don't know his name, but he is a small guard.'

'What?' Grosmal leapt to his feet.

Hermitage leapt back.

'A small guard, you say?' He looked at Wat. 'You saw him too?'

'Oh yes,' the weaver said.

'So he's real?'

Wat and Hermitage exchanged looks at this. Looks that said so many things about Normans and this Norman in particular.

'Oh yes, sire,' Wat said in that assuring voice used to tell children there is no bogeyman. Just before you scare them awake in the middle of the night pretending to be the bogeyman.

Ethel appeared at the doorway of the room with Simon in tow. Literally, as Ethel had hold of the monk's belt and was virtually dragging him along.

'Ethel,' Grosmal called enthusiastically.

'Sire?' The retainer responded without any enthusiasm at all.

'That woman.'

'Which one, sire?'

'The one in the dungeon?'

'Ah, Lady Foella, yes, sire.'

'She was telling the truth. There *is* a small guard.' Grosmal seemed surprised and delighted.

'How disappointing for you, sire.'

'Where is this man?' Grosmal asked Hermitage.

Oh well, in for a penny, thought Hermitage.

'He's hiding out in the woods to the north.' Hermitage felt he retained some honour by not mentioning Scarlan and the rest of the band.

'Not with that idiot Scarlan and his stinking men?' Grosmal almost laughed.

'You know mister Scarlan?' Hermitage was shocked.

'Of course. You don't think a band of so-called Saxon fighters could hang about in my woods without me knowing?'

'How come they're still there then?' Wat asked.

'Because they're useless. They couldn't do damage to a dandelion head. They entertain me. I kill one of them every now and then to keep my hand in, let them plan an attack and give my men some practice, that sort of thing. Not that it's much practice fighting that lot.'

'Ethel,' Grosmal gave orders.

'Sire?'

'Send a detachment of guards to bring Scarlan's bunch in. Needn't be a big detachment. In fact, send them without any weapons. Be good for them. Then release Foella and bring her here.'

'Sire,' Ethel nodded and left, pushing Simon into the room as he went.

'Ah, Brother erm.' Grosmal spoke to Simon, but looked at Hermitage.

'Simon,' Hermitage prompted.

'Yes, Brother Simon.' Grosmal's words came out like a snake selling apples to a lady in a garden. 'A brace of monks, eh? Walk with me, both of you. This one,' he gestured at Hermitage, 'seems to have pertinent information concerning the death of my good friend de Turold. I would have him explain this to me. You,' he looked at Simon, 'you've got some explaining to do as well.'

He led them both from the hall with an arm around their shoulders. Neither of them felt comforted. They weren't meant to. Grosmal was wondering if this was the opportunity he'd been waiting for. His Bending Iron hadn't had an outing in several months, and it was always his favourite. He just hoped it had been cleaned up after the last time.

Caput XXV

Four-thirty: Castle Takes Wood

CARLAN AND HIS MEN, AND BOY, were recovering from their expedition. Well, Sigurd was recovering. The rest were gathered in Scarlan's tent, sitting on the floor reminiscing about the fantastic job they had done.

The small man retold how he shot deliberately wide to drive Hermitage and Wat into the hands of Sigurd.

Cotard reported that his waiting out of sight behind some trees ensured the two fugitives had no escape route.

Scarlan bathed in his strategic brilliance, which ensured their enemies had once more been defeated. This time by a devious scheme to throw them into the hands of the hated Normans.

'Our enemies' enemy is another enemy,' he explained.

Durniss nodded at this profound thought.

Sigurd son of Sigurd wanted his father to get up and play axes.

Sigurd the father wasn't going anywhere for a while. He had made it back to the camp, being sick against most of the trees on the way. As they were walking through a forest, this was quite a lot of being sick. Once in his tent he had collapsed and fallen asleep.

'Why don't we fetch a physick?' Durniss suggested.

They all looked at one another and shook heads.

'We're lonely fighters against the evil invader,' Scarlan explained. 'We don't have a physick.'

'Monks usually know a bit about healing and the like,' said Cotard. 'We could get the, erm, oh...' He ground to a halt as he remembered they had just delivered their only monk to the

Normans. 'I'm sure Sigurd'll get better,' he concluded.

'You don't suppose the monk and Wat will give away our location?' Cotard added after a moment's thought. There was worry in his voice, and he looked like he was ready to start packing.

'Probably,' Scarlan replied, 'not that they'll want to, of course, but Grosmal will get it out of them.'

'He will that,' the small man said. 'You should see some of the stuff he's got in his dungeon. He could get a quack out of a chicken.'

'We'd better move.' Cotard stood, ready to leave at a moment's notice.

'Oh, sit down,' Scarlan was relaxed. 'It'll be hours before they've got any useful information. Then it'll be dark. Then they'll have to actually find us. We'll move at dawn.'

'I could go on ahead?' Cotard offered.

'For goodness sake, Cotard,' Scarlan was losing some patience, 'our camp is completely secret. The monk and Wat will have to think hard about the directions, and the Normans haven't got the first idea where we are.'

◆　　◆　　◆

In the castle of Robert Grosmal, a map showing the exact location of Scarlan's camp was being studied by a large contingent of Normans.

The head guard was actually a Saxon called Carac, who had been in William's service since he was a child. Any parent selling their child to Duke William would have known he wasn't coming back.

Carac went over the map in detail and described the landscape, as he'd been there several times himself.

It was quite a large gathering as volunteers had rushed to the task once it had been announced. When their lord's instruction to go unarmed was revealed, even more turned up.

'Are we finally going to finish them off?'

'Got to bring them back alive, boys,' Carac responded, fierce with instruction.

Moans and boos rustled round the group, and one or two slipped out of the room as they lost interest.

'Lord Robert will want to do something horrible to them here.'

That brought a few of them back.

As they got ready to go they filed past Carac, handing over weapons. Well, explicit weapons. There was a lively debate about what 'unarmed' actually meant. Several of the more intelligent argued that if something was permanently attached to them it didn't count as arms. You couldn't surrender your arms if it was impossible to let go of them.

Knuckle guards, sharpened elbow pads and gloves with large spikes sticking out of them all passed muster. One man who had simply tied a sword to his leg was made to put it back.

Crossing the open land between castle and woods, the expedition to conquer the camp of Scarlan was more like an outing. Guards exchanged victuals and even passed a wineskin round. They chatted with one another and discussed plans.

This one was going to grab Scarlan from behind and accidentally kick him hard in the groin.

Another was going after the big fellow, Durniss, and would bring him down with a special move he'd been practicing on some cattle.

The prize was going to be Cotard. Bets were laid on which of them would be fast enough to catch the man after he got wind of them and ran away.

There was more general respect for Sigurd. He was a real fighter, if a rather old and decrepit one. They would give him his due. Knock him out early and tie him up.

◆ ◆ ◆

Entering the wood, their leader took the troop on a bee line for the camp. Once the smell of wood smoke from the poorly hidden campfire reached his nostrils, he crouched down.

His men did likewise and he signalled they should spread out left and right. He held a hand over his mouth, instructing silence, and scanned the landscape. The late afternoon smudged the shadows, and the grizzled old war horse shook his head at the complete absence of camp guards, look outs or even trip-twines to alert those inside that they were about to fall. He scratched his head, probably wondering what he could do to make this a bit more difficult. Strolling into the camp and accepting the surrender wasn't much of a test for desperate men.

He gestured for his right hand man to join him.

'Alard, we need a captive,' he said.

The man Alard looked at him. It was the look of an experienced man being told to do something comprehensively unnecessary.

'No, we don't.'

Carac sighed. 'Look, if we just wander in there and take the camp, the men are going to be a bit restless, aren't they? No fight, no damage, no blood? You know what happened last time they got a bit restless?'

The look on Alard's face said he remembered very well indeed.

'Lord Robert wasn't happy, was he?'

Alard shivered slightly. 'No.'

'Right. So we need some action. Get into the camp and catch one of 'em. A bit of underhand deception and cheating should give the men something to drink about tonight.'

'Why don't we just storm the place and let them get it out of their systems?'

Carac gave Alard a look now.

'Ah,' he replied, 'bring them back alive. I remember.'

'Go on, then.' Alard's superior nodded towards the camp.

Raising his eyes and shaking his head at this ridiculous situation, Alard stood up and walked off to the camp.

'Sneak,' Carac hissed.

Alard stared at the man, his eyes registering the debt he was now owed.

With very little commitment Alard crouched down a bit and clumped off through the undergrowth.

There was some muttering from the line of men strung out in the woods. Carac smiled that they'd got something to talk about.

◆　　◆　　◆

Less than five minutes later Alard was back. Cotard hung, whimpering, in his grasp.

'That didn't take long,' Carac said, with some suspicion that his man had been cheating at the cheating.

'Found him sneaking out of the camp,' Alard shrugged and threw Cotard to the ground.

'I wasn't sneaking,' the prostrate figure responded. 'I was on a reconnoitre.'

'A reconnoitre?' Carac's disbelief was explicit.

'Yeah.'

'Cotard, you couldn't reconnoitre your own bum. I doubt you even know what a reconnoitre is.'

'I do. I was determining the enemies' disposition.'

'You just copied that off Scarlan.'

'I never.'

'He may know what it means, but he's never done one. Bit too close to the action for him.'

Alard snorted.

'How do you know who I am, anyway?' Cotard asked as realisation of his situation penetrated his self-preservation.

Carac and Alard both snorted at this. 'Cotard, we know all about all of you. You're the most useless bunch of dung sorters we've ever come across. Did you really think you've kept yourselves secret?'

'A traitor in our midst,' Cotard wailed.

'No, we just look out the window and there you are. Sneaking about in the woods, lighting fires, putting on stupid disguises and wandering into the castle thinking you haven't been spotted. It's no wonder we conquered the country with people like you looking after it.'

'Now, look here.' Cotard rose to a seated position and took some umbrage.

'Shut up,' Carac snapped.

Cotard shut up.

'We've got a mission for you.'

'I won't do it.' Cotard was outraged.

'Yes, you will.' Carac wasn't opening a debate. 'Alard, get a helm and shirt.'

Alard smiled as he twigged the plan. He went off into the wood to get the items.

'What are you going to do to me?' Cotard wailed, looking nervously to and fro.

'It's not what we're going to do to you. It's what your own side is going to do to you,' Carac grinned.

Alard returned with a helmet and chain shirt in his hands. He was followed by the owner of the helmet and shirt who was protesting in a stream of Norman French and, with flamboyant gestures, arguing that one of his colleagues was much better placed to surrender his clothing.

'Put them on.' Carac took the items and threw them at Cotard's feet.

The man clearly thought of saying 'I won't' again, but he looked at three large and professional Normans standing over him, one of whom looked very angry at being without helmet and shirt. He put them on.

Even from the inside he looked ridiculous. The Normans had a hearty laugh and Carac showed Cotard up and down the line of men. Laughter giggled from the trees.

'Right, off you go,' he gestured back towards the camp.

'What?' Cotard didn't understand.

'Off to the camp. Go on.'

'But...'

'But quickly.'

'They'll think I'm a Norman.'

'That's right.'

'They'll kill me.'

'I doubt it. Don't think they're capable,' Carac said in disappointment.

'Lord Grosmal said we had to bring you back alive,' Alard explained. 'He didn't say anything about you killing one another.'

'This is,' Cotard tried to think of the word, 'horrible,' he said.

'I hope so,' Carac responded with a hefty kick to Cotard's backside.

◆　　◆　　◆

There was a gentle but audible slow handclap from the hidden Normans as Cotard made his wary way across the clearing. The way to Scarlan's tent was direct, but Cotard's route started to slowly drift.

'And if you try to run off,' Carac's words drifted across the field, 'we will shoot you in the leg.'

Cotard paused.

'It won't kill you, but it will bloody well hurt,' more laughter from the forest. 'Give it a few days to fester. Then it'll kill you. If Lord Robert doesn't finish you off first.'

Cotard resumed his course towards the tent.

When he was within twenty feet or so, he coughed as loudly as he could. He tried to direct the noise to the tent and hoped the Normans couldn't hear. They'd probably shoot him for coughing.

There was no response from the tent so he coughed again.

This time the murmur of conversation within the tent stopped.

'What is it, Cotard?' Scarlan called. 'We thought you'd run off.' This time the laughter was from the Saxon side.

'We have a problem,' Cotard hissed as loudly as he dare.

'Well, of course we do,' Scarlan responded. 'The Norman invader has taken our lands and our liberty. The usurper has taken our throne and our rights and…'

'No, I mean a real live problem. A here and now problem. In fact an "out here" and "about now" problem.'

His walk to the tent had continued and he was now just a couple of steps from the entrance.

The flap was thrown back and Scarlan stuck his head out.

'Normans!' he yelled as he ducked back into the tent. There was much noise and bulging of the tent sides as the people inside scrabbled around with one another.

Eventually the flap opened again and the small man stood there with his crossbow. 'Just point me at 'em,' he yelled.

'I don't have to point; he's right there,' Scarlan called from the safety of the tent.

'It's not Normans, it's me,' Cotard called.

His call was too late. The anger and hatred in the small man's eyes, coupled with the dangerous weapon in his hands, sent a crossbow bolt screaming into the air.

Cotard felt it fly by his ear and he ducked, far too late to be of any help had the shot been on target.

The bolt headed off for the wood.

'Arrgh,' came back from the wood as a Norman who had just had his helmet and shirt taken off him stopped the bolt with his chest.

'The bastards have shot Le Prevost,' the cry went up.

'Get 'em, lads,' Carac called, aware that he wouldn't be able to contain their enthusiasm any longer. The entire Norman force leapt from its hiding place and headed for Cotard, the small man with the crossbow being hidden from sight.

'Oh, bloody hell,' the small man said as he dropped the crossbow and headed off across the camp ground, making for the opposite woods.

'What the hell is going on?' Scarlan demanded as he stuck his head out of the tent flap and around the bulk of Durniss, who he had made go first.

He caught sight of Cotard once more.

'All right, we surrender,' he said, as he glanced from Cotard to the advancing horde.

'It's me,' Cotard said, removing his helm.

'Cotard?' Scarlan was stunned.

'Yes.'

Scarlan drew himself up to his full height and emerged from Durniss's shadow. 'You traitor,' he spat, 'no wonder they found us.'

'I'm not a traitor. They dressed me up like this.'

'Why would they do that?'

'It's a trap.'

'I can see that.' Scarlan waved an arm to indicate the thirty-odd Normans, who were now very close.

'I don't think they're very happy,' Cotard helpfully observed.

'You don't say.' Scarlan folded his arms and waited for death.

'Alive, remember,' Carac's voice called out, 'Lord Robert wants them alive. Any man who kills one of them will be spending the rest of his short life helping his lordship test the equipment in number four.'

The charge faltered to an amble as the Normans took the threat seriously.

'Where's Sigurd?' Carac demanded as he reached the tent. Here were the trembling Cotard, the resigned Scarlan and the puzzled Durniss.

'He's not well,' Scarlan reported. 'He got injured in a fight with some outlaws.'

'What? Real ones?'

The conversation was interrupted by a very large Norman appearing out of the gloom behind the tent. He was carrying something under his arm.

'Let me go, you bastard,' the something under the arm cried out. 'I'll cut your bloody head off.'

The large Norman deposited the small man at Carac's foot.

'All safely gathered in then,' he observed as he peered into the tent and saw the slumbering figure of Sigurd, guarded by the son of Sigurd with his wooden sword.

Carac looked back at his men with puzzlement.

'What are you all doing?'

Alard spoke. 'We aren't supposed to kill them,' he shrugged.

Carac nodded in recognition. 'I said I didn't want them dead. I didn't say they couldn't be a bit damaged.'

Alard smiled and the group advanced, spiked gloves at the ready.

Caput XXVI

Five-o-clock: Bed to Dungeon

LEANOR AND WILLIAM woke up in bed. Foella's bed.

After a bit of groaning and moaning as their heads relayed events from the log store, they opened their eyes.

Eleanor was the first to risk a blink or two and she quickly took in their surroundings and their situation.

'Ahh,' she squealed and sat upright, clutching the bed cover to her neck.

'What, what?' William came fully to his senses. He too looked around, saw where he was, grinned, and rested back on the pillow.

'We're in bed,' Eleanor wailed in anguish.

'Yeah,' said William, with a good deal of something that certainly wasn't anguish in his voice.

'This is awful,' Eleanor went on. 'In bed?'

'We must've been put here after the logs business. Nice of 'em.'

'We can't be in bed,' Eleanor said, although she made no attempt to stop being in bed. She seemed frozen in place. The bed cover was clutched even tighter to her neck, protecting her from the outside world.

'Oh, I don't know. I can think of worse places to be.'

'Don't be disgusting.'

'What now?' William was puzzled.

'We can't be in bed, it's not decent.' Eleanor was sincere in her horror at the situation.

'Decent?' This took William back a bit. 'We've done a good

number of things that aren't decent. Bed's the normal place for most of 'em.'

Eleanor risked a peek under the bed clothes. 'At least we're dressed.'

'Soon put that right.' William tried to give her a nudge, but the bulk of bedding got in his way.

'You're filthy,' she accused.

'I'm filthy?' William was aggrieved at this accusation. 'What about you at the top of the tower in the rain? That was filthy.'

'But this is bed. You don't do bed 'til you're married.'

'What?' William really was stunned. 'You've done everything there is to be done when you're married. And you ain't married. What difference does it make doing it in a bed?'

Eleanor wasn't listening. 'I've been in bed with a man,' she howled, and her wails got louder. William looked anxiously to the door, expecting someone to come in and see what the noise was about.

He sat up. He couldn't get a comforting arm around Eleanor as she was hunched up tight.

'It don't count for nothing,' he said, trying to be encouraging.

'I'm not pure any more,' Eleanor cried through her sobs.

William had a response to that comment on his tongue, but thought better of it.

'No one needs to find out,' he said instead.

Eleanor swallowed a sob.

'I mean who knows, only you and me?'

Eleanor seemed to take some comfort from this.

William thought for a moment. 'And the man who put us here, of course. And his chief.'

Eleanor set to howling again.

'But they won't tell.'

She took breath.

'I won't tell, and you won't tell, obviously. And they won't tell 'cos they put us here against our will.'

'Really?' Eleanor blubbered slightly.

'Oh yeah,' said William full of confidence. 'Go very bad for them if they was found out. It's all right knocking people on the head. You have to do that sometimes. Putting them in bed, though? That's not on.'

'Do you think so?'

"Course I do. And, like I said, we was put here against our will. No one could hold it against you. You was dumped here. Not like you climbed in.'

'I suppose,' Eleanor sniffed. 'And you really won't tell?'

"Course I won't.' He patted the part of the bed where he thought her knees might be. 'Anyway, if the worst comes to the worst...' he left the sentence unfinished.

'What?'

He swallowed. 'I could always marry you.'

Eleanor stopped all her sobs and looked across at William. He was smiling encouragement and comfort, and there was a light of hope dancing in his eyes.

She patted the covers where she thought his knees might be. 'Ha, ha,' she laughed, 'very kind. Except, of course, I could never marry you now,' she gestured to the bed, 'not after this.'

She threw back the covers and sprang from the bed.

William controlled his sob.

Eleanor walked across the floor and very carefully opened the door to peek out.

'Come on,' she hissed at William, beckoning him to join her.

"Right,' William humphed without moving.

'What's the matter with you?'

'Oh, nothing,' he said with big points on it, 'nothing at all, I'm sure.'

Eleanor shook her head in puzzlement.

'Oh, bloody hell.' She closed the door quickly and quietly.

'What?' William was still in bed.

'It's that Ethel. He's in the corridor and it looks like he's coming here.'

This did get William out of bed and he smoothed it over, trying to make it look unused. 'On the floor,' he said.

'Not now,' she snapped at him.

'No, on the floor, like we haven't woken up yet. Like we've been knocked out and dumped here.'

'Oh right.' She got the plan and joined him at the foot of the bed where they lay on the floor, waiting for Ethel.

'Only not in bed obviously,' William whined sarcastically, "cos that would never do.'

'What is your problem?' she demanded in a whisper.

William never got the chance to reply as the latch was lifted, the door opened and Ethel walked in.

He took in the sight before him and let out a light sigh. 'For goodness sake,' he said, 'try to be a bit discreet. I mean, I know you're young and all, but really.'

William did a very good groan-of-pain and slowly raised a hand to the back of his head.

Eleanor saw him and copied his groan.

'What's going on?' Ethel said, in the tone of a man who was not going to be taken in by some charade.

'Oh, sir,' William said, dragging himself to his knees, 'we've been attacked.'

'By one another, it would seem.' Ethel folded his arms.

'Oh no, sir. In the log store, it was. Look.' He gestured to the back of his head where he hoped there was a large wound.

Ethel came closer and looked.

Eleanor was moving now. Helpfully she pointed to the back of her head as well.

'The log store, you say?' There was still disbelief in Ethel's voice, but it was wavering.

'Yes, sir. They said they was the Brotherhood of the Sward.'

'Sword?'

'No, Sward. Definitely Sward. They was going on about the trees and the land and stuff, and how the Normans was spoiling it all.'

This gave Ethel some pause for thought. He was all seriousness now. 'And who exactly were these people?'

'There were two of them.' Eleanor had got to her feet now and was swaying quite convincingly. 'A little odd one who looked like one of his own logs, and a big fellow, well dressed.'

'And why did they leave you here and not in the log store?'

'Don't know, sir,' William replied. 'There's a passage from the Lady Foella's wardrobe down to the log store. They must have brought us back up it.'

'And why did you go down it in the first place?'

'The big man,' Eleanor explained with some reluctance. 'He came to my lady's chamber and told her not to marry Lord Grosmal.'

'A commendable suggestion,' Ethel observed.

'So I thought he might be able to get her out of the dungeon.'

'I'm on my way to do that now. It seems she didn't kill de Turold.'

'Oh, what a blessed relief,' Eleanor sighed. 'See,' she said to William, 'I told you she never did it.'

'No, you didn't,' William said honestly.

'I said she could never have done anything like that,' Eleanor went on.

'No, you didn't,' William was a bit more animated now, 'in fact you said it was perfectly possible...'

'Do you know what?' Ethel interrupted in a quiet voice that made them stop and listen.

'What?' Eleanor asked.

'I don't care. I don't care what you said or what you thought. Or even who you are. The fact is Lord Grosmal has instructed Lady Foella to be released and I have come to get a coat for her.

She's been locked in the dungeon for some time and was in a fragile state when I left her.'

'I'm her maid, Eleanor. I'll fetch her winter wrap, that'll keep the chill out.'

'Not the sort of chill she's had,' Ethel snorted, 'but it'll have to do. Bring it along.'

Eleanor went to fetch the coat from the wardrobe, picking it out very cautiously in case there was anyone in there.

'And your excuse?' Ethel asked William.

'Oh, er, yes, erm…'

'I thought so,' Ethel turned to the door. 'You'd better come as well. Lady Foella can be excitable, and if she is, she can do it to you.'

'Thank you, sir,' said William, not entirely sure what he was being grateful for.

Eleanor emerged with the coat, and the three of them hurried from the room.

◆　　◆　　◆

Through winding ways and tortuous tracks the band made its way to the dungeons. William led the way, and knew some shortcuts Ethel wasn't aware of, but he took careful note. Bypassing the courtyard completely, which Ethel swore wasn't possible, they popped out of a wall near the steps down to the cells.

They could already hear Foella.

Cries of rage and wails of despair alternated so quickly that the Saxon lady had invented a whole new way of expressing two contrasting emotions at the same time. It sounded like it was doing her mind no good at all.

'Oh, lord,' Eleanor winced. 'I've never heard her make noises like that before.'

'I don't think I've heard anything make noises like that before.' Ethel looked worried. 'Guard. You can go first.'

'Thanks,' William grumbled.

'You're very impudent for a guard.' Ethel's voice was sharp now, ready to stab something.

'Don't mind him, sir,' Eleanor stepped in. 'He's in a funny mood. Has been since he was hit on the head. I think it might have affected him.'

'I can affect him some more if he doesn't do what he's told.'

'Oh, he will, sir.' Eleanor pushed William in the back.

'Oh yes, William, do as you're told,' William mumbled so that only Eleanor could hear. 'Do this, William, do that William. Never mind what William wants.'

Eleanor made the madman sign to Ethel and raised her eyebrows.

William stepped cautiously down the steps, into the full force of the howling wail.

'She's in number four,' Ethel called out from the top of the steps where he and Eleanor had stopped.

'With all that stuff?' William questioned. 'Was that wise?'

'Funnily enough…' Ethel paused for William's response.

'Funnily enough what?'

'I don't care again. Just open the door and get her out.'

The mumbles of William were not nearly enough to drown out the screams of Foella, but they added a bass note which gave the whole cacophony a life of its own.

'My lady?' William called through the locked and barred door. 'Lady Foella?'

The screaming stopped. William hoped. The door resounded to an almighty crash from inside.

'Bloody hell, she's strong,' William called out as he leapt back.

'Yeah,' Eleanor called down. 'Make sure there's nothing heavy she can throw.'

'In there?' William's voice rose. 'Do you know what's in there? There are things in there what are built for throwing at people. And doing them damage. How am I supposed to get her out?'

'Quickly,' Ethel instructed.

'My lady,' William spoke to the door. 'I've got Eleanor here, your maid.'

'Don't you bring me into this,' Eleanor called down.

William ignored her. 'She wants you to come out. It's all right now. Everything's been sorted. We know you didn't kill mister de Turold.'

Words emerged from the cell. They were clearly words, William recognised them as words. They were very bad ones, though, and he didn't want to see the thing that made them.

'Who killed him?' the words growled through the woodwork, probably killing worms as they passed.

'Who killed him?' William called up the steps.

'A small guard,' Ethel called back.

'Really?' William asked. 'Have we got any?'

'No, but apparently...' Ethel stopped himself. 'Never mind the explanation, just tell her.'

'It was a small guard, my lady,' William repeated.

'Ha!' The word alone was almost enough to shake the door again. 'I told them. I told them there was a small guard, but did they believe me? No, they didn't.' Sanity crept its way back into the voice as it went on. And on.

'And now what? Now I've been humiliated, locked in a dungeon without just cause? Now they come up with the small guard. I'm a Saxon, Lady Foella, a noble: my word should be enough, but is it? No, it isn't, it seems. By God, I shall have my retribution for this insult.'

There was a long pause behind the door, so long that William got worried again. 'My lady?' he asked.

The calm voice of the Lady Foella was entirely sound and measured now. William could tell that she was straightening her hair and her dress, preparing to rejoin civilised society. She coughed lightly and in a very ladylike manner. 'So,' she said with some pleasure, 'Grosmal will have to marry me now.'

Caput XXVII
Half past Five: End Game

A S THE LIGHT OF A MOST EVENTFUL DAY finally faded gratefully into the west, the courtyard of the Castle Grosmal became the confluence of those with an interest in the death of Henri de Turold.

From the fields and forest, the group of individuals that had been the band of Scarlan was herded in by laughing Normans.

The band was not a band any more.

They were all injured in one way or another, the only one to escape a direct assault being Sigurd. He was back on his feet, but seemed in no condition to do anything other than put one of them in front of the other. The son of Sigurd still tagged along, but, infected by his father's malaise, the young boy was withdrawn and quiet. Without his father going 'yargh' every now and again, he didn't have a lead to follow.

The robust clip around the ear he got when he told Carac he was going to boil them all in oil might also have curbed his enthusiasm.

The small guard was still struggling and threatening, his threats distributed equally between the Normans and Scarlan. The things he said he was going to do to the Normans were still worse than those waiting for Scarlan, but not by much. He was clearly not impressed by the man's leadership. Nor by his plans, courage, conviction, strength, foresight, honesty, nobility and just plain decency. He expressed his view repeatedly and accompanied each failing with a specific promise of physical retribution.

Scarlan, wincing with every step, could not respond. He was

also clutching himself, having sustained injuries of a very personal nature.

'I've surrendered,' he had said in outrage after the first blow.

'We know that,' his attacker had said, just before the second blow.

Cotard, as usual, was at the back. Due to the death of le Prevost he still had the helmet and shirt; in fact he was trying to melt into the body of the Normans in the hope he would be forgotten.

Durniss, strolling along and looking in fascination at all that was going on around him, seemed unaware of his injuries. Most were superficial, but there were an awful lot of them. The Normans had eventually got bored and tired of trying to bring the big man down. He had followed meekly when they told him what to do.

As the guards meandered their captives through the main gate, Ethel emerged from the dungeon steps.

He was followed by Foella, looking at her most haughty, with Eleanor and William bringing up the rear.

"Allo, Ellie,' called one of the guards in Scarlan's escort.

It was not the innocent "allo Ellie' of a friend or relation. It was an "allo Ellie' full of meaning, much of it crude.

'What does he mean, "'allo Ellie"?' William demanded indignantly.

'I'm sure I don't know,' Eleanor responded, but she gave the caller a little wave.

William grunted.

◆   ◆   ◆

'Where do you want them?' Carac called, seeing Ethel to hand.

'Main hall, I think,' Ethel replied. 'Lord Grosmal was there, bound to want to see them all.'

Carac used this instruction as excuse to move his captives along by kicking them heartily. Even though they were already going in the right direction. Well, he kicked Scarlan and the small man. He took no notice of Sigurd, thought better of kicking Durniss, but did look around for Cotard.

'Get that man out of our clothes and bring him to the front.'

Cotard was relieved of his disguise and bundled in with the others. 'I was only looking after them,' he grumbled.

◆　　◆　　◆

Arriving at the Great Hall, Ethel looked around for his master. He saw the place was empty.

'Bring them all in here and let nobody leave,' he instructed as he went off to find Grosmal.

The guards assumed this instruction meant them as well, so there was quite a bit of pushing and shoving as a huge number of people squeezed into the great hall. The guards outnumbered everyone else about five to one, and caused most of the trouble as they brushed people out of their way.

Foella did her bit as she tried to make sure she got to the fire. As close to where Grosmal would be as possible.

Eleanor and William took up space far from the front and stood quietly. William took hold of Eleanor's hand and tried to hold it conspicuously in front of his colleagues. She snatched it back and moved half a pace away.

'Cow,' said William and folded his arms.

Scarlan's erstwhile band growled at the guards and muttered a bit, but that was the extent of their resistance.

Their leader had to sit down to nurse his injuries as standing made the chafing unbearable. He tried to look haughty from his seat, but it was difficult as he had to keep one hand in his crutch to stop the pain spreading.

Durniss was battered, but seemed not to care. He looked around the place, seemingly in wonder at being indoors.

Cotard limped into the room and forced himself to remain standing. Standing as near to the door as he could, that is.

The walk must have done Sigurd, who had recovered his composure and physical presence, the world of good. With the small man, who had only suffered bruising from being thrown about a bit, kicked and trodden on, sometimes by mistake, he strode across the floor as if taking possession of it.

Sigurd son of Sigurd held his father's hand and made rather half-hearted stabbing motions towards the guards.

They all waited and the time dripped by. Eventually a murmur of conversation started as people realised Grosmal wasn't about to walk in.

'Typical bloody Normans,' the small man's voice piped up from the middle of the room. 'Turn up early for a battle when no one's ready, but can they ever start a meeting on time..?'

There was a pronounced thump from the middle of the room and the small man fell silent.

◆   ◆   ◆

Finally Grosmal's party entered, and the guards did some more pushing and shoving to make room for him.

He was followed by Ethel, as usual. Hermitage and Wat brought up the rear. Brother Simon tailed along, looking with apparent fascination at the structure of the roof.

'I expect you're wondering why I've brought you all here,' Grosmal announced, once seated comfortably in his chair by the fire.

There was a bit of muttering which indicated that yes, they were wondering a bit.

'The monk will explain,' Grosmal said simply.

Simon looked shocked for a moment until Hermitage stuttered, 'oh, er, right, yes,' as he became the centre of attention. He clammed up.

'The death,' Wat hissed at him, 'de Turold? You're going to explain?'

'Ah, yes.' Hermitage got his speech back. 'I am going to explain the death of Henri de Turold,' he announced and stopped again.

The small man stepped forward from Scarlan's group and held up a hand for silence.

There already was silence, so he just looked a bit ridiculous.

Hermitage regarded him with some surprise. 'Oh, ah,' he muttered some more. 'Erm, mister – what is your name actually?' he asked. 'We can't go on calling you the small guard.'

'My name,' said the small man or small guard with great pride, 'is Magnus.'

Hermitage could not control his guffaw.

'Sorry,' he said. 'Magnus?'

'Yes.' Magnus glared at Hermitage. 'You got a problem with that?' He strode right up to Hermitage and glared even harder.

'Not at all,' Hermitage said hastily. 'Did you want to say something?'

'Of course I do. I simply want to say that I killed Henri de Turold.' Magnus pulled himself up to his full height and stuck out his chest.

'Excellent,' Lord Grosmal clapped his hands. 'And you'll say as much to King William?'

'With great pride. And I shall spit on William the Bastard's shoes when I do so.'

There was a muted round of applause from Scarlan's band.

'Even better. The execution will go really well.' Grosmal was clearly relieved at this news.

'He may hang me. He may take an axe to my neck, he may burn me and dance in my ashes, but I shall curse him to my last.'

'Oh, this is really good, this is marvellous.' Grosmal positively glowed with excitement. It was not a pleasant sight. Or smell.

There was a general aura of relief around the room as those who had been in the Norman's firing line sighed. The silence was disturbed as one by one those in the room noticed that Hermitage had his hand up.

Hermitage also had some thoughts in his head. They were new thoughts. They were troubling thoughts. He gave his thoughts some thought, and considered keeping them to himself. He immediately knew this was out of the question, but it would mean contradicting most of the things he had just told Grosmal.

For some reason, looking at the small man made all the information he had fall into place. Different strands, different facts, apparently random and disconnected, suddenly came together into a coherent picture. And he saw the truth.

It was still a pretty despicable picture, but it made sense. It was the only picture that made sense.

But it was the wrong one. Lord Grosmal would not be pleased.

'Ah, my favourite monk,' Grosmal beamed across the room, pointedly ignoring Simon. 'Have you something to add to this great moment?'

'I do, sire,' Hermitage was hesitant. He knew things were going very well. As well as they possibly could. Perhaps not so well for Magnus, but even he seemed happy. Hermitage hated to put a dampener on things, but his thoughts were a real problem. Problems could not be ignored. Not, at least, by Hermitage.

◆　　◆　　◆

'It's about the murder.'

'Yes?' Grosmal was still smiling broadly.

'And who killed Henri de Turold.'

'I've got a sinking feeling about this,' Grosmal muttered to himself. He was not alone.

'I killed Henri de Turold.' Magnus beat his chest and strode round in a little circle, showing his strength to the world.

'No, you didn't,' Hermitage said simply.

'I beg your pardon, mister monk,' said Magnus, highly offended, 'but yes, I bloody well did.'

'No, you didn't, you couldn't have.'

'That's as maybe, but I did.'

Hermitage hated people saying things like that. 'If you admit that you couldn't have done it, you can't then go on to say you did. It doesn't make sense.'

'You don't make sense,' Magnus laughed.

'What?' Hermitage was getting lost.

Most of the audience laughed with Magnus. Wat looked more grim.

'Master monk,' Lord Grosmal said in the voice he used with people who weren't going to disappoint him any more because they'd be dead, 'you told me he did it.'

'I said he confessed, sire.' Hermitage was turning pedantry into a martial art.

'That's good enough, surely?'

'But he confessed to something he couldn't have done.'

'So?' Grosmal clearly couldn't see a problem with this. 'If he wants to confess, let him get on with it.'

'But we could execute the wrong man.'

'I don't follow.' Grosmal was clearly confused.

'If Magnus did not commit the murder...' Hermitage led him slowly.

'Yes?'

'And we execute him...'

'Yes?'

'We'll have killed an innocent man.'

Grosmal paused in thought. 'Nope,' he looked completely lost, 'still don't see why that matters.'

'The real killer would be free.' Hermitage tried coming at it from Grosmal's distorted point of view.

'But we'll have had an execution,' the lord replied, as if this was all that mattered.

'But,' Hermitage began – and stopped. He didn't know where to go. How could you argue with someone who was so fundamentally wrong? In so many ways?

'What do you mean, he couldn't have done it, Hermitage?' Wat asked.

Hermitage found it much easier to talk to Wat. 'Two main reasons. The first is he's a rotten shot.'

'I am not.' All the humour had gone from Magnus.

'Yes, you are,' Hermitage reassured him. 'You had two shots at me when we were escaping from your camp. The first one was difficult, quite a distance, so I wasn't surprised you missed. It was a bit shocking how much you missed by though.'

'You were moving and I had to fire one off quickly,' Magnus defended his marksmanship.

'But then the second time…' Hermitage went on.

The audience perked up again. They seemed to be enjoying the humiliation of the great freedom fighter.

'That was just awful,' Hermitage said sincerely. 'You had a clear shot from about ten feet. You even had time to kneel and take a good sight down the crossbow. All you managed to hit were some leaves.'

The laughter of the room was now at Magnus rather than with him.

'The child put me off,' Magnus sulked.

'Didn't, didn't, *so* didn't,' Sigurd son of Sigurd put in. 'I never did. You're rotten you are, can't shoot.'

Magnus growled at the young Sigurd. His father took hold of him and placed a parental hand over his mouth.

'He missed me as well,' Cotard put in, 'right up close he was. Missed completely. Shot some other bloke.'

'He killed le Prevost,' one of the guards shouted.

'Ha,' Magnus called. 'Magnus Norman killer.' He beat his chest again.

'At least we can hang you for something,' said Grosmal.

'But not for the death of Henri de Turold,' Hermitage said. 'With that record of accuracy in the use of the crossbow, I doubt you could hit a tree if you were sitting in it.' Hermitage didn't intend this as an insult. It was a simple statement of fact.

'Do you mind?' Magnus seemed to have given up on his prowess as an archer.

'So the chances of hitting the backside of de Turold through a small hole, from below, in the dark? As I say, you couldn't have done it.'

'You just stand there, point and shoot,' Magnus explained. 'I might have been a bit lucky, but I got him.' He raised his arms again, but there wasn't much reaction this time.

'Well, that's the other problem. You couldn't have got below him anyway. The hole in the privy is too small for you.'

'I can do some remarkable things,' Magnus boasted.

'He is small, Hermitage,' Wat intervened. 'If anyone could have got in…'

'I grant the fellow is not tall, but he's very fat.'

'Oy,' Magnus bridled. 'Do you mind not talking about me as if I'm not here?'

'Oh, sorry,' Hermitage apologised. 'I was just saying you're very fat.'

'Yes, I heard you.'

'So what's the problem?' Hermitage was confused. Why did people have to be so confusing when they spoke?

'What's my girth got to do with anything?' Magnus rested his hands on either side of his girth. They were quite far apart.

'It's your girth that has to get through the privy hole, not your height. You certainly wouldn't fit sideways.'

'All right, don't go on about it.' Magnus seemed on the verge of giving up. 'Ah,' he came up with something else. 'I didn't say I killed de Turold on the privy, did I? I killed him somewhere else and then put him on the privy. Just to put you off the scent.'

'Interesting expression in these circumstances,' Hermitage observed. 'And why would you want to put me off the scent when you're very proud of the fact you killed him?'

'So I did kill him! You said so!'

'No, you didn't. De Turold was killed on the privy.'

'How do you know?' Magnus sneered.

'Because I know how it was done.'

The crowd in the room seemed to be quite enjoying this. Even though the happy grin had gone from the face of Grosmal. Although that could be because he was having to brush Foella's attention from his breeches quite regularly. He was engrossed by the tale. Even though he probably wasn't following it properly.

'He was shot from below?' Wat asked.

'Oh, yes,' Hermitage nodded, 'absolutely. That much is right. He was shot from below, and it was with a crossbow.'

'So who was down there to pull the trigger?' Wat looked around the room as if expecting someone to make a run for it.

'No one,' said Hermitage.

'Oh,' Wat thought about this for a moment. 'Erm, didn't someone have to do it? Or have they invented a crossbow that can pull its own trigger?'

Someone in the audience snorted at a Norman euphemism.

'Oh, someone pulled the trigger. What I mean is, no one was down in the privy. How could they have got out?'

'Back up through the hole?'

'We've already seen the hole isn't big enough. I don't think even young Sigurd could get through it. And if he did he certainly couldn't heft a crossbow. No one could have come out through the door below, because even burly guards couldn't get that open.'

'The secret passages?' Wat suggested.

'A good suggestion,' Hermitage nodded. Wat smiled.

'But wrong.'

Wat's smile vanished.

'We know there are passages in the castle, but they're all new. Made as a result of Lord Grosmal's building programme.'

Grosmal nodded magnanimously at this acknowledgment of his achievement.

'The old priest's chamber was just that. An old chamber. Part of the original castle, and so there was no passage. Plus if anyone had stood in the lower chamber they would have been covered in filth. Look what happened when the place went bang? There would have been a trail leading from the privy. Or someone would have been noticed because they were covered in muck up to their waist.'

'Hang on a minute.' Magnus rejoined the conversation. 'You're saying no one got into the privy below de Turold?'

'Correct.'

'And that he was shot from below?'

'That's right.' Hermitage was pleased someone was keeping up.

'Ha,' Magnus gave a great laugh. 'You are an idiot, sir monk. Accept the simple fact: I did it.'

'No, you didn't. I thought we'd covered that?' Hermitage shook his head, his hopes dashed. The wretched little man hadn't been paying attention after all.

'So,' Wat's eyes narrowed as he thought very carefully before he asked the next question, 'how was the trigger pulled?'

'That's exactly the right question.' Hermitage beamed at Wat, who beamed back.

'If we could get on?' Lord Grosmal interrupted. 'The King is coming at nightfall and I've got an execution to arrange?'

'Sorry, sire.' Hermitage got back to the topic. 'Wat is right. The first question is, how was the trigger pulled? The second question is, who put it there to be pulled?'

'An answer to anything would be welcome at the moment,' Grosmal growled. He was clearly getting a bit bored and might revert to executing whoever was closest.

'Who pulled the trigger is clear,' Hermitage nodded to himself.

'And that was?' Grosmal snapped.

'Oh, sorry. It was de Turold.'

There was a silence while everyone thought about this.

'He must have had very long arms,' Foella piped up. Everyone stared at her and she glared back.

'The man shot himself in the arse?' Grosmal asked.

Eleanor giggled.

'Not on purpose,' Hermitage explained. 'It was the candle.'

'The candle shot him in the arse?' Grosmal was consumed by confusion.

'The candle was the trigger. I found this in the garderobe chamber when I went in.' Hermitage produced a piece of twine from his habit and held it up for all to see.

To a man, the company shied away from a piece of twine that had been found in a privy.

'And, of course, the pieces of the crossbow were found above.'

'All very entertaining, I'm sure.' Grosmal was getting more and more bored. 'Some string from the privy and bits of a crossbow. I hope this is getting somewhere.'

'It is, sire,' Hermitage said, for once recognising impatience in those who might do him some damage. 'My reasoning goes thus: no one could have entered the lower chamber as the hole was too small. Yet de Turold was shot from below. The pieces of the crossbow were down there, and came up when the place went bang. So, how did a crossbow get down there? Someone put it there.'

'You don't say.'

'I do indeed, sire. Someone leant down through the hole in the privy and lowered the crossbow on the two sturdy ropes. They had cocked the trigger before it went down, and held it in place with the light string here.' Hermitage held the string up again.

'And the candle?'

'We have heard and seen that the candles are very heavy.

The one nearest de Turold was used to hold the string in place. I imagine it had melted low and the wax…'

'It's not actually wax,' Grosmal commented. His face had a shifty look.

'Oh.' Hermitage paused for thought, He didn't like these thoughts, so quickly moved on. 'Well the, er, whatever, had probably stuck the candle to the floor. The string was held under this, and there was a weight on the other end of the string. It was planned that when the candle burned down completely, the string would release the weight. Then the weight would pull the trigger and the bolt would shoot up through the hole. This would frighten people out of using the place again.'

'It certainly stopped de Turold,' Grosmal chortled happily.

'What about the other candle, Hermitage?' Wat asked. 'There was one that was on the floor, one that de Turold brought along and another one.'

Hermitage surprised himself with his picturing-the-scene skill once more. Now that he had explained events to his own satisfaction, all the pieces fell into place. He supposed it was because he knew what he would do if he wanted to shoot a Norman on a privy.

'It was left there so people would see the damage of the crossbow. When the trigger candle expired, it would have released the twine to fire the bolt. It would also have left the garderobe in darkness. No one would have been able to marvel at the audacity.'

'But didn't they think someone would notice a dead body with an arrow up its backside? Sounds pretty audacious to me,' Grosmal put in. But then horses seemed pretty audacious to him. So did the castle's cat, on a bad day.

'I do not believe they expected someone to sit on the garderobe and then set off the crossbow.'

'This is all very fanciful, master monk,' Grosmal sighed as he spoke, 'and it could well be true. Frankly, who cares? The point is, I need to know who did it so I can present them to the King. I already have a little man who wishes he had done it, and that's good enough for me.'

'We did do it,' Scarlan and Magnus spoke up together. The smaller of the two went on, 'I told you already that I did it. So I put the crossbow down the hole, like the monk says. Still killed de Turold, didn't it?'

Hermitage was horrified at such naked untruth. 'No, you didn't,' he insisted. 'You didn't have a clue about any of this. If you had killed him, you'd have said how you did it. Now you're just making it up.'

Magnus didn't have an answer, so he just mumbled to himself. 'Still did it. I wanted to do it, that's what counts. Bloody monks, always twisting things.'

'So who did it?' Grosmal was getting loud and demanding now.

Hermitage had an idea in his head. It was a strong idea and it fitted the facts, but he had no evidence. He could not imagine for one moment expressing a view for which he had no evidence. It would be like trying to speak without your tongue. He got the shivers at the very thought, and was not prepared to sacrifice his lifelong intellectual standards for the sake of satisfying a Norman's curiosity.

One could not speculate. Speculation was the devil's own instrument. Speculation was the key to the gates of hell and would lead the unwary to heresy and damnation.

Grosmal drew his dagger and pointed it nonchalantly at Hermitage.

The monk speculated. 'Well, sire. There's very little evidence for this, but if I were asked to risk a,' he swallowed at the word, 'guess...' The word left a nasty taste in his mouth.

'Yes,' Grosmal responded, 'you are.'

Hermitage sighed. He would have to pray for forgiveness later. 'From what I have seen: the threat to the garderobe itself rather than to a person; the fresh carving of the Green Man on the tree outside the castle; the coincidence of the Brotherhood of the Sword being here...'

'Getting to the point would be good,' Grosmal prompted. He showed which bit of his dagger had the point.

'If I didn't know better, I would say this is the work of the Brotherhood of the Sward,' he said, reluctantly.

'I told you,' Scarlan called out.

'Not Sword, not you lot. I mean S-w-a-r-d,' Hermitage pronounced it carefully. 'I studied their ways. They're trying to protect the country and seem to have a thing about modern developments – laundry rooms, kitchens, garderobes and the like. They think we should all live in the woods.'

'Just like us,' Scarlan insisted. 'It doesn't matter how you pronounce it.'

'It most certainly does.' A new voice boomed out from the back of the room, and the well-dressed man from the wardrobe stepped forward. He was followed by Logs, holding a log.

'Who the hell are you?' Grosmal barked. 'Just how many more strangers are there skulking around my castle?' He glared at the guards, who shuffled uneasily.

The stranger pressed his way into the middle of the room, surveyed his audience and nodded a slight bow to Ethel. Wat noticed this, and sidled over to the stiff stick of a retainer. The new arrival faced Grosmal and, with slightly less of a bow, he spoke. 'I am of the Brotherhood of the Sward and I am the killer of Henri de Turold.'

Magnus grumbled some more.

'Are you really?' Grosmal demanded, wondering if everyone in the room was going to claim the credit given long enough.

'Yes. And I'm terribly sorry.'

'Sorry?'

'It was an accident.'

'Oh, well, that's all right then. If it was an accident... Tell you what: you accidentally killed a Norman so I will deliberately execute you. How's that?'

'Obviously I'd rather you didn't. This other fellow seems rather keen on that option.' The man nodded towards Magnus.

'I've changed my mind,' Magnus retorted.

'Well, that's settled then.' Grosmal said, rubbing his hands together and standing up. 'A small queue of people wanting to have killed de Turold. I'll just pick the one who stood up last. What do you think, monk?'

Hermitage looked around the room. All this reasoning was fine and, well, reasonable. He'd almost enjoyed some of it, and the figuring out of what could and could not have happened. But now? Now it was leading to execution. Someone might die because of his wretched reasoning. Wat was right. If they ever got out of this, they would never speak of it again.

At least it wasn't him being threatened with execution this time, but even so…

He caught the eye of the man in the middle of the room who nodded encouragement that this was all right. It wasn't Hermitage's fault and he shouldn't blame himself.

'If this man is from the Brotherhood of the Sward, it would seem to be the reasonable conclusion,' Hermitage finally mumbled, his head down.

'Excellent,' Grosmal beamed. 'The King will be here at any moment, so we can arrange the execution of, erm. I suppose we'd better know your name?' He raised an eyebrow to the most recent confessed murderer.

The man held himself upright and took on a somewhat haughty stance. 'I am Aethelingus,' he announced. 'Aethelingus of Saxmundham.'

'Is he?' Wat whispered into Ethel's ear, 'not very dead then, after all? Perhaps he had the same commitment that prevented you fighting for your King when you were asked?'

The room was totally silent.

Caput XXVIII
Six-o-clock: King's Gambit

HERE WAS A DISTURBANCE outside the doors of the main hall before they were flung almost off their hinges and some really impressive guards entered.

These had colourful uniforms bearing a coat of arms. They bore shining weapons and wore the very latest in armour. Flowing red capes hung from their shoulders.

'Oh, they're smart,' said Eleanor, turning her back completely on William.

The new arrivals brushed the guards of Grosmal aside like swans taking over a duck pond.

Forming an honour guard, they cleared a passage from the door to the fireside, squeezing the existing occupants of the room even closer together.

Even Grosmal got to his feet. He brushed his clothes with his hands and madly twiddled his fingers.

Foella flicked her hair back and tried to look especially beguiling.

There was a moment of silence before, striding down the middle of the space, came another man in uniform. He had his helmet under his arm and surveyed the room. Satisfied with what he saw, he left again and there was some muttering outside.

A further figure entered, an older man with a bald head. Scars socialised on his unshaven face which glared at everyone, daring them to speak or move. No one did.

He gestured back to the door where two more of the smart guards appeared and stood either side of the door.

'How many of you people are there?' Magnus's voice floated out.

The older man made a gesture to one of the honour guard who disappeared into the crowd to do something to the speaker.

Standing to one side, the man brought himself to attention. 'The King,' he announced.

All the Normans in the room bowed their heads.

Scarlan's men did not.

Magnus would have shouted something abusive if he hadn't had an honour guard's fist in his mouth.

Hermitage and Wat exchanged awkward glances from their position immediately behind the front row of the honour guard.

King William entered the room.

◆　　◆　　◆

Hermitage looked at him and weighed him up. He took account of the man's bearing, his clothing, his manner of walking, the way he entered the room and his reaction to the other people there.

Oh dear, he thought. Oh dear, oh dear. This man looked the sort who took no nonsense. Or rather he would probably take nonsense round the back of his castle, where he would beat it to death.

Even Hermitage could see this was a soldier's soldier. That usually meant he could kill anyone who faced him, and would probably enjoy it.

William had the standard Norman haircut, but on him it just added a horribly violent authority rather than a touch of humour. Hermitage thought that if this man even glimpsed a touch of humour he would grab it and break its fingers.

He exchanged another glance with Wat. From the look on the weaver's face, his assessment of the man was much the same. He had the sort of upside down smile on his face that said, 'oh 'eck, here comes trouble.'

On meeting King Harold, Hermitage had been impressed by the man's natural authority. He had been small, but he commanded the room with presence alone.

King William commanded the room because he bloody well said so.

◆　　◆　　◆

After two paces William stopped. Grosmal scurried forward like a starving rat that has spied bread. He knelt at his King's feet and lowered his head.

'Your Majesty,' he said.

'Yes.' King William acknowledged the title. He looked around the room. 'Rather a large reception party? I sent word that I wanted peace and quiet.'

'There have been events, Majesty,' Grosmal simpered. 'All dealt with now, but I had to take action against a number of Saxons.'

'Action, eh?' William clearly liked the word. He beckoned Grosmal to stand.

'Yes, Majesty.' Grosmal got back to his feet. 'We are to have an execution.' He said this as if announcing presents at a children's party.

'Ah.' William's response suggested that he expected presents, but was rather bored with them always being the same. 'Why?' he asked.

Grosmal took half a step back and lowered his head. 'A shameful murder has been committed, Majesty.'

'Not usually anything shameful about a murder,' William said brightly.

'This was of a Norman of your court, by a Saxon,' Grosmal said. He went on rapidly before William could react. 'However, I have resolved the matter. I have found the culprit and have been keeping him for your justice.'

William was not happy. His lack of happiness radiated from

him, blackening the room as a candle of darkness would blight the sun.

'Who has been killed?' William asked in specially pronounced words. Each one carrying more than its own weight in menace.

Grosmal took another step back, helped himself to a deep breath and let it out. 'Henri de Turold.' He half closed his eyes, waiting for the explosion of rage that could take everyone in the room with it.

'Who?' William said, in a much lighter tone than expected.

'Er, Henri de Turold?' Grosmal repeated. Hope raised a cautious eyebrow in his brain.

William dropped his chin in thought. 'No, can't say I know him.'

'Really?' Grosmal tried not to sound too delighted. Wat and Hermitage exchanged a wary glance.

'De Turold.' William tried the name out, as if putting it in his mouth and chewing on it would help his memory. 'Rings a vague bell.'

'I, erm…' Grosmal hesitated. Should he help or not? 'I, erm, thought he was your favourite fletcher?' The lord of the castle's voice went up to a squeak at the end of the sentence.

'My favourite what?'

'Fletcher? The chaps who put feathers on arrows?'

'I know what a fletcher is, you impudent dog. Why the hell would I have a favourite fletcher?'

'I'm sure I don't know, your Majesty. Maybe he makes specially nice arrows?'

'Good God. There's probably a man who makes the points, a man who makes the shaft and a fletcher. I don't care who any of them are as long as the arrow goes into people and kills them.'

'Aha, yes, quite, your Majesty.'

William puzzled a bit more.

'Who told you he was my favourite fletcher?' There was a

frown on his face as if something was coming back to him.

Grosmal looked to Ethel, who did nothing, probably because he had just noticed a spot of dirt on his boot.

'I, er, I suppose he did,' Grosmal muttered. This was not going so well. Hope closed both eyes and groaned softly.

'Hum,' William rubbed his chin. 'Did this fellow tell you he was a hunting companion of mine as well?'

'As a matter of fact…' Grosmal started.

'Le Pedvin,' William called to the old man of scars who stood by the door. He approached and bowed.

'What was the name of that idiot who went round telling everyone he was a close friend of mine? The one who got people to put him up as a guest, claiming he had my ear so would put in a good word?'

'Ah yes, Majesty.' The old man's voice had scars in it as well. He clicked his fingers as he tried to bring the name to mind.

'He had a month in the house of Langlois. Cost them a fortune until he just disappeared one night.'

'It'll come to me, Majesty.'

The captain of the guard, the one with the helmet under his arm, leant forward from behind. He whispered briefly in the old man's wizened ear.

'Ah yes,' the man spoke up. 'De Turold.'

'De Turold,' William said with relief. 'I knew I'd get it. You've been fooled, Grosmal.'

Grosmal's face and body were in an awful state. It was clear that he wanted to do something. He needed to do something, and if his King had not been there he would have got straight to it. It would have involved shouting, hitting, stabbing and causing the widest variety of pain to anyone within reach.

As his King was there, however, he had to show restraint. And this was killing him.

'Ha, ha,' the King laughed.

'Ha, ha.' Grosmal made the same noise, but it certainly wasn't a laugh. 'At least he's dead now,' he snarled through his chuckles.

'Good job too,' William said. 'Stop him bothering people. If he'd carried on I'd have had to do something about him myself.' A thought occurred to the King. 'You've done me a favour, Grosmal.'

Robert Grosmal beamed at this, all uncontrollable murderous rage forgotten.

'There was another death as well. A Saxon shot one of my guards.'

'Oh well,' the King was still happy, 'these things happen. Let's execute him then.'

◆　　◆　　◆

Through all of this conversation, the audience had been silent. And rapt.

Hermitage was particularly fascinated. As usual. He thought it absolutely fascinating that de Turold turned out to be the bad man. This was a new revelation. The bad man could also be the victim. He would have to remember that if he ever had to deal with anything like this again.

Please God he never had to deal with anything like this again.

He looked at Wat. The weaver's eyes were wide in surprise as well.

All that fuss trying to find out who did it. All the threats. From both sides. Dragged out into the country, being held prisoner, escaping, being shot at. Worse than that, all his careful investigation, his analysis, his piecing together a complex web of facts, and no one cared. At the end of the day it didn't matter. How infuriating.

He didn't hear Magnus piping up, claiming to be the killer of de Turold any more. Probably because he didn't want to be seen doing King William a favour. He'd still be executed for killing the guard, though. That would keep him happy.

Hermitage did reason that Lord Grosmal would not be

pleased at being duped. Might be best to slip away if the opportunity came. Still, it had been a most interesting investigation which all turned out well in the end.

'Anyway,' the King was saying in a happy tone to Grosmal, 'you say you've got de Turold's killer. How did you do that?'

'I had a monk,' Grosmal responded. 'Where is he?' He cast his eyes about the room.

'Oh,' thought Hermitage with some resignation, 'it's all going to end horribly after all.' His stomach gave a familiar twist.

'Here I am, Majesty.' The monk spoke up loudly and stepped through the rank of guards to stand before the King.

'Not you,' Grosmal said to Brother Simon, 'you're an idiot. I meant the other one.'

'Erm, here I am, sire.' Hermitage raised a hand and hoped that he could stay where he was. Grosmal beckoned him to join them. One hope dashed.

Squeezing between guards, who melted away before him, Hermitage made his way to the presence of the King.

'And there was another character with him. Better dressed.' Grosmal cast about the room.

'I am here, sire,' Brother Simon called insistently.

'There.' Grosmal pointed to Wat.

The weaver turned and scanned the crowd, apparently anxious to help Grosmal locate the person he sought.

'Get over here,' Grosmal said simply. Wat reluctantly complied.

'So,' the lord said, once they were gathered, 'explain to the King.'

'Well, sire,' Hermitage began, 'some time ago in the monastery of De'Ath's Dingle…'

'I think Lord Grosmal means about the garderobe,' Wat interrupted. 'Not the full history of the monastic movement in these parts, the development of techniques for the identification of miscreants and accompanying observations on the authority of scripture. Just a thought.'

'Oh.' Hermitage stopped. He paused. He gathered his thoughts. He despatched most of them and worked out what really was the kernel of the matter. It didn't make for a very illuminating version of events, but he supposed Kings like William preferred things short. He didn't look the type to enjoy a good chat. Or appreciate the beauty of carefully crafted argument. Shame.

'In short sire, the Brotherhood of the Sward put a crossbow down the privy. Henri de Turold accidentally set it off and it killed him.'

'Very good,' Wat complimented quietly.

The King was looking with wide eyes. 'You mean he shot himself up the arse?'

'Well, yes, I suppose so.' Hermitage thought this was an unnecessarily crude description of events, even if it was accurate. But Kings were probably like that. This one, anyway.

'Or rather this Brotherhood,' William spat out the word, 'made a Norman shoot himself up the arse?'

'I suppose so, yes.'

The room held its breath and waited.

William's mouth seemed to twitch of its own volition. Thoughts could be seen bobbing in his eyes, which narrowed. Guards prepared themselves for action, ready to cast more death around at his word. Eventually he drew a breath. And burst out laughing.

The room relaxed, and some hardy souls laughed as well.

'Serve him bloody well right.' The King honked. He had a most peculiar style of laughter. It probably only ventured out when horrible things had happened, and so didn't mix with the laughter of ordinary people.

✦   ✦   ✦

When William had recovered, he spoke to Hermitage again.

'And what sort of Brotherhood is this that goes around putting weapons in privies?'

'Erm…' Hermitage began.

'We protect the country,' Aethelingus's voice came from somewhere deep in the crowd.

'No, *we* protect the country,' Magnus objected. There was another thump from his vicinity. He stopped objecting.

'Bring that man out here,' William called. 'I must say Grosmal, this is most entertaining.'

Lord Grosmal beamed a beam wide enough to hold up a whole new castle wing.

'When do we get to the execution?' the King asked.

'As soon as you like, Majesty. Perhaps we could have two?' he offered, as if pressing William to another pear.

Aethelingus now stood before the King. It was getting to be quite a crowd.

Grosmal looked at him and a frown came to his face. 'You look a lot like Ethel,' he said, switching his gaze from one man to the other.

Ethel had cleaned his boot, but he'd now found something interesting at the back of the crowd to examine.

'So, Master Brother of the, what was it, Sword?'

'No, Sward,' Aethelingus said. He sounded rather bored with making this correction.

'What, the greenery and stuff?'

'The spirit and body of the land.'

'Ah,' William recognised the description. 'Druids,' he nodded.

'We are NOT Druids. Why does everyone think we're Druids?'

'If it walks like a Druid and talks like a Druid?' William left the question to answer itself.

Aethelingus just snorted.

'Whatever you are, what are you doing putting crossbows in privies? Dangerous and stupid as far as I can see.'

'We are preventing the evil of the garderobe.'

'I know some of them can be pretty rank, but *evil?*'

'We've calculated,' Aethelingus began.

'You've what?'

Aethelingus was puzzled. 'Erm, sorry?'

'You said you've done something.'

'Yes, we've calculated.'

'What does that mean?'

'Oh, er.' Aethelingus searched for a better word. 'I suppose, added up.'

'Well, why don't you say "added up"? It's a perfectly good expression. Why make up a new one just to show how clever you are? Typical Saxon doggerel.'

Hermitage thought about pointing out that 'calculated' was the original word, coming from the Greek as it did. It was a shame for a King to be ignorant. Then he looked at William and concluded he probably didn't want to know.

Wat nodded another congratulation to him. This time for keeping quiet.

'Oh, right.' Aethelingus was off again. 'We've added up that if the use of the garderobe continues, in three years the entire country will be covered in human waste to a depth of two feet.'

'What rubbish.' This time Hermitage couldn't help himself.

William raised his eyebrows at this interruption.

'He does seem a bit learned, Majesty,' Grosmal explained, as if being learned was deeply shameful.

William nodded that Hermitage could go on.

Hermitage took a moment to take this in. He was actually being encouraged to argue a point. In public. With people watching and everything. People who weren't going to get up and leave. People who weren't allowed to get up and leave. How marvellous.

'How many more people are there in the country now than there used to be?' he asked Aethelingus.

'Many,' Aethelingus replied confidently.

'I hardly think so,' Hermitage responded.

'What about all the Normans?' The Saxon nodded at the King, Grosmal and the guards.

'And what about all the people who aren't here any more as a result of the Normans arriving?'

William and Grosmal exchanged grins at this.

'So?'

'So there isn't suddenly a huge number of people producing waste that wasn't here before.'

'But they're doing it in garderobes.' Aethelingus clearly thought this was enough of a killer argument.

'Instead of doing it straight on to the land. If anything the garderobe is going to reduce the amount of waste on the land. Well, it will do if they're built wrong like this one.'

'I beg your pardon?' Grosmal bristled, but Hermitage was off.

'It's the same amount of waste, just in a different place. You've calculated as if every garderobe was a person. In fact many people will use one garderobe. Your adding up is completely wrong.'

Aethelingus was looking at the ceiling and mumbling numbers. He expressed them by waving his hands around and making chopping motions.

'And for this you shot a Norman up the backside.' William was contemptuous.

'Er,' was all Aethelingus could say. He clearly couldn't get the sums straight in his head any more.

'So,' said William brightly. 'On with the execution bit then.'

Caput XXIX

Half past Six: Capitulation

T A NOD FROM GROSMAL the guards ushered everyone from the room. There was a bit of an argument between Grosmal's own men and those of the King about who was in charge of ushering, but it didn't really make any difference to those being ushered.

After several mis-usherings, which drove people down entirely wrong corridors and into dead ends from which they had to be removed, the King's men gave up and handed over to those who knew the place.

The entire party almost immediately emerged into the courtyard, causing some in the King's troop to speculate they had been deliberately misdirected.

This speculation was quite loud and covered the lineage of Grosmal's men in some detail. These men in turn responded with some very disparaging remarks about the decline in the quality of King's guards the days.

No one confessed to striking the first blow, but Le Pedvin, William's scarred retainer, struck the final one very quickly. As one of Grosmal's men was taken away for burial, the group looked at what the courtyard had become.

'Where did that come from?' Hermitage hissed to Wat as a large gallows imposed itself on their view.

'He probably keeps them made up ready,' Wat replied, grimacing at the structure.

Next to the gallows was a pile of kindling that looked more than ready to kindle someone personally. Next to that was a simple tree trunk, complete with a not so simple executioner's axe embedded firmly in it.

'I thought we'd have a selection.' Grosmal smiled and laughed with William as they strode into the scene and headed for an observation station which consisted of a wooden platform, raised above the mud of the floor.

'Do we have enough for one of each?' William asked.

'I think we might,' Grosmal considered. 'We could hang the one who killed le Prevost. That's a fairly straightforward murder. Then we could burn the one who did for de Turold. I think there's something a bit suspect about protecting the trees. Sounds like witchcraft to me.'

'And the axe?' William asked.

'Oh, I don't know,' Grosmal speculated. 'Perhaps we could chop the head off the useless monk. You know, the other one?'

Brother Simon looked around the crowd for another monk. Then he realised everyone else was looking at him.

'What is this about monks?' the King asked. 'Why does everything here have to involve a monk?'

'Ah that's very interesting, your Majesty.' Grosmal, having embarked on an explanation, rapidly lost his way. 'Monk,' he called to Hermitage, 'explain to his Majesty.'

'Erm?' Hermitage said from the courtyard floor as he looked up at the King and Grosmal. 'Explain about what sire, I mean King, er, Majesty?'

'This King's Investigator business.' Grosmal was brusque.

'Ah.' Hermitage stole a glance towards Brother Simon. The glance was arrested as Simon was nowhere to be seen. Casting his eyes around, Hermitage spotted a habit sidling towards the main gate.

'King's Investigator?' William enquired. 'I never knew I had one.'

'Indeed, sire,' Hermitage humbled himself, 'King – erm, your, erm, predecessor saw fit to appoint me his investigator. Someone who would look into matters of confusion. Murders mostly, it seems.' Hermitage looked inward and gave a resigned shrug at the evil necessity of telling a new King that he could investigate murders for him. 'Although I've only done one,' he hastily added, having an awful presage of where this might be leading. 'And that had a lot of help from other people.' He paused. 'Anyway, that appointment is obviously null and void with your, erm, arrival?'

William regarded Hermitage with a serious eye. He seemed to contemplate this statement carefully and considered his response.

'Well,' he said, 'if Harold had one, I want one.'

'Majesty?'

'This King's Invest-in-mater.'

'Yes, sire?'

'You're it.'

'Oh.' Hermitage's heart sank. So much for welcome obscurity. So much for not saying a word about any of this. He looked to Wat for encouragement.

Wat did not give out encouragement. He gave out desperation and resigned hopelessness. His look said simply, 'Hermitage, did you have to?'

Hermitage shrugged. What were you supposed to do in front of Kings who had just conquered your native land? 'No thank you, sire, I'd rather not' was hardly an option. He simply nodded and slipped back to stand next to Wat, whose expression did not change.

◆　　◆　　◆

'So,' said William with gusto, 'who shall we do first?'

'I always find a hanging starts things off nicely. Perhaps the beheading next and then the fire to warm us for the night,' Grosmal suggested. 'Should we hang the murderer first?' He gestured offhandedly to Magnus.

'As you please.'

'Bring up the little man,' Grosmal commanded.

'Get your hands off me.' Magnus thrust out at those who came to take him to his final opponent.

Before he was delivered to his death, he was presented to the King.

Scarlan, Sigurd and his son looked defiantly on, daring Grosmal to name them as well. Durniss appeared to be admiring the construction of the gallows.

Cotard, on the other hand, was near the gate and on the verge of departure. He seemed to be idly chatting with Brother Simon.

'William,' Magnus called as he was taken, with very little resistance, towards his silent stage.

'Uh, huh?' William was suddenly shy.

'I defy you to my last. I take your sentence of death and cast it in your face. Come here and I will fight you.' Magnus's face lit up with realisation. 'In fact I challenge you to trial by combat.'

'Yargh!' Sigurd yelled from somewhere at the back.

'Don't be foolish, little man,' Grosmal laughed. 'The King will not fight a convicted murderer in combat.'

'I will fight you in combat,' William shouted. The prospect of action had knocked shy off its perch and stamped on it.

'The King will fight you in combat. Magnificent!' Grosmal applauded.

At a gesture from William, one of the guards gave Magnus a sword. He swung it round once and it clashed on to the ground. It was clearly too big for him.

'Where's my sword?' Magnus demanded.

'Where is his sword?' William called.

After much mumbling among the crowd, one of them eventually produced something that looked like a cross between a sword and a dagger.

'I was only looking after it,' the guard who had been holding it whined.

'Present it to the man and clear a space,' William command-ed as he stepped down from the dais. He held out his hand and a uniformed guard slapped the most enormous weapon into his glove.

It was the sort of sword that takes weeks of training just to lift.

The crowd gasped.

William swung the thing round his head a couple of times to loosen his muscles. The action also loosened a lot of the air as it gave a low whoop, getting out of the way of the passing blade.

It was clear that if this thing hit you, you would be dead. It was clear to the crowd that if this thing hit small Magnus the results would be spectacular. They gathered closer.

Magnus looked at the whirling tree trunk of metal death which scythed above him.

'Typical,' he said defiantly, 'bloody Normans.'

He crouched into a fighting stance and held his sword at the ready. The thing looked like a device for scraping the mud off the grip of William's sword. 'Come on then,' he snarled at the Nor-man King.

William looked at the man in front of him and lowered his own sword. He put one shoe forward and rested the point of his weapon on his foot, not wanting to blunt the killing edge on the ground.

Several people grimaced at this and wiggled their toes in sympathy.

From its upright position, William's sword looked down on Magnus. Probably by a good two feet.

The crowd waited for William to bat his opponent across the floor with a simple flick of the wrist.

'Ha ha,' William roared, 'I like you, man. You have guts.'

'I'll have your guts,' Magnus retorted.

William roared again. 'Le Pedvin,' he called, and the scarred old man was at his side immediately.

'Sire?'

'This little chap's a vicious bastard. He has no fear and very little sense. I reckon we could use him.'

'Sire?' Le Pedvin did not seem so sure.

'He could get into all sorts of places unnoticed and then...' William made the ever familiar knife-across-a-throat gesture.

Le Pedvin nodded.

'I'll never work for you, you Bastard,' Magnus spoke through gritted teeth. 'I'll protect England to my last breath.'

'Very right and proper,' William replied. 'But what if I gave you a piece of England of your own? Quite a large piece. You could protect that.'

Magnus was still. Magnus was thinking. Magnus lowered his sword. 'Yes, I could do that,' he said, neatly balancing his morals against the weight of William's argument. Not to mention his sword.

'Magnus,' a plaintive wail came up from Scarlan.

'Traitor,' Sigurd barked.

'Who said that?' William commanded. There was a moment's silence. 'Come on, who said that?'

Guards were bounced aside as the figure of Sigurd strode centre stage. 'I did,' he boomed, quite back to his old self now. He even bashed his own chest again.

'I thought I recognised the voice,' William muttered to himself. 'Sigurd!' he cried with some joy, and stepped forward to embrace Sigurd in a mighty clasp.

'William,' Sigurd replied, with a lot less joy.

'Oh, now come on, Sigurd. What's this "William"? It was always Wills and Uncle Sigurd.'

'Uncle Sigurd?' Scarlan's wail was now disbelieving. 'You're his bloody *uncle*?'

'Not a real one,' Sigurd defended himself. 'His father just knew my father and they sort of, well, got on.'

'I don't believe this,' Scarlan cried out. 'First one gives up for a parcel of land and the next one turns out to be the enemy's bloody family.' He wasn't having a good day.

'Sigurd son of Sigurd, you dog. So you're the enemy, eh?'

'I am.' Sigurd stood his ground.

'Sigurd son of Sigurd?' Wat whispered to Hermitage with a slight snigger. Hermitage thought this was not the time for jollity.

'That means his son is Sigurd son of Sigurd son of Sigurd.' Wat smiled broadly. 'I'll have a guess what his father was called as well.'

'Ah,' William stepped back and looked at Sigurd with a friendly face. 'Always good to have family on the end of your sword. Makes it all a bit more personal. So you're with this bunch, are you?'

'I am. And you've turned out to be a bad lot, William.'

William leant in close, but spoke so that everyone could hear. 'Turned out to be a bad lot, William, your Majesty,' he said, emphasising the final words.

'Humph.' Sigurd acknowledged the title reluctantly.

'I could tell you a few home truths about your precious Harold if you really want to know,' William promised.

'He was the King.'

'Always a loyal family, the Sigurds. Your father, Old Sigurd, would be proud.'

'Told you,' Wat hissed at Hermitage. He had.

'Well, we can't be executing you, can we? Being family and all. Banishment, that's more like it. What about the rest of your band? Don't seem to be much of a threat any more.'

'Never were,' Grosmal laughed.

'Really?' William asked in interest.

'Completely useless, the lot of them.' Grosmal cast his eyes around the courtyard. 'Their leader is a craphead who only knows the way to the back of a battle. Then there's one who usually runs away.' He scanned the crowd, not seeing Cotard. 'In fact guess what, he's run away already. There's a big fellow who doesn't know which end his head is, the little one you've already taken and that leaves Sigurd and his son.'

'Sigurd son of Sigurd, I assume?' William gave Sigurd a knowing look.

Sigurd just nodded.

'You're going to have to stop that some time, you know,' he said kindly.

'Tradition,' the old fighter mumbled.

'Tell you what,' William announced, 'I will not execute this band, who it seems are very little trouble anyway; they certainly didn't kill de Turold. Instead, they shall be exiled.'

There was not much reaction to this. Scarlan was resigned, Sigurd was stoic and Durniss clearly didn't know that what was going on had anything to do with him.

'They clearly nurture loyalty to the usurper Harold, along with a hatred of all things Norman,' William went on. 'So my decision is this.' He left a dramatic pause until he had everyone's attention. 'I banish them – ' another pause for effect – 'to Normandy!'

'Oh, bloody hell,' Scarlan called out in the offended tones of a child punished for something he hasn't done.

Sigurd took out his sword and threw it on the ground in disgust.

The rest of the courtyard had a good laugh, which Durniss joined in with.

He stopped when a number of guards grabbed his arms and escorted the band to the cells to await removal. His smile reappeared as if he had just been offered a guided tour.

✦   ✦   ✦

Grosmal was looking a little crestfallen. No hanging, no axe man. The day was turning out very poorly.

'Well, Majesty,' he said, 'we'd better get on with burning the witch.' Before that goes belly up too, his expression said.

'Ah yes,' said William with enthusiasm, rubbing his hands. 'Bring forward the witch,' he commanded.

Two of his own guards brought Aethelingus to the front and stood holding him firmly, if cautiously. They seemed fearful of becoming infected with witchcraft if they got too close.

'Put him on the fire,' William gestured.

'I say,' Aethelingus protested as the guards dragged him towards the kindling.

At this moment Ethel sidled away from Grosmal and towards the King's ear. He seemed determined to reach the ear quite quickly and slip something important into it.

William noticed him approach. He frowned.

Wat, ever watchful of Ethel and his movements, nudged Hermitage to pay attention.

Ethel leant in close to the King and whispered some short words into his ear.

'What's going on now?' Wat whispered.

'I imagine mister Ethel is pleading for his brother's life,' Hermitage speculated.

'Doesn't look like there's much pleading going on to me.'

William had heard Ethel's words and turned to look at the man. There was surprise on his face and he looked Ethel up and down as if sizing him for a new tunic. Which would certainly be a good plan.

With a wave of the hand, William halted the procession towards the pyre.

'Hello, here we go,' said Wat to himself.

William next gestured to Grosmal, who stepped over. The three men got their heads together in a huddle. There was whispering so quiet it was hard to tell if anything was being said at all. Their bodies suggested some of the whispering was quite fierce.

At one point Grosmal's head emerged from the huddle and

looked at Aethelingus. He then took half a step back and looked at Ethel. He looked backwards and forwards between the two men a couple of times before shrugging and rejoining the discussion.

William next turned to regard Aethelingus, who stood like a rabbit caught in a cart's torchlight.

He went back to Ethel and held his hands out, conveying 'what can I do?' or 'don't blame me, mate' to anyone who saw the gesture.

This time Ethel shrugged and whispered a few more words in William's ear. The other one this time. The approach to the King's organ was more confident now.

The King stood up from the huddle and said something quiet but decisive.

Grosmal threw his hands in the air and stomped away.

'Bring the man back from the fire,' William instructed. It was clearly an instruction he wasn't keen on.

'Well, well, well,' Wat said to Hermitage. 'What on earth do you think brought that about?'

Hermitage was fascinated as well. 'It's like the time we saw mister Ethel talking to that man outside the castle.'

'It is, isn't it? What secret could Ethel possibly have that would persuade King William not to burn a witch?'

'Well,' Hermitage began, 'actually the Brotherhood of the Sward are not witches. They share a number of traits and behaviours with some of the Druidic movements, but...'

'Yes, I'm sure they do,' Wat expertly stopped the flow. 'But what would stop William burning anyone he was looking forward to burning a couple of moments ago?'

'Ah,' Hermitage realised, 'I see your point. Ethel must either hold some sway over King William or William owes him a favour.'

'Good thinking,' Wat nodded.

Hermitage smiled.

'I can't believe that Ethel has any authority over William.

Who does? After all, the man's killed most of the nobles in the country, as well as bishops, freemen and anyone who gets in his way. It must be a favour. What could Ethel have done for William that came at so high a price?'

'He didn't turn up at Hastings – perhaps William's rewarding those who stayed out of it?' Hermitage speculated, knowing absolutely nothing about what nobles and the like were supposed to do in battles.

'He didn't, did he?' Wat said slowly. He thought some more.

Aethelingus had now been released completely from his capture and was exchanging quiet words with Ethel. Logs stood loyally to one side, looking at the pile of wood that had been ready to take his life. There was almost disappointment in his face.

'Just standing on the sidelines isn't enough,' Wat concluded. 'There had to be more.'

They stood in silent contemplation.

'You know what I've always thought was odd?' Hermitage broke the quiet and asked, as if he was about to comment on the finer points of church regalia.

'What's that?'

'Why William attacked *when* he did. When King Harold came to De'Ath's Dingle he was very angry that William had arrived unannounced. Harold had to come running down from the North.'

'And?' Wat wasn't getting this.

'How did William know Harold was in the North?'

'It wasn't a particular secret, and anyway these Kings have spies everywhere.' Wat's sentence ended with wide eyes.

'Do you think…?' Wat asked Hermitage.

'Oh, frequently,' Hermitage replied, 'but it usually gets me into trouble.'

'No, no. I mean, are you suggesting that Ethel is a Norman spy?'

It was Hermitage's turn to look shocked. 'What? Good heavens no, of course not. Why would you think I was suggesting that?'

'You asked how William knew Harold was in the North?'

'Yes, it was just a general observation. As I said, it puzzled me. I mean, I like being puzzled, but I need an answer as soon as possible. I thought we'd finished talking about Ethel.' Hermitage looked around, hoping that no one had heard this conversation.

'But it fits,' Wat conceded. 'If Ethel was William's spy it would explain why he's still alive, and what favours he can call in.'

'That's awful,' Hermitage said as his despair returned in strength.

The King's party were getting ready to go back inside.

'Majesty, we have no one left to execute,' Grosmal whined. He was fed up.

'Ah,' William recognised the problem. He scanned the courtyard and watched as everyone suddenly found something important to do, or look at.

'Where's that other monk gone?' Grosmal demanded, seized by sudden inspiration.

'He ran off with Cotard,' one of the guards called from the gate.

'Oh, merde.' Grosmal spat.

William clapped him on the shoulder. 'Never mind, let's go and examine de Turold's body, ha ha. That'll cheer us up.'

As the party left, Wat touched Ethel on the arm. The Saxon turned his meagre and disinterested attention to the weaver.

'So, Ethel. You persuaded King William to change his mind, then?'

'So it seems.'

'You must have been powerfully persuasive. Must have been a significant favour he owed you? And all around the same time you and your brother never quite made it to Hastings. When

William seemed to know that Harold was in the North.'

Ethel just raised his eyebrows, clearly considering Wat's statement needed no response.

'So?' Wat wanted an explanation.

Ethel sighed and leant into Wat, preparing to leave. 'Mister Wat. I'm still alive. You're still alive. Your monk friend is still alive and seems to have acquired a royal appointment. The little band of rebels without a hope is still alive, and yet you want to complain. Why exactly?'

'I hope you can live with yourself,' Wat bit back with feeling.

'For many years. Someone has to keep Grosmal's estates under control.'

'Keep Grosmal's estates under control?' Hermitage wasn't keeping up with the conversation anyway, but this made even less sense.

Ethel tapped his nose. 'Grosmal is a dangerous loon. He has his uses to King William, though, and I am assured he will soon be off fighting again. Someone has to be steward of the estate while he's gone. Perhaps never to return. I'm told things like that can be arranged."

'You old...' Wat tailed off in disgust.

'It'll be nice to be in charge of the old place again.'

Wat had to gape a bit before he could speak. 'Steward of your own estate? By God. Happy under a Norman yoke, eh?'

Ethel shrugged. 'Don't forget, I only held the estate for Harold anyway. Steward under a Saxon King or a Norman King.' Ethel held his hands out as if he were balancing two equal weights. Two weights of something equally distasteful. 'It's a life,' he said, and wandered off after King William, his brother in tow.

As the party disappeared into the castle, Hermitage and Wat watched Foella run after them. Her gentlemen's gown had acquired a few more rips at strategic places, and her hair had an unnatural lustre. A whiff of Ethel's candles followed her.

'So, King William.' Foella was simpering loudly at the King's elbow, fluttering her eyelashes and thrusting bits of herself forward. 'It's really lovely to meet you,' she trilled. 'Tell me, is there a Mrs William...?'

Epilogic Prologue

HERMITAGE AND WAT EXCHANGED LOOKS as the darkness of the courtyard took over from the departing crowd.

The guards went back to guarding. Scarlan's band were in the cells, and the King's party were probably back by the fire.

'I suppose we can go now?' Hermitage suggested hopefully.

'I suppose we can. And Athan let you go from De'Ath's Dingle, remember, so there's no need to go back there.'

'Do you think that would be all right?' Doubts were creeping back into Hermitage's mind. The events at Castle Grosmal had put his old monastery, and his old abbot, completely from his mind. How remarkable.

'Yes, Hermitage, I do.' Wat was emphatic. 'Do not go back to that place. You'd be defying your abbot's direct instruction. That must be a pretty serious sin.'

Hermitage nodded and a smile broke his face. 'I suppose it would.' He felt liberated and rather bad at the same time. Was he just taking advantage of the situation? He was sure that Athan had not meant him to simply wander off after the business at the castle had been resolved. Still, if Athan didn't know, how could he object? Hermitage couldn't decide if Wat was a good or bad influence. Or both. And what were his tapestries really about?

'So,' Wat said, rather awkwardly. 'I suppose this is it. The plan to not say a word and go our separate ways.'

'Oh.' Hermitage felt a shock run through his system. He had grown used to Wat's company and couldn't really imagine what he would do without him. If he didn't have a monastery wall around him, he imagined the problem would be what the world would do to him.

'Where will you go?' Wat asked, although Hermitage thought there was some reluctance in his voice.

'Oh, er.' Hermitage had absolutely no idea where he was going to go. Or how he was going to live. Or even for how long he was going to live.

They were completely alone in the courtyard now, the silence of the night falling around them. Surely this was not the time to be going anywhere. Hermitage decided to find a corner of the castle to sleep in and see what the morning brought. He remembered he was now the King's Investigator. Perhaps some bread might come with that.

Before he could say anything a lone man ran across the drawbridge and into the courtyard.

The man stopped and bent double, getting his breath back from a long run.

When he stood upright he looked around the space and saw Wat and Hermitage.

'Is Wat the Weaver here?' the man panted.

'Could be,' Wat responded coolly.

'Of course he is.' Hermitage spoke up, wondering why Wat had given such an odd answer. 'This is Wat.'

'Thanks, Hermitage,' Wat muttered under his breath.

'Thank God I've found you.' The man strode up to Wat and rested a hand on his shoulder.

'What is it?' Wat asked with some resignation in his voice.

'I've been sent. You have to come immediately.'

'Sent by whom? Why? And come where? I don't do calls in the middle of the night. Nor can I turn out tapestries that quickly.'

'It's the market at Baernodebi,' the man said, as if this was sufficient explanation.

'I'm sure it is,' Wat sympathised. 'Bit dark for a market though.'

'We only found him when the market closed.'

'Found who?'

The man was sombre. 'There's been a death.'

Hermitage and Wat's looks were a combination of shock and resignation.

'Not another one? Are they following us around?' Wat asked angrily.

'It's Briston the Weaver – he's been murdered.'

This really took Wat aback.

'Briston? Bloody hell. How?'

'Not nicely,' the man responded.

'We need to go, Hermitage,' Wat said, sincerely saddened and worried.

'Of course,' Hermitage said, supporting his friend. 'As you said, it is a bit dark though?' he added, looking with concern past the drawbridge towards the dark wood.

Wat tutted.

'Why did you come here?' Hermitage asked the man, trying to move on from his natural caution. 'Are you seeking the aid of the castle? Why did you ask for Wat particularly?'

'Special instruction. Briston left a note.'

'So he could write?' Wat was sharp in his surprise.

'Obviously,' the man retorted, rather rudely.

'And you can read?' Hermitage answered back, and immediately regretted it.

'Yes,' the man huffed. 'Well, the big letters. Some of them. The stonemason did most of the difficult bits.'

'And this note said "If I'm murdered go and fetch Wat, he's at Castle Grosmal", did it?' Hermitage was incredulous.

The man was very impressed. 'How did you know?'

FINIS

For the next Chronicle of Brother Hermitage, see
The Tapestry of Death
In which is unravelled the murder of Briston the Weaver.

Also available in The Chronicles of Brother Hermitage:

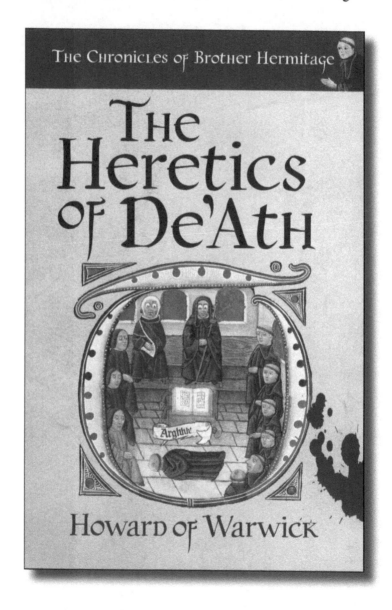

ISBN 978-0-9929393-0-4

£7.99

The Heretics of De'Ath

England 1066...

During an utterly pointless debate at the austere monastery of De'Ath's Dingle, a monk dies in mysterious circumstances. Standing accused is Brother Hermitage, who needs to work out who did it before he's executed. More medieval than detective, he finds a companion in Wat the weaver, producer of tapestry to make Beowulf blush. Naive and blindly deferential, Hermitage is helped through events by Wat, coming to a conclusion as startling to him as anyone. With monks, nobles and even a King, *The Heretics of De'Ath* does for the medieval crime genre.

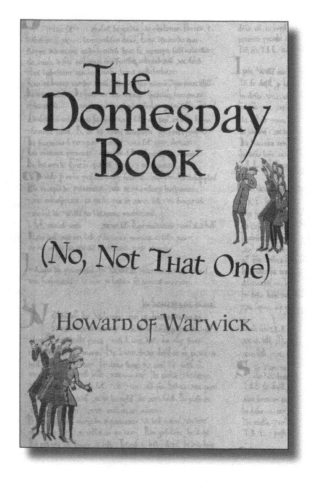

The Domesday Book (No, Not That One)

William of Normandy ...

... has just won the Battle of Hastings but has lost something precious; so precious no one must even know it is missing. Reluctantly assembling a team of incompetents, he sends them on a mission of recovery. But his secret is out and another band is after the treasure. In a race across a savage land, through a population of confused misfits, against the clock and against one another, two forces hurtle towards a finale of cataclysmic proportions; all in 29 concise and entertaining chapters.

ISBN 978-0-9929393-2-8   £7.99

And coming in 2015:

The Magna Carta (Or Is It?)

The Tapestry of Death

England 1067...

Briston the weaver has been murdered – in a very special way – and it is up to his old friend Wat to avenge his death. Brother Hermitage will support his companion, but the number of suspects keeps rising.

When events take a turn for the truly bizarre, Hermitage and Wat find themselves up to their Saxon socks in people who want them dead, people who want one another dead and people who seem to want everyone dead.

They must find a missing maiden, placate a giant killer and reveal the awful secret of the Tapestry of Death before matters are resolved.

With a monk, tradesmen, priests, Normans and Saxons, *The Tapestry of Death* should be a solid, traditional medieval who-done-it, but it isn't. Really, it isn't.

Read the first chapter →

Caput I

HE BODY OF BRISTON THE WEAVER was tied up. Definitively, comprehensively and indubitably, tied up. All over.

Even Brother Hermitage, who didn't like to disturb the practical details of the world as they passed him by, could see this was the case. In fact there was more tying up than body, which raised interesting questions of nomenclature.

The fellow who had summoned him and Wat the Weaver to this gloomy place stood respectfully by the entrance of this canvas mausoleum. Perhaps out of respect for the dead, but more likely because Wat had said 'Move and you're dead' when they entered the tent.

'Not Briston.' Wat's voice was intense as he looked down on the tied up Briston.

Hermitage gave his companion a few quiet moments for contemplation, while he pondered the problem. Perhaps it shouldn't be tied up Briston at all. Maybe Bristoned tying up? He looked over at Wat and thought this might not be the moment for syntax.

The dull light of an oil lamp, hanging from the centre of the tent, dropped slowly on to a sad scene, somehow made more poignant by the early hour of the night. Poor Briston's body had expired with the setting of the January sun, leaving his soul to make its journey through the long darkness of a winter night.

The lamp was old and the oil was cheap. The light was not

comforting, either; it seemed to hang on Wat's drooping shoulders.

'We've been forced to look into two deaths now, Hermitage, and I couldn't have given a hoot about either of them. But Briston?'

Hermitage, still panting from the rush of getting here, had no breath to chide his friend for thinking ill of the departed. Albeit the departed to whom he referred had been an aged monk, soon to die anyway, and a rather despicable Norman.

Nor did he like to interrupt. For once. He appreciated that there was real emotion in the weaver's words.

Hermitage relied on Wat as his rock. A firm, steady presence in the face of life's travails. Wat could always find some note of optimism, even when Hermitage's execution was being arranged – usually for the murders he was trying to investigate, which was something he was going to have to work on.

Now his lungs were complaining that they hadn't been full since running off from Castle Grosmal, only round the corner really. He was still young, even a couple of years younger than Wat, but life had prepared Hermitage for mental rather than physical exertion. He had viewed his role as the King's Investigator, appointed first by Harold and now by William, as an opportunity for careful thought and analysis. If the job was going to involve a lot of running around, he might have to resign.

He imagined resigning from a job that the Norman King William had given you was quite straightforward. You died, then you didn't have to do it any more. If you were too young for death, or just weren't keen on the idea, you carried on.

'We go so far back,' Wat was still shaking his head, 'and he was my age.' He seemed to find this fact particularly unbearable, and ran his hands over his face in despair. 'At twenty-four you think you've got a good few years left. Ten, at least.'

On their journey Hermitage had tried to get more information about the victim, and Wat's relationship with him. He also wanted to know about weaving in general. Wat always seemed reluctant to discuss his trade.

'All will be revealed, Hermitage,' was all his companion would say. 'All,' he added firmly, as if the Book of Revelation itself was going to be explained. Not that this was needed by Hermitage, to whom it was already as clear as day.

'You,' Wat snapped, emerging from his reverie and striding across the tent to the man by the entrance, 'what do you know about this?' Grasping the man firmly by the throat, he gestured to where Briston lay, like some awful caterpillar.

The ex-weaver's tent was the last thing standing from that day's Great Market of Baernodebi – a title so far adrift from reality that it had floated over the rainbow. It may have been great once upon a time, but certainly never in living memory.

Which was odd, really, as this was a time for trade. The truly great markets of Lincoln or Nottingham, bubbling with the raucous energy of a hundred tradesmen going about their bustling business, were magnificent places. Still further afield, markets in Norwich or the amazing London were simply dazzling. Exotic goods and people jostled with rich merchants, nobles and the ordinary man. Even if you had nothing to buy you would go, simply to gawk at the marvels brought to your doorstep.

If you wanted to gawk, you could also go to Baernodebi.

You'd want to gawk from a distance, preferably up a hill and most definitely up wind. If you chose to gawk close up, it was essential you didn't touch anything. Quite apart from the risk of disease, the merchants were a jealous lot. The slightest hint of a sale would have the purse out of your breeches before you could mutter 'do you mind?'

Hermitage had noted the place was deserted when they arrived. Only Briston's tent remained standing in the small square field surrounded by hovels. If just three hovels can surround anything, that is.

True, everyone else had departed with the falling sun, but it was also the case that Briston was the only one with a tent.

'What do you know?' Wat repeated slowly, having had no reply.

Hermitage gently touched his friend's arm. He indicated that the man in Wat's grasp was being most effectively throttled, and couldn't get a word out.

Wat let the man go, but a glare kept him in his place.

'Nothing,' the fellow croaked. 'I just brought you the news. I found him after the market closed. Everyone else had gone, but his tent was still up. I thought he was probably doing business and obviously didn't want to get too close.'

Hermitage frowned at this piece of information. This sounded like some sort of contagion, yet it was only weaving. Perhaps Briston did business with nobles and well-to-do folk, and so couldn't be interrupted.

Then he remembered the market field and the hovels, and thought it highly unlikely a noble would come anywhere near the place. The Normans had been in the country for months now, ravaging, pillaging and just plain stealing everything that wasn't nailed down. Even they hadn't touched Baernodebi market, and their standards were remarkably low.

'And when you did get close?' Wat demanded.

'We found him. Like this. All weaved up.'

Hermitage thought this a fine description. It was indeed as if Briston had been woven to death.

He squatted at the side of the body and examined the rope. Except it wasn't actually rope. It was tapestry thread, the thin delicate strand from which great beauty would spring. In this case, however, many strands had been wound to make a thick cord. The only bits of Briston visible through his bindings, his boots at the bottom and a clump of hair at the top, certainly didn't look beautiful.

Most incongruously of all, the colour of the thread was flesh pink...

'It's called the Tapestry of Death,' Wat explained.

Hermitage thought this was a fine expression, but no explanation. He turned his head to his friend and raised eyebrows in question.

'It's the ritual of execution for those who breach the code of the guild.' Wat was sombre and serious. 'There's an awful lot of ritual in the guild. Books and books of the stuff, but this is the end of it all.'

Hermitage nodded sagely. Then he had some more thoughts.

'Weavers?' he said, incredulity creeping into his voice.

'Yes,' Wat snapped back.

'The guild of weavers executes people?' The incredulity had gone up a notch and been joined by an undertone of mockery.

'A significant body,' Wat insisted.

'Oh, absolutely,' Hermitage agreed, not wanting to offend his friend. 'To maintain the standards of the craft. Ensure the proper training and appointment of apprentices. Show prospective customers that their weaver is a man of quality. Perhaps even see off those of inferior workmanship, or expel people in the most abhorrent cases. But execution?' Hermitage found it hard to believe that the guild of weavers had an office of murderers.

'I mean,' he went on, 'it's a bit harsh, isn't it?'

'Only in the most extreme circumstance, obviously.' Wat sounded rather defensive.

Hermitage was still pursuing his train of thought. 'A guild of assassins I could understand. Certain chivalric orders, perhaps the guild of spies? They might have to kill their own members. Quite often, I suppose. But for a bit of mucking people about and being a, what did you say, a chancer?'

'It's about more than that,' Wat said with insistent significance, 'much, much more than that... It was Briston's subject matter.'

Hermitage struggled to get his head round this. 'You mean, he was executed for what he did tapestries of?'

'Exactly.'

'Good heavens. They must have been pretty unique to get this done to you.'

'Believe me, they were. And even though I know it was the guild, there are still questions. Someone actually did the Tapestry of Death to poor Briston, and there aren't many who can. So he's the first one I want.'

'Ah.' Hermitage didn't like the sound of that. Wat's tone wasn't of a man who wanted to resolve an intellectual puzzle. It was the tone of a man who wanted to hit things. And if there was a first to be hit, there would probably be a second.

'Then there's the guild master who ordered it done. He's second on my list.'

Now there might be a cartload. 'You have a list…' Hermitage tried to sound supportive, but it came out as a bit of a squeak.

'And there could be a third man.'

'Another one?' Hermitage was concerned that this list was quite long.

'It's possible someone asked the guild to do it.'

'Ah.' Hermitage was hoping the list would come to an end soon.

'Unless there was some sort of group,' Wat speculated. 'A number of the aggrieved getting together, for example, and deciding to take action.'

'Let's stick with two for now, shall we?' Hermitage suggested. He had a bad feeling about this.

Wat nodded a sombre acknowledgment. 'One at time,' he mused threateningly, 'one at a time.'

'That's the spirit.' Hermitage knelt once more at Briston's side and laid a hand on the man's head in blessing.

As he touched the large topknot, the body overbalanced and rolled on to its back.

Wat nodded as the whole structure was revealed. 'Definitely guild work.'

♦   ♦   ♦

Wat had become thoughtful. 'This only doubles the force of my promise', he declared, coming to some sort of conclusion.

'A promise?' Hermitage hadn't heard any promise. Wat had promised a couple of things to the peasant who brought them here, but Hermitage thought them inappropriate at the time. They were certainly not relevant now. What else could the weaver be talking about? He rubbed the death note between his fingers and pondered. The old familiar sinking feeling had descended on his stomach. 'These notes?' he asked, a slight tremor in his voice.

'They were promises', said Wat. 'Promises that if either of us died and left the death note, the other would avenge.'

'Oh.' Hermitage didn't like the sound of that at all. Suddenly it seemed even darker in the tent. He noticed Wat's fists were tightly clenched – another alarming sign. Investigating he could do. Well, he could do it now. After all, he'd done it twice before, and neither time had actually resulted in his own execution. Although both came close. But avenging sounded much more dangerous.

'Avenge by bringing to justice, perhaps?' he offered, trying to subdue the image of avenging which had sprung into his mind. This involved running around with swords and getting in ferocious fights, all of which he lost. Painfully.

'No,' Wat snarled, 'avenging by hunting down the men who did this. The guild master who invoked the ritual and ordered Briston's death, and the paid killer who did it. I'll get them if it takes my last breath. And I will dispense the only justice possible.'

'Ah,' said Hermitage. 'So we're hunting down a professional killer then. Marvellous.'

Notes pages for questions you might like to discuss
at your book group:

Why? Why not? Who and where? How come? Never again?